WHAT REVIEWERS, AMAZON AND GOODREADS READERS ARE SAYING ABOUT BARBARA BRETT'S BOOKS

SIZZLE
Where the boardroom meets the bedroom

"[A] battle fraught with…the dirtiest of tricks…the stuff that destroys marriages, people, lives…. Sizzle through the summer with *Sizzle.*"—*The Salem News*

FIVE STARS
Powerful and Page-Turning

"*Sizzle* has it all: corporate greed, sex, and glitz, mainly in Manhattan, but with snapshots of the exotic places you have always wanted to visit—the French Riviera, Paris, Amsterdam (including its red light district), elegant shops, fancy restaurants, expensive hotels, and seedy dives. With vivid storytelling, the author creates a fascinating cast of characters who gravitate around a ruthless woman using appalling tricks to get what she wants: money and power. She faces formidable foes and has just enough vulnerability to make her interesting and unpredictable…. *Sizzle* is a page-turning, hair-raising look at the eighties' materialism that set the stage for our lives today."

FIVE STARS
A Fun, Sexy Read

"*Sizzle* is a juicy, fun, sexy read. It's perfect for summer (or any season). Barbara Brett does a terrific job of creating the eighties Manhattan setting for this story of intrigue in the publishing world. Marietta is my new favorite heroine!"

FIVE STARS
Sizzle for Summer and Every Other Season

"How far will the glamorous and ruthless heroine go to get what she wants? There seems to be no limit on the tricks she'll try—and succeed with—but that's what makes her and her world of 1980s materialism fascinating to the reader. *Sizzle* is a book that's difficult to put down. But why put it down? Just surrender to the author's "sizzling" imagination and vivid writing."

BETWEEN TWO ETERNITIES
Some loves are meant to last forever

"The facts are cold; the story that unravels is warm and extremely moving.... Brett handles it impeccably."—*Publishers Weekly*

"...Heartfelt, poignant, and—surprising—even uplifting at many unexpected points, *Between Two Eternities* will captivate any reader interested in life, death, and transition points in between"—*The Midwest Review of Books*

"This is one book that everyone should read to understand that time is short and we need to live and love life to the fullest because you just never know..."—Fran Lewis, *Just Reviews*

FIVE STARS

"Barbara Brett tells us the story of a love so strong that in order to maintain that strength one person has to lie...has to keep the truth from the dying partner and, in some way, perhaps, to also protect himself from the reality of the inevitable. Brett's skillful handling of the 1970's setting, its steadfast rules and regulations, its mores and its concept of how and when to live and die, takes us back to another time and place and Robert's final act of love – his farewell to Marcie – will leave you in tears but also with a sense of finality and a question: would you, could you, have done the same?"

FIVE STARS

"Would you tell your spouse s/he is dying of a terminal disease? That is the central question of this tale of timeless love. Things fall apart as the husband tries to shoulder the burden of keeping it a secret from his wife, mother-in-law and children. The characters and atmosphere for this endearing story are well drawn. The husband is a college professor up for tenure. The wife is an artist with an inquisitive mind who needs to better understand her illness. These are characters we care about. The author knows how to weave a good story."—Barbara Mitchell, DCH, author of *10 Powerful Stress Busters*

FIVE STARS
A Must Read for Inspirational Content and Good Story

A book commensurate with my belief in ongoing life. The story has an intriguing, well-written story line with inspirational quality. I quoted the author in a book I wrote: *Prelude to Eternity*

SECRET AGENDA

Who's Castrating the Wolves of Wall Street?

Barbara Brett

For Hy

"'Till all the seas gang dry"

LATE SUMMER—EARLY AUTUMN 2005

PROLOGUE

Moonless nights are made for mischief, especially the sexual romps of Golden Guys like Tony Portman. They are also made for mayhem, and retribution. But that never occurred to Tony as he signaled his bodyguard to stay behind in the cocktail lounge. All evening he had been burning to screw Ilsa Grant, and at about eleven o'clock, when she slipped away from the party through the French doors, he followed her out onto the beach. Pursuing her at a discreet distance, he looked up at the stars and smiled, his groin stirring in anticipation. Slowly, he closed the gap between them. He pitied guys who needed Viagra, and couldn't imagine a time when he himself ever would.

Alone in the night, holding her Chanel sandals by their slender straps, Ilsa looked like merely another broad for the taking and not an invulnerable sex goddess, which was the image currently being cultivated by her PR guy, the same bald little genius who advised Middle Eastern and African strongmen, the President, corporation CEOs, and messiahs from the Orient and the Bible Belt. The wind was blowing in from the ocean, and as Tony began to speak, it was an effort for him to shape his usual suave tones.

"Hi, Ilsa. I see that we both had the same idea."

Montauk was reputed to be safer than Manhattan, but men, even billionaires, are the same everywhere, and she looked startled as she whirled around. It took a moment for her to get her act together, and she began with the ravishing smile from the ads for her latest film, *Shades of Passion*.

"Hello again, Tony." She looked down at her toes. "You've caught me without my shoes."

He would rather have caught her without much more of her attire. "I hope I didn't frighten you," he said, and grinned as he did in the TV commercial for his luxury hotel and spa in the Virgin Islands.

"Of course not. I recognized your voice right away." She added, "It's so distinctive, you know."

He knew that very well, because early in his career he had studied with a voice teacher, aspiring to a repertoire of styles that would, above all, enable him to charm beautiful women and intimidate stubborn businessmen. As for those men and women who were amenable only to more forceful methods, he felt no compunctions about using those same methods in both work and play. At forty-six, with a backbreaking work schedule, he had no time to waste on other people's games, and he had learned from studying the careers of several recent Presidents that with the right PR and spin doctors, you can wallow in shit and come out smelling like an American Beauty rose.

Still in his vocal mode with Ilsa, he turned and gazed across the mounds of sand at his latest achievement, Portman Condos in the Clouds, which rose far higher and wider than the neighboring hotels and condos and would soon make the Hamptons passé as a playground for the rich and famous. More than the usual number of naysayers had predicted that it couldn't be done here in Montauk, with its vested interests and its maze of zoning and conservation laws. But once again he had summoned his lawyers, politicians and, most helpful of all, a few of his old fraternity buddies, who, after twenty-five years, were still adhering to their slogan borrowed from the Three Musketeers, "One for all and all for one." The name of the game was hardball, and in tune with the business and political climate of the new millennium, the Golden Guys, as they had been known in college and ever since, had added some embellishments that would never have occurred to d'Artagnan and his simpleminded buddies.

"Doesn't it look just great from here?" he said, employing the boyish enthusiasm that his pollsters had identified as his most positive trait.

"I'm sure your tower looks great from anywhere."

As if paying homage to Freud, his penis stirred at her use of the suggestive word *tower* rather than the more neutral *building*. With his thick black hair and custom-tailored tux he had an image that oozed potency. He was as attractive a guy as she was a woman, and quite probably their libidos were on the same wavelength. Anyhow, *People* magazine was always selecting him as among the ten sexiest men in the world. This was going to be easier than he had thought, and for a fleeting moment, he regretted that their coupling would lack that added zest of having to overcome an initial reluctance.

"I started planning this complex at the dawn of the new millennium, and it took five years to see it through to completion," he informed her. "Of course, it would have taken any other builder fifteen."

She nodded as if she were a subscriber to *Architectural Digest* and had read all about him in the latest issue. "I certainly admire your energy and drive."

"And I yours, Ilsa. Needless to say, I've followed your career."

"Thank you, but it's nothing to compare with yours."

"Oh, I wouldn't say that," he lied.

"Really, a career in show biz is as volatile and shifting as these mounds of sand."

As he turned round to view the sand she was nudging with her pedicured toes, he saw also the marble pavilion that he had contributed to the community in a trade for a few zoning variances, and he began to entertain the idea of having her *al fresco* instead of in one or another of the model apartments in Portman Condos. From a one-room studio to a terraced penthouse, each unit was currently supplied with a bottle of Dom Pérignon in the color-coordinated GE fridge, so that his sales reps could keep clients in a happy haze until the sale was finalized.

Ilsa was saying, "An actress is only as good as her last few performances, and there's always someone younger and prettier who's dying to push you out into the cold. I firmly believe that all actresses under twenty-five should be drowned in a vat of Diet Coke."

Tony looked astounded by her remark. And then, not at all lasciviously, but like a connoisseur examining a Renoir masterpiece at Sotheby's, he let his eyes pass in approval over her short blond hair, and blue eyes and full lips, and graceful throat and shoulders, and her full bosom and rounded hips. She wore a sleeveless black evening dress of a luxurious simplicity, and amid the shimmering satin, lace peepholes invited the eye to linger and lust. He ended his pleasure cruise at the string of pearls round her neck, as if this classic ornament certified her true and eternal beauty.

Now that he had fed her the carrot, it was time for the stick, and he sounded more businesslike as he brushed a mosquito from his sleeve and said, "To be candid, Ilsa, it was not my own idea to engage a spokesperson for the residential division of Portman Enterprises."

"Oh...?"

"But once the idea was proposed by my task force, I quickly saw its merit, and since we were looking for a unique image of beauty, charm, glamour, and intelligence, the choice was obvious."

"What can I say but thank you? I'll certainly try my best to come through for your firm."

"I'm sure you will, Ilsa. And with flying colors." With a hand to his chin, he nodded as if he'd just made one of the ten big decisions of his life. "As a matter of fact, your contribution has such potential that I think it would be a good idea if you reported to me directly instead of to Bill Strausse."

"Are you sure Bill won't mind?" She turned and looked back at the towers. "At the party, I got the impression from him that he was my contact."

"I'm sure that Bill won't mind a bit. Besides, his wife is a very jealous woman, so we'll be doing him a big favor and keeping his marriage intact." He smiled as if he had just saved Bill and Dora from the exorbitant fees of divorce lawyers.

Like a proper lady, she looked perplexed by this allusion to her capacity for wrecking a marriage. She murmured finally, "You know best, Tony."

"Yes, I like to think I do. Trust me, Ilsa."

"Of course I trust you."

Suddenly he took a mighty swipe at a mosquito. "Damn these bugs. I think we've stopped in the middle of their convention center."

"It may be my perfume."

He stepped closer to her, then sniffed and smiled. "I don't blame the critters for wanting to hang around you. But since they're unlikely to go, may I suggest that we move on from here?"

When he took her hand, she allowed it to be held, but she offered no favorable signal, no pressure that she would welcome a more intimate contact. He felt a surge of annoyance, because, if nothing else, he was her employer, and employers were entitled to certain perks. Damn it, it was not only the American way but also the way of the whole world. Whenever he heard of the recreational screwing that went on in Thailand, he had an urge to transfer his corporate headquarters to that center of ancient wisdom and cheap labor and tax breaks, and he would probably do so one of these days. He envied his buddies in manufacturing and the service industries who were able to outsource so much of their payroll. But you couldn't erect buildings via phone calls to India and China. Of course, he did the next best thing by hiring contractors who kept costs down by employing undocumented day laborers.

"You're right," Ilsa said. "I should be getting back."

"Not yet." His grip tightened on her hand. "Those pests who are doing the documentary about me and my buddies are getting on my nerves. Help me hide from them a little longer. Come, I'll show you my pavilion. It's my 'public space' contribution to the community, but I intend to get a lot more than a tax break out of it."

"I can see it from here."

"But not well enough. I built it with you in mind—*for* you. That's where we're going to tape most of your commercials. You have to see it up close. Pity there's no moon tonight. No doubt Diana knew you'd be out here and couldn't face the competition. The stars are out in force, though, just to light your way."

Unlike every other woman who had heard a variant of this tarnished line, she did not smile and shed a few inhibitions. He sensed her reluctance to accompany him, but he pretended he was unaware of the stiffness in her hand and arm as he tugged her along behind him.

A minute later, when they had climbed the steps and were

standing between two of the graceful Ionic columns, he said with pride, "If I say so myself, even the Greeks couldn't have built a temple more worthy of Aphrodite, their goddess of love and beauty." He sat her down on one of the long stone benches, and then waved his other hand in an all-encompassing gesture. "And what more fitting setting for you, our American goddess of love and beauty?"

He had her now. He saw the glow of vanity in her eyes, the swell of pride in those tempting, voluptuous breasts. He sat down beside her, moved closer, put his arm around her. He brought his face nearer, and his voice, a soft whisper, blew gently in her ear. "After a few commercials, this will be known not as Portman's pavilion but as the temple of Ilsa Grant."

That clinched it. Slowly she turned her face to his, ready to accept the homage of this supplicant.

Her lips were soft and satiny, a delicious appetizer to the feast to come, and as he pulled her closer, her breasts sent his blood pounding to his ears in a crescendo that drowned out the thunder of the ocean's waves. Closer. He had to get closer. And be inside her.

But as caress turned to crush and his tongue and hands began to reach for her intimate places, she stiffened in his arms. This was not the humble offering of a worshiper. This was a classic Hollywood rape, whether upon a producer's couch or a bank-roller's patio.

"Tony, stop it!" she said, having managed at last to wrench her lips from his. "That's enough! I'm a married woman and my husband is your guest."

But he already had her back pressed down against the bench. He grabbed her hair, so hard that she thought her scalp would come off. "Who the hell are you telling to stop?" he growled, and his lips crashed down on hers again as he pulled her legs up beneath him with his other hand. "You want this as much as I do," he said, his lips working their way down to her breasts.

"The hell I do! Let me go! I'll scream!"

"Scream away. Not even the fish can hear you above the roar of the waves." Desire was a white-hot pain shooting from his groin to his chest, a pain made more delicious and exquisite by Ilsa's struggles. He reached beneath her dress. What a relief that, unlike in some of his previous encounters, she wasn't wearing those goddamn pantyhose. He grabbed her thong and started to tear it off.

"No!" she cried, trying to wriggle away, trying to knee him. "No!"

But he was more than twice her weight and his body was like iron. Her cries were lost in the hot cavern of his mouth, and her struggles only served to make his harsh, rhythmic thrusts all the more pleasurable.

"You son of a bitch!" She beat at his chest, but he grabbed her fists and pinned them down.

"Save the dramatics for the movie screen. You're no blushing virgin. You didn't give me anything you haven't given to dozens of other guys."

"You're right. I didn't *give* you anything. You took it, you bastard."

"Watch your language, honey. Remember that you're working for a blue-chip corporation with entrée to the White House and both parties in Congress."

"Not for long." She began to stuff her breasts back into her gown.

"We have a contract."

"I'll get out of it. That's what lawyers are for."

"Try it and you'll never work again except at McDonald's. All I have to do is pick up a phone and exert a little pressure in the right places. It wouldn't be the first time."

The hatred in her eyes blazed brighter. "You think you're so big, so all-powerful. But maybe this time you've met your match. You seem to have forgotten who my husband is."

A year ago, in a three-ring circus of a wedding, Ilsa had plighted her troth (the third troth for her, the first for him) to Vittorio Capperrelli, the former Olympic wrestler from Italy. The muscle-bound Capperrelli now made his living from public appearances, cameo roles in the movies, and as a spokesman for vitamins, health foods, and a line of macho sportswear.

Portman laughed. "I haven't forgotten that overgrown macaroni-brain. If you tell him about what happened here, and I doubt that you will, because in his macho Italian way he's sure to blame you and not me, I suggest you keep in mind that the same goes for him as for you. If he ever dares to raise one muscle-bound finger against me, I'll be on the phone with my fraternity brother whose conglomerate owns both HeartHealth Foods and Chuck Chandler Sportswear. If he wants to continue to afford his spaghetti and meatballs, he'd better keep his peace."

"You bastard."

"You're repeating yourself. Your conversation has become as boring as sex with you turned out to be." He took out his Speert pocket comb from Switzerland and handed it to her. "Now get back to the party and do your duty as spokeswoman for Portman Condos in the Clouds."

She hesitated, but pride and big bucks won out, and she snatched the comb and ran it through her hair. After thrusting it back at him, she stood up, straightened her dress, and picked up her shoes. At the steps of the pavilion, she paused and turned to glare at him, still sitting relaxed and unconcerned on the bench.

"I'll get even with you one day."

"I doubt it. You have more to fear if word got out about our little rendezvous. I can either deny it and say you're lying in order to get publicity to save your career from going in the toilet. Or, a simple businessman who is unacquainted with women and their wiles, I can tell the world that you seduced me—and turned out to be a lousy lay. Either way, you lose big."

She paled and started down the steps.

"Also," he called after her, "I'd tell the world, starting with Page Six of the *Post,* that your tits are much smaller than they appear on the screen. Who's your stand-in for nudie scenes? Obviously, it will be great publicity for her."

Ilsa took the last two steps at a run.

Tony reached into his pocket for a Marlboro, the cigarette of real men, and regretting that he didn't have access at the moment to one of the horses at his Duchess County estate, he sat back for a leisurely smoke. When he tried to blow one of his perfect and exquisite smoke rings, the wind blew the smoke back in his face.

He listened to the crash of the waves and luxuriated in his power. Like the ocean, he was an irresistible force. Nothing could stand in the way of what he wanted. Too often, there was no challenge; sometimes he didn't even have to finish articulating what he wanted before it was handed to him on a silver platter. How delicious it was to be a real man and take it by force, as he had just done with that impertinent and unappreciative bitch, Ilsa Grant. He looked forward to exercising his dynamism on the political scene in a couple of years, when his old school buddy Lyle Wayne became President and would appoint him to the Cabinet. Or maybe not. It wouldn't make any difference. What mattered was that he and his pals would be where they wanted to be, running things, the way they had been planning it for years. It would probably be better for most of them not to be too visible. They would have more control that way.

His cigarette finished, he sighed and rose to his feet. It was time he returned to stroking his guests. There was almost as much money and power at Portman Condos in the Clouds tonight as at a Washington banquet sponsored by the American Pharmaceutical Association. It was the cream of Wall Street and society, which included, of course, most of his fraternity brothers. He laughed to himself. Too bad that he couldn't, as in the old days, take the Golden Guys aside and tell them that he had just fucked Ilsa Grant. But now was not the time. It would make a good story, though. Maybe he would save it for their anniversary party in a few weeks. Yes, that would be a good time to share the experience. Just as he had a few minutes ago, they were bound to get a big bang out of it.

He was almost at the steps, and still chuckling at the pun, when he became aware that someone had silently entered the pavilion from the back or side and was now creeping up behind him. He froze, and the hair on the back of his neck stood up. Should he make a run for it, or turn and confront the intruder? The son of a bitch would probably run for his life when he saw who his intended victim was.

But in the split second it took him to consider his options, the options disappeared. A black-clad arm clamped over his neck from behind and started squeezing the air from his lungs. And from the corner of his eye, Tony glimpsed something sharp and shiny being held against the hollow of his throat. It pricked him, and he felt a warm trickle. The body pressed up behind his was tall, and the arm felt as strong as iron. He could feel hot, warm breath in his ear, and the fact that the breathing was smooth and controlled made his situation seem all the more ominous.

Never had he felt so alone. Never had he felt so helpless. Never had he felt so afraid. He tried to struggle, but the grip only tightened. The knife pricked deeper.

"Do you know who I am?" he screamed under his breath.

"Tell me." It was a whisper, and he felt the words in his ear.

"I'm Tony Portman."

"Too bad, Tony."

"Take my wallet, my Piguet," he managed to gasp out with the little breath he had left. "Who are you? One of Mario's guys? I explained to him about the carting contract. If he's not happy, I'll try to do better. I *will* do better! What the hell—it's only money. And I'll also cut him in on my next project. Just don't kill me. Please!"

"I'm not going to kill you." The whisper of that controlled breath near his ear turned even more menacing. "But when you wake up, you're going to wish to God that I had. Sweet dreams, lover boy."

The pressure tightened around his neck. Then, as he vowed to hunt down this maniac and exact the cruelest revenge that the world had ever known, everything went black.

CHAPTER 1

A LOCAL FLORIST had been stabbed and robbed a few days ago, and when Tom Berenson heard the door of his bookshop open and close, he excused himself to Mrs. McEvoy and hurried up front. Like many of the local shopkeepers in Brooklyn Heights, he was licensed to keep a gun, and his .38 was in a drawer beside a first edition of *Little Women,* which he had been commissioned to sell by a customer who had been downsized out of a job. After looking down at his fourth corpse, he had vowed never again to shoot to kill, but good intentions were often forgotten in the heat of a shootout.

The visitor was a tall, well-dressed man in his mid- to late forties, and he didn't look at all like the grim, menacing figure in the police sketch that had been circulated throughout the neighborhood. Tom relaxed, but not completely. While still on the police force, he had always believed that the expressionless, black-and-white sketches made the public too trusting of real-life strangers who wore the bright smiles of political candidates and other professional do-gooders.

"Nice little store you have here," the man said in an authoritative voice.

With his mind on villains rather than benefactors, it took a few seconds for Tom to recognize Dr. Albert Foster. Until today, he had seen the doctor only at his Park Avenue office, dressed in either a dark suit or a white lab jacket. Today he was wearing a tan cashmere jacket, gray slacks, and tasseled loafers. Tom wondered what the city's best and most expensive urologist was doing in Brooklyn. Here in the borough of churches and bagels, it was common knowledge that upwardly mobile Manhattanites would rather be caught dead in a Sutton Place brothel than alive in Brooklyn, even in a church.

"Is my father-in-law okay?" Tom asked.

"As of his most recent checkup, Max is holding his own nicely."

Tom smiled with relief. "For a moment, I was afraid that you had some bad news about him. But, of course, it's unlikely that you'd come all the way out here to tell me that."

Foster's own smile suggested that for a decent guy like Tom, he would make a house call to the ends of the earth, or at least to Coney Island. "Has Max been drinking his eight glasses of water a day?" he asked.

"And wishing they were beer."

"Well, an occasional glass of beer wouldn't hurt him. Upon second thought, better make that a light, low-carb beer." Foster laughed at what he evidently considered a joke.

"We both appreciate the good care you've been taking of him. His previous urologist hadn't done much for him."

Foster nodded his head of thick blond hair. "That's gratifying to hear. I'm not one to knock a fellow healer, but I guess that in every profession there are some who just don't measure up. By the way, I understand that you were a terrific detective until you retired."

Tom waved aside the compliment, not that he would have disputed it. "Nowadays I'm concentrating on becoming a terrific book dealer."

"I just passed a mega store on Court Street. Do you get much competition from them?"

"They hardly know I'm here. Does the Four Seasons worry about a hot dog vendor down the block? We concentrate on rare and used books, not the latest bestsellers. Most of the credit for the store's survival, though, has to go to my wife. When she started it, she believed that it should have a specialty, and she decided to feature books about Brooklyn—its history and famous inhabitants."

"Name one."

"Walt Whitman."

"Ugh. I had to write a paper on him in college, and whenever I see a leaf of grass, I feel like stamping on it."

"We also have Mae West, Spike Lee, Barbra Streisand, Sandy Koufax, Lena Horne, Carl Sagan, Rosie Perez, Woody Allen, and Justice Ruth Bader Ginsburg to name just a few. And there's Ilsa Grant too, although, judging by her recent commercials for Portman Condos, one would think that she was born in the throne room of Buckingham Palace."

"I met her at a party recently."

"It must have been a pleasant evening for you."

"Not really. My wife at the time was with me. She didn't officially walk out until a week later."

"Well, the social season is still young."

Though they proceeded to share a manly grin, Tom was a little surprised by this personal side of the famous urologist. While his own wife, Beth, was still alive, he would never have expressed or even felt an interest in other women. And currently, with Beth gone from him for almost two years, he still felt her presence all the time, especially on his rare and disappointing dates. He was thankful that Beth had survived until their daughter was into her teens, sparing him the problem of providing a stepmother.

"Excuse me," he said to Foster, and turned to Mrs. McEvoy and her little brat, who were emerging from the children's section. The woman was holding a slender book the way a butcher does a cleaver, and it was only inches above the child's head.

"Barry has decided on *Winnie the Pooh*," Mrs. McEvoy said with determination.

"*You've* decided on *Winnie the Pooh*," the child corrected her.

"I thought that you'd finally made up your mind, which you probably inherited from your father. If you don't want *Winnie the Pooh*, what do you want?"

"I want a Terminator gun like the one on TV."

"Over the dead body of Arnold Schwarzenegger! I'm sure that Grandpa Harry wouldn't want you to buy a gun with your birthday money. Knowing him, he would probably want you to have a book of Bible stories." She said to Tom, "Grandpa Harry is on the Jewish side of the family. We'd prefer a storybook that has both the Old and New Testaments, if you have it."

"No! No!" Barry screamed. "I do want *Winnie the Pooh.*"

"In that case, shut up before Mr. Berenson decides to sell it to a boy who's better behaved."

After the departure of Barry and his mother, Tom laughed and said, "Maybe I should have asked you to give her the name of a good child psychologist."

"Even the best of doctors can't work a miracle," Foster said with a weak smile. "Recently, I myself, with all my years of training...." He shook his head. "Man, what a nightmare. I'm in the middle of a doctor's dilemma that was never discussed either at GMU Medical School or at Massachusetts General Hospital, where I did my residency."

Tom smiled. "In that case, may I show you my selection of self-help books?"

Foster put his hand on Tom's shoulder. "I think that you can be more helpful to me than any of your books. Max is always bragging about his son-in-law, the cop who cracked so many tough cases when he was a lieutenant on the police force."

"Is this a criminal matter?"

"It's probably the crime of the century."

"Then you should go the police immediately."

"That's one thing I can't do."

Tom knew that there was a lot of drug addiction among doctors, and he wondered if Foster had succumbed to the filthy habit and, perhaps, gotten in trouble with his supplier. Certainly it would explain his presence and rather peculiar behavior. For the time being, it was probably best to humor the guy, and leaning against his counter, he suggested, "How about going to the FBI?"

Foster shook his head sharply. "The cops and the FBI are out. News would leak to the press and the public."

"I'm sure that if an eminent physician like you insisted on secrecy, they would go all out to accommodate you. You could use your clout with patients in high places. Speaking as a former insider, I can assure you that it's done almost every day. Would you like a few names at Police Headquarters?" Tom grinned. "As a clincher, you could promise to maintain their potency into old age."

What started as a nervous laugh suddenly seemed to become uncontrollable. As Tom stared at him, Foster pressed his arm, and when he was able to speak again, he said, "I think you'll agree with me, Mr. Berenson, that the worst thing that can happen to a man is the loss of his capacity for sex."

"Sure. At least for most men."

"*All* men."

"I was thinking of certain clergymen."

"Balls!" Foster glanced at his Patek Philippe. "Listen, we can't talk here with people coming in and out. I'll take you to lunch. You mentioned the Four Seasons before. Let's go."

Tom looked at his fifteen-dollar Rolex rip-off from a sidewalk vendor on Fulton Street. "I can't leave the store for that long. It'll have to be a neighborhood place."

Foster grinned. "Actually, my next choice is a Subway or a Karl's Kajun Kitchens. Do you have one of them nearby?" At Tom's raised eyebrows, his expression grew sheepish and he confessed, "Don't tell my patients, but ever since medical school I've had a weakness for fast food." He sighed. "I guess that's not such a great idea for today, though. We need privacy and don't want to be rushed. Take me to a good local place, if such a thing exists."

Outside, a traffic agent was sticking a summons under the windshield wiper of the white Lexus that was double-parked on the narrow street.

"Officer! How can you do such a thing?" Foster cried plaintively. "Didn't you see the *MD* on my plate? I was attending a critically ill patient." He whirled round and pointed to a window on the third floor. "Acute nephritis," he added for good measure.

"In that case, you must be the last doctor in town who still makes house calls."

"I suppose I am, but I feel it's a duty I owe my patients. The Hippocratic Oath and all that."

"The Hypocritic Oath, if you ask me," she said. "Okay, I'll give you the benefit of the doubt this time."

"Thanks. You've just confirmed my faith in our great Civil Service." Foster winked over her shoulder at Tom as she removed the summons and placed it in her pocket. "Dumb broad," he mouthed.

Suddenly, Tom didn't like the rich and famous doctor from Park Avenue, and he had an intimation that he was getting involved in something foul and slimy.

CHAPTER 2

"THE FOOD here is much better than the decor," Tom assured Foster.

Across the red-and-white checkered tablecloth, the urologist was gazing quizzically at the amateurish mural of the Leaning Tower of Pisa. It was leaning about fifteen degrees more than in real life, and looked about to fall upon the carefree strollers in the Piazza dei Miracoli.

"Actually, I rather like this place," Foster said. "The ambiance reminds me of a joint that was popular with my fraternity back at GMU." He sighed. "Golden memories—golden guys. That's what they called my friends and me, you know—the Golden Guys. We were the crème de la crème of Beta Alpha Beta Phi. Neither before nor after did a class at Gouverneur Morris University have so many members who were tops in both brains and brawn. I'm sure you've heard of it—it's one of the oldest, most prestigious fraternities in the country. Which one did you belong to?"

"I worked days and attended Brooklyn College at night. I had no time for a fraternity."

Foster nodded sagely. "In a place like Brooklyn College, there probably aren't any worthwhile fraternities, anyway. Still, you should have made the time, because belonging to one, even one that's obscure and mediocre, is an opportunity that comes just once in a man's life. In a fraternity, a guy makes friendships unlike any others either before or after. It's male bonding that's stronger than Crazy Glue, and endures forever. Certainly longer than the usual marriage, and I speak as a man who's about to terminate his third."

Sal Bevilino, the owner of the restaurant, appeared with a bottle of wine and two glasses. He nodded to Tom, and then, after introducing himself to Foster, said to him, "From the bottom of my heart, I'm truly sorry that we don't carry any of those fancy wines you ordered from your waiter, but I trust this Bardolino will satisfy your obviously discriminating palate." He leaned his huge, wrestler's frame forward and revealed with a smile, "We order it special for that great man of God, Bishop Tomasulo, who honors us at regular intervals."

"What's good enough for the bishop is certainly good enough for me. Thank you," Foster said solemnly.

"My pleasure, I assure you." Sal opened the bottle and poured a specimen for Foster.

"Superb," said Foster, his eye on Sal's bulging biceps.

"I felt confident you would like it, sir." After pouring the wine for his guests, Sal placed a heavy hand on Tom's shoulder. "I appreciate the fact that it's a bestseller and gonna be made into a movie with Scarlett Johansson and Brad Pitt, but I'm not too happy about that novel you sold my wife."

"What's wrong with it?"

"All the characters make love all night every night, and the women always have these great four-star orgasms. My wife is jealous, and after thirty-seven years without complaint, she suddenly thinks there's something wrong with me, or with our marriage that has produced six children and nineteen grandchildren."

"Wait till she reads the last chapter," Tom assured him. "She'll learn that magnificent orgasms don't always bring true happiness. In fact, they're usually a prelude to disaster."

"No kidding? Well, I'm certainly relieved to hear that." Sal nodded and put the bottle on the table. "Next time, though, I'd appreciate it if you'd steer her toward a book that won't make problems for me in the bedroom."

As Sal walked away, Foster stared into his glass and said, "I know a few great guys who have real sexual troubles."

"I'd think that, being a urologist, you'd know more than just a few."

Foster looked up. "I'm talking about great guys—people close to me."

"Your fraternity brothers."

Foster nodded, and then swallowed most of his glass of wine. "Not bad. If I were the Pope, I'd elevate that bishop to a cardinal." About to speak further, he broke off and turned his attention to the waiter, who was setting down their scampi and spaghetti.

"Hot plates!" the waiter warned. "Enjoy your lunch, gentlemen."

Foster waited till the waiter was out of earshot, and then refilled his wineglass. He gazed down into its contents as if searching there for the words he needed. Suddenly he looked up again and blurted:

"There's a maniac loose—and he's been castrating my fraternity brothers. We want you to catch him before he strikes again."

The words were so unexpected that Tom wasn't sure Foster was serious. He sipped his wine while he gathered his thoughts and studied the man sitting across from him. His years as a cop had made him a better-than-average judge of human nature, or so he liked to believe, and he saw before him neither the cool gaze of the pathological liar nor the excitement of a man who has just gone around the bend. Foster was serious, all right. Tom had never been on a castration case and he had no intention of handling one now. Nevertheless, the cop in him was curious and wanted to hear more.

"What exactly do you mean by 'castration'?" he asked.

"The maniac doesn't actually cut off their penis or testicles, but he does render them sexually incompetent. There's no hope of reattachment. The Vas deferens and efferent ducts are detached in such a way that they shrivel up and disintegrate. What's almost equally tragic, some of his victims begin to lose their male characteristics."

"Surely, testosterone injections should counter that. And what about Viagra—and that other one that's advertised on TV? The one that claims to be strong enough to cause a side-effect of a four-hour erection—though I doubt that some guys would consider that a negative reaction."

"These guys no longer have the equipment to respond to Viagra or Cialis. As for testosterone, it helps, with the feminization, but the injections don't work on everyone. No one knows what the prolonged side effects will be, either. And they certainly can't reverse the castration."

"How is it done?"

"I wish I knew. My friends came to me for help. They wouldn't have dreamed of going to anyone else. We were all in the class of '80 at GMU."

"As a doctor, isn't it your duty to report these crimes?"

"I was afraid you'd say that."

"I am saying it. You have your code of ethics and I have mine."

"Ah, but you're no longer a regular cop."

"I guess that once a cop, always a cop."

"Admirable, and yet rather inhuman." Foster leaned across the table. "Please don't tell me what my duty is. In the present instance, I believe that I have a greater duty to my friends and patients, and they've pledged me to secrecy. As a cop, surely there were occasions when you didn't abide by the absolute letter of the law."

"Who are the victims?"

"They're all prominent. You'd recognize their names immediately. Do I gather that you're interested in the job?"

"I'm interested in hearing more."

"If I tell you their names, do you swear never to reveal them to anyone else?"

"Not even if I'm ever interviewed by *Sixty Minutes.*"

Foster pointed to the mural of the Leaning Tower of Pisa. "How the mighty are fallen. The most recent victim was Tony Portman."

"Is that Tony Portman, the master builder of our age, the guy who once said that Rome wasn't built in a day because he wasn't in charge?"

"Yes."

"How the hell could anyone get near enough to touch him? My group can't even get through to him in the mail or on the phone."

"What group is that?"

"The Pineapple Street Merchants Association."

"The name is so quaint that he probably thought it was a gag."

"The situation is no gag to the merchants involved. Portman is trying to buy up every foot of real estate on our three blocks from Clark Street to the Esplanade. He's going to throw us all out and build a fancy mall where none of us will be able to afford the rents."

Foster tried to look sympathetic, but his easy shrug negated the expression. "Enterprise—that's the name of the game."

"That's the name of *his* game, and he can have it."

"He does have it. And, if you'll pardon my saying so, that's what makes the millions of dollars of difference between the two of you."

"But I've still got my balls," Tom couldn't resist saying. "Tell me how he lost his, and tell me about the others."

The two other victims were Bob Michaelson, known on Wall Street as the Hedge Fund Honcho, and Neal Barnard, the lead negotiator in the law firm that had recently successfully defended Luxxon Oil in a class-action environmental damage suit for more than two billion dollars.

"How can you be sure they were castrated? Isn't it possible that they're victims of some new virus or degenerative disease that the medical profession hasn't diagnosed yet? There was a time not all that long ago when no one had heard of AIDS and even more recently when SARS and bird flu weren't in our lexicon. Couldn't it be something like that?"

"I ran every possible test, and it was castration without any doubt. Besides, on two of the victims I could still see the puncture wound with my magnifier. On the third, it must have healed before he realized something was radically wrong and he sought my help. None of the guys associated their impotence with the attack until I questioned them about foul play because of the puncture wounds I'd spotted on those two."

"How could they not have realized it?"

"This weirdo obviously knows what he's doing. There was no blood, or very little. When the guys returned to consciousness after the attack, they all felt like they'd been kicked in the balls, but they didn't think it was serious enough to run to their doctor or a specialist about. And they all received the same anonymous note the next day. It said, 'You're not the man you thought you were.'

But they all thought it referred to being caught unawares, not to a sudden termination of their sex life. It wasn't until they couldn't get an erection a few times, then noticed that their scrotum was shriveling that they panicked and consulted me. I'm the one who put it all together and spotted the pattern. And once I'd pointed it out to them, they realized it was true. They weren't suffering from a disease they'd picked up in Rio or Las Vegas. They'd been castrated when they were mugged."

Tom shook his head. "I still don't understand how it could have happened. Guys like that are always surrounded by bodyguards and gofers. What were they doing at the time—exploring in the dark in the wrong bedrooms?"

"If you take the case, you can ask them that yourself."

"In his interviews and TV ads, Portman comes across as a powerhouse. Surely he could have taken on an attacker. Where did it happen to him?"

"Out in Montauk, on the night of August twenty-seventh."

"In whose bedroom?"

"You seem to have an obsession with bedrooms. It was nothing like that. Tony was throwing a party to celebrate the completion of his latest condo. At about eleven o'clock, the room became stuffy, and Tony, who's devoted to clean and natural living, went out on the beach to clear his lungs. That's where and when it happened."

"Any witnesses?"

"Not to the crime itself. But I was at the party, and I saw him go out and then come back about a half hour later. Come on, Tom! We both know it's a jungle out there. The tabloids and even the *Times* print articles every day about innocent people who are assaulted by thugs. These three guys didn't know they were in danger until the mugger was squeezing the life out of them with one hand and holding a knife to their throat with the other. Powerhouse or not, Tony is a man of peace. He didn't stand a chance against an armed criminal." Foster leaned across the table, his voice urgent: "Now the damage has been done, and we need your professional help before someone else gets hurt."

The words brought Tom back to his own situation. He wasn't a cop, and hadn't been one since a rampaging crack addict had sent a bullet through one of his lungs. He hadn't been sorry to put it all behind him. And he had no desire to risk his life and return to the dark and violent world of crime. Certainly not for the likes of Tony Portman and his rich and powerful pals.

"I'm not a private investigator," he told Foster. "I'm a shop-keeper and it's time I got back to my shop. I can't afford three-hour lunches like you and your friends. My daughter is still in high school, but her college tuition is already giving me nightmares. Thanks for the lunch." He put down his napkin. "Tell your friends that I advise them to go to the police. That's what they pay their taxes for. If rich guys like them do pay taxes."

"I've already told you they can't do that. The police would ask questions and want to examine them. This is a traumatic thing that has happened to them. They've been violated in a most hor-rible way. No one should expect them to talk to strangers about it, to submit to physical examinations by police doctors who were too incompetent for private practice."

"Why not? We all expect women to do it when they've been raped."

"Though it's a great trauma, rape is different, because once it's over, it's over. After a few sessions of counseling, the woman can pick up the pieces and go on with her life. But what's hap-pened to these men is irreversible. They'll never be the same."

Tom thought of the rape victims he had seen, both the dead ones and the so-called lucky survivors, some of whom had been battered beyond recognition and needed to have their vaginas rebuilt surgically. All would have benefited from extensive psycho-therapy by real pros instead of a few pep talks with social workers. But few could have afforded state-of-the-art therapy. The memory made him sick, and he took a swallow of wine to push down the nausea. Then he stood up and said, "I gave you the best advice I have to offer."

Foster pointed to Tom's chair. "Give me another minute. Please. Thanks," he said when Tom complied. "Even if we went to them, the police would take forever. They'd have to sandwich us in between all their other cases. Time is running out. Neal Bernard, one of the nicest guys I know, can't tolerate the testos-terone injections. He's already losing his facial hair and starting to grow boobs. The others could probably escape that fate, but they'll never again be real men. And this weirdo obviously has a vendetta against *all* my brothers. You've got to get him before he strikes again."

Tom shook his head. "Look, I'm sorry for Portman and the others. I don't like to hear about anyone being the victim of violence, even people I have no use for. These are men who chew up and spit out guys like me every day before lunch. When I was a cop, I was under oath to help all comers. But I'm not a cop anymore. I can pick and choose what I do. I do not choose to undertake a private investigation, certainly not one for the likes of Tony Portman and his friends. Frankly, they're not worth the risk of my life and the expenditure of my time."

"We'd make it well worth your time. You mentioned your daughter before. You'd come out of this with enough money to put her through the best college and, if she's an old-fashioned girl, still have plenty to spare for her wedding reception. No matter what her grades, though I'm sure she's as brilliant and talented as Condoleezza Rice, we'd get her into GMU or Harvard or Yale or any other school of her choice. And if she's interested in sororities, as she should be, we'll get her into the most exclusive one on the campus."

"Sorry, but I'm not interested." Tom tried to soften this final turndown with a smile. He didn't want to screw things up for his father-in-law, who still needed a good urologist. "Thanks again for lunch." He rose and started for the exit.

Foster tossed some bills on the table, rushed after Tom, and caught up with him at the door. "I beg you to reconsider," he said, putting his hand on Tom's arm. "This is no time to indulge in personal convenience or preference. I didn't bring this up before, but it's also a matter of national urgency. Senator Lyle Wayne is one of our members. He's gearing up to run in the Presidential primaries and is bound to win the nomination. With that in his pocket, he's a cinch for the White House. A lot of important people are backing him. His presidency would change life for us all."

"It sure as hell would change life for me," Tom said. "And not for the better. As far as I'm concerned, Wayne is so far to the right that he makes Dubya and Cheney look like card-carrying liberals."

"That's because you don't understand his new vision for the nation. But that's not really the point. The point is that the people have a right to a meaningful choice, and if this maniac gets to Wayne, there's no way he can run. Who would vote for a politician who starts growing effeminate before their eyes? Even if testosterone covered it up for him, there's always the danger that the attacker would leak the truth to the press. And then there are the goddamn physicals the candidates have to take to show how hale and hardy they are now even though they once had enough infirmities to avoid the military. You've got to help us."

"Sorry, but I haven't heard a single word that could possibly change my mind. I think you've been seeing too many reruns of old private-eye movies with Humphrey Bogart."

Tom turned to go, but Foster tightened the pressure on his arm. "What if, in addition to your fee and expenses, I can get a promise from Portman that he'll stay away from Pineapple Street when he's building this damn mall?"

Tom looked Foster in the eye. Obviously the doctor had just played his trump card. "Not good enough," he said. "Get a written guarantee from him that he and all his stooges and dummy companies will stay the hell out of the entire neighborhood—and for good. If our lawyer gives it the okay, we may have a deal."

Tom retrieved his arm from Foster, but softened the gesture with a smile. His step was light as he walked out into the sunshine. He was sure that he had set impossible terms.

CHAPTER 3

O N HIS WAY down the corridor to apartment 5B, Tom began
to smell Max's chili, and soon he could hear the mating
shrieks of one of Stephanie's rock singers. He said hello to Mrs.
Alexander when she emerged from 5F and headed toward the
trash-compactor room with a plastic bag of garbage. She was an
attractive widow of anywhere from fifty to sixty, depending upon
her attire and makeup. In recent weeks, Max had come to believe
that she had designs on him, because they had met in the laundry
room three Thursday mornings in a row. Further, on one of those
occasions, she had poured her All-Temperature Cheer into his
wash, assuring him that it was more effective than his economy
brand from Pathmark. "But you can't really be sure that she's
coming on to you," Tom had told Max. "No," Max had agreed
with a wink. "Not until she offers me her Downy too."

Now, Mrs. Alexander smiled and returned Tom's greeting.
"The whole building smells like a fast-food joint in Acapulco," she
said. "Are you having Zorro and the Cisco Kid to dinner?"

"Well, you never can tell who will drop in."

She laughed. "If you run out of Maalox Plus, don't hesitate
to ring my bell."

After opening his door, Tom stood in place and let the scent
and the sound wash over him. This was his world now—this
apartment and the bookstore. He had been right to turn down
Foster although the case might have been more entertaining than
a vacation. For one thing, unlike in the old days, he wouldn't have
to spend most of his time writing reports.

Holding aloft a wooden spoon, Max emerged from the

kitchen in the COME 'N' GET IT! apron that Stephanie had given him for Chanukah. His round face was flushed from working at the stove, and when he smiled, he looked like a bald and bespectacled cherub who had somehow gotten steroids mixed in his ambrosia and grown to a burly six-feet-two.

Tom's father had died when he was ten, and Beth used to tease him that he had married her to get Max as a father-in-law. Such a thought had never entered his mind during the brief, beautiful two months that they dated before they married, but Max *had* been an unexpected, four-star bonus, and over the years the two men had grown as close as any father and son could be. When Max came up from his Florida condo to share the strain of Beth's last weeks and the grief that followed, he had simply stayed on, knowing intuitively how much Tom and Stephanie needed him and he needed them. Not to fill the aching gap in all their lives that Beth had left behind, but to create a new corner of love and caring.

"Hi," Max said. "Hope you brought your appetite."

"I had a big lunch, but there's always room for your chili. One of these days you're going to blow a hole through the ceiling with all those spices."

"If Stephie doesn't do it first with her music. That singer sounds like I felt when I had those kidney stones."

"I'll go say hello if she can hear me above the racket. Meantime, want to pour us a beer?"

His knock was muted by the roaring blast of the CD, and Tom waited a few seconds and then opened the door. As usual, the room was strewn with socks and sweaters, books and CDs. Stephanie was slouched over an equally messy desk, her long chestnut hair falling in a curtain around her face as she took notes from a book for a paper Tom knew would be articulate and accurate, and earn her usual A. She was a good kid who worked hard in school and at the shop on weekends, and who willingly did her share around the house. Tom saw no reason to criticize the appearance of her room. It was her space, her world, her business, her mess.

"Prince Andrew is on the phone," he shouted. "He wants you to join him on the royal yacht."

"Tell him that after doing that report on *Moby Dick,* I'm staying far away from boats." She turned to face him, and, as always, he felt that sweet, sad tug at his heart. There was so much of Beth in her smile, in her warm brown eyes. Only moments before she died, Beth had gripped his hand and promised, "I'll always be with you." Every time he looked at their lovely daughter, he knew what she had meant.

"Hi, Dad. Have a good day?"

"Fair. And you?"

She shrugged. "Same old stuff."

On the windowsill, Gertrude, their orange tabby, snoozed between a stuffed panda and a beat-up Raggedy Ann. Tom walked over and rubbed the cat under her chin. She opened one eye, gave him a bored look, then closed it again. She had always considered herself Beth's cat, and for a while after Beth's death, Tom had been sure that Gertrude would soon follow her to the grave, as she used to follow her around the house. But, eventually, she began to eat and live again, if only half-heartedly. Sometimes, he would see her stiffen suddenly, all senses alert, as though watching and waiting for one more glimpse of Beth. He knew how she felt.

"Chili for dinner," he announced.

"I never would have guessed. I'll give you guys ten minutes for your beer. Then I'll race you to the stove."

In the living room, Max had the two glasses waiting on the coffee table. "Hear anything from that bastard Tony Portman?" he asked when Tom had settled himself on the recliner.

Tom nearly choked on his first swallow. How could Max have known? Then he realized that his father-in-law was referring to the attempts of the Pineapple Street Merchants Association to contact Portman. "I'm beginning to believe that guy talks only to God and Citibank. No, make that just Citibank. After creating our planet, God probably doesn't dabble in real estate anymore."

"Has your lawyer come up with any new tactics?"

"Of course, but not as many as Portman's eight guys, one of whom is Neal Bernard, who recently got Luxxon Oil off the hook." To change the subject, he asked, "And how was your day?"

Until retiring, Max had taught math and science at Garfield High in Coney Island, a job, he said, that needed more of his brawn than his brain at the end. Now he spent much of his free time working with elderly illiterates, a second career that he found more rewarding than his first despite the lack of payment. He was giving a glowing report on the progress of an eighty-two-year-old great-grandfather from Guatemala when Stephanie joined them and they headed for the chili.

Having used up her cell-phone minutes, Stephanie was on the home phone most of the evening, and when it rang again at ten-fifteen, Tom made no effort to answer it, sure it was just another call for her. A few seconds later she was in the living room, her face pale, her eyes worried.

"It's for you, Dad," she murmured, glancing over at Max, who was dozing in front of the TV. She lowered her voice even more. "Dr. Foster."

The sound of that name, like Pavlov's bell with Russian dogs, always caused a strong reaction in Max. Instantly he was awake and alert.

"Relax." Tom tried to look and sound casual as he got to his feet. "It's probably just a question about your health insurance."

"At ten-fifteen at night? And what about all his office assistants? He has enough of them for a basketball team. Or, more likely, a mini-harem."

Max and Stephanie followed him out of the room, and Tom resigned himself to having an audience.

"Do you know that your phone has been busy for the last hour and a half?" Foster spoke with the pique of a doctor who considers himself too important to be kept waiting.

"Longer than that, actually. Obviously you don't have a teenager at home."

"I do, as a matter of fact. But she has her own cell phone."

"So does mine, but she's used up her minutes for the month."

"Then get her unlimited minutes like mine has. It's worth the price when you factor in all the nagging and whining it saves you from."

Realizing that Foster wanted to continue the conversation he had walked away from in the restaurant, Tom felt obliged to warn him: "My father-in-law is standing right here. Are you sure he's not the one you want to talk to?"

"Of course not. You know what this is about. I— Oh." He got

the message. "I'll make it brief. I talked to Tony and he's ready to accept your demands. We want you to meet with us tomorrow at—"

"Wait a minute." Tom couldn't be sure he had heard right, but now was no time to ask for a repetition, not with Max and Stephanie hovering behind him. And he had no intention of being bulldozed into anything. "I may be able to get the books for you, but I don't have the relevant catalogs here. Why don't you call me at my store tomorrow, and we can talk about it then? I open at ten."

"But we expected you to meet with us at nine."

"Sorry." He wasn't the least bit sorry. On the contrary, it was rather gratifying to keep a guy like Tony Portman waiting. "There's nothing I can do until I have all the information at my fingertips. Goodbye. Call me in the morning." It had been difficult to refrain from preceding the last words with, "Take two aspirins and…"

"What was that all about?" Max asked.

"Some out-of-print books he wants me to get hold of for him."

"Don't tell me that Brooklyn was once a great center of urology?"

"His mother-in-law collects books on the theater, and she's currently in the market for anything I can get about Mae West, who was from Greenpoint."

"How do you like that guy's nerve? Can you imagine how he'd chew me out if I called him at home instead of at his office? And he'll probably expect you to make a house call with those books too!" Shaking his head, Max returned to the living room to resume his nap in front of the TV.

THE PHONE RANG before Tom even had a chance to turn on the lights in the shop. He knew it would be Foster, so he continued to the rear and flipped the light switches and hung up his jacket before answering.

To Tom's amazement, Foster agreed at once to an up-front fee of one hundred thousand dollars, and he added happily, "That's in addition to the thousand a day plus expenses that the guys are putting up. Speaking as a friend, however, I think you'd come out miles ahead if you were paid in stock in one of their corporate entities in an Asian tiger like Singapore or Taiwan. That way, your accountant could arrange all sorts of advantageous—"

"Thanks, but I try to keep my finances simple these days. I'll take the cash and suffer the consequences on April fifteenth. And I want Portman's guarantee in writing about staying far away from my neighborhood."

"An agreement like that would probably be hard to reduce to writing. Anyhow, Tony's word has always been his bond."

"Yes, but we live in the age of junk bonds. It's to be iron-clad, with no possibility of a dummy corporation moving in."

"That would never have occurred to a square-shooter like Tony. So you're taking us on?"

"I'm willing to hear more. Where and when can we meet? Make it after six. I can't afford to just lock up my shop and take off."

"Nine o'clock tonight. At Tony's apartment on Park Avenue. Parking's impossible. Would you like to be picked up and returned in his limo?"

"Is it a stretch?"

"What do you think?"

"I've always considered them ostentatious, but what the hell? Limos are usually safer than the subway at night."

Foster laughed dismissively. "I wouldn't know about that. I haven't been on the subway in decades."

CHAPTER 4

TOM WAVED to the TV monitor as he stepped off the elevator and into the vestibule of Tony Portman's penthouse on the fiftieth floor of Portman Plaza on Park Avenue. From the floor to a height of about eight feet, the walls were lined with mirrors that reflected his image to infinity. Turning around in place, he noticed four identical doors, and he began to feel like a character in a fairy tale.

"Hi," he said to the man who emerged from one of the four doors and glared at him. "The name is Berenson. I'm expected."

Closer to seven feet than to six, and standing like Arnold Schwarzenegger ready to take out all the bad guys in the *Terminator* movies, the man was obviously a bodyguard. Certainly Tom couldn't imagine him performing the usual duties of a valet or a butler.

To Tom's relief, Foster came out of the door too. He smiled at the bruiser and said, "It's okay, Boris. We'll let this one live."

Boris shrugged as if life or death made no difference to him. And as Foster led Tom toward one of the other doors, Boris continued to glare at him.

"He looks like a capable man," Tom told Foster.

"You should see the guy on the morning shift."

"I can see his resemblance to Karloff when he played the Frankenstein monster, but is his name really Boris?"

"Absolutely. He's Russian, and the human equivalent of a pit bull. Rumor has it that in the bad old days he was a loose cannon in the KGB. Comes the revolution and Yeltsin picked him as his personal bodyguard. When his former boss, Putin, came in, Boris thought it wise to do a disappearing act and come over here and try our brands of vodka and democracy."

"He might be getting a skewed look at them from this lofty vantage point."

Foster shrugged. "Depends on what you want to see."

"Where was Boris when Portman was attacked in Montauk?"

"As we've come to learn, even presidents are vulnerable."

"You're not answering my question."

"Tony wanted to be alone on the beach."

"His bodyguard could have remained at a discreet distance. I gather that wasn't the case."

"No, it wasn't."

"Why?"

"You'll have to ask Tony that."

"Do *you* know the answer?"

Foster sighed. "Being his friend as well as his doctor, I find myself under a double burden. But you definitely must ask Tony about why he wanted to be on the beach alone. It might go a long way in your investigation."

Tom followed Foster through a succession of corridors that were lined with statuary and end tables and chests, and hung with paintings so modern that they looked as if the artist had merely thrown a can of paint at his canvas and then gone to bed with his model. Recognizing what looked like a Brancusi, he asked Foster, "Where does he keep the Rodins?"

"Rodin isn't in his period for the time being. Maybe, in a few years, he'll expand his horizon, aesthetically speaking."

"I'll bet that the art dealers can't wait. Are we almost there?"

"Actually, this is the shortcut."

"How many rooms does he have here?"

"Originally, there were twenty, but he's always expanding and contracting. His principal interior decorator is Irene Chamfort. I guess you've heard of her."

"Who hasn't? She recently suggested that the White House needs a different color."

"Blue, as I recall. She's a little steep, but you get what you pay for in this world."

"Right. I'll remember her the next time my cat chews up the curtains."

"Here we are." Foster had stopped before a door in Wedgwood blue and surmounted by a lintel with a urn on each end. "While motoring through England after closing a big deal in London, Tony was impressed by a door in the Duke of Cumberland's palace."

"Did he buy it from the Duke?"

"The door or the palace?"

Tom shrugged. "Both."

"He couldn't. The palace and its contents are a national trust."

"Dumb question. I'm pleased to hear, though, that there are still things that money can't buy."

"Not as many as you think. The duke is Tony's spokesperson in Britain, just as Ilsa Grant is now becoming here in America." As he reached for the doorknob, Foster added softly, "So far, the testosterone shots are working and there are no obvious physical changes, but I can't convince Tony of that. He's hypersensitive and can't believe they won't show up any minute. Don't be surprised if he doesn't come forward to greet you. He prefers dim lights and the shady side of the sofa."

In size and style of furnishings, Portman's living room reminded Tom of the sets in the Fred Astaire-Ginger Rogers films that he watched with Max when they were shown on Turner Classic Movies. Stephanie's excuse for not joining them on those elegant occasions was that the feathers and spangles on Ginger's gowns always made her feel like a slob in her sweatshirt and jeans.

Across the room, looking pudgier and shorter than in his TV commercials and interviews, Portman laid aside the clipboard that was one of the good-impression props suggested by his PR men, and then, after a token rise of a few inches from the yellow and green sofa, he pointed casually, almost indifferently, to an easy chair a few feet away. He was a broad-shouldered guy who held himself proudly erect, determined that others be aware of every inch of five-feet-eleven, every ounce of muscle. His square jaw was just beginning to turn to jowl, and his black hair was both blow-dried and parted low on the left to give the illusion of more fullness on top. Perhaps from the habit of narrowing them in an attempt to read the hidden and obviously selfish motives of others, his gray eyes seemed small for his face.

"I'm Tony Portman. Glad you could make it, Tom."

Tom wanted it to be clear from the outset that he was not here as another of his gofers, and though it made Portman look uncomfortable, he strode over to him and shook his hand as though they were meeting as equals. "Al told me that I'm the guy to help you with your problem. I guess we'll soon find out if he's right."

Portman's handshake was limp, as if Tom weren't worth his energy. "Can I offer you a drink?"

"A ginger ale would be nice. My father-in-law made chili yesterday, which means that we'll be eating it for the rest of the week."

"No kidding? I've had a couple of fathers-in-law, but none of them ever made chili. Only demands on my money."

"Well, lucky in real estate, unlucky in fathers-in-law."

Portman said somberly, as if he were delivering his own eulogy, "A lot of hard work went into my success." He removed a BlackBerry from a pocket of his sports jacket, and after an inquiring glance at Foster, who asked for a brandy, he pressed a button and ordered the two drinks. Then he turned back to Tom. "How much has Al told you?"

"Merely some background. I'd like to hear a lot more about your experience."

Suddenly Joel Grey sang out "Come to the cabaret, old chum," and then a panel in the wall opened. "I'll get it," Foster said, and fetched the two glasses.

"Amazing." Tom shook his head. "When I ask my daughter to get me a drink, she usually stops off for an hour of phone calls." He nodded toward the wall panel, which had by now slid closed and was indistinguishable from adjacent panels. "I'll bet that was one of Irene Chamfort's ideas." He sipped the ginger ale, which tasted different from though not better than the house brand at his supermarket.

"I order it from Fortnum & Mason's in London," Portman informed him, though Tom hadn't been interested enough to inquire.

Tom nodded as if he intended to do likewise when he was next in the market for a bottle or two. "Go on."

"It isn't easy to talk about."

"Maybe a drink would help," Foster suggested.

Portman leaped to his feet. "What the hell is it with you?" he roared. "First you tell me that a drink could counteract my medication. Now you tell me the opposite."

"I'm taking a holistic approach."

"Fuck that! You're really telling me that you don't know what the hell you're doing."

"Not at all. I have high hopes for your recovery. I really do, Tony." Foster's compassionate smile must have been a major component of his bedside manner, because, even from afar, it quickly pacified Portman.

"Sorry, Al. Maybe this thing is affecting my mind too." Portman sat down and groaned. "I still can't believe that this has happened to me. It's the work of a maniac. I've always been a square-shooter with everyone."

"Did you ever offend anyone in the Mafia?" Tom asked.

At first Portman looked as if he had never even heard of the word, but as Tom stared quizzically at him, he leaned forward and said finally, "Okay. After this incident, I did have a talk with a guy whose name I'd rather not mention, but he swears on the life of his mother and all the saints that he and his associates consider me a *paisano* and would sooner hurt the Pope than me."

"Well, we're starting to make some progress," Tom said. "Tell me exactly what happened to you. It happened in Montauk, right?"

"But it could have happened anywhere. And in case you're in the market, I'm sure it's still the safest of all communities for a real estate investment."

"That's reassuring." Tom took out a ballpoint and the spiral notebook he had bought at a local stationery store that morning. "By the way," he said, "I assume that I have an expense account."

"Sure, but it doesn't include trips to Paris."

"At this point, I don't intend to go farther than Montauk, about which you're now going to tell me more."

"I had thrown a party there to celebrate the opening of my

new development. At a certain point, I went out to the beach to inspect the pavilion that I'm contributing to the community."

"What time was this?"

"About eleven."

"Do you often do your inspecting at that hour?"

"I wanted to see it by starlight."

"By starlight?" Tom raised an eyebrow.

"Why not? I've always prided myself on having a touch of the poet. This very building we're now in—I was inspired to build it while reading a poem."

"'Ozymandias'?"

Portman's eyes hardened. "No. Longfellow's 'The Building of the Ship.'" He shook his head. "I can't understand why Longfellow isn't more popular these days. As far as poets go, he's always been tops with me. 'A Psalm of Life' is probably the first poem I ever learned, and frankly, I don't think I've ever heard a better one since."

"Go on," Tom said, expecting to hear more bullshit.

"As I was saying, I was on the beach, and suddenly I was attacked from behind."

"How many guys were there?"

"I don't know. I was aware of only one guy, but his pals may have been hiding behind the pavilion or one of the dunes. I got the impression that he was huge."

"Why?"

"I'm nearly six feet tall." Portman stretched his neck up, as if to give himself that extra inch. "For him to tackle me at all, he had to be at least as big as I am, don't you think?"

"One of the nastiest hit men I ever arrested was hardly taller than five feet. I needed three guys to help me pin him down."

Portman shot Tom a look of disdain. "That was you. A little guy I could take on in a minute. This bruiser was a human dynamo. He made Mike Tyson look like a patsy."

"Did you see his face?"

"No. He was behind me all the time and had his arm around my neck in a hammerlock. In his other hand was a knife, and he was holding it to my throat." Gingerly, as if it still hurt, Portman pointed to the spot. "Finally he cut me with it." As Tom started toward him, Portman gestured him away. "It's healed now."

"Did you see the knife?"

"I couldn't."

"How about his hands? Anything distinctive about them?"

"He wore gloves."

"What kind?"

"They were black. He must have been wearing a black sweater or sweatshirt too. All I could see was black."

Tom turned to Foster. "Was it you who treated his neck wound?"

"It was about five millimeters."

"Just a small puncture, in short."

"But it was deep!" Portman yelled. "And I bled like a pig." Foster looked like he was about to contradict him, but Portman glared at him and rushed on: "After that, I was knocked out, either by the guy or his buddies."

"Any signs of concussion?" Tom asked Foster.

"None at all. Not even a bruise. It could have been a karate chop."

Tom turned back to Portman. "What about his voice? Did he speak?"

"Yeah, but it was disguised. A kind of hoarse whisper."

"What did he say?"

"That he wasn't going to kill me. But that when I woke up, I was going to wish that he had." Portman stared at his crotch. "He was right."

"What else did he say?"

"Nothing!" Portman jumped to his feet. "He'd made his fucken point! Enough with these dumb questions. Go out and find the son of a bitch. He's got to be punished!"

"Sit down! Tell me about when you came to."

"I was still in the pavilion. I'd been out for about fifteen minutes. I felt groggy, disoriented, weak."

"Did you call for help?"

"I was alone. Anyhow, I didn't want to create a scene. I made it back to the party." He pointed to Foster. "Luckily, Al was still around."

"After a crime, it's a citizen's duty to inform the police. Why didn't you?"

"Are you crazy? It was the last thing I'd do. Who'd buy a luxury condo in an area where you can't step out without getting mugged? Also, I've spent years and a fortune to create my current image as a powerhouse." Portman ran a hand over the loosening flesh on his cheeks and jowls. "During the execution of my project in Montauk, a lot of officials out there misinterpreted my motives and ideals. If I'd informed the cops, all those bastards would have learned everything, and they'd have blabbed to the media and all its garbage-disposal outlets.

"Besides suffering personal embarrassment, I would have been harassed by all the banks that were supplying capital and greasing politicos for my various projects all over the world. They would have doubted that I was still the guy for the job, and would have started to call in the loans that they had begged me to take out in the first place. Sure, my lawyers would eventually send those human pit bulls back to the kennels, but it would cost me millions in legal fees."

"Okay, you said you bled like a pig. Didn't your friends and security people notice your condition and rush out to search for the perpetrators?"

"Tony, either the guy was lucky or he knew where to cut," Foster reminded him. "There was just a little drop of blood on your neck, nothing on your shirt."

If looks could draw blood, Foster would have been drenched in it. Portman shrugged dismissively. "So maybe I exaggerated a little bit about the blood. I guess I didn't look different enough that anyone would notice. Besides, I didn't want to call attention to myself and spoil the party or give potential buyers the idea that the area might be unsafe. But the knife was sharp and the wound hurt like hell."

"Was anything taken from you?"

"Nothing. At least, nothing in the way of cash, jewelry, and credit cards. I wish that robbery *had* been his motivation. Robbery I can understand." He looked down at his crotch. "But not a devastation like this."

"Tell me about the guests at your party. Any trouble with them lately or even long ago?"

"If I'd ever had any serious trouble with them, they wouldn't have been there in the first place. Anyone who tries to screw you once will certainly try it again. These were all as kosher as a Hebrew National hot dog, either personal friends or close business associates."

"How come your security was so lax that night?"

"No way!" Portman yelled. "I pay top dollar for security. I had men both inside and out."

"A lot of good it did you. Where were they when you got jumped?"

Portman's shrug was too casual. "They know I like my privacy and don't want them hovering over me. They keep a safe distance between us."

"Safe for you or for them? If I were you, I'd replace them with guys who aren't afraid to risk their necks."

"It wasn't their fault." Portman's eyes slid away from Tom's steady gaze. "I told you, I like my privacy. They respect that."

"Who was the woman?" Tom's tone remained as steady and relentless as his gaze.

"What woman?"

"The woman they were respecting your privacy with."

"I don't know what you're talking about."

"Cut the bullshit. We both know that your security guys wouldn't let you out of their sight if you were simply taking a stroll alone on the beach. But no doubt they have standing orders to get lost if they see you coming on to a woman, especially if she's from your own circle and the wife or mistress of a friend or politician who can screw up one of your projects."

Portman didn't answer. He picked up his clipboard and began to inscribe big doodles. Tom was sure they were daggers.

"I've read a lot about you, Tony, but you're never mentioned as chivalrous. Surely you're not trying to protect the woman's reputation. Or is it yours you're trying to protect? Did your assailant attack her too—and did *she* manage to fight him off?"

"That's crap!" Portman's eyes flashed and his cheeks turned red. "If I couldn't take on that bastard, then no woman in the world could have, either. She was long gone when I was attacked."

"But on her way, she may have noticed someone. Who is she? And please don't say it was a near-sighted mermaid."

Portman groaned. "I was afraid of this. Al told me you were a discreet guy, so don't make a liar of him."

"Heaven forbid."

"It was Ilsa Grant."

Foster told Tom, "Even back in college, Tony had excellent taste in women."

"Don't sound so impressed. She's a lousy lay."

Foster shrugged. "I've heard otherwise. As usual, you must have come on like Tony the Tiger during the mating season."

"Is there any other way? I think that fancy fucking went out with Cary Grant. And there's one thing I know about women. They prefer to be subdued and treated rough."

Tom cut them off. "How long were you with Ilsa Grant?"

"Maybe twenty minutes."

"Where did your encounter take place? On the beach?"

"In the pavilion that I've built for the community, just as here in town I've built miniparks and plazas for the comfort and delight of my fellow New Yorkers."

"Is it one of those open-air structures with widely spaced columns?"

"It's a replica, more or less, of one I saw in Greece when I was cruising on my yacht with friends from Washington."

"And the lady was willing?"

"And how she was willing! What broad wouldn't be with Tony Portman? I've been on *People*'s list of the ten sexiest guys for the past eight years."

Tom had picked up the split-second hesitation as to the lady's willingness, but he decided not to pursue it just now. Ilsa Grant was about five-four and probably weighed no more than a hundred and ten pounds. There was no way she could have performed an intricate surgical castration in the midst of being raped, or even afterward.

"Tell me what happened next."

"You know damn well what happened next. That's why you're here."

"I mean immediately after your encounter with Ilsa Grant.

Did you sit and hold hands? Or gaze at the stars while you talked about your next tryst?"

"Almost immediately, she came down with a chill and went back to the party. We thought it better not to walk in together, so I stayed behind in the pavilion for a smoke and to enjoy the ocean breeze."

"I know that she's married to Vittorio Capperrelli, the former wrestler. Was he at the party too? Was he the reason you didn't want to walk in together?"

"Why go looking for trouble?"

"Were you in the pavilion long enough for her to have told her husband, and for him to come out and jump you?"

"I've already told you, she was as willing as a virgin with her dream guy. She would never have told him."

"Okay. But Capperrelli doesn't give me the impression of being the patient and understanding type. He's all muscle and all macho. Maybe he followed the two of you out to the pavilion, and when his wife left, he took his revenge."

Foster said from across the room, where he was studying a framed photograph of Portman and Tom DeLay at a barbecue, "If castration had crossed his mind, I doubt that he'd have been so meticulous about it. He would probably just have pulled off his prick."

Portman glared at his friend. "Olympic wrestler or no, I could take on that guy in a fair fight any day."

Tom turned to Foster. "Did you see him at the party at the time in question?"

Foster pondered awhile. "I know I saw him from time to time, always holding a full plate, but I can't be sure when. I didn't know then that I should have been checking my watch and taking notes. Besides, considering the fact that others in our group have been attacked at different times and places, isn't it more likely that it's an outsider?"

"On the contrary. The fact that the victims are part of a specific group makes it look like this is someone you all know."

Both Portman and Foster looked appalled at the idea. Portman cried, "Bullshit! No one we know would do anything like this. We don't hang around with criminals and creeps!"

Tom resisted the temptation to mention Portman's buddies at Enron, WorldCom, and Tyco, and asked instead, "With security men roaming around, how did an outsider get inside?"

"The Atlantic Ocean has a long coastline," Foster reminded Tom. "And let's face it, there's really no protection against a determined maniac."

"It's much too early to rule out any possibilities. I'll need a list of all the guests, and I'll have to talk to the other victims. Outsider or insider, there's something that connects this man to all of you, and when we find out what it is, we'll know who he is." He put his pad and pen into his pocket.

"So you're taking our case, then," Portman said.

"Not till my lawyer has received and examined the paper we discussed."

"You'll have it in the morning. But remember, this is a strictly private matter for all of us. With the exception of a few frat brothers, and Foster will tell you who they are, no one is to suspect what you're investigating, or that you're conducting an investigation at all."

"That may be a little difficult."

"No, we have it all worked out," Foster told him. "Maybe you can think of a better one, but your book business has suggested an adequate cover to us. There's a sociologist and fraternity brother out at Stanford, Blair Whitney, who's writing what he claims will be *the* definitive study of fraternities and the ongoing influence they have on the lives of members. We've gotten his okay for you to say you're doing research for him. It will give you an excuse to be seen hanging around us and attending all our functions, beginning with our twenty-fifth reunion weekend at GMU next week."

"Is Whitney a Golden Guy too?"

"No, he was three years behind us. We told him that we want you to investigate something secretly, but we didn't tell him what."

"And he wasn't curious?"

Foster glowered as if the question were an insult. "Members of Beta Alpha Beta Phi respect one another's privacy and trust one another."

"In addition to Ilsa Grant, I want to speak with the other two victims. Are they attending your reunion at GMU?"

"Only Bob Michaelson is coming. Neal Bernard is so depressed about the change in his appearance that he's becoming a recluse. I suggest you look him up as soon as possible, before he goes around the bend completely."

"Does he live here in town?"

"He has a town house here, but I'm pretty sure that he's holing up at one of his other residences. I'll call his wife and get back to you at your shop."

"How many residences does he have?"

"About six in the United States and three abroad in places like London, Rome, and the south of France. I call them 'residences,' but except for the town house, they're real estate operations and provide him with a nice chunk of income that is virtually tax free. He doesn't even have to pay extra water tax for his indoor swimming pool in Rome."

Tom got to his feet, and so did Portman and Foster.

"Find that son of a bitch and find him fast!" Portman ordered. "We have to get him before he gets to Lyle Wayne and wrecks his chances for the Presidency. For obvious reasons, I want to stay on the sidelines on this, so you'll report to Al. But when you get the bastard, you come directly to me, whether it's day or night."

Tom groped for a diplomatic reply. He didn't believe in vigilante justice. When he found the assailant, he intended to turn him over to the police, along with the evidence against him. But that was in the future, and he saw no particular harm in Portman's demand that he come to him first. He held out his hand and said, "All right. Agreed."

"And stay away from Ilsa Grant and her big Wop! I've told you everything about Montauk! There's nothing more to learn from them!"

"I'd like to find that out for myself."

"How will you go about it? I demand to know."

"The man's a pro," Foster reminded Portman. "I'm sure he has his bundle of tricks, just like the rest of us do." Foster chuckled.

"Shut up, Al!"

"Sorry." Foster started to smile, then gave up the idea.

"I'll think of a way to question them," Tom informed Portman. "All I want from you now is their address. And my check, of course."

"Foster will give them both to you. If you dare to cause me any embarrassment, it'll be the end of you, Berenson!"

"In what way?"

They stared at each other awhile. Portman began to breathe faster. The silence lay as heavy as a cement coffin between them. Finally, Foster nodded to Tom and then led the way to the door. In the corridor, as they started toward the elevator, Foster shook his head, sighed, then said in a faintly puzzled voice:

"Poor Tony. This affliction is causing sharper mood swings than I had anticipated. I hope he won't wind up requiring a psychotherapist. Despite all their self-serving crap about being as secretive as priests, they're the biggest blabbers in the profession, with the possible exception of the plastic surgeons who specialize in celebrities. I want to apologize for his occasional abruptness with you. Ordinarily, he's the sweetest guy you'd care to meet."

Boris was standing beside the elevator, and as they entered the vestibule, he swung open its door. Foster handed Tom his check in a plain white envelope, and, after nimbly manipulating a smartphone that was no bigger than a playing card, he gave Tom the phone number and home address of Ilsa Grant.

"Do you have me on it too?" Tom asked.

"You bet. And also the governor and the President."

"My father-in-law wanted to give me a more modest version for my birthday, but I told him that my life was too simple to require one."

Foster laughed. "Now that you're working for us Golden Guys, it may not be so simple anymore."

As the elevator door closed, the last thing Tom saw was Boris's icy glare.

CHAPTER 5

BACK IN THE living room, Foster sat down on an easy chair near Portman on the sofa.

"What did you think of our private eye?"

"He left me underwhelmed. I haven't seen a cheap suit like that in years. And his shoes weren't even polished. This guy has no special qualifications or credentials. He was obviously just a dime-a-dozen New York City cop."

"But he was a particularly good one. Neal made inquiries in all the proper quarters. When Tony Blair was threatened by the IRA during a visit to the UN, Giuliani had Berenson assigned to guarding him."

"Big deal! I'm sure he was also being guarded by his own security people and the FBI. This guy, working all alone, can't possibly have the capability of our usual investigators."

"Granted, but as I still insist, and Lyle and Neal both agree, a loner is less likely to leak information about your condition than a team of investigators working for an agency, and I don't care how discreet they're supposed to be. If word ever got out that you're... vulnerable, investors would switch projects you've been counting on to Donald Trump."

Portman's face grew red with rage. "Don't mention that guy to me! Him with his TV shows, his Miss Universe contests, his hairstyles—"

"What is it with you? No need to go ballistic every time his name is mentioned. There's enough cash slushing around in this city and country for both of you to swim in. You'll keep getting your share as long as we can put a lid on all this." He looked off at a photograph of Portman shaking hands with George Bush, Laura beaming wide-eyed beside them. And why not? She'd just seen Portman's check for the Bush Library.

Portman acknowledged the merit of the argument with a grunt. But then he frowned and said, "I still don't like the idea of this guy going around knowing what he does. Once he tells us what we need to know, he goes."

"Meaning…?"

"You know exactly what I mean. And his father-in-law and the kid—we want them taken care of too."

"Is it really necessary? He's not the kind of guy who would blab to anyone. We're paying him enough to keep his mouth shut."

"Not all of that money is in advance. We've got better things to do with it. It's not like you to be so damn naïve. This is business. Big business. Forget about the Hippocratic oath, if that's what's bothering you. You read every day about poor people who die because they're turned away by doctors and hospitals."

Foster sighed. "I guess you're right. But it is too bad. I kind of like Max, his father-in-law. As a kid, he always preferred my father's brand of liverwurst to Braunschweiger, Oscar Mayer's, and every other big-name brand."

"I'm touched." Portman clenched a hand. "When the time comes, we keep it in the family. No outsiders. We want you to take care of it."

Foster blanched. "Come on, Tony! You can't mean that. What about Boris? This is right up his alley. If he was good enough for the KGB, he's good enough for the Golden Guys."

"Not after a few vodkas with those thugs in Brighton Beach. It's been decided. It has to be one of us, and you're the one who has the best access."

"How come I wasn't in on this decision?"

Portman shrugged. "I guess you weren't available that day. You were probably in the operating room, enlarging the cock of one of your celebrity patients. I hope you've taken my advice to charge them by the inch."

"You should have waited for me. You guys are always leaving me out, and it isn't fair. You know I can't do something like this."

"Cut out the shit. You'll damn well do it." He held up his hand to head off another protest. "And don't tell me you've never killed anyone. You Park Avenue doctors have plenty of blood on your hands. Think of all the desperately ill patients you've turned away because their insurance won't cover your fancy fees. When was the last time you took on a charity case, or some poor slob on Medicaid whose life could have been saved by your expert skills?"

"That's different, Tony!"

"The hell it is. Now stop whining. You sound like when we were back at GMU and we forgot to let you know about a gang bang or beer bust. You're not a kid anymore. You'll get used to the idea. On second thought, maybe we can give Berenson's family a pass. We'll let you know."

"No. We'll decide that together. No more decisions without me. I mean that, Tony."

"Sure, sure. We'll have a conference." Portman relaxed against the sofa. He took out his BlackBerry. "I'll have that drink now."

"Make it two," Foster said. "And have him bring in the bottle. And some corn chips."

CHAPTER 6

W HEN BETH'S illness began to take over their lives, Tom had hired Phil Howard, a retired librarian who lived in the neighborhood, to work part-time in the shop and fill in for him as needed. He arranged for Phil to open up on Friday, and at ten he left for his appointment with Ilsa Grant and Vittorio Capperrelli. Rather than risk being delayed in traffic, he took the subway to Sixty-eighth Street and Lexington Avenue, then walked over to their Fifth Avenue apartment. The doorman announced him, and told him to take the elevator to the tenth floor.

As the door to 10C opened, Tom was stunned to find himself so close to someone so tall and so wide. It was like standing on the corner of Fifth Avenue and Thirty-fourth Street and looking up at the Empire State Building.

Vittorio Capperrelli was aware of his effect upon strangers, and he tried to mitigate it by offering a hand and a broad smile to his visitor. Tom took the big hand gingerly, but found it less overpowering than that of the guy who handled his insurance.

Instead of his usual TV attire, a jogging outfit full of logos and patches for his multitude of sponsors, Capperrelli wore a pendant with a huge gold cross, a yellow turtleneck, and gray slacks. Over his deep, large eyes, which *Vanity Fair* had compared to Rudolph Valentino's, he wore the dark-framed eyeglasses of the successful Italian businessman or professional.

"Come in, come in," he said in a soft, cultivated voice, and with much less of an accent than in his commercials or public-service appeals for a cleaner environment and a drug-free society.

"Thank you, Mr. Capperrelli. It's good of you to see me on such short notice."

"My beautiful wife will be with us shortly. You pronounce my name just like an Italian. Are you a *paisano?*"

"No. But I have a lot of Italian friends."

"Friends are as important to our well-being as the right food, vitamins, and exercise, and my wife and I are always so happy to try to help out a good friend like Tony Portman." After a solemn nod he went on cheerfully, "We were very sorry to hear of this unusual theft, and in Montauk of all places. I hope that Tony's prospective tenants there don't hear about it. But I am sure it is just an isolated incident. Come into the parlor. Everyone in New York calls it the living room, but my wife, who's from a rather quaint little town in Vermont, insists on calling it the parlor."

"I thought that she came from Brooklyn."

"That was just her biological birthplace. But for interviews and such, she now prefers to be from Vermont. It's true of a lot of other celebrities."

Tom nodded as if it were all crystal clear to him. Feeling very short at six-one, he accompanied Capperrelli along a foyer hung with landscapes in watercolor.

"They're all very beautiful," Tom said.

"Yes, and they're all of Italy. The poet Robert Browning said, 'Oh, to be in England now that April's there.' But he was a wise poet, and chose to write the poem while he lived in Italy. By the way, who do you think painted these pictures?"

"Someone with a lot of talent, I'm sure. They remind me of John Singer Sargent."

"Thank you. The fact is, I myself painted them."

"Congratulations. You're a man of many talents. A real Renaissance man."

"Except that I've never poisoned anyone—yet. Yes, I've been very blessed. Maybe the Good Lord is rewarding me for being a choir boy for so many years. I was allergic to incense, and almost sneezed whenever the censer was swung in my direction. And it was a very painful decision for me when I had to choose between singing and wrestling. Fortunately, my priest was also the chaplain for the Italian Olympic team, and he convinced me to change to wrestling."

At the end of the foyer, Capperrelli threw open the French doors and, with the lavish gesture of Don Giovanni welcoming his latest conquest to his bedroom, he implored Tom to precede him into the huge, bright, colorful room. As Tom complied, he felt that he was stepping into a painting by Matisse. Certainly the picture over the plum sofa looked like a Matisse. It depicted a nude woman watering the plants on her windowsill. Back in Brooklyn, Max was in charge of watering the plants, and he would have praised Matisse's nude for attending to her window garden even before attending to her own attire.

"Beautiful room, isn't it?" Capperrelli said, and coiled his powerful arms across his chest. "My wife and I designed it together, with a very minimum of professional help. When we decided to get a dog, we chose one whose colors—white and gray—would harmonize."

Tom wondered if Capperrelli was kidding him about the dog, but he suppressed a smile. "It's absolutely gorgeous," he said truthfully.

"Wait!" Rather dramatically if not operatically, Capperrelli lifted a forefinger as he retreated to the door. "I think I hear the arrival of someone who is even more gorgeous." Then he called out, "In here, *cara mia*. And Mr. Berenson is here too."

Ilsa Grant paused briefly in the doorway to scrutinize Tom, and perhaps also to give him a chance to scrutinize and admire her. Then, satisfied that he didn't appear to be a threat or problem, she smiled and completed her entrance into the room. Wearing a red jumpsuit and a pair of immaculate white Mercurys, the jogging shoes endorsed by her husband, she managed to walk with more sexuality than an expensive Park Avenue call girl in a negligee.

"Hi. I'm Ilsa Grant." Her short blond hair looked perfectly attractive, but she frowned and pursed her lips as she patted and poked it for a suitable period. "I just came in from this awful wind, so please excuse my appearance."

Tom hoped his smile said that her appearance required praise rather than excuses.

She turned around in place and glanced at the cocktail table and other areas. "I see that my husband hasn't offered you any refreshment yet."

"I'm so sorry about that," Capperrelli said to Tom. "Can I bring you a Tiger's milk shake, or some herbal tea?"

"And I think we can also rustle up some of the more conventional drinks," Ilsa added with a smile.

"Just joking," Capperrelli informed Tom. "People always expect me to act like a health freak, so I try not to disappoint them."

"And you usually succeed quite well, dear."

"Living with an actress, I've come to learn some of the tricks of the trade."

"We prefer to think of it as a profession."

"Thank you," Tom told her, "but I really don't want anything."

"You're here, I know, about Tony Portman and some peculiar robbery at Montauk, but I really don't understand anything about it."

"It happened late on the night of August twenty-seventh."

She turned to her husband. "Vic, refresh my poor memory. Was I in Montauk then?"

"We both were. That was the night of the big bash for his condos. Condos—what a silly idea. To own a property with a hundred other people is like not owning it at all."

"Poor Vic. You will never understand the real estate business."

"Do you, *cara mia?*"

"I understand enough to know that it pays for our new apartment." She sat down on the sofa and indicated an adjacent easy chair to Tom.

When he was settled, he leaned forward and addressed them both: "I assume that Mr. Portman has spoken to you about this robbery."

"Not a word," Ilsa said. "But I'm becoming quite intrigued."

"I don't think I've seen him since that night," her husband said. "Actually, we're not that close. I know him only through my wife, who is his spokesperson." He laughed. "Spokesperson—what a peculiar occupation."

"That's what you are, and for many things. Do you object to my being one too, dear?"

He swiveled his head to observe the apartment and its contents. Then he sat back on the sofa and extended his long arm across its top. "If you're happy, I'm happy," he murmured.

"At about eleven o'clock," Tom began, "Mr. Portman left the party and went out to the terrace for some fresh air. Since the night was so pleasant, he decided to take a stroll along the beach. After a while, his shoes were so full of sand that he went into the pavilion to empty them. While there, he was assaulted and robbed. On behalf of his insurer, I'm trying to get some information from his guests that evening."

"It's absolutely shocking," Capperrelli said. But he looked more amused than shocked.

"Poor, poor Tony." As Tom was speaking, Ilsa had turned away to rearrange some flowers on the cocktail table that didn't need rearranging. She didn't raise her head as she asked, "Was he hurt badly?"

"He was hurt badly enough to need some medical attention."

Now she did look up. For a second, her eyes were impenetrable. Then she widened them to tragic dimensions. Tom was sure that she regretted the lack of a handkerchief, so that she could express all sorts of deep and heartfelt emotions with it. "I hope his injury wasn't serious."

"It's still being evaluated, I believe."

"He's a big and powerful guy," Capperrelli said. "It must have taken a whole gang to attack him."

Ilsa leaned forward. "What was he robbed of?"

"His watch, money, and credit cards," Tom said gravely. "And, what's most important to his insurer, a negotiable bond for a considerable amount of money."

"How does that differ from a regular bond?"

"It's the equivalent of cash."

"Why was he carrying it around with him so late at night?" Capperrelli asked.

Tom was prepared for the sensible question. "He'd just received it in payment for a particularly desirable condo."

Ilsa nodded knowingly. "That's the way these big wheelers and dealers operate," she informed her husband. "They're not like you and me, who, when we want something, we pay real money for it. These guys pass around bonds and pieces of paper so that they charge everything to their companies, or so that they don't have to pay taxes."

Capperrelli shrugged. "So what else is new? We had that in Venice and Florence even before America was discovered in 1492. By, of course, an Italian."

"Who was the big operator who paid with this valuable bond?" Ilsa asked Tom.

"I'm sorry, but his identity is confidential." Tom made an apologetic smile, and spread his hands in a gesture of helplessness.

"I bet it was Bernie Madoff," Capperrelli said. "He wouldn't bother talking to me. I don't have millions in my pocket to invest in his funds. But someone told me he was there to look for an apartment for one of his sons. That guy must walk around with a bunch of those bonds in his pocket."

Ilsa shook her head. "He's out of our class, dear, but I've heard from one of my directors, Carl Hochman, that he's a straight shooter and wouldn't do anything underhanded." She snapped her fingers. "I bet it was Tony's buddy Bob Michaelson. He gets such a kick out of these tricky financial maneuvers that if he wanted a chocolate cupcake, it would never occur to him to go directly into a bakery and buy one. First, he would buy the bakery and then he would put his brother-in-law in charge."

Tom laughed at her joke, which was not that far from the truth, and then he said, "I'm hoping that one or both of you saw something that evening that may help us to apprehend Mr. Portman's assailants. My company is offering a reward, and Mr. Portman will also be very appreciative of any help."

Capperrelli's eyes narrowed. "Did he suggest that you question either me or my wife in particular?"

"Your names are included on a list that he had compiled. He did say to me that upon his return from his ordeal on the beach, he happened to see you both in the banquet room, and unlike so many of the other guests, you both looked sober and alert."

"I am *always* sober and alert," Capperrelli announced, and he expanded his chest with a deep breath. "Last March or April, I attended the Passover Seder of the author who's helping me with my autobiography. There I had four little glasses of that red

Jewish wine called Manischewitz. But I haven't had any wine or anything alcoholic since then."

"That's my good boy." Ilsa leaned over and kissed his cheek.

"At the seder, my author mentioned that Jews are big readers, and it would be nice if we could find some Jewish relatives or pay tribute to the Jews in my background."

"Not a bad idea." Tom cleared his throat. "And did either of you see anything?"

Ilsa and her husband went through the motions of pondering. Almost at the same moment, they turned to each other and looked long and hard for a signal. Finally, Capperrelli turned back to Tom and shrugged.

"I was across the room at the time," he said, "but I did see Tony come in through the French doors."

"What time was this?"

"About midnight, because I'd just taken my zinc tablet. I don't know about you, Mr. Berenson, but whenever I have to stay up beyond my usual bedtime of ten-thirty, I make it a point to have an extra zinc tablet, and sometimes a kelp and ginger capsule too. When he came in from I don't know where, maybe to look at all the wonderful stars, or maybe to keep a date with Miss or Mrs. Montauk, Tony seemed in good shape, not like he'd been roughed up and needed a doctor. And though his *paisanos* Dr. Foster and Senator Lyle Wayne—America's next President, God save us all—were not that far away from the door, he did not hurry right over to them as if he needed help immediately."

Tom smiled and said lightly, "Do I gather that you're not a big fan of the senator?"

After a glare at her husband, Ilsa laughed and said in a rush, "It's just one of his pet peeves. He blames the senator for the big tariff on his new line of silk shirts from Milano."

"I can't keep up with him and those other crooks down there in Washington!" Capperrelli roared. "In Italy, a deal is a deal with a politician, and it usually lasts until he's assassinated or caught in a scandal and has to leave public life for an election season or even two. But here in America, the land of the free and the home of the brazen, nothing at all is free, and certainly not trade. They keep asking for more and bigger campaign contributions every year." He thumped his chest so that it sounded like a bass drum. "I am merely a small businessman, not the owner of Fiat or the House of Gucci."

"How about you, Ms. Grant?" Tom asked. "Did you see anything out of the ordinary that night?"

He was sure she blanched. But a split second latter, she shook her head vigorously. "I'm sorry. I neither saw him go out nor did I see him return. I'm the spokesperson for his residential properties, and so I was hard at work all evening, charming clients and chatting up the media. At about midnight, when I felt that even my wrinkles had wrinkles, Senator Wayne, who had loused up my husband's shirt deal, had the audacity to suggest that we pose together for TV."

"And so neither of you saw anything or anyone suspicious from one of the windows in the room, or from outside on the terrace or on the beach."

"At perhaps that time," Ilsa said, returning to her flower arranging, "I did step out for a breath of air for a minute or two, but I remained on the terrace and saw nothing there."

Tom had been watching Capperrelli while Ilsa was speaking. Capperrelli seemed lost in thought, and his gaze slowly descended one of her legs to the slim ankle above her white shoe. Suddenly he realized that it was his time to speak, and he said quickly, "I never went outside to the terrace or beach that evening. In my teens, I was a lifeguard at a beach on Capri, and I developed there an aversion to amorous old women and to walking on sand that could be contaminated with condoms and cigar and cigarette butts and rotten foods. I did look out the window a few times, but I saw only an infinity of darkness."

"But otherwise you saw nothing strange?" Tom prodded.

"On the contrary, everything I saw there was strange."

Ilsa laughed like a mother whose little boy has said something improper. "Don't mind my husband. Everything that transpired that night was absolutely normal and usual for a gathering of that sort. The writer who's helping him with his book once wrote a biography of Krishnamurti, the Indian mystic or whatever, and Vic has been reading it in bed recently."

"I recommend this book very highly to you," Capperrelli

told Tom. "Unlike such people as Tony Portman and his friends, Krishnamurti spurned power and wealth and desired to live the simple life of a traveling guru. One of these days, Tony and his friends are going to reap the whirlwind."

"That's possible," Tom said. "But currently, it looks very unlikely, don't you think?"

"Maybe it has something to do with the change in the ozone layer, but haven't you noticed, my friend, that things are changing more quickly than they used to? As recently as the mid-eighties, no one predicted the sudden end of the Soviet Union and its satellites, or the sudden victory of Japan over the United States and General Motors, the biggest corporation in the world. A few years ago, who would have thought that China would become one of America's biggest lenders, buying up your treasury bonds and companies? Who would have dreamed that fanatics would crash planes into the World Trade Center, or that instead of being quick the war in Iraq would be quicksand?"

That was a more profound answer than Tom had expected from a man more famous for his muscles than his mind. He looked inquiringly from Capperrelli to Ilsa Grant, then persisted: "But who would want to harm Tony and his friends? They may have their little faults or excesses, but all in all, the American public regards them as national heroes. Everyone wants to become billionaire wheelers and dealers like them."

"That's very true," Ilsa agreed. "The ones I've met are not only men of achievement but fine gentlemen. You know, a documentary is being made about them. People were filming for it right there at the party. Tony and his friends were called the Golden Guys when they were back in college, and the name has stuck. Everything they put their minds to seems to turn to gold."

As her husband snickered, she tried to glare him into silence. But it was like a kitten trying to intimidate a bear. First, he took her hand and kissed it. Then, holding the hand, he told Tom, "I know of at least one man who really hates the guts of those Golden Guys and wouldn't mind ridding the earth of every last one of them."

Ilsa pulled her hand free and leaped to her feet. "That was just your impression, Vic, because you're so very Latin and macho."

"Who are we talking about?" Tom asked lightly.

"It makes no difference!" Ilsa cried.

"What's the big secret here?" her husband asked her. "Is Tony Portman going to accuse a big and famous guy like him of stealing his negotiable bond?"

"Of course not. But this conversation is making me very uncomfortable."

"You just work for Tony Portman, and you work damn hard for him, and you don't owe him any special favors or loyalties so that you can't speak your mind. Those you owe only to me, your loving and devoted husband, just as I owe them only to you."

"I know that," Ilsa murmured. She sounded rather overwhelmed by the implications of his remark.

He drew her back to the sofa, and then sat her down beside him and stroked her cheek. "Now try to be quiet and good while I explain to our guest. The man who made those remarks about the Golden Guys," he told Tom, "was Lou West, the famous football coach at Gouverneur Morris University. I was introduced to him by Ed Siegler, the writer who's helping me with my book. He also helped Lou with *his* book, which is a national bestseller and may even become a miniseries on TV. But Ed tells me that my own book should be even more popular, because I have more charisma and sex appeal." He raised his cross to his lips and kissed it. "God has been very good to me. I work for Him and He works for me. Some people criticize me for not fighting against AIDS. But as I once explained on *Sixty Minutes,* the Lord must punish these evil transgressors who misuse their genitals."

Never much of a fan of the rough, Machiavellian Lou West, Tom had merely read the blurbs and merchandising tips for *Coach!* when the book arrived in the store a couple of weeks ago, and he couldn't recall any material about West and the Golden Guys.

"I would have thought that Lou West and the Golden Guys got along like spaghetti and meat balls," he told Capperrelli. "Why don't they like one another?"

"I don't know the details. We met one afternoon at a birthday party for Ed at the St. Regis. Ed's such a big publicity hound that the ASPCA should make him wear a license. A couple of the TV channels agreed to cover the party if he supplied enough celebrities to make it worth their while, which is understandable."

Ilsa leaned forward and struck a sophisticated pose. "I refused to attend this crummy and utterly commercial affair," she said to Tom.

Capperrelli enveloped her in a hug that came close to crushing her. "That's because she knew that though I could have my choice of all the gorgeous women there, I would remain two hundred percent faithful to her, just as she, under similar circumstances, would remain faithful to me. There is a spiritual as well as a physical affinity between us, and if one of us does anything wrong or sinful, the other soon knows about it."

Tom smiled his approval of their ideal relationship, his eyes on Ilsa, who was smiling wanly. "You were going to tell me about Lou West and the Golden Guys."

"I really have nothing more to add. On these occasions, as you surely know, everyone drops all the famous names he knows and has ever known even slightly, and after mentioning George Bush and Justice Scalia and those charming ladies, Queen Elizabeth of England and the late, lamented Mother Teresa, I happened to mention Tony Portman, who had dropped by earlier. Lou had been drinking a lot, and he seemed to be more asleep than awake, but he suddenly jumped up and began swearing at me, saying I shouldn't mention such scum in the same breath as the one that had pronounced the name of the sainted Mother Teresa.

"I don't think anyone else noticed. We were off in a corner by ourselves, and Ed calmed him down immediately. It was really strange, though. Only an hour earlier he'd been horsing around and posing for publicity photos with Tony and a couple of other Golden Guys who had brought the Gouverneur Morris football team and Lou himself to glory when they played." He shook his head.

Ilsa forced a tinkling, disparaging laugh. "Vittorio still can't interpret macho American behavior when it comes to hard drinking," she told Tom. She patted her husband's hand. "I'm sure it was just the liquor talking, dear. Lou West has probably forgotten the incident."

Capperrelli looked doubtful. "I certainly haven't. I can still see the hatred in his eyes. *In vino veritas,* as we've said in my country since the time of the Caesars."

CHAPTER 7

"**W**HY ARE WE stopping here?" Tom asked Neal Bernard's chauffeur, a tall and husky black man who had introduced himself as Sam at the airport.

Tom had been flown to Nantucket in Tony Portman's Cessna, and after being met by Sam and the pale-blue Lexus that matched the sky on this windy afternoon, he had expected to be taken directly to a mansion overlooking the sea. Instead, Sam had just pulled into a parking lot behind a gabled inn on Gardner Street, which was only a short walk from the downtown shops and restaurants. Ten years ago, this same inn, The Captain's Bounty, had exuded much more atmosphere than the out-of-the-way little hotel where Tom and his family were staying, but after inquiring about the rates here, he and Beth decided that it wasn't really for them despite the inn's claim to preeminence in comfort, decor, service, and cuisine, including the best scones and muffins on the island. However, they agreed to make reservations at that vague but inevitable time in the future when they would be rolling in dough.

Sam emerged lithely from the car and opened the rear door for Tom. "This is where Mr. Bernard resides on Nantucket," he said. He stared with concern until his passenger was safely out of the car. Or maybe he was afraid that Tom's head would dent the Lexus.

Holding his new and impressive Samsonite three-gusset briefcase, which contained his laptop, pads and pens, Tom accompanied Sam toward a side door of the house. The gravel was multicolored, and noisier than usual. Only two cars—a Mercedes and a Saab—were in the parking lot that could have accommodated about twenty. A striped cat peered but did not grin at him from the branch of a silver birch, and a German shepherd gazed at him from one of the white chairs around a lawn table. The dog uncurled himself, rose, and barked once. Then, having established his credentials, he resumed his siesta.

"I've heard that Nantucket is being turned into isolated fiefdoms for billionaires," Tom said. "I had pictured your boss in one of them, something more befitting a man of his wealth and sophistication."

"His other places are certainly like that, sir, but here on the island, he prefers to live the simple life of his ancestors. They settled here before the Revolutionary War."

"Do you know which side they were on?"

Sam suppressed a grin. "Google might tell you that."

Tom smiled too. "Anyhow, this place sounds like a sensible idea to me. I guess a man needs a change even from luxury."

"And since he spends so little time here, Mr. Bernard converted the old homestead into an inn, and he merely retains a suite in a wing on the top floor, where he can maintain his privacy from the paying guests." Sam glanced at his watch. "I'm supposed to ask whether you'd prefer to have your lunch before or after your conference with him."

"I guess it's too late for your famous scones and muffins."

"I'll check it out in the kitchen."

"It makes no difference when I eat. Which would be better for your boss? I know that at upwards of five grand an hour, these topflight lawyers have rigid schedules."

"He always has his cottage cheese and toast exactly at noon, so I'm sure he's already partaken of his luncheon."

"In that case, I'd rather see him as soon as possible. That plane is coming back for me at three-thirty, and I want to have time to pick up a few souvenirs."

Sam led him through a side door and then up two flights of narrow and thumpy stairs. Tom wondered whether this was where Bernard had been assaulted. But Foster had told him again and again that he must not question any of Bernard's people, because they weren't to know about his injury.

"Is this a private staircase?"

"Yes, sir. Only Mr. Bernard and his visitors use it. And maybe a few ghosts."

"How about the staff?"

"They're discouraged from using it."

"Does he get many visitors?"

"He gets a few." Sam turned his head and looked curiously at Tom.

As they reached the landing, an alarm began to ring. "Oh, shit!" Sam rushed over to a moose head upon a wall. There he pressed the animal's nose and shut off the alarm. "Sorry about that. Usually it's turned off in the morning, but the boss wants it on all day today for some reason."

"I once read in *New York* magazine that the first thing he does in the morning is consult his astrologer. Maybe his astrologer warned him about danger today."

Sam grinned. "That's possible."

"So it's true that he's an astrology fan."

"Absolutely." He thumped his chest. "The most important qualification for my job is that I'm a Leo. I hope your sign is compatible. If it isn't, you may have wasted a long trip from Brooklyn."

"How did you know I'm from Brooklyn?"

Sam didn't answer at once, and when he did, he spoke quickly: "I guess I heard the boss mention it." Before opening the last door on a long corridor hung with dark, depressing pictures of whalers and lighthouses, he said softly, "I'll inform Mr. Bernard that you're here. Don't feel offended if he sits apart from you. It isn't because he's unfriendly. He's recovering from a bad case of the flu and is avoiding other people's germs."

Sam was gone for a minute, and then reappeared in the doorway and beckoned Tom to enter. Full of dark leather furniture and shelves of the sort of thick books that impress visitors and justify the fees of lawyers and doctors, the room was a lawyer's working office such as Tom had often visited professionally as a cop. Sitting in one of those modernistic ergonomic chairs that are advertised to cure, for starters, slipped discs and pinched nerves, Bernard was switching off a computer. Then, as he rose and started rather feebly toward a recliner across the room, he motioned

Tom to a wing chair in front of a framed photograph of himself with Lyle Wayne and George Bush. "Welcome to Nantucket," he said. "Ever been here before?"

"Three times."

"Then you're my kind of folks. Disneyland is for...for those who like that sort of thing." Bernard turned to Sam. "That's all for now. I am not to be disturbed unless it's my wife, or Dr. Foster, or Senator Wayne." He motioned Sam to wait, then turned to Tom. "Would you like a drink of some sort? We're famous for our cider."

"I had something on the plane. Thanks."

As the door shut behind Sam, Tom said, "He looks like a formidable man. I assume that he's also your bodyguard."

"I was told I could be frank with you. There's not that much to guard anymore."

"I wouldn't say that. For one thing, you still have your mind, which is supposed to be the sharpest in your profession."

"Thanks, Berenson, but it isn't as if I were a priest or a celibate. The loss of his pecker diminishes a man out of all proportion to its size, not that mine was ever anything to write home about."

With an obligatory smile, Tom conveyed that Bernard was being too modest, and that his pecker no doubt belonged in the *Guiness Book of World Records*.

"Sam has been with me only two months. I wish I'd had him around on the night I was attacked."

"Bodyguards didn't help Tony Portman."

"Tony Portman goes around looking for trouble."

"Can you explain that a little, Mr. Bernard?"

"I was referring to his lifestyle. For one thing, he doesn't hesitate to pursue the wives of other men. Ordinarily, I wouldn't mention that to a stranger like you, but Al Foster wants me to tell you everything that can possibly help your investigation." Bernard leaned forward and tensed his brow. "Before we go any further, would you mind telling me your sign?"

Tom nodded matter-of-factly. "Not at all. I'm an Aries."

"Fine. Good enough. A Libra would be just a bit more advantageous for present purposes, but I don't see why an Aries shouldn't be compatible too."

"Thank you. Al Foster is right about the need for you to co-operate." Tom unzipped a pocket of his briefcase and removed a ballpoint and a legal pad. "Who are these wives and men?"

"Since I've been happily married for eighteen years and philander very infrequently and in very different circles, it's unlikely that the same jealous husband would be after both me and Tony. Some of his women are young enough to be his daughter. Not that I fault him for that. I like them young too, but I stick to girls who will depart gracefully and not too expensively when the relationship has run its course." He smiled roguishly. "By the way, I read recently in a biography of Voltaire that his favorite mistress was his own niece."

"I'm sure she was also his favorite niece."

"Further, the church didn't consider such a relationship to be incestuous."

"*Autres moeurs*, etc. Especially in France. Those names, please...."

"How far back shall I go? To our college days?"

"Was he already active back then?"

Bernard raised a well-trimmed eyebrow. "Aren't all college guys, then and now? You name it, and Tony was doing it. We all were."

"How about rape and sodomy?"

Bernard laughed. "Obviously, I was exaggerating a little."

After that, he quickly named fourteen women, ten of whom Tom knew from TV and the press, including *The National Enquirer*. One was a popular author and advocate for ultra-conservative policies on gays, abortion, and family values. Tom was especially amused to hear the name of New York City Deputy Mayor Ginger Pritman, who had pushed through a forty-nine-million-dollar tax subsidy for Portman's contemplated project in Brooklyn Heights, and he looked forward to passing along Ginger's name to his lawyer.

"I think that's enough for starters," Bernard said. "Foster has told me some great things about you, Berenson. There's a maniac on the loose, and we've got to catch and dispose of him."

"I think that disposing of him should be the job of our legal system."

"That's what I meant, of course." Bernard looked perplexed about something, and Tom wondered what it was.

"Al Foster tells me that you have no enemies."

Bernard looked upward as if he were communing with angels. "That's true." He lowered a hand to his crotch. "Believe me, I've pondered and pondered until my head aches, but I can't think of anyone who would want to do such a thing to my poor friend Elmer."

"Not even Clara Claiborne?"

"Why do you bring her up? Have you uncovered any evidence about the bitch? Nothing would make me happier than putting her behind bars for the rest of her unnatural life. She always harangues us about keeping everything pure and natural, but the fat bitch never appears in public without a ton of makeup. And according to my informant at Bloomingdale's, it's not a brand that doesn't experiment with animals."

"I have no evidence about her involvement, but she's certainly been saying some pretty nasty things about you ever since you defended Colonial Mining and won. Immediately after the Colonial trial, she said on PBS's *NewsHour* that, like her native Maryland countryside, you deserve to be destroyed by one of Colonial's bulldozers."

"Don't believe a word she says about me. I'm worth a fortune to her, and she hates me all the way to Citibank, where her various foundations and organizations have their accounts, and they amount to a considerable sum, let me tell you. Do you know that she also has a personal account in a Swiss bank? She used to be a mere consumer reporter on a paper in the wilds of Ohio, but since latching on to the environment issue, she has become a national celebrity, and probably her only real problem these days is whether Glenn Close or Meryl Streep should portray her in the movies. I'm sure she was delighted when I moved on to defend Luxxon Oil. All the more money for her."

"Is that what she has told you, Mr. Bernard, or are you just interpreting or evaluating her conduct?"

"Since we are not exactly intimates, the woman has never confided in me that she is as greedy as anyone else in business, the professions, and government, but I take it for granted that she is."

"Nevertheless, I'll have to check her whereabouts during the time of the assault on you."

"Are you demented? She could never have taken me on. But you should check up on her hatchet man, Charlie Ludlow. During the Luxxon trial, I had occasion to see him close up outside the courthouse as he was giving a pep talk to the traveling troupe of professional picketers that he probably pays to follow him around. He struck me as being the embodiment of evil, and as a guy who's not in full control of himself, unlike Clara, whose every word and move is calculated, I'm sure."

"Do you know Lou West?"

"I'm proud to say that I do. He was the greatest coach ever at GMU, and a great American. About a year ago, he also became a client of our firm. When I heard that he was writing a book, I immediately recognized its enormous potential, and suggested that he get in touch with our Chuck Fenlow, who's the top literary lawyer in the country. A week never goes by when one of his clients or her dog or cat isn't on the best-seller lists. Where does Lou come into this?"

"He was recently heard bad-mouthing Tony Portman."

"I'll bet he was under the influence at the time." Bernard laughed as Tom nodded. "Something happens to poor Lou when he has even a single drink. He's always been that way."

"Would he have any reason to harm Portman?"

"None at all. Nor, certainly, would he want to harm me. For Christ's sake, I introduced him to the investment counselor who was instrumental in making him financially independent for the rest of his life! Some of these counselors are nothing but rip-off artists, but I told Schuyler Price that Lou was an old pal of mine and was not to be screwed like an old fart of a senior citizen who'd answered an ad in the financial section of the Sunday paper."

"Al Foster told me that the assault on you occurred on the evening of Saturday, May seventh."

"That's right. I'll never forget that date."

"Tell me what happened. And in detail."

Bernard winced, then sighed and began:

His wife, Erica, was away in Milan, where she was researching her next novel, based on the romance between Wanda Toscanini and Vladimir Horowitz. Bernard was spending the weekend here in Nantucket with a few friends. On the night of May seventh, he was walking alone on Cliff Beach when he was attacked from behind and knocked out. When he recovered, he was surprised to discover that he hadn't been robbed, not even of his Rolex and his wallet. He could think of no other motive for an assault on his person, not on Nantucket, not anywhere. Naturally, he reported the incident to the police. They didn't find the assailants although he was sure that they had tried their best for him, a benefactor of the police and of the whole island.

"I never really expected them to," he finished his story.

"Why is that?"

"Their resources are limited, and they were bogged down at the time on an arson case. I trust that you'll have better results for me."

"Do you recall the name of the detective on the case?"

"I certainly do. His name was Watson, and I couldn't help wishing that it was Holmes."

"Who were the friends staying with you?"

"Tony Portman, and Doug McGrath, and Senator Lyle Wayne. Portman you've met, I believe. McGrath is the movie superstar. Even his muscles have muscles. And I don't have to tell you about Senator Wayne."

"Did they come alone or with a wife or girlfriend?"

"Without."

"Without what?"

"Without their wives."

"How about girlfriends?"

"Is that relevant?"

"It might be."

Bernard sighed. "Portman and McGrath brought girlfriends, but the girls didn't stay here. They wanted more glitzy accommodations, and I was able to get them something more suitable elsewhere."

"That sounds a little odd to me."

"In what way?"

"Why bring along girlfriends on a trip if they're not around to do their thing on demand? I'm of course assuming that these women weren't intellectual companions, or experts on whales and whale-watching."

"I see what you mean. You'll have to ask Portman and McGrath about that. But I was just as glad to have the girls off the premises. They were both young enough to be the daughters of the two guys, and this is basically a family hotel. Besides, staying with us that weekend was Daniel Escott, head of Faith, Family and America's Future. Whatever his own morals, he expects everyone else to be as pure as the driven snow."

"I know that Escott isn't a Golden Guy. Is he a member of your fraternity?"

"Yes. He was a few years ahead of us at GMU."

"Is he a friend as well as a guest?"

"Yes. And I'm also one of his lawyers."

"So I assume that he is also acquainted with Portman and McGrath."

Bernard nodded. "And they'd also had a variety of business dealings. For instance, Portman was the prime contractor for God's Great Cathedral City in Arkansas. And McGrath is the front man for the city's annual two weeks of rodeos and barbecues, which attracts tens of thousands of the faithful and keeps Dan's armored cars rolling to the bank. Two things that Dan Escott will never preach are kindness to animals and vegetarianism."

"But he does preach against the evils of abortion and stem-cell research, I know."

"You can say that again. During his fund-raisers, he makes the Pope sound like a liberal."

"How sincere is he?"

"What you really want to ask is whether he cares enough about his beloved fetuses to castrate a poor sinner like me."

"Well...?"

Bernard shook his head sharply. "Not a chance. Like most of our saviors both in and out of government and religion, he has found a profitable niche and jumped into it. If Dan ever castrated anybody, it would be because he found the guy screwing his young blond so-called secretary, who has tits like Dolly Parton's. She's his private property."

"And I assume, Mr. Bernard, that you and the secretary...."

"You assume correctly. Nobody lays a finger, no less a pecker, on any of the girls in Danny's holy harem." Bernard winced suddenly, and he sat up in his recliner and leaned over to massage his thigh. Then he jumped from the chair and began to pace the floor almost frantically. "These damn spasms!" he cried. "They started a few days after the attack. Previously, I'd never had one in my life except when I jogged too much. Catch that fucken son of a bitch! I know that you've made certain arrangements with Foster, but I'm prepared to give you a generous bonus." After pacing another minute, he took a few deep breaths, sat down on his recliner, and resumed massaging his thigh.

"How well do you know Ilsa Grant?" Tom asked him.

"Not well enough to screw her, which I assume is what you want to know. First of all, I don't want to tangle with her husband, who could take on all of us Golden Guys single-handed in a fair fight, not that we ever fight fair." He bared his teeth in a grin. "That was just a joke, and off the record. Second, since the woman works for Portman, I assume that he will get all the bedroom privileges, if and when there are any going around. The first and last time I ever met her was at the bash for Portman's condos in Montauk."

"Did you notice anything unusual that night?"

"Unusual in what way?"

"That was the night Portman was assaulted in much the same manner as you were here in Nantucket."

"I get the picture. What time frame are we talking about?"

"Between eleven and midnight. But you may have seen something significant either earlier or later."

"Sorry, but I was gone by ten-thirty." Bernard stared down at his crotch dolefully. "By that week, I was already feeling the effects of the attack. But, as Portman's lawyer, I felt I should be on the spot for legal clarification of any problems that might arise with potential clients. For instance, a certain CEO whose name I dare not mention was interested in a suite for his girlfriend, but could it be charged to his corporation as a hospitality suite for visiting clients from Japan or wherever?"

"And could it?" Tom asked out of curiosity.

"You can bet your red, white, and blue ass on that. The

practice is as American as Trojan condoms." He shrugged. "I assume that they're still manufactured in New Jersey. It may well be the last first-class product still manufactured in New Jersey, or in the States. But I have no pity for American workers, who became too greedy and priced themselves out of the labor market. Where was I? Oh, yes...by ten-thirty I was exhausted and had to leave. And I'm exhausted right now too. I really have to rest. Is there anything you have to know right away? Here's my card. Call me at any hour if something pops into your head." When Tom reciprocated with a card, Bernard glanced at it and smiled. "Very impressive," he said. "Is there really such a bookshop, and in Brooklyn, of all places?"

"Of course."

"But I assume it's just a cover for your investigation agency."

"You might say that."

"My law firm frequently hires private investigators from a certain prominent agency, but I can't recall that their cards have ever identified them as anything but what they are."

"What's the name of this other agency?"

"Denning and Pankhurst."

"They're the best and biggest in the business."

Bernard nodded. "My partners and I have always been more than satisfied with their work." He established a strong eye contact with Tom. "Needless to say, if you solve this current assignment to my satisfaction, I'll make it my personal commitment to see that you get a decent share of our work in the future."

"Since you already have a business relationship with Denning and Pankhurst, why didn't Tony Portman and Al Foster hire them for this case?"

"I wondered about that too, until Tony told me that you have unique qualifications that make you the ideal man for this job. He'd better be right."

"If he's not, there's always Denning and Pankhurst. Or, better yet, the police, as I've been recommending from the beginning."

Bernard was the first to look away. He shifted his gaze to his watch. "I'm overdue for my afternoon rest period, not that it has been helping me. Anything else?" He began to stretch out on the recliner.

"Do you trust all your employees here?"

Bernard shot up again, and leaned forward. "Funny you should ask me that. Ten days ago, I would have told you that I trust every single one of them. And I would have added that I trust them even more than any of my partners or the staff at my law firm."

"And now?"

"When I visited our Washington office recently, one of the partners based there informed me that Pablo Valdez, the man who has been managing my dining facilities here for several years, used to be a minor official of the Sandinistas while they governed—or, rather, misgoverned—Nicaragua during the eighties." Bernard raised a hand to his brow, and then shook his head. "But Valdez is a real gentlemen, and I really can't believe that he would harm me or anyone else."

"Why would he harm you?"

"Back in the eighties, my firm did a lot of legal work and lobbying for the Contras and all those private and governmental front groups and councils and fund-raisers that were supporting them. I was just a junior back then, joining the firm right out of law school, but I think it's safe for me to say that without us the Contra movement would have been stillborn, especially since the Reagan-Bush Administration was being so sneaky with its support instead of acknowledging that the Contras was their baby to begin with.

"But all that is water under the bridge, I'm sure. The fighting down there is long over. Nicaragua has quieted down and is becoming a showplace of democracy and the free market system." Bernard winked at Tom. "Back in the eighties, that's how we defined any Central or South American government that shot fewer than a thousand of its union leaders, peasants and even priests in a calendar year. And we still do, I suppose." He lowered himself to the horizontal. "I'm really very tired now. Good luck, Berenson."

THE LUNCHEON HOUR was long over, and Tom ate alone in the dining room of the Captain's Bounty. He was enjoying the small Scottish scone and the huge oat-cranberry muffin, but he would have enjoyed them even more if Beth were sitting across the table from him.

By the time of his arrival in the dining room, all the waitresses were performing other duties, but Pablo Valdez had assured Tom that it would be an honor for him to serve a special guest of Mr. Bernard's, as Sam had introduced him. Valdez was a tall, thin man in his late fifties, and he wore a white shirt and snug black suit that made him look like a cross between a priest and a flamenco dancer. As Valdez dashed from one chore to another, Tom recalled the alleged figure in black who had assaulted Tony Portman at Montauk.

While eating, Tom tried to chat with Valdez as he came and went, but he learned principally that the man was not only extremely polite but also extremely reticent, and would not even commit himself to a weather forecast.

Presently, Valdez emerged from the kitchen and wheeled over the gleaming cart of pastries that had been resting near a portrait of a sea captain who looked like a more ruthless or merely less inhibited Neal Bernard. For the dessert course, which Tom hadn't ordered, Valdez had, for some reason, put on a pair of white gloves, and they seemed to accent his uncommonly long fingers. After picking up a pair of tongs, he smiled approvingly at Tom's clean plate, and then said gravely with a slight Latin accent, "What may I offer you now, sir? The New England apple cobbler is very nice today. It is baked right here on the premises."

"It does look very nice, but I've had enough. Just a little more coffee, please."

Having served the coffee and replaced the carafe, Valdez returned to Tom and said, "Perhaps, sir, you would like a doggie bag for your apple cobbler or any other dessert of your choice." He executed a suave gesture toward his cart and its high-calorie goodies.

Eager to keep up the conversation with the reticent guy, Tom nodded. "That's a great idea. Thank you."

"My pleasure, sir. I would suggest the cobbler, unless of course you have a long trip ahead of you. Washington, I suppose."

Suddenly, Tom had the impression that Valdez, in turn, was trying to learn something about *him*.

"Actually, I'm based in Brooklyn."

"Brooklyn!" Valdez exclaimed. "I lived there for a while. Dangerous here and there, but also wonderful. Coney Island! And the Botanic Garden! And Prospect Park with its lake and fields that take you back a century. Walt Whitman lived there. He's the greatest United States poet after Edgar Allan Poe. I'm an admirer of both of them. And of Arthur Miller, your greatest playwright, who also lived in Brooklyn."

"I sell books there."

"Books are wonderful, one of mankind's greatest blessings. I'm referring, of course, to literature and books of learning, not to the sort of garbage that is no better than the movies or television."

"I try to sell only the books that are blessings, but one must deal with the other kind too."

"Yes, I know exactly how it is. At best, life is a series of compromises."

"My name is Tom Berenson." He extended his hand.

The hand of Valdez was strong and warm. "Pablo Valdez."

Tom pointed to the chair opposite his. "Join me for coffee. It's always a pleasure to chat with someone who likes both Brooklyn and books."

Valdez smiled, then shook his head. "That would not be correct, sir. You are a guest—and Mr. Bernard's guest, at that."

"My presence here is no big deal, really. Actually, I'm just doing some work for Mr. Bernard. So in a way, we're both employees of his." Tom thought it would be going too far, and perhaps even attract suspicion, if he referred to the two of them as "comrades."

Valdez looked unconvinced by this explanation, but he eventually smiled as if humoring a Weight Watcher who questioned the number of calories in her toast. Then he went over to the serving counter for a cup of coffee and returned and sat down opposite Tom.

"Thank you," Tom said. "I have a reason for not wanting to sit here alone." He went on to tell of his inquiry years ago about the rates here, and of his frustrated hope of returning with Beth one day.

"I'm so sorry, Mr. Berenson. That is a sad story. I know how it feels to lose people who are near and dear. May I offer you something stronger than your coffee?"

"No, thank you. I drink very little, and never in the afternoon."

"That is wise. As Poe would have said, 'Wine turns men into fools and assassins.'"

"I'm certainly not one of Mr. Bernard's wealthy clients or business associates, who must have their two martinis for lunch. When you mentioned a doggie bag and Washington before, I hope you didn't think I was a member of the Beltway set." Tom leaned forward and lied confidentially, "Both of my parents were socialists, and they would turn over in their graves if I ever sold out to the capitalists and their stooges in government."

"Perhaps it's better that they're in their graves at present. Socialism seems to be a lost cause."

"I'm sure it will revive in a few years, or a few decades. I see no other solution for the ills of undeveloped countries like those in Latin America."

"Until now it has always failed."

"You're forgetting about Hugo Chavez in Venezuela. The United States and the CIA and the World Bank took more than the usual number of steps against him, but he has been holding on."

With his brow drawn, Valdez stared at Tom as if he had never heard of the CIA and the World Bank. Then he shrugged. "What you say may be true, sir, but I really know nothing about such matters."

Across the room, Sam strode through the open doorway and then stopped rather abruptly. For a few seconds he stared at Tom and Valdez sitting together. "I suggest we go now if you want to have time for those souvenirs."

Immediately, Valdez leaped to feet and rushed off. "I'll fix that doggie bag for you," he informed Tom.

AT THE FOUR WINDS, Tom bought matching blue and white sweatshirts with spouting whales for Stephanie, Max, and himself. Then he asked Sam to take him to the police station.

Sam stared at him curiously, and then said, "You have a plane to catch, sir. I'm not sure we'll have time. Maybe it's something I can help you with." His tone made it clear that he didn't want Tom to go the police station.

"There's enough time," Tom said, getting into the car. "But if you're concerned, while I'm inside, you can contact the airport and tell the pilot to wait."

"I'm not sure he can or will. I happen to know that he's on a pretty tight schedule."

"Then I'll just have to make other arrangements about a flight back to New York. Let's go!"

THE DESK SERGEANT didn't look up or even acknowledge Tom's existence with a grunt or a nod. But as soon as Tom said that he represented Neal Bernard, the sergeant smiled and established a heartwarming eye contact as he snatched up his phone.

Not five minutes later, out in the squad room, Watson beckoned Tom into his cubicle and then pointed to a chair with a suspicious brown stain on the seat. "Don't mind that," the tall detective said. "It's nice and dry by now, but please don't ask me how it got there."

Tom introduced himself as an insurance investigator, because he knew from experience that cops loathed private eyes with their expense accounts and lousy imitations of Humphrey Bogart, and nothing made them happier than to put these overpaid interlopers on a false trail. He continued, "It's in relation to the assault on Mr. Bernard."

"That was certainly a terrible thing, and very rare. As you probably know, he and his folks are part of the history of Nantucket." Watson touched the green folder on his desk. "I have his file. What kind of insurance is involved here?"

"Health."

"Health? I just refreshed my memory, and I'm not aware from my reports that he'd suffered any injuries to speak of. By the way, do you represent Mr. Bernard personally or some insurance company?"

"Mr. Bernard, of course. It was he who suggested that I visit you, and he had his chauffeur, Sam, drive me over. Sam's waiting to take me to the airport, and if you'd care to look out a window...."

"Oh, I believe you all right."

"At first, his injuries didn't seem to amount to very much, and they may not even be mentioned in any detail in your report."

"They aren't."

"But if you've ever been in any kind of an accident, you'll know that today's trivial bump or bruise can be tomorrow's trauma and debilitating injury."

Watson leaned forward and rubbed his lower back. "You can say that again. And I'm sure sorry to hear that Mr. Bernard was hurt that night. If you have some relevant medical data on you, I'll include it in his folder."

"Why didn't I think of that? Give me your number and I'll fax the information when I get back to the office. Meantime, I have to verify this for my report. According to Mr. Bernard, you're trying your best to catch his assailant, but haven't had any luck so far. Do I have it right?"

"That's true, unfortunately, and I sure wish we could have had better results for him." Watson opened the folder again. "Since his assault on May eighth, we—"

"Excuse me," Tom interrupted, "but aren't we talking about the *seventh*?"

"Are we?" Watson flipped through several sheets in his folder, and then shook his head. "I have Sunday the eighth in all of these. Sergeant Crowell on the desk got the call at ten thirty-nine."

"I guess I heard it wrong," Tom said. But he knew that he hadn't.

THE DISCREPANCY IN dates bothered Tom, and he wanted to discuss it with Bernard. Reluctant to use his cell phone in the car and be overhead by Sam, who probably wasn't a confidant of his boss, he waited till he was at the airport.

Maybe it was only because he had been aroused from his nap, but Bernard was cold if not caustic, and almost a totally different person from their meeting only two hours before. In answer to Tom's simple question, he shouted:

"The seventh! The eighth! What difference does a single day make? Is this what you're calling me about? I don't recall giving you permission to speak with the police. This is supposed to be a *private* investigation. Didn't Portman and Foster impress that upon you?"

"Well, which day was it? This is very important. A suspect may have an alibi for one day but not for the other."

"How should I know what day it was?"

Tom wondered if the castration was affecting the guy's brain. "Come on, Mr. Bernard. There must be a way you can check. Think back. Consult your appointment book, or the friends who were staying with you. If you're tired or busy, I'll be happy to call them myself. May I have their phone numbers, please?"

"I can see that you're not going to leave me alone on this trivial matter."

"I don't consider it trivial."

Bernard was silent a long time. Finally he cried, "Okay, it was the seventh! It happened on the seventh, and exactly the way I told you."

"Then why did you wait twenty-four hours before informing the police?"

"They got the date wrong."

"There was a lot of paperwork by different personnel, and it's unlikely that every one of them didn't know the date."

"Shit!" Bernard draw a deep breath. "Okay, I'll tell you. After gaining consciousness from that assault, I certainly did want to call the cops at once and nail those bastards to the cross. Nobody touches Neal Bernard and gets away with it! But then I remembered that my three fraternity brothers were staying with me, and I didn't want the cops and, inevitably, the media to learn of their presence here."

"Why not? I thought that publicity was the life blood of politics and show business."

"It usually is, but McGrath had told his official mistress, as it were, that he'd be hunting that weekend in Montana, and Lyle Wayne had informed the press that he was taking only his Bible and German shepherd and going off alone to the Grand Canyon, there to meditate until God informed him whether he should run for President in the next election." Bernard snickered, and took another deep breath. "Although I didn't yet know the full extent of my injury, I felt worse and worse on the eighth, and I certainly wanted the cops on the job, so as soon as my buddies took off in their plane, I called the police and told them it had just happened. Honestly, I thought that was the simplest solution."

Convinced that Bernard was lying to him, Tom wanted to question him further, but his pilot had rushed into the waiting room and was yelling at him:

"Let's get going! There's a storm coming up, and if we don't leave now, we may have to hang around till about midnight."

"We'll be talking again," Tom told Bernard. Then he followed the pilot out into the wind.

CHAPTER 8

DURING HIS BRIEF stints as a Christmas stock clerk at Saks Fifth Avenue back when he was juggling jobs and going to college at night, Tom had become aware that the rich and privileged of all nations have a glow and a posture that make them stand out from other people. Maybe it came from their access to the best food and health care. Or maybe it was that, because they never had to knot up their gut about paying the rent, their glands had the leisure to manufacture a unique hormone. Whatever its source, the whole room seemed suffused with that glow as Tom walked into President Colbert's reception, by invitation only, for the Beta Alpha Beta Phi Class of 1980.

His entrance was unnoticed by Al Foster, who was deep in conversation with Colbert. Recently, on the PBS *NewsHour,* Colbert had called for tougher punishment for students who defaulted on government-insured loans of any size. His opponent in the discussion, a Harvard educator, then asked Colbert about the punishment he was suggesting for the banker on his board of trustees who had arranged a collateral-free loan of a half billion dollars to secret business partners in a Mexican resort whose TV commercials featured their gambling casino and swimming pool filled with bathing beauties in bikinis. Trippingly on the tongue, Colbert replied that his trustee's only possible fault was that he had perhaps been overeager to stimulate trade with America's friendly neighbor to the south.

After accepting a glass of champagne from a passing waiter, Tom slipped off to a corner where he could observe unobtrusively for a while.

The reception was being held in Aldburgh Hall, an ornate Victorian building that had been named for Phineas Edward Aldburgh, who bequeathed his alma mater a part of the fortune he had amassed by gunrunning to the Confederacy during the Civil War. Cocktails were being served in the Walt Whitman room, which was decorated with a Mauve Decade lushness that would have provoked the poet to rush out and commune with grass or any other flora except orchids. Its current occupants, however, looked as at home among the marble mantels, crystal chandeliers, velvet sofas, and Bouguereau paintings as their Victorian forebears must have been.

There were about fifty people in the room—the fifteen Golden Guys, and the top-echelon GMU administrators, and the women attached to the groups of men. All the men were in evening dress, and the women in the sort of designer gowns that Tom usually saw only, and unintentionally, in the advertising pages of the *Sunday Times Magazine*. But they all looked more comfortable in their clothes than he felt in his rented tux from a shop on Kings Highway back in Brooklyn. He shrugged his shoulders in an attempt to make the jacket set better. Harry the fitter had assured him that he looked exactly like a movie star, but he had been afraid to ask Harry which one.

He smiled as he remembered how Stephanie had helped him with his bow tie. Since GMU was one of the colleges she would be applying to in the hope that she might be awarded financial aid or a scholarship, she had accompanied him up here for a look at the place. They had spent the afternoon being guided around the campus by a premed student named Mark Vincent, who was now giving Stephanie a taste of campus nightlife.

He sighed and told himself to get back to business. Once more his eyes swept the room, taking in the Golden Guys at their most charming. Though he had met only a few of them so far, he had done his homework and could put names to all the faces.

Holding court by one of the fireplaces was Senator Lyle Wayne, not one gleaming blond hair out of place, assuming that his hairs had been arranged for an effect of down-home sophistication, of combining everything that was best about prairies and skyscrapers. He was not as tall as some of his courtiers, but his broad shoulders and gigantic ego made him appear to tower above them.

Over near a window stood Doug McGrath, the football hero turned blockbuster movie star. From his loud laughter and the way he was draping his arm around the naked shoulders of a woman, Tom surmised that he was on his way to getting drunk. And from the dark looks of the woman on McGrath's other side, Tom surmised also that Ms. Naked Shoulders was not his wife. Professor Jason Gilbert, the Golden Guy who had won a Nobel Prize and now headed GMU's chemistry department, didn't look too happy, either. Perhaps Ms. Naked Shoulders belonged to him.

As Gilbert suddenly broke into a sunny smile, Tom shifted his gaze and saw that the scientist was being approached by a tall young woman with a camcorder and a taller, slender, older woman in black velvet evening pants and a sequined jacket. While the younger woman aimed the camcorder at Gilbert, her companion began to speak with him. With a hand to his short, graying beard, Gilbert listened intently and sagely, and then he threw back his head and gave what, from a distance, appeared to be brilliant answers, the sort that would be quoted at least as long as Albert Einstein's.

The interviewer, Tom realized, must be Nora Malcolm, the director-producer of the Biography channel's documentary on the Golden Guys in their twenty-fifth year after graduation. Foster had told him about her and promised an introduction, noting that she could be helpful with information. Her team had been on the TV project for months and was doing in-depth research on the fraternity, just as for previous projects for PBS and HBO, they had researched the Bronx Zoo, women athletes, the secret lives of whales, and the family and mistresses of Pablo Picasso. Hearing about her, Tom had feared that she would be one of those young media celebrities who lived in Brooklyn Heights and periodically ravaged his stock without buying anything, and he had not looked forward to the meeting. He was pleased to see that he had jumped to the wrong conclusion. She appeared to be in her mid-thirties, with short-cropped blond hair that curled softly around her face. Though she was not beautiful or pretty, at least to a disinterested beholder like Tom, her crisp and attractive features suggested a woman of distinction.

Her chat with Gilbert had stolen McGrath's attention from the woman at his side, and like a jealous sibling, he ambled over to her, snaked his arm around her waist, and whispered into her ear. She handled him like the pro she obviously was, laughing as though he had just made a clever remark. How she managed to slip from under his arm and turn the embrace into a warm handshake, Tom would never know, but it was a maneuver he would always admire. She then moved the two fraternity brothers closer together and nodded to her assistant, who stepped back for a two-shot.

Gilbert had been glowering at McGrath's intrusion, but she soon had him smiling again, and after recording for posterity what appeared to be some good-natured ribbing between the two men, she moved off with her assistant to find another subject. Like countless other cops, Tom had picked up some lip-reading during his many stakeouts with and without bugs and binoculars, and he was sure he saw the woman say to her assistant, "Jesus, he's the biggest schmuck of the lot."

"Sorry I didn't see you come in. Have you been here long?" Foster's voice came from Tom's right and took his attention away from the two documentarians.

"Barely long enough to finish a drink." Tom put his empty glass on the tray of a passing waiter and took another. Without a drink he would have looked less affable to people with information. "Is the gang all here?"

"Hail, hail. All except Tony Portman and Neal Bernard, of course. When I spoke with Neal a few days ago, he expressed great confidence in you, but he was rather pissed that you visited the police afterward without consulting him first. As you may recall, your investigation is supposed to be extremely confidential."

"My visiting the police station was no big secret. He'd reported the attack to the police, and I assumed that his loyal chauffeur would tell him that I'd made the side trip. Anyhow, I told the cops that I was interested only in the insurance angle."

"Did you learn anything from them?"

"No." Tom didn't see any need to mention the discrepancy in dates to Foster.

"You were certainly the busy bee in Nantucket. You also spoke with Valdez, the dining-room manager."

"After Bernard's mentioning his connection to Nicaragua, I felt that I had to check him out."

"And...?"

"The time was too brief for me to learn anything. I may have to get back to him."

"Neal likes and needs the man, so let's forget about him for the time being."

"Do the rest of the Golden Guys know what has been happening?"

"Not really. We didn't think it would be wise to tell them all. We clued in Lyle Wayne, of course. And Doug McGrath. They're both public figures and may be in more danger."

"Come on, we're talking Golden Guys here. You're all public figures."

"Maybe so, but there's no need to start a panic. After all, you're bound to have this wrapped up quickly."

"I wish I shared your optimism. Is Lou West here tonight?"

"No. At least, I haven't seen him."

"Do you know if he was invited?"

"Colbert was in charge of that. It's hard to believe that he didn't invite good old Lou, who's become a bigger celebrity than ever in his golden years. Why the interest in him?"

"I've heard that he isn't particularly fond of one or more of you guys."

Foster made a dismissive gesture. "Something did happen once. But that was eons ago. It's hard to believe that Lou has held a grudge so long. Who told you about him?"

"One of my sources."

"We don't like anonymous tattlers. And for the money we're paying you, we expect your complete cooperation."

"What is Lou West's beef against you guys?"

"It's a long story of teenage pranks from the dim past, and utterly irrelevant to what's going on. Anyhow, this isn't the time and place."

"In that case, let's get started on those introductions."

A minute later, as Tom extended a hand to Doug McGrath,

he expected a crushing and he got it. McGrath smiled afterward, as if he had enjoyed inflicting pain.

"Always nice to meet one of my loyal fans. Pretty boys like Brad Pitt and Matt Dillon come and go, but Doug McGrath endures forever."

During his introduction, Tom had not mentioned that he was a fan. Even when they were available free on TV, he would never have dreamed of viewing one of McGrath's old thrillers or westerns.

"I hope you've caught my latest," McGrath went on. "I have three leading ladies, and I banged every one of them."

One of the men around him asked, "Off screen or on, Doug?"

McGrath nodded toward the woman who had been glowering earlier. "That's not a question you should ask me in front of my adoring wife." Then he winked and added in a stage whisper, "Get me later."

Everyone in McGrath's audience laughed, including his wife. But Tom noted that the woman's smile was forced and her eyes were bright—with anger or perhaps a hint of tears. She was considerably younger than her husband, and much more beautiful and voluptuous than Ms. Naked Shoulders, who had since wandered off with Gilbert. Blessed with such a variety of striking attractions, she probably had theatrical ambitions of her own, which no doubt was why she had married McGrath and continued to stick around.

After explaining that Tom was helping good old Sanford Whitney with his long-overdue study of the elite fraternities, Foster introduced him to the other brothers who were kibitzing with McGrath: Philip Winchester, heir to the throne of the Winchester Trust; Nicholas Hammond III, CEO of Hammond Enterprises; and Bob Michaelson, known alternately as The Whiz of Wall Street and the Hedge Fund Honcho. He was the genius who dreamed up the subprime loans and derivatives that were currently shooting earnings on Wall Street to dizzying heights and which would no doubt remain there forever, thanks to the rating agencies and to the former Wall Street colleagues who were now in Washington and supposed to be regulating them.

Being the castrator's second victim, Michaelson had been informed of Tom's real mission, and he shook hands with a special fervor. His hand felt soft, and his cheeks had a smoothness that might not be from a sharper blade or a richer lather.

"Sounds like an interesting project," the financier said, his eyes holding Tom's. "Maybe I can give you a tip or two. Let's have a drink later."

"Thanks. Sounds good."

Next, Foster set off with Tom toward the fireplace where Lyle Wayne was still holding court. On their way, Foster paused and touched the arm of a tall man with broad but slightly stooped shoulders. He was the only man present who was not wearing a tuxedo, and Tom wondered why he hadn't noticed him before. As the man in the black serge suit turned to face Foster, Tom saw his clerical collar.

"Arnie, when did you arrive?" Foster asked, shaking the man's hand. "I was afraid you were going to stand us up because of a previous engagement with Jesus."

"And miss an opportunity to hit all my brothers for donations? Not a chance. You should be so lucky!" The man's blue eyes sparkled, and he laughed good-naturedly as he returned Foster's handshake. "I had to leave later than I'd intended. We had a little emergency at the mission."

"Only a *little* emergency? That's a switch." Foster's smile and tone were filled with affection. He nodded toward Tom. "Arnie, I'd like you to meet Tom Berenson. He's working with good old Sandy Whitney on his history of fraternities."

"Ah, yes. That's been taking longer than Gibbon's *Decline and Fall of the Roman Empire*. Let's hope he finishes it while we still have an American empire, or even a United States of America. The way this country is going—"

Foster slapped him on the back. "You've been drinking too much sacramental wine of a dubious vintage. But don't worry, I won't tell your flock. Tom, this is Arnold Simon, Beta Alpha Beta Phi's token failure. He's the only Golden Guy who actually turned his back on the gold. He was a Wall Street wizard until he gave it all up to fight Satan instead of the IRS."

Simon's handshake was as hearty as his laugh. "The Buddha tells us to exchange our worldly goods for a begging bowl at fifty. I was just a little precocious, that's all."

"Some begging bowl," said Foster. "Your fund-raising is more elaborate and computerized than Lyle Wayne's."

Simon placed his palms together, and he said with mock piety, "In my Father's house are many bowls."

"I've contributed to your various campaigns," Tom said. "Keep up the good work."

"And you keep up the contributions. Remember, my friend, there really is a hell for sinners." Simon's eyes were gleaming with delight.

As they walked away, Tom said to Foster, "Does he actually believe in hell or is he softening me up for his next barrage of junk mail?"

"Of course he believes in it. Like most clergymen, he's got quite a loony side."

"Don't we all?" Tom asked.

"Certainly not. My psychiatrist says that I'm completely cured."

Tom's next introduction was to Lyle Wayne, who not only shook his hand but also clapped his shoulder as if Tom were delivering a block of votes that would ensure his victory in the next election. His deep voice, used to addressing multitudes instead of individuals, vibrated in the air as he said, "Al has mentioned your research into the great fraternities of the land. It sounds like very important work." He threw out an arm. "Every man in this room will testify to the importance of fraternities, especially to Beta Alpha Beta Phi. In union there is strength, and fraternities bring together men with common interests and ideals. Anything I can do to help?"

"Al says you have some good stories about Beta Alpha. I know that Whitney can use as many as possible to juice up his book."

"Nothing would give me more pleasure. And there's no time like the present, I always say."

Ignoring the pleas of the people around him that they wanted to hear the stories too, Wayne led Tom and Foster to a relatively secluded part of the room. He had just turned his back on his companions as if they no longer existed.

"They're all pains in the ass," he said to Foster. "By the way, what am I doing here when I could be on a junket to Switzerland?"

"You're running for President."

"That's right, come to think of it." He winked at Foster, then turned a sharp eye on Tom. "After the big buildup from Al here and Tony Portman, I'm expecting great things from you, so you'd better not let me down. Any bright ideas yet?" He stared at Tom as if he expected to hear at least a dozen.

"I'm still gathering information."

"Heavy is the head that aspires to the presidency. I assume that I'm a prime target of this maniac."

"It's possible."

"Every morning when I wake up, I immediately rub my pecker to make sure it's still in working order."

"How was it today?"

Wayne glared as if Tom had overstepped the bounds of their relationship. "Any suspects yet?"

"None to speak of."

"Well, get with it, fella."

The threat in Wayne's icy blue eyes probably sent his assistants scurrying for cover, but Tom met it impassively, and he smiled and said, "Even the FBI needs time to solve a case. Sometimes it takes them a decade or more. And sometimes, as we know from 9/11, even when clues have been handed to them on a silver platter, they still manage to screw up. But you can turn this investigation over to them whenever you want to." It was a delicious feeling not to have to play the public-servant role of a cop anymore. He could walk out on these guys any time he chose. And they knew it.

Attracted by Wayne, others in the room began to wander over, and Foster took the opportunity to make more introductions. Tom had met all the Golden Guys by the time a gong was struck somewhere and then President Colbert and his wife joined elevated hands and strolled ostentatiously to the doorway, indicating that dinner was about to be served and it wasn't going to be pizza on paper plates. From behind him, Tom heard a young woman whisper:

"Jeez, Nora! I feel like I'm living a scene in *Masterpiece Theater*. I'm back in those jolly old days when the British ruled the world."

"Well, these guys and their ilk rule it now."

"Yeah. But the good news is that generations come and go. These guys too will pass away."

The speaker was Nora Malcolm's assistant, and as he started toward the dining room, it seemed to Tom that she had sounded utterly delighted about the passing away of the Golden Guys.

CHAPTER 9

FOSTER HAD attended to details, and as Tom had hoped, he was seated at a table with Nora Malcolm on his left. Also at their table were Nora's assistant, Denise Jackson, and three GMU administrators and their wives. Denise was the only African-American in the room except for the servers, and Tom recalled a black cop's wedding reception where he and Beth had been the only whites present. And a Pentecostal naming of a friend's daughter where they had been the only Jews.

After the usual general chitchat that follows round-the-table introductions, conversation broke down into smaller groups, and Tom was finally free to concentrate on the TV producer who had become an expert on the Golden Guys. But before he could start their tête-à-tête with regards from Sanford Whitney, she said to him with a bright but unintimidating smile:

"I know you're not a Golden Guy, but I bet you belong to Beta Alpha."

"Do I really look that rich and successful?"

"Sure. Don't tell me you aren't?"

"It must be the suit, which I rented from an establishment on Kings Highway in Brooklyn. I've never belonged to *any* fraternity, let along Beta Alpha. I hope you won't think the less of me for that."

"On the contrary. And to prove it, I'll let you in on a secret. I never belonged to a sorority while I was in college. Do you live in Brooklyn?"

"Absolutely. So that I'll always be close to the source of my formal attire."

"It must be pleasant to live there."

"Not always."

"I suppose you're referring to the crime." She sighed. "It's happening all over now. Last year, my purse was snatched in Kensington Gardens in London."

"I'm sorry. But since you were so close to Harrods, you had a perfect excuse to go in and buy a new one."

She laughed. "How did you know that?"

"People from Brooklyn are very intuitive."

"So I've heard from Barbra Streisand. Have you ever met her?"

"No," he admitted.

"If the funding comes through, one of my forthcoming projects will involve Brooklyn."

"Lucky you."

"That remains to be seen. It'll be about the home life of a few leaders of the Mafia and Murder, Inc."

"Quite a change from the Golden Guys."

"Maybe not as much as you think," said Denise, who had been listening to them.

"Hush," Nora told her. "If one of them heard you, they might take away your dessert."

"It'll probably be baked Alaska, which I'm not crazy about, anyhow."

"Well, life can't be all Twinkies." The two women laughed, and then Nora turned back to Tom. "What do you do besides attend formal dinners?"

"I own a bookstore."

Her eyes sparkled. "Really? I love old-fashioned neighborhood bookstores, but I hear it's tough going for them these days."

"You heard right, but I help things along as a free-lance researcher."

She nodded knowingly. "We hire them from time to time. Can't afford a staff researcher on our budgets."

"Currently I'm working for Sanford Whitney, who's doing the definitive history of fraternities. That's why I'm here this weekend."

"We read some of his earlier works before embarking on this

venture. Can I have your card? If you're not too expensive, I may throw some business your way."

"Thank you. I'm not expensive at all." He removed his wallet, took out a card for the bookshop, and handed it to her.

"Pineapple Street," she read, and then shook her head and laughed. "I can imagine there being such a street in Honolulu, but not in Brooklyn."

She was even more attractive close-up. Her eyes were the vivid blue of a rain-washed sky, and though they now sparkled with wit, he could sense intriguing depths behind them.

When the *jardin à la Provence* was set before them, he informed Nora that his daughter, Stephanie, called it simply fruit salad back in Brooklyn, and then he added, "She came along with me to look over the campus."

"I'm familiar with that routine. I think my own daughter dragged me to every campus in the country before she made her decision. At least it felt that way, and my arches have never been the same."

"And where does she want to go?"

"She's already there, at Johns Hopkins. She's a junior and loves it. It's a great school. Tell your daughter not to overlook it."

The reference to her daughter's being a college junior made Tom revise his initial conjecture about her age. Obviously she was closer to forty than she looked. And maybe even on the other side of it. Her maturity, and the absence of a wedding ring on her finger rather pleased him. It was a sensation from the past, one he hadn't felt about any woman since Beth's death. Also, it confused him, and he wanted to stop to examine it, but he was obliged to continue the conversation.

"Stephanie's not interested in medicine. She's more inclined toward the literary professions, or what's left of them."

"Don't let all those Hopkins doctors who are always being quoted in the *Times* fool you. Hopkins has a strong liberal arts department. John Barth, P. J. O'Rourke, Russell Baker, and NPR's Michele Kelemen are graduates. Gertrude Stein, Ayn Rand, and Rachel Carson are famous alumni too. Of course, I'm prejudiced about the school because I studied there." She smiled. "If you decide to check it out, let me know. I'm sure that Leslie would be happy to show you and your daughter around."

"Thanks. I'll keep that in mind. Is Leslie your only child or are you going to have to hit the campus trail all over again with another one soon?"

"She's my one and only. How about you?"

"Same here. I have a friend with four teenagers, but he has a wife and so they'll be able to divide up the trips." As a cop, he had become used to asking blunt questions, so he had no clever idea how to learn Nora's marital status without blurting a question she might take as intrusive. He wondered if this approach was too subtle.

Either it was or she wasn't biting. She simply nodded and said, "It certainly helps when there's someone to share them with. I take it you're no longer married."

"My wife died a few years ago."

"I'm sorry. I'm in the same boat...have been for several years. It isn't easy to raise a child alone." She gazed into her wineglass, then raised it and took a sip. When she put it down, she smiled and asked about Stephanie's interests. From that, they passed on to their own interests, and by the time grace was offered by the Reverend Simon and they picked up their forks, they had agreed to meet for tennis in the morning.

During their Nantucket fish chowder, a traditional dish of the fraternity, Nora explained to Tom that the dinner itself wasn't being filmed because the variety of wines and the expensive foods and chinaware might not go down well with one or another of Lyle Wayne's present and future constituencies. She went on: "Since a single picture is supposed to be worth more than a thousand words, we have to make sure that the viewer sees the correct and desirable picture."

"What if the correct picture isn't the true one?"

Nora laughed. "That's the sort of question we used to discuss in Communications 101."

"Were there any good answers?"

"Let me put it to you this way. This film wouldn't be made at all if I didn't agree to follow certain...guidelines." When Tom went through the motions of looking just a little surprised, she added, "I'm sure it's much the same for writers, whether of books, magazine articles or newspaper stories."

During the entrée of *boeuf à la reine Charlotte,* Denise arose, bent down, and whispered to Nora, "Gotta get ready for the great oratory. Any final instructions?"

"You know the shots better than I do. Be sure to get plenty of low angles for that look of power and dynamism, and the ability to stop hurricanes and tornadoes." Nora clenched her hands and tried to look fierce. "In short, the senator's keynote should come out looking mucho macho. Did you check with him about makeup?"

"We're off the hook. He has his own guy, who used to work for Reagan and can make a mummy look like Mr. America."

"I can believe that. Good. We don't want the senator blaming us if he comes out looking like a pimp from Montmartre." As her assistant rushed from the room, Nora turned to Tom and said breezily, "A little shoptalk, as you may have gathered."

"Only one camera for the great speeches?"

"Are you kidding? We'll be having five of them. One will be for close-ups of the left side of his face, which he believes is more craggy and resembles a young Clint Eastwood's. Honestly. Don't laugh. It was a stipulation of our grant from Winchester Trust, whose CEO, Philip Winchester, is a Golden Guy." She sighed. "There was a time when I wanted to be the American counterpart to Ozu, the Japanese director who dealt with the joys and sorrows and sake drinking of so-called average people."

"Perhaps you will be one day."

Dessert was followed by a welcoming speech from President Colbert, who, with great pride and passion, recalled his first encounter with the Golden Guys when they were freshmen, and then he proceeded to name and glorify their accomplishments ever since. Finally, he turned the microphone over to Senator Lyle Wayne, who, he assured his audience, was currently working like a demon to realize the great American dream of permanently eliminating the capital gains tax.

Wayne's speech was a more polished repeat of Colbert's, with the difference that he mentioned only his own accomplishments, which had begun with a recitation of the Pledge of Allegiance at the age of two, or so his Irish nanny, Katie O'Neill, had always assured him. Katie was still alive and well on the Wayne family estate, and every year on her birthday he presented her with a bouquet of violets, her favorite flower, which reminded her of her native Galway.

"Oh, brother!" Nora groaned under her breath, but when Tom looked at her, she rolled her eyes and shook her head.

To Tom, the speech had all the earmarks of a campaign kick-off, and it probably was. If future speeches evoked only a fraction of the enthusiasm of this one among conservative Republicans, Wayne would have the nomination in the bag.

The speeches were over by eleven-thirty, but the evening was not, and the company moved on to Beta Hall, the magnificent brownstone that was home to the GMU branch of the fraternity. Irish coffee and brandy had been set up. Most of the Golden Guys were staying in the opulent guest rooms on the third and fourth floors. A few of the overflow gave in to nostalgia and decided to spend the night in a room usually occupied by a current fraternity brother. The rest opted for rooms or suites in the Sheraton about three miles away rather than in the nearby motel where Tom and Stephanie were staying.

Tired after a long day, Tom longed to sit down and relax, preferably with Nora Malcolm. But Nora and Denise had work to do, and he reminded himself that he did too. He picked up an Irish coffee and began to circulate.

Over in a corner, Bob Michaelson was staring moodily into his brandy snifter as though expecting to find revealed in its depths the liquid assets of his next corporate victim. He had been away in Delaware, preparing the legal infrastructure for a hostile raid on a food-and-entertainment conglomerate, and Tom had not yet had a chance to interview him.

"Is this a good time for that talk?" he asked.

Michaelson looked up. It was a few seconds before recognition flashed in his sharp brown eyes. "Not here," he snapped. He rose and turned around in place. Then he pointed to a door and led the way through it and down a long, carpeted hallway into a small sitting room with upholstered chairs and two ornately carved writing tables. Centuries ago, when the tables were new, they had held staff pens and inkwells. Apple computers now stood upon them.

Michaelson closed the door behind them and sat down on one of the chairs. Tom leaned against a table, because standing would give him an edge with a megalomaniac like Michaelson. There was no need for preambles. "Tell me how and when it happened."

"Didn't Al tell you?"

"I prefer firsthand information. Important details get lost with every narration."

"It was the damnedest thing. It happened at two in the morning in a hallway of a prominent and respectable hotel. I'd been at the annual meeting of a society I belong to, and was on my way to bed."

"What was this meeting? Where was it held? And who attended it?"

"It was held at the Devonshire Plaza in New York. That's why I was staying there."

"And the name of the society and the names of the people who were there?"

"That's irrelevant. No one there would have harmed me. We're all brothers."

"So it was a Beta Alpha meeting."

"No."

"But you just said you were all brothers."

"Look, I told you that the group's irrelevant."

Tom straightened to his full height. "That's for me to decide. If you guys want me to look into this matter, then you have to level with me—and that means about *everything*. If you're not prepared to do that, then I'm prepared to walk. I don't have time for bullshit. And, judging from what's been going on, neither do any of you."

He strode to the door, and was reaching for the knob when Michaelson found his voice:

"All right. But this is in confidence."

"Which makes it no different from anything else I've been told so far." Tom retraced his steps. This time he sat down. He had the upper hand now. Michaelson might resent it, but he wouldn't forget it. He stretched out his legs and waited.

"It's Nu Iota Zeta Mu," Michaelson said after some fidgeting. "We meet once a year. It's a secret society, cream-of-the-crop Wall Streeters only." He straightened in his chair, his voice and eyes filling with pride. "It was started back in the Depression, probably to get the guys' minds off their troubles. It's a great honor to be asked to join, and the privilege is extended to only the most powerful people in the financial world."

Tom got the picture. Some of the nation's wealthiest citizens assembled to do good works in secret—donations to charities, scholarships for the underprivileged, homes for the homeless. Michaelson began to rise in his estimation. "And you seek anonymity for your good works," he said.

At first Michaelson looked blank. Then he laughed as he caught Tom's meaning. "Hell, not good works—good times! We kid that the letters stand for 'Nutty, Insane, Zany Millionaires.' Our motto is *Cantamus et Potatum*: 'We Sing and We Drink.' You can't believe what a ball we have!"

"Try me."

Michaelson sat forward, his eyes sparkling with delightful memories. "First, of course, there's the march of the neophytes. All the guys being initiated have to dress up like women and march in together. You should see them staggering around on their high heels." He was laughing so hard that tears came to his eyes. "This year, Bill Calvin of Fenner & Fenner was one of them. He put two melons in his bra! What a guy! What a woman! Just between you and me, I never got such a hard-on from a real broad."

Tom had never been able to understand what some men found even remotely amusing about dressing up as women. To him, wizards of Wall Street who pranced around in wigs and high heels and melon breasts were idiotic and pathetic. While he waited for Michaelson to catch his breath and get his laughter under control, he couldn't resist asking: "And do the women initiates dress up as men?" But he knew exactly what the answer would be, even before he saw Michaelson's expression of incredulity.

"There are no women! This is a *fraternal* society, a well-earned chance for us guys to let our hair and toupees down once a year." And between peals of laughter, Michaelson explained how the initiates must entertain the brothers with skits and songs of their own composition, and the more ribald and scatological, the better. "While they're performing, we razz them and pelt them with food. One guy hit Pete Burton smack in the eye with mashed potatoes. And Fred Hollings of B.L.M. & O. picked up a plate and started smacking the rolls right back at us. One landed in front of Carter Cole of the SEC and splashed his cream of asparagus soup all over his tux. Cole turned his spoon into a catapult and got Hollings right on his tit with a huge black olive. Holy shit, do we have fun!"

The picture Tom saw was of homeless people a few blocks away in Central Park, and all over the city. They foraged in garbage cans for scraps while at the Devonshire Plaza on Fifth Avenue, some of the richest men in the country were having food fights. "Sounds like quite a night," he said. "Who else was there besides good old Calvin, Burton, Hollings, and Cole?"

Michaelson's smile faded. "I told you, these guys are brothers. None of them would hurt me."

"And I told you, I draw my own conclusions. I'll need a list—a complete one. And I'd like it in the morning."

Michaelson's mouth and eyes hardened. But he nodded finally.

"You said you left at about two a.m. Who left with you?"

"Who can remember? Hell, I was stewed. A bunch of us walked to the elevators together." He gazed into space a moment. "I remember saying good night to Burton. He offered me a lift in his limo, but I said I was staying at the hotel in my firm's hospitality suite. Immediately I was sorry I'd said that, because he suggested that we make the evening really memorable, and organize an orgy."

"Why didn't you join him?" Tom asked out of curiosity.

Michaelson flinched a little at the question, and then he stared down gloomily at his crotch. "Until this incident occurred, I liked a good orgy as much as the next guy, but Burton goes in for some *really* kinky stuff, and I'm afraid that one day he'll go too far and a call girl will send her pimp after him. Besides, I was so plastered that the only thing I wanted to do in bed that night was sleep." He folded his hands virtuously on his lap. "I guess I'm old-fashioned at heart."

"You and Little Lord Fauntleroy."

"Exactly."

"Tell me about the attack. Where did it happen, and when?"

"I said good night to Burton and took the elevator upstairs to my floor. Reaching my door, I took out my key, one of those electronic cards that I hate and despise and have never quite gotten the knack of. But I said to myself that I was going to do it slow and steady and open the damn door within only a few tries."

Michaelson looked down at his fly soulfully, and then he raised his eyes to meet Tom's. "The next thing I remember, I was inside and lying on the floor. My head ached, and so did my prick and balls." He clenched his fists. "You've got to get that bastard! He didn't even give me a fighting chance. He crept up on me and grabbed me from behind."

"Did you get a look at him?"

"I told you, he grabbed me from behind. I remember only his breathing, and his pressing a dark hand over my mouth. I don't know whether it was dark gloves or the color of his skin. But he must have been huge to have overpowered me, even if I was drunk. At first, I didn't realize what had really transpired, because I hadn't been robbed of anything. Although it was hard for me to imagine it happening at the Devonshire, I thought that I had fallen victim to one of those maniacs who are increasingly prevalent in the land because we're no longer allowed to toss them in the nut house where they belong. It wasn't till the next night, when I was with my favorite femme and couldn't get it up in any of our pet positions that I began to suspect foul play. And then a day or two later I got that psychotic note in the mail: *You're not the man you used to be.*"

"Have you still got it?"

"No. I threw it out. A guy in my position often gets these letters and phone calls from weirdos and misfits. I didn't connect it to what had happened until much later, after the other guys had been hit. They told Foster about their notes, and he made the connection and asked me if I'd gotten one too."

"Describe it."

Michaelson shrugged. "It was a photocopy of poor quality. Like in the old movies on TV, the guy had cut out the words from magazines and pasted them down. Because of the very distinctive lettering, I recognized two of the words as being from an ad for ABC, the baking company that I had to take over last year."

"I'm very stupid when it comes to big business. Why did you *have* to take it over?"

"Because it was part of a conglomerate, and it's always simpler and more profitable for me to buy the whole shebang and then dispose of the entities I don't want to keep. ABC, formerly the Abbington Biscuit Company, was one of them, and when the *Wall Street Journal* reported that I was buying it only to sell it to another baking company that planned to close it and eliminate competition, you can just imagine the flack I had to take from Democrats, labor, and the media. If those rich and compassionate congressmen and millionaire columnists were really concerned about all those lost jobs, they would have pooled their money and topped my offer from Dixon Baking."

"Okay. So you had to buy it. Let's move on. Do you, Portman, and Bernard have any enemies in common?"

"Are you kidding? Guys like us would need the latest supercomputers to count all our enemies, and there are bound to be plenty of crossovers. Not that we've ever done anything to earn the enmity of any rational person who believes in the free-market system instead of a socialist slave economy. It's envy, pure and simple." Michaelson sat back in his chair and looked virtuous and at peace with himself.

"What about Vittorio Capperrelli? Did you ever screw around with Ilsa Grant?"

Michaelson shook his head. "Not that I wouldn't like to. God, that broad is built! Lucky Tony. Now that she's working for him, I assume that he gets a discreet piece of ass upon occasion. Maybe my time will come one of these days."

And then he remembered that, in the absence of a miracle from his friend Dr. Albert Foster, his time for Ilsa or any other woman would never come. He sat up straight, his hands grasping the arms of the chair so hard that his knuckles gleamed shiny and white. "You've got to find that son of a bitch, Berenson!"

He looked around the room before continuing. Caught up in emotion, he forgot to adjust his vocal cords, and his voice rose at least an octave to its new and higher pitch. "My wife is the original assertive woman and feminist who knows every single one of her rights. She walked out on me a month ago because I couldn't get it up anymore, and she suspected it was because I was screwing too many other women. It's just as well. Being one of the Carringtons of Virginia and therefore independently wealthy, she married me more for my virility than my wealth, and after those glorious years of screwing, I couldn't let her see me like this. Shit, *I* can't stand to see me like this!" Tears filled his eyes. "The only thing my pecker's good for now is peeing and blowing in the breeze. Dammit! One of the drug conglomerates I took over is coming out with what will deliver more juice than Viagra and its two competitors, but it won't do a goddamn thing for me!" He jumped to his feet.

"One more question. Have you ever done anything to offend Lou West?"

"Yes!" Michaelson cried. "On the rainiest, muddiest day in years, I fumbled a fucken ball and cost us a victory over Yale. And do you think that twenty-five years later he still holds it against me and has castrated me for my sin on the field? Lou has a compulsion for being number one, but that's going too far, even for him. Enough, goddamn it! Let's get out of here. I need a drink!" He rushed from the room like he was being pursued by demons.

Tom followed at a more leisurely pace. He paused at the entrance to the reception hall. Michaelson was already at the bar, staring at the bartender who was preparing his drink. Most of the others were still there, laughing and talking, full of gourmet food, expensive liquor, and themselves. Apparently Nora and Denise had packed up their equipment and called it a night. Tom felt a stab of disappointment, and realized that he had been hoping for a nightcap and a quiet talk with Nora in one of those cozy rooms or alcoves along the corridor.

He walked toward the exit. When he opened the door, Ms. Naked Shoulders—Jason Gilbert's wife or girlfriend—dashed inside and past him without even a nod. It was unlikely that she had noticed him, for she appeared to be distressed and intent on rushing down the hall. Before he could ask if she was okay, she had disappeared behind the door of the powder room. He shrugged and continued on his way.

Outside, the night air felt cool and refreshing. The breeze also brought the hard rock from a nearby frat party, along with youthful laughter, male and female. He became conscious of yet another sound as he walked along the path to the road. To his left, across the lawn and behind a tall hedge, two or more grown men were cursing and yelling as if they weren't aware they were on the campus of a noble institution of learning, the "cradle of presidents past and future," as President Colbert had remarked only an hour ago.

Ordinarily he might have thought twice about interfering in what was no doubt a private quarrel, but since he was getting his best pay ever to protect Golden Guys, he rushed across the lawn. Soon he heard scuffling, and a man yelled, "I'm going to cut your cock off, you son of a bitch! Guys like you don't deserve to live!"

As he came to the hedge and ran alongside it in search of an opening, Tom wished that he had brought along his gun.

CHAPTER 10

BEYOND THE HEDGE, a spotlight illuminated a statue of Gouverneur Morris, one hand outstretched in oratory, perhaps at the very moment of declaring his famous opening to the preamble of the Constitution, "We the people of the United States...." And it also revealed two struggling figures in black.

As Tom ran toward them, the taller and broader of the two, who certainly fit Tony Portman's depiction of his assailant, punched the other one in the stomach. The shorter man groaned and doubled over. He remained that way a moment, and then tried to knee his assailant in the groin. With a laugh, the taller man grabbed the knee, twisted it, and hurled his opponent to the ground.

From closer, Tom saw that the fighters were two of the fraternity brothers—Doug McGrath and Jason Gilbert. Gilbert was the first to see him coming. He tried to sit up but couldn't. "My back and spine!" he cried. "Oh, my God!"

"I thought all you scientists didn't believe in God," McGrath said. "It would serve you right if He punished you."

After another attempt to rise, Gilbert placed his hands over his eyes. Leisurely, McGrath turned round and nodded to Tom. He placed his hands on his hips and spread his legs in an obvious attempt to appear cowpoke casual while keeping Gilbert in view. Then he made the crooked grin swiped from Clark Gable that his fans had been adoring for almost two decades.

"Howdy, pardner," he said. "To what do we owe the pleasure of your company?"

"To my wish to prevent mayhem." Keeping an eye on

McGrath, Tom pushed past him and knelt down beside Gilbert. "Lie still," he ordered. "You may have internal injuries. How's your breathing? I'll get Dr. Foster."

Gilbert took a few deep breaths, and then placed a hand over his lower right ribs. "I'll be all right. And if I need a doctor, it won't be Foster."

"What was going on here?"

"It's none of your damn business!" McGrath roared. He rushed over to Tom and pulled him up. "Who the hell are you and where did you come from? If you're another one of those spies from the gutter press, I'll tear you limb from limb. My private life is my own, damn you!"

"Keep your hands to yourself." Tom shoved him away with such force that McGrath landed on his behind next to Gilbert. "I'm Tom Berenson, not some Hollywood extra who's paid not to fight back. Al Foster introduced us before. Remember? I was passing by and heard shouting."

McGrath got to his feet and squinted as he stepped closer to Tom. "Right, right." He blinked a few times. "My left contact seems to have popped out. Always nice to meet one of my old fans. The fact is, I was showing Jason how I handled that bunch of ornery honchos in my latest Western, and I misjudged the length of my arm." McGrath squatted down beside Gilbert, and made a smile as bright as in the TV commercial for the brand of beef jerky he promoted. "How are you douching, buddy? You're okay, ain't you? Sure you are. I never saw you looking better. Come on, I'll help you up."

"Go to hell! I expected better behavior from a brother."

"Let's not expose our dirty linen in public."

"I'll get up by myself. And I'm not going to forget this."

McGrath laughed. "What are you going to do? Too bad the Nobel Prize isn't a statue like the Oscar. You could hit me on the head with it."

"Whatever it is, you can be sure that the punishment will fit the crime."

"You're blowing this whole thing up out of proportion. It's not my fault that women keep throwing themselves at me. It would be impolite not to take what they're offering."

"You goddamn son of a bitch! Cassie was *not* throwing herself at you! You were all over her from the moment you were introduced."

"Come on, buddy. I always gave you credit for more sophistication, especially after your visit to Sweden where they have all those gorgeous blondes. No broad is worth fighting for, especially if you're a Golden Guy. There's always a new crop ready for the plucking." McGrath rose and started back to Beta Hall at a leisurely pace, whistling "Gonna Fly Now," the theme song from *Rocky*.

Still on the ground, Gilbert rejected Tom's hand, and struggled into a sitting position. There, with a hand rubbing his abdomen, he glowered at his foe until he disappeared into the building.

"Thanks," he muttered. "Sorry you had to see my embarrassment. But I'm glad you came along when you did. It was stupid of me to appeal to that bastard's sense of decency, because after twenty-five years I should have known that he doesn't have any. But sometimes a man has to do what he believes to be right, regardless of the consequences."

"I agree. And I didn't see anything that should embarrass you."

"Thanks."

Tom chose his next words with care. "During your fight, did you ever get the impression that McGrath intended to harm you seriously?"

"What do you mean? Did you see that punch he gave me? That was serious enough, I think."

"I mean, did he try to hit you in the groin?"

Gilbert looked at Tom as if there were something odd about him. "Actually," he said, "*I* tried to hit *him* in the groin. Too bad I missed, because it would be a very appropriate injury for that... satyr." He extended a hand to Tom. "I'll take you up on that offer now."

Once upon his feet, Gilbert swayed a moment. He shook his head when Tom offered to accompany him to his room. "We're not staying over. We live not far from here. I'll go get Cassie and she'll drive us home. I'll be back to normal in the morning," he assured Tom as he started on his way. After a few slow and difficult steps, he turned and added, "Of course, as Hume says, we can never be sure that morning will ever come."

Hoping to end their encounter on a positive note, Tom replied, "And if it doesn't come, we'll be saved the trouble of getting out of bed with a hangover."

"That's a thought, but not a particularly cheerful one. Good night, my friend. And I look forward to returning your kindness one day."

With a sigh, Tom resumed his walk back to his motel. Soon he became aware of the pulsating beat of rock music all around him. Responding to a beat of their own, a couple was making out—or whatever kids called it these days—behind the statue of Judge Horace Pitkin, a benefactor of the law school, and also of women under fourteen, because, as a state senator, he had advocated legislation barring their employment in mines and factories for more than twelve hours a day. He heard glass breaking in the distance. And the roar of youthful laughter. Then male voices broke into a bawdy song about beer and beds and blondes.

It occurred to Tom that Stephanie would soon be part of a college scene like this. The thought chilled him. Was she ready for it? Was he? He quickened his steps.

Amid the wind and crunched leaves, he could hear Beth reminding him, "She's growing up, honey. She needs a dad, not a cop. It's time to let go."

He slowed his steps and raised his eyes to the starry sky. The memory of her wisdom and her laughter warmed him the rest of the way.

CHAPTER 11

TOM HAD hoped that Stephanie would be sound asleep in her adjoining room, but he wasn't really surprised to find it empty. After washing up, he got into bed with the psychology textbook on male sexual aberrations that he had been reading since he agreed to take the case. It couldn't have been easy for the two authors, a man and a woman, to make their subject as dull and incomprehensible as his IRS booklet on the depreciation of office equipment, but they had managed to do it, even with the chapter on breast envy. According to the two authors, breast envy, a subject often ignored by colleagues, was the male counterpart to Freud's more famous penis envy in females, and a key to understanding the psyche of males in postindustrial societies. Despite his motive for reading, an excuse to wait up for Stephanie, he found himself dozing off.

At last, approaching footsteps and then muffled words and laughter outside brought him back to full alertness. Quickly he doused his light and slid the book and himself under the covers. The words and laughter continued. That wasn't so bad. It was those pauses in between that got on his nerves and finally made him send telepathic messages to Mark: *She's only sixteen. Leave her alone. Go flirt with the co-eds back in your dorm. They know how to handle smooth guys like you.*

Finally, thankfully, he heard footsteps retreating along the gravel road, and then the click of the lock next door. With a giant sigh of relief, he turned over on his side.

A minute later Stephanie walked through their adjoining bathroom and switched on his floor lamp. He kept his eyes closed.

"You're a lousy actor, Dad," she said with a laugh. "Besides, I saw your light when we got back."

"Foiled again."

She sat down on the edge of his bed. "So how was your night among the high and mighty?"

"Long and boring."

"Did you bring me back a doggie bag?"

"Of course not. I wouldn't insult your palate. It was just a lot of junk food for the elite. Nothing like your grandfather's cooking. Though it may have sounded gauche, I couldn't help remarking to my neighbor at the table, 'Oh for a bowl of my father-in-law's chili.'"

"What did he say to that?"

"It was a she, and she said that she'd heard that the food and everything else about Brooklyn was very interesting if not intriguing."

"I'm surprised that she'd even heard about Brooklyn. Was she a Golden Girl, if that's what the wives of Golden Guys are called?"

Tom smiled as he considered Golden Girl as an accurate description of his neighbor at dinner. "It was Nora Malcolm, who's making the documentary about the Golden Guys."

"I know who she is. One night after the pro tennis matches, Channel Thirteen showed her documentary about great women players of the past. I don't usually collect autographs, but if you happen to see her again...."

"As a matter of fact, we're playing tennis tomorrow."

"Interesting." Stephanie smiled, and fixed her gaze upon him, obviously waiting for details.

He shrugged. "No big deal. We both hope to work off tonight's meal."

"Sure you do."

He added quickly, "I also met Lyle Wayne, one of your favorite statesmen."

"Did you punch him in the nose for me and tell him that what I do with my body is my own business?"

"I knew there was something I forgot to do."

She sighed. "Never mind. As you're always telling me, if you want something done, you have to do it yourself. Who else was there?"

"Mostly guys who get a lot of attention in the *Wall Street Journal*. But there was one real superstar—Doug McGrath."

"That old man?" Stephanie made a face. "He should have been put out to pasture along with his horses from years ago. Why are you hanging around these guys, anyway? I can see you working on a book about crime or Brooklyn, but fraternities? That's weird."

"My work on this book is going to pay your tuition bills at the college of your choice, even if it's Oxford. By the way, Ms. Malcolm extols the liberal arts program at Johns Hopkins, where her daughter is a student. But enough about *my* evening. How was yours?"

"Great!" Her eyes lit up. "Mark is the student president here of one of Mom's favorite causes, Friends of the Planet."

"That reminds me. If and when we go to Baltimore for a look at Johns Hopkins, we can drop in at the National Aquarium. You're probably too young to remember, but as a member of Save Our Oceans, your mom once adopted one of the tortoises there."

"I remember Teddy the Tortoise very well. I used to consider him my much older brother, because he was about eighty. Okay, it's a date for Baltimore, but as I was about to tell you, Friends of the Planet invited Clara Claiborne to speak tonight. I think she's fantastic, and I've never had a chance to hear her speak in person."

"Many summers ago, your mother and I left you with Aunt Pat for a weekend while we went up to Nantucket and joined a whale and dolphin watch that was organized by Clara Claiborne. What was she saving tonight—redwood forests or ring-tailed rhinos?"

"Don't make fun of her, Dad. You're gung-ho on saving the environment too."

"Yes, but I don't gung along with her militancy in recent years. She encourages her followers to break the law and even endanger their lives to make their points."

"Sometimes that's the only way to get the media and the politicians to listen. Too bad those Wall Streeters you were with tonight weren't with *us*. Clara would have torn them apart. Her whole speech was about how big business is raping and ravaging the country, the entire world. If something isn't done to stop it soon, we'll all have to pack our bags and find another planet to live on."

"Claiborne's known as a windy woman, but surely she wasn't lamenting the state of the environment all this time. What did you do afterward? Something that was more fun, I hope."

"We went to a frat party first."

"*First?*"

She made a face. "Don't look so worried. Anyhow, I didn't like it much. Too much drinking and…other stuff. I was afraid I'd look like a baby if I said anything to Mark, but he got the message and he asked if I'd rather go to the campus disco."

Mark shot up a notch in Tom's estimation. "And how was that?"

"Great!" She stretched. "Is it okay if we don't have breakfast together? Mark wants to take me to this place in town where all the kids go for bagels Sunday morning."

"Enjoy. I'm hoping to hit the road before three. Think you can get Mark to part with you by then?"

"I'll be back and packed and waiting." She leaned over and kissed his cheek. "'Night, Daddy." As she flipped off his light on her way back to her room, she added, "Thanks for bringing me along. It's been a great trip."

"Have you formed any impressions of the school yet? How does it compare with Penn, for example?"

"I think Mark dances much better than the guy who showed me around at Penn." She blew him a kiss.

He pulled the covers up. He was glad that one of them was having a good time.

Stephanie had already closed the door when she opened it again and said, "I sure hope that Senator Wayne brought along a bodyguard."

"Why the concern about him?"

"There was another speaker at the meeting, a weird, hyper guy named Charlie Ludlow. Clara Claiborne introduced him as the chairman of her action committee. He was really mad about the energy bill that the senator pushed through Congress, especially all the giveaways to the oil companies. He threatened to tear the senator limb from limb if they ever met."

"Sounds like a rhetorical flourish to me."

"Maybe, but you should have seen his face when he said it."

As he turned over on his side and awaited sleep, Tom reminded himself that, strictly speaking, it wasn't Wayne's limbs that he had been hired to protect.

CHAPTER 12

DOUG MCGRATH'S knuckles were sore as he returned to the Beta Phi house. But it was a good kind of sore, the kind that comes when your punch has hit its mark and delivered your message with a resounding *crack*. He headed upstairs for the room one of the current kids had turned over to him for the night. Of course, it would have been more satisfying if Gilbert wasn't such a pushover, drunk and out of shape. The most exercise the guy probably got was lifting test tubes and pushing around Bunsen burners. McGrath chuckled to himself as he opened the door. Nobel Prize winner or not, Gilbert was a schmuck. He had to be out of his fricken mind to think he could take on a *real* man.

At the basin, McGrath ran some water on his hand. Who the hell did Gilbert think he was, coming after him for making passes at his nebbish of a wife? Gilbert should have gone down on his knees and thanked him for giving her what had to be the biggest thrill of her life. It was obvious Gilbert wasn't man enough to keep the skinny bitch happy. But Gilbert was always a thin-skinned prick. What can you expect from a Jew? McGrath had fought against inviting him to pledge for the fraternity, but, no, they had to kowtow to National and open the doors a little wider. Fuck that.

Lucky that detective guy had come along when he had. Otherwise, Gilbert might be dead by now. Serve him right. He splashed some water on his face. Shit. Was that a bruise coming out under his eye? He squinted and touched the area tenderly. What the hell. As long as the eye didn't close up, it would be okay. Add a little mystery. Prove he was the don't-mess-with-me guy everyone with half a brain took him for. Besides, it was nothing that his Dior Cannages couldn't cover up.

He ran a comb through his hair, brushed off his jacket, took a quick look at his Hublot Big Bang. Twelve forty-two. He still had about three quarters of an hour to kill. Might as well go back downstairs, have a couple more drinks, shake a few more hands, squeeze a few more behinds, spread around that old McGrath charm. No matter what their bank accounts or academic credentials, every man in that room downstairs wished he were Doug McGrath. And every woman longed to be screwed by him in a dozen different ways. He flashed his trade-mark smile, checked that there was no food caught on his teeth, turned from the mirror, and headed downstairs.

BY ONE-THIRTY there were only a few stragglers left, hardly worth wasting his charms on. Most of them were too bleary-eyed to notice him slipping away. And if they did—so what?

He strolled leisurely over to Thomas Fitzsimmons Walk, his footsteps only a little unsteady from all the alcohol he had consumed. The old-fashioned lampposts, so conducive to getting girls in the mood in his undergraduate days, had been replaced by bright fluorescent lights, meant to discourage muggers and perverts. Definitely not a sign of progress. He was pleased to hear whispers and grunts coming from the bushes. He smiled. The brighter the lights, the darker the shadows. These kids could always go back to their dorms to screw, and the administration wouldn't give a damn. But there was something so invigorating about fucking al fresco.

He stepped off the walk, preferring to make his way in the shadows. No need to have someone recognize him. All he needed was to have some kid waylay him for an autograph when he was on his way to meet the president's wife. He wished he and Midge could do it al fresco, as they sometimes had in the old days. What a piece of ass she had been back then—twenty-five and with curves that were wasted on a graduate student on her way to a Ph.D. in philosophy. Of course, those delicious curves also helped her achieve her other goal—an MRS with Colbert. He had been a dean back then, but everyone knew he was on the president track. She broke up his marriage faster than you could say Friedrich Wilhelm Nietzsche, her favorite philosopher and the author of her favorite self-help book, *The Will to Power*. But she always had time for old Doug whenever an event brought him back to the campus.

Up ahead, he saw a figure dart out from behind one of the huge white oaks, probably full grown when Morris drew up the Constitution, that kept the campus looking rural and idyllic, and worth the high fees. She stopped behind the next one, the one where they had agreed to meet. McGrath quickened his steps. But not too much. No need to seem eager.

Midge was still in the sexy black velvet gown she had worn to the reception and dinner. Back then, though, she had worn a long-sleeved black lace jacket over the strapless top, which declared to the world: "I'm the reserved and respectable wife of a university president, but even at fifty I'm still his sexy trophy wife." Now the jacket had been replaced by a stole to keep off the evening chill.

She melted in his arms, as women always did. But when he reached into her bodice for her breast, she pulled away. "Not here, darling." She jiggled a key ring. "I have the keys to the Morris museum." She took his hand and they dashed over to the building at the end of the walk. "Stay back." She pulled the stole over her head, went to the entrance, quickly punched in the code to turn off the alarm, then opened the door a crack. Once again, she motioned him to stay where he was, then reached through the open door, obviously feeling for some equipment on the wall beside it.

Finally, she waved him over, took his hand, and led him inside. "All's clear. Alarms and security cameras are off."

After a moment to accustom their eyes to the dark, she led him quickly through the entrance hall and exhibits beyond.

"Where the hell are we going?"

"Shh! Not to worry. I know this place like the back of my hand." They wove between statuary and display cases. "You don't want to screw on the floor like undergraduates, do you? Watch out for Ben Franklin up ahead. The dirty old man's left hand is sticking out at just the right height to give you a surprise goose." Finally, she paused before a door at the end of a corridor, unlocked it, and threw it open with a flourish. "My office."

"What happened to the one in the philosophy department?"

"It's still there, but it's hell to get to in the middle of the night. This is more convenient, and comfortable. They gave it to me when I volunteered to help plan events."

"What kind of events?"

"All kinds. But this is my favorite."

He didn't need to ask if this was the first of those "favorite" events. She knew her way around in the dark too well to pretend that she had wangled this set-up just for him.

She tossed her stole on the desk. "Want to unzip me—or do you still prefer a striptease?"

"A strip, of course."

"What is it with you guys? You never grow up." She closed the drapes and turned on the desk lamp. Next she reached around, unzipped her gown, and slowly wiggled out of it. "Sorry I can't provide music, but you can hum something appropriate."

She was wearing a black lace teddy with long garters that were attached to sheer black stockings. She sat down on the edge of the desk and struck a pose. Slowly, she detached the garters and rolled down the stockings, turning each one into a silken ball that she tossed to him. He caught them and put them into his pocket. Then he pulled off his jacket. Before it had hit the floor, she was in front of him, slowly unbuttoning his shirt, kissing her way down his chest.

"Jesus!" he said. "My cock is going to break my zipper."

"Tell it to wait," she whispered, slipping his shirt from his shoulders.

She undid his belt. Slowly, agonizingly, she drew down his zipper, then pulled his trousers and jockeys down in the same movement. As he stepped out of them, she kissed his navel. He took her head between his hands and tried to force it down farther. But she slipped free and stood up, placing a light kiss on his lips to soften the movement.

"No." She shook her finger at him gently, like a teacher admonishing a favorite preschooler. "Me first. You later. I've learned that the hard way. No pun intended." She lay down on the leather sofa, taking the same position as Goya's "Nude Maja."

"Now, do you think you can get me out of this thing without ripping it?"

No, he couldn't. But neither of them really gave a damn about that flimsy piece of material. Then they were lost in a whirling frenzy of arms and legs, mouths and tongues. Occasionally, muffled by either her flesh or his, Midge was panting, "Easy, easy!" But all McGrath chose to heed was the sound of the blood pounding in his ears and the throbbing flames in his loins. They crashed off the sofa in the chaotic fury of his thrusts and lunges.

"Baby, that was great." McGrath rolled over, gasping for breath, running the back of his arm over his sweaty forehead.

"For you."

"What the hell does that mean?" Actually, he didn't give a damn. He was Doug McGrath. At her age, she was lucky he was willing to waste his precious juices on her. He only did it because they went back so many years. And, well, because, even at fifty, her tits were terrific and she was a better piece of ass than most of the stuck-up starlets he screwed.

She raised herself on an elbow, smiled, and sighed. "On screen you're a great cowboy, but in bed you've always been just a rookie bronco buster—quick to mount and even quicker to fall off."

The rage he felt shot him to a sitting position. "That's crap! Women throw themselves at me, begging for it. If you've got problems, it's because you're over the hill. Menopause must have turned off your switches."

"Baby, I've got news for you. Menopause turns them on. All they need is a guy smart enough to flip them. And watch out who you're calling over the hill. I'm only a few years and a couple of steps ahead of you on that mountain."

"For men it's different."

She laughed. "So men like to delude themselves." She reached over and began making little circles in the hair on his chest. "Now quit sulking and lie down like a good boy, and I'll give you that treat I promised you."

He obeyed, and it was a treat indeed. No one gave a blow job like Midge.

He was ready to go another round, but as the Webster Hall clock chimed two, she got to her feet.

"Gotta go."

"Aw, come on. Once more, for old time's sake." He gave her his trademark McGraw smile, the one that melted the heart of every damsel in or out of distress, and reached for her hand, trying to pull her down beside him.

With a shake of her head, she extricated her hand. "Sorry. Poor Bob's deep into the prostate years. His only action in bed is get up to pee, and he has to do that at least three times a night. I made sure he had enough scotch to knock him out for a while, but Nature will be calling him any minute now. I want to be in my usual place, curled innocently beside him, when he heeds that call."

"Why?"

"Because I like being the president's wife. And I also like Bob."

"But look at all you're missing."

She laughed. "That's a funny thing for a middle-aged naked guy to say." She wiggled into her evening gown, zipped it up, and slipped into her shoes. "Baby, there are plenty of guys around who are only too happy to see to it that I don't miss a thing. Sorry to disillusion you, but you're just one of many." She tossed his clothes to him. "Come on. Get dressed. Time to get out of here."

While he got into his clothes, she retrieved her torn teddy and rolled it up in her stole. Then she held out her hand. "Stockings, please."

"No souvenirs?"

"Just your memories, which I'm sure will get raunchier with every passing day." She tucked the stockings into her stole, turned off the lamp, reopened the drapes, and headed for the door. "Stay close. It's an obstacle course out there."

All the way to the exit, he could smell her perfume. By the time they reached Ben Franklin, he could feel the ache in his groin all the way up to his back teeth. He grabbed her, wrapping his arms around her breasts and shoving his fiery genitals against her buttocks. "Here. Let's do it right here. In front of this old lecher. Show him what a good fuck really is."

"Not now! I have to get back." She struggled to get away, but he was too strong for her.

"It'll only take a minute." With one hand he pulled up her skirt. Then he shoved her over. He was wrong. It took less than sixty seconds.

"There," he panted. "That will show the old bastard what a good fuck is really like."

"*You're* the bastard," she said, straightening up. "And you don't know shit about what goes into a good fuck. Now zip up your fly and follow me, or I'll lock you in the museum with all the security turned on. It would serve you right." She rushed away from him before he could grab her again.

At the exit, she opened the door and pushed him out. "You first. We don't want to be spotted together. These horny kids are all over the place."

Outside, he huddled near a tree and waited. It took a moment for her to turn all the security codes back on, then she slipped through the door, locked it, and pressed some more buttons. She didn't bother to turn to see if he was still around. There was no wave or blown kiss. She just rushed off toward the safety of home, keeping to the shadows.

That's gratitude for you, McGrath told himself, also sticking to the shadows, but heading in the opposite direction, for Hoover Walk. No way could that lying bitch have had such good sex since the last time he was on campus for that film forum a couple of years ago. Menopause must have messed up her brain as well as turning off her juices. At her age, she was lucky he was willing to give her a tumble. The more he thought about it, the more furious he became. He could use a drink.

He paused and took out the gold flask his last ex-wife had given him on their first Christmas. The Macallan went down with the warmth of a golden sunset, making his anger recede in a liquid haze. Midge had been kidding, of course, when she said those nasty things. It was just her weird sense of humor. They had always had great sex together. Great sex. He thought of those luscious tits, that sweet, round ass. Who was he kidding that she was dried up? She wasn't like those skinny stuck-up starlets who thought only of themselves. Midge was willing to try anything, do anything. Like wine, she just got better with age.

He took another swig from his flask. As the scotch reached his belly it seemed to merge with all the other liquor he had consumed that night and revive it. God, he wished she was still here so they could have another go at it. It would be great down there on the grass. Chuckling at the thought of it, he brought the flask to his mouth and took another gulp. Not a good idea. Now he had to take a piss.

He staggered over to a tree and leaned his shoulder against the huge trunk. His head nodded and it was hard to keep his eyes open as he relieved himself. Oh, Jeez, that felt good. The liquor made his fingers feel like they belonged to someone else. He had to struggle a bit to grasp the tab of his zipper. Before he could get it halfway up, a black-clad arm came out of nowhere and he found his neck caught in a tightening lock. He reached up to grab the arm, but he suddenly felt a prick against his neck. From the corner of his eye, he saw the flash of a knife.

"Don't even think about it, cowboy." The raspy whisper was even more threatening, more frightening than a full voice.

"It's my flask, isn't it?" He could barely talk with that arm cutting off his air. "You saw it. It's gold. Take it." He struggled to turn, to see his assailant. But the scotch had turned his legs to rubber and he couldn't move. "My watch. Wallet. Take them. Just don't hurt me. Please!" Talking made it even harder to breathe. But he had to do something, say something to protect himself. The creep obviously didn't know who he was dealing with. "For Christ's sake! Do you know who I am?" he gasped.

"Sure. You're Doug McGrath. And you're about to ride off into the sunset." The pressure tightened around his neck. Then a bright red haze turned to black.

CHAPTER 13

NORA MALCOLM looked as attractive to Tom in a white Windbreaker and denim shorts as she had in her evening attire. Maybe she looked even better, because now he could see her shapely legs as she rose from one of the benches near the enclosure of four tennis courts. Only two of the courts were occupied, and all six players, like Nora, were in correct attire. Feeling rather a disgrace to the game, and also an embarrassment to Nora in his old chinos and a yellow Shetland sweater over a T-shirt, he broke into a jog, hoping that he could at least impress her with his exuberance, his athletic spirit.

"Am I late?" he asked.

She laughed and motioned him to slow down. "Not at all. I'm just an early bird and have already been out for a run." She was taller than she seemed last night, when he had attributed a few inches of her height to the assumption that she was wearing high heels. Now he realized that she must have been wearing flats, for in her white tennis shoes she was only about an inch shy of his own height. She tilted her head to one side and studied him, for so long that he began to wonder if she had learned the ulterior motive for his presence at GMU, not that it would have been a calamity. He assumed that since the Golden Guys were cooperating so wholeheartedly with her documentary about them, Portman, Wayne, and the rest had given her their imprimatur and considered her a person who wouldn't betray them if she came across any of their dark and dirty secrets, past or present.

"You look different today," she said at last.

"I know I do, but I was afraid to wear Harry's expensive tuxedo on the tennis court."

"It's more than that."

Tom couldn't bring himself to admit aloud that the difference might be due to their being together this morning. Nora picked up the two rackets on the bench. "You can have your choice."

"I assume that one of them belongs to Denise."

Nora sighed. "Once she got up here, she realized that she'd be too busy to play. Well, that's show biz."

It occurred to Tom that the two women might be practicing certain traditional wiles on him, an unattached male. But he brushed aside the flattering thought. Though he might possess such underappreciated qualities as wit and charm, and considered himself a leading authority on Robert Benchley and Will Cuppy, probably because there were few authorities left, he was forty-four and neither rich nor handsome. A talented and attractive woman like Nora Malcolm could definitely do much better for herself than to get involved with the likes of him. Nevertheless, since destiny had brought them together, it would be wasteful not to make the most of their tennis date. He would have liked to look longer at the way the sun caught the golden highlights in her short hair.

"First a run, then tennis," he said. "What have you scheduled for this afternoon—horseback riding?"

"How I wish. Unfortunately, Denise and I will be trailing around after the Golden Guys all this afternoon, capturing them in their native habitat."

As she smiled and pulled off her Windbreaker, he was conscious of a throbbing at his temples and in his chest. She tossed the jacket over a bench, and strolled onto a court. Her pale-blue sweatshirt depicted Alice in Wonderland and the Cheshire Cat, and as Tom studied it, she explained, "Early in my career, I did a short on Lewis Carroll for a short-lived educational program on one of the networks. To my chagrin, the producer and his star were more interested in Carroll's sex life than in his literary works. That's when I decided to become an independent producer one day." She started across the court. "Okay if we volley a bit first? I'm out of practice, not that I'm any sort of player even with practice."

Once he saw the power and accuracy of her strokes, he

realized that she was giving him a chance to warm up without having to be the one to suggest it.

But warming up couldn't help him when they retreated to their positions and began to keep score. She was by far the better player, of at least superstar caliber at the courts in Prospect Park, and after she won the set without his even winning a single game, they agreed to keep the ball in the air rather than try to score points.

"That's the best game I've had in ages," Nora informed him as they walked off the court.

"Same here," Tom said, probably more truthfully. The sun was high overhead, he was leaving at about three, and he hadn't even attempted to learn whether Nora had come across any dark secrets about the stars of her documentary. "How about a cup of coffee?"

"I never drink coffee," she said, "But I'd sure love a cup of tea."

"Great. Let me take those rackets from you."

"Ah, chivalry isn't dead."

"Only male superiority on the tennis court."

"You were having a bad day."

He refrained from telling her that, on the contrary, he was having his best day in years.

Nora led him to the nearest eating place, which was in the basement of an ivy-covered, early nineteenth-century building that housed the school museum as well as Webster Hall, a national-landmark auditorium where Daniel Webster used to speak and debate. According to Nora, the great statesman had, one night in 1847, orated for almost three hours against the morality of America's seizure of Mexican territory.

"Three hours!" Tom said. "Recently I had to address a small group in Brooklyn, and after about three minutes I couldn't think of anything else to say."

"What was the occasion?"

"About a real estate mogul's attempt to seize territory in Brooklyn Heights."

"Webster failed, but I hope you have better luck."

From her booth in the vestibule, the cashier told them to

take any table. They were about to enter the dining room when a very distinctive man and woman emerged whom Tom recognized from news photos and TV appearances as Clara Claiborne and Charlie Ludlow. A chunky redhead of about fifty, and with theatrical make-up on her full lips and heavy-lidded eyes, Claiborne wore baggy jeans and an orange Windbreaker with a picture of a dolphin. Towering above her, Ludlow, reputed to have been an enforcer for the Winter Hill gang in Boston before his parents died of salmonella poisoning and he became a born-again environmentalist, was dressed in a plaid mackinaw and green corduroy pants. The pants were tucked into the sort of tall shiny black boots that could conceal a knife or gun. His attire was immaculate and suitable for a Barney's ad in *Vanity Fair,* and with his neatly trimmed gray-brown hair and beard, he looked like an actor impersonating a woodsman.

While Ludlow looked on benevolently, Nora and Claiborne called out in delight to each other, then hugged and began chatting animatedly. Obliged to do something during this display of affection, Tom and Ludlow exchanged a grin that said, *Well, it's nice to see someone so happy.*

Nora was saying: "I'm sorry I missed your lecture yesterday, but I was tied up with my documentary about the Golden Guys."

"The Golden Ghouls, if you ask me. Don't let Doug McGrath get too close to you."

"He tried to feel me up yesterday, as a matter of fact."

"That guy acts so macho that I wouldn't be surprised if he's impotent, or gay."

"I have no intention of finding out."

"My spies tell me that neither Portman nor Bernard showed up for the big bash yesterday."

"Yes. Senator Wayne explained that they had important business abroad."

"I guess the time has come to sell the rest of the country to the foreigners. Maybe one of these days you'll remember your old friends and you'll also do a full-lengther about me and Charlie and the movement."

"I'd like nothing better. Find the money and I'll do it tomorrow."

"How's Denise these days? Did she get over her father's accident or whatever it was?"

"It takes time."

"Give her my love. And remind her that time heals all wounds."

Ludlow observed with a grin, "And it also wounds all heels."

Claiborne suggested, "But time needs a hand sometimes."

"No problem."

Finally, the women introduced their companions, and Tom proceeded to praise Claiborne and her work and Ludlow did the same with Nora and hers.

Nora pointed to the dining room. "Do you really have to leave now?"

"I'd love to join you, but I can't," Clara said. "I hardly slept last night, and tomorrow morning at nine-thirty I have to be in Federal court in Milwaukee."

"Who is it this time?"

"Hanover Lumber, and I have much better hopes than with my previous target, damn them to hell."

Ludlow bared his large teeth in a gloating smile. "For one thing, Hanover won't be represented by that legal slime, Neal Bernard, who seems to have an inside track with all these judges." He rubbed his large hands together. "I know that he spends a lot of time in Nantucket. One of these days when he's out swimming, I'm going to sic one of my pet sharks on him."

Clara said to Nora, "I was really surprised to hear of your association with those bastards. Shame on you, Nora."

"And shame on you, Clara, for implying a drop in my standards. Would you have said that to Orson Welles because he was making a movie about William Randolph Hearst?"

"You're right. I'm sure this is going to be a satire on the bastards." Clara opened her huge purse. "And to make amends, I'm going to give you one of these pins of Danny the Dolphin that we usually give only to patrons who contribute at least five hundred bucks."

"Thanks. How about one for Tom?"

"Okay, but he'll have to promise never to buy Treasure of the Sea tuna, which is still using those death nets."

"That's right, pal." Ludlow showed his teeth to Tom.

"I promise," Tom said. "Not even when it's on sale at my local Key supermarket on Montague Street."

Wearing their new silver pins, Nora and Tom entered the dining room and chose a table near the fireplace. When Nora learned from the waitress that only Lipton's was served, she deplored the management's presumption as to her preference in teas, and after removing a small tin from her Channel Thirteen tote bag, she examined its assortment of tea bags and selected one with a purple tag. Tom leaned back in his chair, and as he looked around the cozy room, he tried to picture Stephanie here and on the Morris campus.

"Provided that you bring along your own tea bags," he observed to Nora, "this must be a great place to go to college."

"Only if you're born to it. Outsiders are always outsiders in a place like this. Scholarship money can buy them the education, but not the connections." She glanced over at a group of students laughing and talking at a nearby table. "My daughter, Leslie, was accepted here, but I'm glad she decided not to come. I think she would have been miserable among kids like these."

"Maybe you've been hanging around the Golden Guys too long and have let them make you cynical."

"And maybe you've been working in your bookstore and shut off from the real world for too long. People don't change as they get older, they just become more of their essential selves." Her smile and tone softened the disagreement. She nodded toward the students at the nearby tables. "It's my bet that these kids are chips off their old blocks."

Tom was pleased that his bookman persona was working. "You're probably right. We book people do tend to get a little isolated from things." He smiled before adding, "Anyhow, we're certainly a lot different from your Golden Guys. Since starting this project, you've probably learned much more about them than you can possibly depict in your film."

"It's always that way. I'm sure it's the same way with you and your research. Al Foster told me about your assignment a few days ago, and asked me to help you if I can. He and the rest of the Beta Alpha brothers are really in there pushing for

Wayne. How'd you meet Foster? You seem to live in such different worlds."

Tom was prepared for this moment of truth, and also of deception. "Foster's a customer of mine, and I keep my eye out for rare old medical books for him. When his fraternity brother, Professor Whitney of Stanford, mentioned he was looking for someone to help him out with research on the East Coast, Foster thought of me. With college fees coming up for Stephanie, I figured I'd better grab the opportunity. Independent bookstores aren't exactly gold mines these days. In fact, it might help if Clara Claiborne put us on her endangered species list." He shrugged. "I'd appreciate any help you can give me. As I'm sure you know, the book will be a scholarly study of fraternities and their influence on their members and society. Whitney wants his centerpiece to be the GMU Beta Alphas of '80, who seem to have achieved the full potential of the fraternity system in America."

"That's more or less the point of my documentary too."

"How did *you* get tied up with these guys?" Tom couldn't resist asking. "My daughter's a fan of yours, and she pointed out that this doesn't seem to be your usual hard-hitting journalism. Unless there's more than meets the eye, and you're going to delve beneath the surface and expose all their nasty hidden agendas."

"It's all absolutely aboveboard. This came along when I was between projects, and I took it because I can use all the big bucks these guys are shelling out to help me with more important work after I wrap this up. We all wind up having to do that now and then in this business." She smiled, and a delightful glint came into her eyes. "Of course, I wouldn't be sorry if I found an unobtrusive way to suggest that some nasty business has been conducted to keep these guys' gold glowing and growing."

"All that glitters...?"

"But it would be hard to slip it past them and their lawyer and PR guys."

The waitress returned with their orders. Nora opened her teapot and shook her head "The water isn't even steaming."

"It's not my fault. Do you want a different pot of water?"

"Do you think it'll be an improvement over this one?"

"I can't guarantee it. Like me, the short-order cook is here on work-study. He's a philosophy major."

"He might be studying the preparation of the hemlock that killed Socrates. I'll stick with what I have."

The waitress smiled gratefully, and glanced over her shoulder at Tom. "Let me get out of here before your husband tries his coffee."

They watched her depart, and then they turned to each other and smiled.

"I wonder what made her think you were my husband?"

Tom shrugged. "She probably thinks that couples our age must be visiting parents. Also, we're wearing matching Danny the Dolphin pins."

"How's your coffee?"

"It has some added ingredient that I can't identify."

"Maybe ash from one of Daniel Webster's old cigars."

When the grandfather clock began to chime, Nora groaned and jumped to her feet, "I'm really sorry, but I have to run. I'm meeting Denise in twenty minutes and I can't trail after the Golden Guys dressed like this."

Tom stood up too. "Thanks for the game. About that help you might be able to give me...."

"Right." She took his pen, removed a business card from her wallet and wrote down a number.. "The front's my office, the back's my home number. If I'm not in either place, my machine will take a message and I'll get back to you. And that's not phony TV-land talk. I really do return calls."

He extended his hand. "I'm glad we met, Nora. And that's not phony book-land talk."

She looked surprised and then pleased by his words. They smiled at each other. She shook his hand, scooped up her things, hurried off, stopped suddenly, turned round, withdrew her wallet again.

"Please!" Tom protested.

She hesitated a moment, but didn't argue. "Thank you, Tom. Good-bye"

For a minute, he just sat and thought and basked in her afterglow, but then he reminded himself that he, too, had work to do.

Some of the other Golden Guys he could get in touch with in New York, but while he was still here, he wanted to talk some more with Jason Gilbert, who lived nearby, and with Doug McGrath, who was in from the Coast.

Back in his motel room, he changed out of his tennis clothes, checked his cell phone for messages (there were none), and called Gilbert's home. The woman who answered sounded definitely older and crankier than Gilbert's wife. She told him that Gilbert was on campus, working in his laboratory. She thought it peculiar for Tom to have expected to find him at home, even on a Sunday morning.

"After all," she said sternly, "my son didn't win a Nobel Prize by sitting around in his jammies and reading the Sunday funnies."

Foster had provided Tom with a VIP visitor's pass, and it proved sufficient to admit him to the Simon J. Cragley Science Center, a glass and steel skyscraper that looked ephemeral amid the older buildings of brick and stone.

Though he had no idea of Gilbert's specialty, Tom expected to find him in a long white lab coat and pouring steaming liquids from one bubbling beaker into another. Instead, clad in a baggy sweat suit, the Nobel laureate was sitting at a desk in an office cluttered with books and journals. Computer printouts were spread before him, but his attention was on the bottle of Johnny Walker from which he was pouring a hefty slug into a mug on which was depicted a mad scientist holding a test tube. It was obviously not his first drink of the day.

There was no sign of recognition in his bleary eyes when Gilbert looked up from his cup. Tom reminded him of their meeting the night before, and continued, "We were both dressed a little differently."

"Oh, right. I'm sure that McGrath wanted to kill me. You certainly arrived in the nick of time. Were you ever with the United States Cavalry in a John Ford movie?" He gestured lavishly toward a chair piled high with bulging filing folders. "Just toss away those things and have a seat. Al Foster says you can use my help on a book you're writing. Are you connected with Nora Malcolm? Not that we have anything to hide up here, but for the past two weeks, she and her crew have been poking all over the campus, into all our nooks and crannies. If she wants to continue in television, I hope she bears in mind that Lyle Wayne expects her work to be sheer puffery and not an immortal masterpiece by Ken Burns."

"No, I'm working with Sanford Whitney, a Beta brother of yours out on the Coast." Tom lifted the folders, and at Gilbert's shrug, placed them on the floor. "He's writing *the* definitive study of fraternities and their influence on American education and society. I'm helping him with research on your group—what you've all been doing, awards you've won, and worthwhile things like that."

Gilbert extended the bottle. "Join me? There's another cup around here someplace."

"Thanks, but I think I'll pass."

Gilbert shrugged. He downed what was in his cup and refilled it. "I know Sandy. He's a bright guy. Why is he wasting his time on bullshit like that?"

"I assume he got a lucrative contract for the book."

Gilbert grimaced. "Lucrative is the operative word—for all Betas."

"Surely not for Arnold Simon, from what Foster told me about him."

"Saint Arnie of the Inner City." Gilbert's face softened. "No, not for him. Sandy would be making a bigger contribution to society if he wrote a biography of Arnie. He's a bit of an embarrassment for most of the brothers. Like them, he had it all going for him. Old family, old money—and one day he just turned his back on it. Even though he made lavish provisions for them, his Social Register wife divorced him, and his kids have refused to have anything to do with him. He spends his life down in the ghettos, working with the people his Beta brothers like to pretend don't exist, probably because they're responsible for a hell of a lot of them being there."

"What happened to the 'All for one, one for all' spirit I keep hearing about? Sounds to me like you're talking about your Beta brothers as though you're not really one of them."

"Even among insiders there are outsiders. Everyone knows that, or should know it." Gilbert took a swig from his mug and tried to focus his gaze on Tom. "Are you Jewish?"

Tom nodded, sensing where the conversation was going.

Gilbert nodded too. "I thought so. We Jews can usually sniff each other out."

"I've never tried to hide it."

Gilbert held up his hand. "No. No. Of course not. Neither have I. I'm proud of what I am and where I come from. I'm sure you are too. It's just that...." His voice trailed off, and Tom hoped that he wasn't about to take another swig from his cup. He wanted Gilbert at least halfway lucid.

Gilbert waved his hand and went on. "Just that...all those centuries of being 'the other.' We can sense that in one another."

"And?"

"And so you'll understand what I'm talking about." He ran his fingers over the rim of the mug. "This information is not necessarily for your book, and I reserve the right of approval prior to publication."

"Fine. That's the way I always work."

"I came to Morris as a brilliant science major on a full scholarship and with a plethora of high school awards from corporations like Du Pont and Allied Chemical. When I got on the football team and then was invited to try out for Beta, I thought I had it made both on campus and forever after. I won't lie about that. Up till then, my brain had always made me an outsider. Now I was going to be an insider in one of the most influential fraternities in the country."

He gazed off into space as if lost in memory. Then he poured more Scotch into his mug and set the bottle down with a thud. "What I didn't know at the time, but soon figured out, was that the national organization was leaning on the GMU chapter for being too parochial at a time when the civil rights movement was already history and affirmative action was moving ahead full steam. I was their token Jew. At least I was a brain, and my skin color blended nicely with the rest of them. No one would notice the difference in a crowd as long as I didn't drop my pants and wiggle my penis. That's as far as it has ever gone for me. I'm not part of their old-boy network. Everything I've accomplished, I've accomplished on my own. I don't owe shit to Beta Alpha Beta Phi."

"Why haven't you quit?"

"Why should I? It guarantees me fat grants, and invitations to big-money seminars all over the world, and I like the way it looks in my bio in *Who's Who*. Besides, there are some nice members. Arnie and Foster, for instance. Until his big success with the prostate of Edwardo Bevalino, who couldn't hit a high C without fear of wetting himself on the stage of the Met, and then his flood of innovations in urology, Foster was always a little on the outside too, because his nouveau riche family had immigrated from a so-called lesser-developed country and committed the sin of making its fortune in trade. There are circles within circles, you know, but I'm sure that's true of all groups, including the National Association of Book Researchers, if there be such an outfit."

"There certainly is."

Gilbert shook his head so that his cheeks and jowls vibrated. "Tough shit for all of us outsiders. We're not going to be invited to share in the spoils after the revolution."

"What revolution is that?" Tom was beginning to wonder whether he was being confronted with a case of alcoholic paranoia or of *in vino veritas*.

Gilbert's lips turned down in disdain. "The Lyle Wayne revolution. Didn't you watch that installment of *Frontline* on PBS? That fucken son of a bitch is going to be our next President. But *Frontline* doesn't know the half of it, or maybe they do know it but know also where their future grants will be coming after PBS is dumped. Old Lyle will be taking a lot of his favorite brothers along with him to the White House. They will be a secret Star Chamber that will treat the whole country as their private cookie jar."

He took a swig of Scotch. "They always swore they would do it. From the time they were snot-nosed sophomores they had their secret agenda. They said they'd take over the country before they were fifty and then proceed to run things the way they should be run. Stinking cabal. They've got it all planned. That's what they had the secret meeting about in the spring. Like Antony and Octavius and that third Roman whose name I can never remember, they were going to divide up the country and all its provinces and conquests among them, figuratively speaking."

"The third Roman was Lepidus."

"Thank you. I owe you sixty-four thousand drachmas. Wonder whatever happened to old Lepidus."

"He died in his bed, no doubt with his sandals on." But this was no time to discuss ancient history. Tom needed to know about current events, though it was clear that politicians and their tactics had changed very little if at all over the millennia. "So, did this meeting take place in Nantucket at Neal Bernard's place?"

"How'd you know that?"

"When I interviewed Bernard for Sandy Whitney's book, he mentioned a gathering of the Golden Guys in May."

"But I'm sure he didn't tell you the purpose of that gathering in the merry month of May."

"He implied it was devoted to fun and games."

"Some fun. Some games. Actually, to be more exact, the real meeting took place on Nicky Hammond's yacht about a dozen miles out in the Atlantic, but a few of the guys were staying at Bernard's place. Wayne and Portman, Michaelson, Hammond, Winchester, and McGrath were all there. Ask them what they talked about. No, you can't ask them. It was a secret meeting, like that famous Mafia convention in upstate New York in the fifties. But information leaked about that one, and now the same thing has happened about the one off Nantucket. I found out about it, as I've found out many things, through our—how shall I say it? —our international academic information network." Gilbert pointed to a computer under an elaborate poster of Mendeleev's periodic table of the chemical elements. A crafty look came into his eyes. "I'm pretty sure that Thucydides said it first: 'Powerful men have powerful enemies. It cannot be otherwise.'"

Tom nodded, then asked lightly, "Who are these enemies of the Golden Guys?"

"They're all over, I would think."

"Does their enmity extend to physical harm?"

"I sure hope that it does. After all, what better harm is there for an enemy? Just between you and me, I can't wait for a certain Golden Guy to get what's long been coming to him."

"Doug McGrath?"

"Even the rest of them hate him, because he's screwed all of their wives and mistresses and will boast about it if he's accused. The man has the morals of a bull in heat. But until the election, they'll need him to go out and win votes for Wayne. And after the election, unless they eliminate him, they'll have to give him a fucken big piece of the pie. They'll hate like hell to do it, but they'll have to do it anyway. Serve the bastards right."

"Are the Golden Guys capable of murder?"

"They're capable of anything—murder, rape, theft. Wayne isn't even president yet, but he's already using his clout with politicians and the media and friends in the Administration to help Portman grab a part of Brooklyn that'll be worth billions in only a few years." He put a hand to his forehead. "Jeez, I don't feel too good. There's a nice soft sofa in the lounge down the hall. Will you give me a hand? I think I'd better lie down."

Out in the corridor, Tom asked Gilbert if his academic information network had ever mentioned the name of Pablo Valdez.

"Who's he? A spokesman for a new brand of Colombian coffee?" Gilbert laughed at his joke.

"He was involved with the Sandinistas in Nicaragua."

"Is there a connection with Wayne and the other guys?"

"There might be."

Gilbert thought a moment, then nodded. "Sure there is. Bernard's law firm has a history of working for South American dictators. It would probably have been before his time there, but I'd bet they were involved with the Contras and their money-raisers. And Wayne has always been one of the biggest supporters in Congress of South American dictatorships. A couple of years ago, when McGrath wanted to branch into Sylvester Stallone-type roles, Portman put up the seed money for a movie starring McGrath as a CIA agent who poses as a priest in order to enter Nicaragua and kill all the Sandinista biggies." Gilbert stopped, and placed a hand on Tom's shoulder. "I know I owe you one, and I like you, but I can't help thinking there's something fishy about your being here."

Inside the faculty lounge, which seemed to have free billiards and computer games, Gilbert passed out the minute his head touched the handsome leather sofa. Tom left the building, his own head spinning. What kind of a cesspool had he stumbled into?

Back at the motel, he reached into his pocket for his cell phone. He was about to call Foster to arrange a meeting before his departure. But the phone rang in his hand.

It was Foster. Doug McGrath had been hit last night. Foster had him under sedation, but McGrath was coming out of it now and would be alert enough for questioning.

CHAPTER 14

DOUG McGRATH looked very different and deficient without his curly brown toupee, and Tom tried not to stare at the top of his head. Except for a few sad wisps, it was as bald as Max's. Max, however, had never tried to conceal his condition, and in his thirties used to play second base on a softball team called the Brooklyn Baldies.

"It was the crowning indignity!" McGrath cried. He parted his pajama top and revealed a gold cross on a heavy gold necklace, and then he raised a sleeve and pointed to his gold Hublot Big Bang and his gold bracelet. "I wouldn't have minded so much if they had taken these. They're all insured."

Foster indicated the door. "A kid or one of the hired help is going to hear you out there. Do you want Page Six of the *Post* and the media slime machines to learn about this?"

"No. You're right, Al."

When his cell phone rang, McGrath told Foster to answer it.

"Hello.... No, this is Albert Foster.... Oh, I didn't know you were still here.... To be candid, Nora, Doug leads a rather sedate life despite all the sensational gossip about him, and last night he forgot himself and celebrated a little too much. That's why I'm with him now, to give him something for his head and stomach. Please hold on a moment." Foster clamped a hand over the mouthpiece. Then he groaned and said to McGrath, "Nora Malcolm and her crew are downstairs for some nostalgia shots of the joint. They want to come up and interview you on how it feels to be back in your old room, etc."

"Tell her to go to hell."

"Doug is really sorry," Foster said into the phone. "He says that he's in even worse shape than in the climax of *Last Stage to Tombstone*." He chuckled. "Under the circumstances, he hopes that you'll give him a rain check on a one-on-one interview.... Yes, I have your card, and I'll certainly give your number to Doug.... That's true. A guy like him is never down for long. By the way, Senator Wayne and the rest of us are delighted with your work, and we all have high hopes that it'll eventually appear in theaters and on Showtime instead of just the History Channel. Good-bye."

Foster put down the phone. "That takes care of her."

"Thanks, old buddy." McGrath massaged his crotch. "If I were feeling good, I would certainly like to take care of that young black chick who works with her." He turned and stared at the bed. "Boy, we used to have some great times in this place. Those ancient Romans never had anything on us, eh, Al?"

Foster grinned. "Berenson is likely to think we went in for orgies."

"Well, we did, didn't we?"

"Doug is exaggerating," Foster assured Tom.

"Like hell I am!" McGrath cried. Leaping from the bed, he clenched his hands and began to pace the floor from the bed to the door, which was covered with a poster of a nude redhead cupping her huge breasts and offering them to the viewer. The poster had Oriental lettering here and there, and a picture of a package of condoms. Upon his second trip to the poster, he raised his hands and ripped it savagely from the door. He held it to his eyes for a second. And then, with a yell, he ripped it into little pieces.

"You shouldn't have done that," Foster said. "It belonged to some kid who was nice enough to lend you his room."

"The hell with him. Why should he still be able to fuck and masturbate while I can't?" McGrath rushed over to his thick wallet on the chest of drawers. He removed a few bills and slammed them down on a copy of Stephen King's *The Dark Tower*. "Okay, now he can buy some new posters. Variety is the spice of life." He looked down at his crotch and grasped his penis.

"It's incredible!" he cried under his breath. "They should have killed me instead. Never again. Never again. There's a blonde bitch from Texas in my current film. She's been a little cold and aloof, but on Thursday, just before leaving for here, I had Mel Breen, the screenwriter, put in a scene in which I rescue her from the bad guys and put her on my horse. I was sure that once she felt my big cock against her cute little ass and then my arms around her tits, she would be begging me to screw her."

"Don't be so pessimistic," Foster urged. "Since the first incident occurred, I've been in touch with some of the greatest specialists in the world. Together, we're establishing a data bank that will surely lead to a cure for your condition."

"You hope. I don't want one of those contraptions that have to be inserted in my dick and then pumped up with distilled water that's been boiled and sterilized."

"Of course not. I think we have more going for us than just hope."

"Are any of these specialists from China or Japan? I've heard that they have all sorts of secret knowledge there that we can't even begin to imagine. When I was making *The Cowboy and the Geisha,* my leading lady told me that a Jap once screwed her twenty-four times in one night, and each time she got a terrific orgasm. It made me want to take the first plane out to Tokyo."

Foster looked unimpressed, as doctors will by anecdotal evidence instead of pages of statistics. "Could have been the brand of sake. But it wouldn't hurt to look into the Oriental therapies. Meanwhile, Doug, you should try to tell Tom Berenson everything you know."

"I've had some unpleasant experiences with private eyes. Do you give me your word he's discreet?"

"Absolutely. Tony and Neal have given him the okay. If you trust me, you can trust him too."

McGrath touched his groin. "The pain is back. Maybe I should have another injection."

"At this point, I'd rather that you held off till you've spoken with Tom."

"I'll try." Gingerly, with a prolonged ouch, McGrath sat down on the edge of the bed. He sighed. "And to think that I used to be able to sit in a saddle for hours. The crew used to call me Iron Ass McGrath."

"They will again, Doug," Foster assured him.

"First of all, Berenson, despite our little brawl last night, this couldn't possibly be the work of Jason Gilbert. In the heat of the moment, he may be capable of taking a swing, but the guy's a coward physically, and he's always been one. Right, Al? I suppose you remember that incident." McGrath laughed for the first time since Tom's arrival.

"What incident is that?" Tom asked.

Foster came to a sudden stop in his chewing of an Oreo cookie that he had picked up from a package on the night table. "It happened a long time ago," he said. "I can't imagine its relevance to what happened last night."

"But it was really this morning, wasn't it?" Tom asked McGrath.

"Right. It took place about two-twenty."

"Did you look at a clock?"

"About a half-hour earlier, I heard the clock atop Webster Hall chime two." McGrath looked up inquiringly at Foster, who was eating another Oreo.

"Tell him everything," Foster said. "He's the only one who can help us. Or do you want to go to the police?"

"That's all I need. But how about Neal's outfit?"

"We considered them, Doug. Take my word for it, they're unsuitable in the present instance."

"Who or what are we talking about?" Tom asked, though he was sure they were referring to Denning and Pankhurst.

Foster grimaced and shook his head sharply. "It's some utterly inadequate flea-bag of an operation. Go on, Doug."

McGrath touched his crotch. "Oh, my God! It's already getting smaller!"

"It's not getting smaller. That takes months. Hopefully, I'll have a cure for you by then. If Dubya and his gurus hadn't put the kibosh on stem cell research, we might have had the answer to this and a hell of a lot of other things by now. But we're checking out other angles. "

"I'll pay you anything, Al."

"Okay, half of your Swiss bank account."

"Fuck you."

Foster shrugged. "It was you who made the offer."

"Yeah, but I was sure you'd consider that we were brothers."
McGrath stared at Foster as if he were seeing a new side of him.
"Maybe some of us are brothers by adoption instead of by blood."

Tom said, "Okay, you heard the clock strike two. Where were
you?"

"Inside the Morris museum."

"Unusual time to be in a museum."

"Maybe for looking at pictures and old charters. But not for
humping."

"I gather that you were with a woman."

"You gather right, pal."

"And she wasn't your wife."

"My wife returned to the city right after the banquet."

"I have to ask you who the woman was, in case she saw something of what happened later. I'm sure she'd want to cooperate."

McGrath made his famous crooked smile. "No problem,
buddy. It was Midge Colbert, also known as Mrs. Robert Colbert."
As Foster looked in pain suddenly, McGrath shrugged and said,
"You told me to tell him everything."

"I didn't know you were screwing Colbert's wife." Foster added to Tom, "Here at Morris, it would be like having sex with Laura
Bush. I guess that nothing's sacred anymore."

"You guess right," McGrath informed him. "Actually, it's been
going on for a long time. It started back in my freshman year. And
it's become our own little tradition. One of the things I love about
this school is its variety of traditions. It has a tradition for everything." He grasped his crotch. "If this becomes a permanent condition, I think I'm going to miss her more than any other woman I
ever had. Other women get older, but Midge keeps getting better
and less inhibited. There's nothing she isn't ready and willing to
try. Bob Colbert is a damn lucky man, because I know that, in other
respects, Midge is a devoted wife to him. If she ever found a hole
in one of his academic robes, she would darn it herself."

"Okay," Tom prodded him. "The clock struck two. What
happened next?"

"The next ten or so minutes were busy—*very* busy. In my
present condition, it would break my heart to try to elaborate on
what we were doing."

"Did you leave the building together?" Tom asked sharply, hoping to speed up the recitation.

"Of course not. Even at that hour there are always a lot of kids screwing around outdoors when they should be doing the right thing and sleeping or studying, and Midge has her reputation as GMU's grande dame to consider. I left first. I waited a moment, till I saw Midge come out and head for home. Then I started out along Hoover Walk, which is not exactly the shortest way back to the old dorm, but I always like to stroll along between the ancient trees that remind me of my grandfather's old estate in South Carolina." He shook his head. "For years I've been trying to interest my studio in a remake of *The Birth of a Nation* that would be palatable for today's audiences. Some of the scenes could be shot on that estate, which is still in the family, I'm proud to say."

"Meanwhile, back on the campus...."

"Suddenly, as often happens after a fuck, I had a desperate urge to take a leak, and since my doctor back in Beverly Hills once told me that it's not healthy for a guy my age to hold it, I left Hoover Walk and stepped behind a tree to do my thing." He gave a prolonged sigh. "At least that bastard was gentleman enough not to attack me till I had finished my piss. But why did he take my hairpiece? I wouldn't be surprised if he's a pervert."

"Did you see him at all?"

"He was like a ghost. It was dark. The nearest light was from a lamppost on Hoover Walk, which was maybe ten yards away. Suddenly this black hand was holding a knife to my throat. If it was a black guy who did this, it would be very ironic, because my ancestors were always as kind as they could be to their slaves, considered them a sort of extended family." McGrath banged his fists together, and then tugged at his fringe of hair and cried out in anguish, "When we pay our usual ceremonial call on the Colberts later, I can't bear to have Midge see me looking like this."

"You'll skip it," Foster said. "And I'll tell them you had to rush back to the Coast."

"I hate to disappoint Midge. She particularly enjoys those secret little feels and gooses. I wouldn't be surprised if they give her an instant orgasm."

"She'll just have to be disappointed, like other women all over the land."

Tom felt like banging their heads together, but he kept his voice calm as he brought the conversation back to where it belonged. "Have you ever had a run-in with Vic Capperrelli the wrestler?"

"I've met the big Wop. He's Ilsa Grant's husband." He rubbed his palms together. "Ah, memories. I did have an affair with her, but it was very brief and while she was still married to another guy."

"Who was the other guy?"

"A disc jockey named Art Costigan or Art Conrad or something like that. But he's been dead for years. The story goes that he was killed by one or more members of a psychotic Latin rock group whose music he was allegedly boycotting and badmouthing. If the case doesn't ring a bell, it's because the rock group was big at the time and their handlers and lawyers were able to hush it up to far more than the usual extent." Suddenly McGrath's hand shot up. "Speaking of psychotic Latins, there's one who—" McGrath turned to Foster. "I'll bet it's him."

"Go on," Tom said. "Who's *him*?"

McGrath ignored him, and addressed Foster. "It must be that Spick son of a bitch! I'd bet my last million on it!"

"Tell Berenson about it. He's the trained investigator."

"Okay. It happened in Nantucket. Have you been in touch yet with our buddy Neal Bernard?"

"Yes. And he told me about your get-together at his hotel in May."

"Did he also tell you about Carmen?" McGrath snickered. "I can tell from your look that he didn't. What a gorgeous piece of ass! And in using that noun, I am thinking of more than just her literal ass, if you get my drift. She was a sort of general helper at the hotel. The first time I saw her she was in the garden, bent over and trimming a bush. I knew immediately that I had to get into hers. And she wanted sex with me too. I can always tell that about a broad. It's a gift I—"

"This is going to be as long as *Gone with the Wind!*" Foster cried.

McGrath grabbed Foster by the lapels and yanked him forward. "This is *my* story! Do you mind if I tell it my own way?"

"I do mind, because I have to be back in the city in a couple of hours." Foster glared at McGrath until he released him. Then he told Tom, "Doug has told me it was one of his standard seductions, now tender, now a little more ardent. The girl says it was rape, and she went running to dear old dad, who was also one of the hired help. Being one of these emotional Latinos, he went after our pal with a cleaver."

"Were you present during the cleaver incident?" Tom asked Foster.

"It wasn't just an incident!" McGrath yelled. "It was attempted murder!"

"There were no eyewitnesses," Foster told Tom. "I heard this from Neal Bernard."

For the first time since Tom took the repulsive case, his instincts told him that he was on to a likely suspect. The volatile father, proud and watchful of his family honor, might well have hated his employer and Michaelson and Portman, probably regular visitors to the hotel. He quickly removed his notebook and a ballpoint from his pocket. "The guy has an adequate motive, all right. Who is he?"

"Pablo Valdez," McGrath said. "Sounds like he belongs in a commercial for tacos or Tabasco sauce."

Tom groaned inwardly. He just couldn't square his memory of the courtly gentleman with McGrath's image of an avenging demon with a cleaver. As he jotted down the name, he told himself to be realistic and to recall the many murderers who were perfect ladies and gentlemen both before and after their crimes. Then, even while he asked the question, he knew what the answer would be: "What was the official disposition of the case?"

"What do you mean?" McGrath said.

"I'm referring to the police. What did they do about the alleged rape of Carmen Valdez and then her father's assault on you?"

McGrath screwed up his face as if he were hearing a proposed film script in which he was a villain who kicked dogs and ignored damsels in distress. "This had nothing to do with the police. Never at any time did I force myself upon that kid, who has probably seduced more guys than there are bananas in her homeland. She was hysterical, a pathological liar."

"Shouldn't you have reported her father's attempt on your life?"

"I decided to give him another chance."

"After his unprovoked attack with the cleaver? That was very noble of you."

"'Noble' is my middle name. Her old man is an immigrant, and I didn't want him deported to the hellhole he came from."

"He's from Nicaragua, which, according to President Bush, is now a model democracy and an example to the rest of Latin America."

"Is that so? I guess I was behind on late developments there. But I realize now that I was wrong in not reporting the guy." Mc-Grath touched his crotch and then pointed to the window. "He may still be on the campus, waiting to attack poor Lyle."

"Why would he do that? Did he suspect that the senator was also trying to rape his daughter?"

"Nobody was raping anybody! It was all in the mind of this demented Latina."

Tom reached into his pocket and took out his cell phone. When Foster and McGrath looked at him, he told them he wanted to call Neal Bernard and find out if Valdez was with him on Nantucket. A minute later, having been roused from a nap, Bernard was saying on his private line:

"What's going on there?"

"McGrath was hit early this morning."

"How?"

"The same as you, it appears."

"Damn. What's happening to this country? A respectable citizen used to be safe, and feel safe. Did you catch the maniac who did it?"

"Not yet."

"What are we paying you for? I knew that we should have used Denning and Pankhurst for this job."

"I'm beginning to think so too."

"I'm afraid to ask—how's Lyle Wayne?"

"He's okay, as far as I know. McGrath tells me that during his visit with you in May, he was assaulted by one of your staff. There could be a connection to these other assaults."

"What did he say happened exactly?"

"First I'd like to hear *your* recollection of the incident."

"We're wasting time, Berenson, because you can cross Valdez off your list of suspects."

"McGrath was hit at about two in the morning. Can you account for Valdez's whereabouts at that time?"

"Absolutely. For every minute."

"Okay, where was he?"

"In a grave somewhere in Nicaragua. Last Tuesday night, he and his daughter were killed in an auto accident on the New England Turnpike."

"How did it happen?"

"According to the police, they had both been drinking, and they piled into a truck that was slowing down. I'm going to miss that man. He was the best in his job on the island and had built up a loyal following. Is Doug with you and in condition for some sympathy from a fellow sufferer?"

While McGrath and Bernard were talking, there was a knock on the door, and McGrath quickly hung up and told Foster to inform the caller, whoever it was, that he wasn't seeing anybody, even if it was a German or Japanese banker who wanted to bankroll him in a 3-D remake of *Stagecoach* with Angelina Jolie as his leading lady.

Foster slipped out and came back with what looked like a small pizza box. "It has your name on it, Doug," he said. "One of the fraternity kids found it in the lobby."

"I didn't order any pizza."

"It may be from an admirer."

"I don't want any, even if it's from Miss America."

"Do you mind if I have a slice or two?"

"Be my guest, although I consider it very insensitive of you under the circumstances. One of these days, all that junk food is going to catch up with you."

Foster opened the box, and then he removed the dark-brown lustrous hairpiece and said, "Well, what do you know? It's come back."

Sitting on the edge of his bed, McGrath stared dumbfounded for a few seconds. But as Foster's words sank in, he rushed across the room, seized the toupee, and continued toward the bathroom.

"There's more," Foster told Tom, and he pointed to the sheet of white paper in the box. Tom doubted that the sheet would contain fingerprints, but he removed it by a corner. He delayed reading it aloud until McGrath returned, wearing his wig and looking more like his old and virile self. McGrath glared at the sheet. "Okay, let's have it," he growled.

Tom read: "'You can put this back on your head, but you still won't be the man you thought you were.'"

McGrath snatched the piece of paper and roared, "That's what *you* say, you degenerate creep!" He pounded his chest and gave a cry like Tarzan's. "You can't keep a real man down." Breathing heavily, he rushed toward the door.

"Where the hell are you going?" Foster demanded.

"I'm going out to get me a woman—even if it has to be a hooker!"

"You're in no condition for that. Please get back to bed. I'm speaking as your doctor."

"Shut the hell up, Al! Even my father never ordered me around!"

McGrath threw open the door, ran out of the room and across the landing to the stairs. Halfway down, his knees buckled, and he went crashing to the ground floor of the frat house.

CHAPTER 15

LYLE WAYNE had been told earlier about the assault on Mc-Grath, but when he learned of the tumble down the stairs, he summoned Foster and Tom to the suite that had been put at his disposal in Fairfax House, the residence of President Colbert. As they hurried across the campus, Tom remarked to Foster that it would have been simpler if Wayne had just come to the frat house.

"Simpler for whom?" Foster said. "Wayne has never given a shit about anyone but himself."

"Then why all this loyalty to him?"

"The Golden Guys are a team, and Wayne is our leader."

"How did that happen? Does he consider himself a master spirit anointed by Ayn Rand? And did the rest of you once vote for him like cardinals do for a pope?"

"Right from the start, we all recognized Lyle as a natural leader. Like Reagan, he has that certain charisma none of us lowly mortals can resist." When Tom looked skeptical, Foster glowered, and went on: "That may sound peculiar to an outsider like you, but I believe it more and more. Lyle was born to lead. I'm sure you'll recognize that, too, when you get to know him better and come to feel his magnetism."

Tom had learned over the years that everyone is a bit of a crackpot, and he refrained from laughing.

They were admitted to Fairfax House by an elderly African-American servant. His three-piece black suit made him look more like a businessman or a professor than a butler.

"Hello, Rutherford. I hope you're feeling as great as you look."

"I certainly am, Dr. Foster. Thanks for all those drug samples."

"Not at all. I figured that they'd eventually cure you if they didn't kill you first."

Rutherford did not look amused by this specimen of medical humor, but he managed to force a smile.

Foster turned to Tom. "I have to be very nice to my friend Rutherford. He knows where all the bodies are hidden here at Morris."

"I have no idea what you're referring to," Rutherford said somberly. "I'll announce you to President Colbert, sir."

"Actually, we're here to see Senator Wayne."

"In that case, I'll announce you to the senator."

"Don't bother. Just point the way."

"Who is it, Rutherford?" a woman's voice asked from beyond the vestibule and to their right.

"Dr. Foster and another gentleman, madam. He's a Mr. Berenson, I believe."

Tom was surprised that Rutherford knew his name even though it hadn't been mentioned by Foster. If there were any bodies hidden at Morris, Rutherford probably did know their locations.

In a few seconds, Midge Colbert came into view, her hand already outstretched for the execution of her social duties. Tom had seen her only from afar last night. Up close, in snug Ralph Lauren jeans and a gray cashmere cardigan over a red turtleneck over a striking bosom, she looked like a desirable woman instead of a grande dame who promenaded like British royalty to *Pomp and Circumstance* when the occasion required.

"Hello, Albert."

"Hi, Midge. This is Tom Berenson, who's helping Sandy with his great opus."

She transferred the hand to Tom. "It's nice to meet you. Please tell Sandy that I can't wait to read it, especially if I get a free copy. Signed, of course."

"I certainly will, Mrs. Colbert."

She turned back to Foster. "I'm so glad I ran into you like this. This weekend has been so hectic that we've hardly spoken to our old friends. Robert and I would like you to join us for cocktails at about five."

Foster's sigh was suitable for turning down an eight-course dinner at the White House. "I'm so sorry, but I won't be here then. A patient at Sloan-Kettering has taken a turn for the worse."

She touched his hand. "I understand. But I'm sure that Doug will be able to make it." She smiled. "I've never know him to refuse an invitation." She added to Tom, "His people are patricians from South Carolina, you know."

"Doug won't be able to make it, either," Foster informed her.

"How do you know?"

"An old back injury of his is kicking up. Just to be on the safe side, I'm checking him into the hospital for a few tests."

"He didn't mention anything last— at the party yesterday."

"It happened suddenly."

"What a shame." She was obviously trying to look concerned, but Tom detected a little curve of her lips that hinted she had a good idea exactly how McGrath injured his back.

IN THE LARGE bright room with a handsome Chippendale desk and built-in bookcases filled with impressive books, Lyle Wayne glared at Foster as if he had done the unforgivable. Then he grabbed his forearm and cried under his breath:

"We're lucky that all those TV people weren't around! He's my oldest buddy. It's a miracle he didn't break his head. How did you let such a dumb thing happen?"

Stung by the insult, Foster began to breathe rapidly, and he returned Wayne's glare before replying. "I'll tell you that when you let go of my arm."

"My, my, Al. I remember you when you weren't so assertive."

"But you were always the same way, Lyle."

"You're damn right, buddy." Wayne grinned and released his hold on the other man's forearm. For good measure, he even brushed his sleeve. "There you are, as good as new. I know that an immaculate appearance is part of your famous bedside manner."

Foster grabbed a handful of popcorn from a green Venetian-glass bowl. "You, of all people, should know how uncontrollable Doug can get about sex. He makes bulls look sedate and shy.

Suddenly he wanted to prove to himself and maybe to us, too, that there was still some juice in the old kazoo."

"And there isn't?"

Foster swallowed the popcorn in his mouth. "I'll explain it to you again if you like."

"Spare me."

"Ever since the misfortunes of Neal and Bob, I've been in touch with colleagues all over the country—over the world. So far, the prognosis is pretty bleak."

Wayne thumped his chest. "I'm a dedicated public servant, and I've lived a blameless life by contemporary standards of morality in the Beltway. It's hard for me to believe that this maniac would want to harm me too."

He stared at Foster for confirmation of his words. Foster hesitated a second, then nodded. "We may not be on a level with the Pope or the Reverend Arnie Simon," he said, "but I think that we're all pretty decent guys."

A few yards away from them, examining the contents of a bookcase, Tom was glad they weren't looking at him for further confirmation of their high opinions of themselves and their other fraternity brothers.

Wayne turned to Tom. He clenched both hands. "I hope that, investigation-wise, your stay here hasn't been a complete waste of time."

"I think I've learned a great deal."

"Good. How about sharing your gleanings with us."

"They need more development."

Wayne turned to Foster in disgust. "Your sleuth has the makings of a great bureaucrat in Washington."

"I was disappointed that Lou West wasn't here," Tom said.

Wayne shrugged. "These days, I hear, he's always off to some book-signing in some god-forsaken place."

"Can either of you tell me why he hates the Golden Guys?"

"Who told you that?" Wayne snapped.

"It was told to me in confidence."

Wayne bared his teeth in a smile. "Everyone is supposed to love us. We certainly pay enough in PR fees and freebies for the press."

"Are you telling me that my informant was lying?"

Wayne and Foster exchanged a questioning glance. Foster shrugged and said, "We're paying Berenson top dollar to get to the bottom of these atrocities. He may be on to something."

"I don't think he's on to much with old Lou."

"Let me be the judge of that," Tom suggested.

"It happened over twenty-five years ago," Foster said. "A terrible accident occurred, and Lou held us responsible."

Wayne glared at Foster. "I can't say that I like your tragic tone. Berenson is liable to get a totally wrong perspective."

"Then, by all means, you tell the story in your own charming way."

"I certainly will." Wayne fixed his piercing eyes upon Tom. Then he clapped a hand to his chest and extended it in a gesture his media expert had no doubt told him denoted total sincerity. "Even though none of us guys were responsible, our hearts went out to poor Lou, and over the years we've made it up to him a hundredfold. For example, it was I who suggested to President Bush that Lou be appointed to head his Emergency Council for Physical Fitness. True, the post is little more than a sinecure, because the medical and food lobbies would never tolerate a real overhaul of existing health practices, but Lou realized a golden harvest of benefits from it."

"I still don't know what happened to Lou," Tom said.

"Lou had a son named Larry. Larry was pleasant and well meaning, but he was missing something upstairs." Wayne tapped his forehead. "Thanks to the clout of his adoring dad, Larry was admitted to Morris, though I don't see how he even finished high school. But that wasn't enough for Lou. He wanted Larry to become a member of our fraternity."

"How did you and your brothers feel about Larry?"

Foster shook his head sadly. "He would have been utterly out of place. He wouldn't have been happy and neither would we. Unfortunately, Lou was adamant. And he was our coach."

"Naturally, Larry had to adhere to our age-old tradition and take the initiation," Wayne said. He shook his head and sighed. "During the cross-country run, he fell, broke his neck, and died eventually. It had been raining that day and the day before. Lou said that we should have postponed that part of the initiation. Time and again we showed him the rule book, which specifically forbids postponements unless the school is in mourning for its president or chaplain." Wayne shook his head again. "I'm sorry to hear that Lou has been bad-mouthing the old fraternity from which he has derived so many benefits."

"Someone should contact him before the next election," Foster suggested.

"I'll be contacting him too," Tom told them.

"Of course," Wayne said. "You should." He strolled over the window and looked off in the direction of his old frat house. "Poor Doug," he murmured. "How the mighty have fallen. Is it safe to leave him alone?"

Foster extended his arms in a dramatic gesture. "First you wanted us over here on the double. Now you're worried about his being alone. I gave him enough sedative to put him out for at least three hours. An earthquake wouldn't wake him up."

"Who's going to tell Christie about his accident?"

"Which one?"

"Both, I suppose. Or don't you agree?"

"Why the delicacy? Do you really think she still gives a damn about him?"

"She knew the sort of guy he was when they got married. Doug has always been too much of a man for one woman. He's unique. Like Niagara Falls and Rush Limbaugh, he's one of our national treasures, God bless him. When I met the Pope last year, His Holiness told me that he has always been a big fan of Doug's."

Foster picked up some more popcorn. "Last night in Whitman Hall, I got the definite impression that Christie has had it with him, especially since he's never tried very hard to help her career along."

"That was just his come-on for the dumb bimbo, and I can't understand how she ever believed him. Like me, you, and any other real man who works hard all day, Doug wants his wife to be at home waiting for him, not at the studio or on location in the Swiss Alps." Wayne made his heartwarming smile. And then he put an arm round Foster's shoulders. "Since I carry aloft the banner of faith and family in our great nation, I can't have any of us involved in messy divorce suits until after the election has come and gone. My enemies will argue that if I have no moral authority over my old friends, how can I be expected to influence the nation at large? Being a doctor, Alberto, you're much better than I in one-on-one encounters with distraught wives. I would certainly appreciate it if you would contact Christie and tell her to be discreet and say only the right things to the media. Tell her also that if she plays ball with us, we'll do for her what Doug never did, and find a good role for her somewhere. Maybe the Marilyn Monroe part in a remake of *Some Like It Hot*. In 3-D, so that audiences can really appreciate her talents from top to bottom."

"Sounds like a good arrangement all around."

Wayne smiled. "And since she won't be getting any cock from Doug, she may care to show her gratitude."

"To you—or to me?"

Wayne laughed as he slapped Foster on the shoulder. "Why not the both of us?"

Tom was revolted by the coarseness of the conversation. The two men were speaking in his presence as if he were invisible. He was reminded of Victorian upper classers who blithely committed adultery in the presence of household servants, because the servants were regarded as nonpersons. And if they ever dared to betray their masters and mistresses, they would be accused and swiftly convicted of such heinous and long-term felonies as stealing pieces of the family silver.

"You look a little pissed," Wayne said to Tom. "Don't worry, fella. If you do a good job for us, we may give you a little bonus and cut you in on the action." He turned to Foster and winked. "He can warm her up for us. Do you remember the old days on this campus? Men were really men back then."

"Sounds like it was quite a place," Tom said. "But what could you do back then that college kids don't do nowadays?"

The smile that passed between Wayne and Foster evoked shared secrets that triggered ribald laughter.

Tom turned away from them in disgust and opened the door. "I have to get back to the city," he told Foster. "Let's check on McGrath before I leave."

Downstairs, before Tom reached the door, Rutherford

appeared. "I'll get that, sir," he said, reaching for the large, carved brass doorknob.

"Thanks." Tom paused on the threshold. "How long have you been working here, Mr. Rutherford?"

He looked surprised by the question, or perhaps the appellation. Maybe both. "Close to forty years. Why?"

"I'm working with Sanford Whitney. Do you remember him?" Rutherford nodded. "I'm helping him collect anecdotes about the Golden Guys for his study of fraternities. Maybe you can remember some good ones."

"Surely, the best people to help you with that are the men themselves."

"They've told me some things, but nothing out of the ordinary. I'm looking for some college antics they may have forgotten, but which would add some dimension, maybe even a few laughs to the book."

Rutherford's smile was genuine, but at the same time, his dark eyes seemed to hold a friendly warning. "If the antics have been forgotten, maybe that's because they are supposed to be forgotten."

"These guys turned out to be so exceptional, though. You must have some special memories of them." Tom reached into his pocket for his notebook and pen. "Let me have your phone number. I'd like to come up and take you out to lunch on your day off." He gave his card to Rutherford. "Or give me a call if you're planning to be in New York."

Rutherford took the card, but shook his head. "It would just be a waste of your time. I've seen thousands of students come and go over all these years. I couldn't possibly remember all the goings-on, or who was involved in them." His eyes said that he remembered very much indeed.

Tom shrugged and returned his pen and pad to his pocket. "I hope you'll see thousands more come and go."

"Oh, surely not thousands, sir. At my age, a man looks forward to a safe and happy retirement."

Rutherford tucked the card into his pocket without looking at it. Tom got the message. He extended his hand. "Then I wish you that safe and happy retirement."

Rutherford's grip was strong, and his eyes never wavered from Tom's. "And I wish you a safe and happy life." It wasn't a wish, it was a warning.

As Tom started down the steps, a chill went up his spine. He was certain that Rutherford had spotted him as a man, possibly a cop, on a dangerous investigation, mixing with dangerous people.

Behind him, he heard Foster saying good-bye to Rutherford, then his quick footsteps as he descended the stoop.

"What was that all about?" Foster clapped a hand on Tom's shoulder.

"What?"

"Back there." Foster pointed a thumb in the direction of the door Rutherford had just closed behind the two of them.

"Oh, just passing the time of day, chatting about changes Rutherford has seen on the campus over the decades."

"Such as...?"

Tom shrugged. "More women. And more minorities for a while. At least until your friends in government and the courts began pulling the plug on affirmative action."

"I'm surprised old Rutherford would say that."

"He didn't. I just inferred it from what he said when I asked about the racial balance of the undergraduates. He's a nice guy, but very reticent."

"He knows his place. How come you shook hands with him?"

"Common courtesy." It took an effort to refrain from adding, *Ever hear of that?*

"He's a servant, for chrissake."

"Not my servant. We were just two guys having a friendly conversation. I'd rather shake hands with him than a lot of people I've met around here. When I feel the need for tips on etiquette, I have a whole shelf of books in my store that I can turn to."

Foster let his breath out in an exasperated hiss of dismissal.

Behind them, Tom could sense Rutherford watching from the window. Just how many secrets did the man know about the Beta Alphas? And did he have his own grudge against them?

CHAPTER 16

"S INCE WHEN did you become such a big football fan?" Max asked.

It was Monday evening, and Tom and his father-in-law were in the living room, where Max had just turned off the critically acclaimed but thoroughly disappointing comedy he had borrowed from the library. Tom had given up on the pathetically puerile attempt at humor twenty minutes earlier, and turned his attention to the copy of *Coach!* he had brought home from the shop. He shrugged. "Just trying to keep up with the reading public's tastes."

Actually, he wanted to see what Lou West had to say about his son's death. So far, he hadn't come across a reference to it.

Max nodded toward Tom's book. "That guy had a reputation for being a real bastard, but he sure knew how to push his teams to victory. Wasn't he the one who said, 'Winning isn't everything—it's the only thing'?"

"That was Vince Lombardi, a real sweetheart compared to West. West is famous for: 'Victory means vanquish; leave no opponent fit to play another day.'"

"I suppose he's made a million bucks from his book."

"More than that, when you add on all the subsidiary rights."

Max sighed. "I guess I chose the wrong profession. No one's interested in reading a math teacher's memoir, even if he did wind up having to learn karate to survive. Still, I don't imagine all that money is bringing much happiness to Lou West, not after what happened to his son."

Tom nodded and returned to his reading, but he looked up

quickly when Max added: "It was a real tragedy. The guy left a wife and two little kids."

"You must have your tragedies confused. West's son was only a kid himself."

"When you're my age, anyone under sixty is a kid, but this guy was in his thirties—it was in all the tabloids a year or so ago. You shouldn't depend on only the *Times* and *Publishers Weekly* for your news. The guy was killed in a white-water-rafting accident. Men with families are out of their minds to take risks like that."

"Anybody want something?" Stephanie asked on her way to the kitchen. The two men shook their heads. They were still discussing the accident when she returned munching an apple. "Who are you talking about?" she asked.

"Lou West." Tom held up the book.

"You met him at the party Saturday night, didn't you?"

"No. He was out on the West Coast, promoting his book."

"That's funny. Mark told me he was there. He was going to be autographing his book in the campus bookstore Sunday afternoon. Mark wanted to take me, but we had to leave. I didn't really care. I think football's stupid. I wonder why he wasn't at the party."

"Maybe he didn't fly in till Sunday," Max suggested.

Stephanie took another bite of her apple and returned to her room, obviously losing interest in the subject. But Tom hadn't. *Had* Lou West been on the campus all weekend? And had the death of his second son put him round the bend, stirring up memories of the death of his first son and fueling a desire for revenge? How had the first boy died? Tom doubted that Al Foster had given him the whole story.

He continued skimming through *Coach!*. There was only one reference to the earlier misfortune: a brief mention that "a tragic accident took the life of my older son during his freshman year at GMU." Was that reticence due to a father's grief, or an ambitious man's pragmatism?

Tomorrow he would try to arrange a meeting with Lou West. He would call Nora Malcolm too. Maybe, as a disinterested party, she would be able to shed more light on the incident. And maybe they could talk about it over dinner....

He went to bed with a feeling of happy anticipation.

BEFORE CALLING NORA the next morning, Tom spoke with Al Foster, who assured him that Lou West had not arrived at Morris until late Sunday afternoon, just before the signing, and then had taken off again for parts unknown. Not to worry, though, he hastened to add; there was really no reason for Tom to be in touch with old Lou. Which, of course, made Tom all the more determined to talk with Lou West. A call to West's publisher revealed that the author would be in New York all day, taping an appearance on *Good Morning America* in the morning, then signing books at a Fifth Avenue bookstore in the late afternoon. So much for "parts unknown." Phil Howard wasn't available till the weekend, so Tom asked Max to keep an eye on the store so that he could attend the signing. He didn't have to arrange every meeting through Al Foster.

The phone at Nora's office was picked up by a young woman with a chirpy voice who informed him that Nora would be working away from the office for the next few days. He was unprepared for the wave of disappointment that washed over him at the news that she was unavailable. He left his name and said he would call again.

As long as he still had the telephone in his hand, he decided to try Nora's home number on the chance that she might still be there. On the fourth ring, an answering machine kicked in with Nora's smooth, husky voice. Sounding both businesslike and silkily seductive, it asked the caller to leave a brief message at the sound of the beep.

Tom complied, afterward wishing he could have thought of something clever to say, something that would have made Nora smile when she played back the message. Now, upon hearing his dull words, would she dismiss the call as strictly business, and unimportant business at that, and not bother to return it? After all, he had said he would call back.

He wondered what had gotten into him, and was unable to understand why he was getting himself so worked up over trying to arrange a simple meeting with a woman he hardly knew.

While he waited for Max to come, Tom set about unpacking an order that had been delivered the day before, and by the time the invoice was checked and recorded and the books were on display, his thoughts were centered on the Golden Guys once more. Before leaving for Manhattan, and while Max was out of earshot, Tom phoned Joe Henley, a friend on the force, and asked him to check into the accident that took the life of Juan Valdez. He left the shop feeling like a cop again.

IT WAS A COOL, clear day, and Tom enjoyed the walk from the subway to the Fifth Avenue bookstore. In the front window, beneath a banner announcing the autograph session, a blowup of a beaming and benevolent Lou West was surrounded by piles of *Coach!*.

Inside, Tom paused to look around at the promotional dumps and displays, the seemingly endless rows of shelves and tables, the laminated jackets on the piles of books gleaming in the bright light. His own little shop could have fit into the fiction section, with plenty of room to spare.

As he watched the customers scurrying to purchase their copies of *Coach!* and join the autographing line, it once again crossed Tom's mind that it was almost a miracle that his store had been able to survive in face of the competition and deep discounts offered by the chains. But Beth had insisted that the megastores were good for business. They kept people interested in books, and they made her store, with its specialty, stand out. She had made Beth's Book Nook a cozy, welcoming place, with the emphasis on variety, customer service, and the Brooklyn specialty. These attractions brought in customers from outside areas and were building up into a respectable mail-order business too.

Still, if Tony Portman ever succeeded with his shopping mall, it would sound the death knell for Beth's Book Nook and many other small merchants and longtime residents in the neighborhood and throughout Brooklyn Heights. Their buildings would be bulldozed, and none of them would be able to afford Portman's astronomical rents.

Tom bought a book and took his place on line behind a silver-haired man in a dark gray suit, perhaps from Brooks Brothers, who turned and began talking football with him. The man, who looked as though he should have been more comfortable discussing litigation or leveraged buyouts, seemed to have the details of every game played since 1970, both college and professional, engraved upon his agile brain, and he spouted plays and scores the way a Sunday-morning TV evangelist can quote chapter and verse of the Bible. Happily, he was disposed to talk rather than listen, so all Tom had to do was nod politely and look interested.

While he pretended to listen, he let his mind and his gaze wander. He smiled at the sight of a young mother with a baby in a back carrier, a toddler in a stroller, and a third clinging to her jacket. She was over in the romance section, had already made three selections and seemed to be deciding on a fourth. He wondered how much more romance a woman with three kids needed in her life. Then he could almost hear Beth laugh and say that it was *because* the woman had three little kids to contend with that she needed a touch of romance.

Beside a table with a display of gourmet cookbooks stood a big bruiser of a man in a navy-blue raincoat with a faded streak of what was probably white paint on the right sleeve. Anyone who judged by appearances would have placed that man on Lou West's line, but no one knew better than an ex-cop how deceiving appearances could be. Tom looked more closely at the man, sure he had seen him before. Perhaps it was on the street as he approached the store. His face was turned too far to the side for Tom to get a good look. Not that it mattered. It was just a little mental exercise to keep his brain from going numb while his buddy on the line gave him a tackle-by-tackle replay of the GMU-Notre Dame game of 1979.

In another few minutes Tom was standing in front of Lou West and extending his copy of the book. He wondered what the poster photographer had done to make the man look benevolent. Certainly the lines etched by nature on his face had not come from an excess of smiling.

Tom stretched his own lips into what he hoped was a charming grin. "Great book!" he said. "I already have my own copy. This one is for my dad, who's also a big fan."

Lou cracked his cheeks in a smile and looked up. When there was eye contact, Tom continued:

"Also, I'm helping out Blair Whitney, who was one of your boys at Morris, with some research. He said you'd be *the* guy to turn to for some information he needs. Would you have time to talk with me when you finish here? It shouldn't take long. We could grab a cup of coffee, and you'd be able to relax a bit after handling this crowd."

Lou turned to a young man in small, wire-framed eyeglasses who was hovering behind him. "Hey, Mike, how much time do I have before I have to be at the airport?"

Mike looked at his watch. "The limo is picking us up out front in a half hour."

Lou turned back to Tom. "Make it someplace close—and make it a scotch—and you've got it."

"No problem."

Lou put his pen into his pocket and stood up. "Sorry, folks," he announced, "but I've got to be on my way. Have to make a plane. Hang in and keep punching."

A groan that turned to a grumble ran through the line, but Lou paid no attention to his fans. He turned his back on them, and as he conferred with Mike, who was obviously from the publisher's publicity department, Tom turned to the woman who was standing behind him.

"Oh, dear!" she said with a deep Southern accent. "My grandson's going to be so disappointed."

"No, he won't." Tom extended his book. "Give him mine. I'll take yours."

"But that wouldn't be fair!"

"It would be more than fair if it helped you to take home a good feeling about New York and New Yorkers."

As they exchanged books, she said, "You may be a New Yorker, sir, but you're a true Southern gentleman at heart."

To avoid being recognized and blamed as the cause of the disruption in autographing, Tom left the store and waited outside for Lou, who joined him a moment later. "Where to?" he asked.

"A half hour doesn't give us much time to be choosy," Tom said, "but there should be a couple of places around the corner."

"Dewar's is Dewar's, no matter where it's served."

They went into the first place they came to, a small Italian restaurant with a bar.

When their waiter had set their drinks before them, Tom raised his glass and tilted it toward Lou. "To your book. Long may it last on the bestseller lists. Thanks for taking time out to speak with me."

"Thanks for rescuing me from that mob back there. What a goddamn pain in the ass all this publicity shit is."

"Sells books," Tom reminded him. "And while we're on the subject, would you do just one more?" He passed his unsigned copy across the table, along with his pen.

Lou grimaced, but he complied. Then he downed his scotch and signaled the waiter for another. "So, what's with Whitney?"

"He's a professor at UCLA now, and he's writing a book about fraternities and the lifelong benefits and effects they have on their members."

Lou made a face. "Sounds like the kind of stupid thing he'd do. He always got his goddamn signals crossed when he was playing, at least in the beginning. I had to come down on him with both feet. But by the time I was through with him, he was a damn good linebacker. The benefits and effects of fraternities? Who gives a shit about stuff like that? He should be writing about the lifelong benefits and effects that come from playing football. That's what builds the kind of *real* men this country needs."

"Like the Golden Guys, from GMU's class of '80?"

Except for a slight narrowing of his eyes and lips, Lou's expression barely changed. "Yeah, like them. I built the best goddamn football team around them that any college has ever seen—before or since. You wouldn't know it to look at them now. Things were different back then too. Kids didn't grow into the giants that coaches have to work with these days. Not one of those guys was over six feet, and McGrath and Simon were the only ones who made it to that height—when they stretched. I had to work my ass off with them. I'm the guy who turned those snot-nosed, puking green kids into *men.*"

Sitting there, his massive shoulders and chest nearly bursting out of his tweed jacket, his scotch glass disappearing inside his huge ham of a fist, Lou West also looked like the guy who could now be turning them into eunuchs.

"Maybe Blair will devote his next book to football," Tom said.

"But meanwhile, he has a nice, fat grant for this one that it would be crazy to waste. He's particularly interested in the Golden Guys and your opinion of how much their membership in Beta Alpha Beta Phi is directly or indirectly responsible for the positions of power they all seem to hold in the country today."

"They learned more from me about how to kick ass to get to the top than they could have learned from that snooty fraternity."

"You certainly taught them the rough-and-tumble end of that. But Beta Alpha gave them the connections for the subtler methods that often have to be employed. It's said that membership is a guarantee for being set up to run with the rich and famous for life. Some kids would kill for an invitation to pledge."

"Or be killed pledging." The knuckles of Lou's hand turned white as he gripped his glass.

"Excuse me?"

"Nothing. Forget I said that." Lou tossed down his drink, and then looked at his watch. "Listen, I don't know shit about fraternities, except that they keep guys in training up too late with drinking and fucking. For that alone they get bad marks from me. Anyway, I gotta go now and catch a plane to Chicago for more of this TV shit."

Tom tossed some bills on the table and hurried after Lou. "But you've kept in close touch with the Golden Guys over the years, haven't you?"

Lou gave him a sharp look.

"I mean, they've never forgotten you and the part you played in their days of glory at Morris. They all think you're a great guy."

"They're great guys too."

"I'll bet you were a guest of honor at their twenty-fifth reunion last week."

If Tom hadn't been a cop experienced in questioning suspects, he might have missed the split second flash of wariness in Lou's eyes before he shrugged and said casually, "Nah. I was out on the Coast signing books. I was at Morris for another signing that weekend, but I couldn't get a plane till Sunday, and I didn't arrive on campus until late Sunday afternoon, after the guys had gone and the excitement was over."

"What excitement?"

"The big party that was thrown for them Saturday night. The one I couldn't make it to."

"Too bad. Were you able to get to the big bash Tony Portman threw to celebrate the completion of his condos out in Montauk?"

For a second, Lou looked as though he might be about to say no, but something obviously changed his mind. "Yeah, I was there. That's some place. I bet Tony put it up just to have a tax write-off for fancy digs for him and his pals to bring their broads to and screw. Those guys never learned how to keep their peckers in their pants."

They hurried back to Fifth Avenue, where a Mercedes limo was pulled up to the curb and Mike was pacing in front of the bookstore. Mike opened the door of the limo. "We'd better get going, Lou. Traffic's going to be a bitch."

Before Mike could climb into the car after Lou, Tom leaned inside and handed him his card. "If you think of anything about the Golden Guys that might help Blair with his book—some funny or even sad story—give me a call."

"Sure, sure." Lou shoved the card into a pocket without even glancing at it.

Tom extended his hand to Mike. "Tom Berenson, friend of an old friend," he said. "Sorry I took him away for a while, but I did get him back on time. And you're...?"

"Mike Lacey, publicity."

Tom kept shaking his hand so he couldn't get into the car. "I guess you're in charge of making all the traveling connections Lou was raving to me about."

Mike looked pleased. "You've got it."

"Too bad you couldn't arrange for him to get to GMU last Saturday for the twenty-fifth reunion of the Golden Guys, some of his best players."

"Oh, I got him there all right. He was just too jet-lagged to go to the party. He asked me to keep it quiet that he was there. He didn't want to offend the guys. If you ask me, I think he didn't want anyone to know how exhausted he was. You know how macho these sports guys are. They—"

"Hey, I thought we were in a hurry!" Lou roared from inside the car.

"Coming!" Mike turned back to Tom. "Listen, you never heard from me about his non-attendance at the old alma mater."

Tom raised his hand in a mock pledge of secrecy. "Have a good trip."

The limo took off, only to have to stop for a red light as soon as it pulled into traffic.

As Tom turned away from the curb, he saw that the man in the blue raincoat had just left the store and was heading for the corner. He wasn't carrying a bag. Maybe he had memorized all the recipes. He had certainly had enough time. Customers like that drove him nuts. Then he smiled. But the chains certainly deserved them.

BACK IN BROOKLYN, Max greeted Tom with the news that he had rung up a whopping forty-three dollars' worth of sales in his absence and had used the down time to fill some mail orders. "And your pal Joe Henley called," he went on. "Said he got that information you wanted. He'll be around till six, if you want to call him back today."

As the door closed behind Max, Tom picked up the phone and called Joe.

"If you were expecting drunk driving or foul play, you're in for a disappointment," Joe said. "There was no sign of either. This guy Valdez was driving with his seventeen-year-old daughter. They were both killed instantly. Rotten shame."

"What time did it happen?"

"About five a.m."

"And the driving conditions?"

"Pretty good. There was no rain or fog or anything like that, according to Sergeant Clyde Finney of the Massachusetts State Police, who looked up the report for me. It seems to be just one of those accidents that shouldn't have happened but did. According to Finney, the driver of the other vehicle said that Valdez kept switching lanes, and he suspected he might be high on drugs or alcohol. But the autopsy was negative on both. The car, by the way, was devastated. And so were Valdez and his daughter."

"What about the other driver?"

SECRET AGENDA | 165

"Walked away without a scratch."

"Quite a contrast."

"Not one we haven't seen a million times before."

"Did you get a dope sheet on him?"

"Finney gave me all the info. His name is Charles Andrew Stoddard. Forty-seven, Caucasian. An independent trucker. Excellent safety record. Driving a Mitsubishi truck that was brand-new and in perfect condition. Until the accident, of course. No charges against him. Excellent character references. Jeez, if he didn't have a wife and three kids, I'd have asked for his phone number so I could introduce him to my sister Fran, who lost her husband last year."

"Did Finney fax you a printout on all this?"

"Yeah. Want a copy?"

"I'd appreciate it. Take another look. Does it list any organizations he belongs to?"

Joe hummed softly as he scanned the information. "The usual—PTA, deacon in his church, a bowling league, belongs to Faith, Family and America's Future, and teaches in one of their Sunday schools. Isn't that the group started by Senator Lyle Wayne? The one that burns books and harasses women who want to enter abortion clinics?"

"That's the one. I don't know whether Wayne started it, but he's certainly their patron saint." Tom expected another coincidence, and he was not disappointed. "Is there any mention of former employers?"

"Just one. Colonial Oil."

"Small world."

"I don't get it."

"Valdez's boss is the hotshot lawyer who helped a multimillionaire pal of his pull off a hostile takeover of that company."

"And you think there's some kind of connection between the death of this poor schnook and his daughter and those two guys?"

"It's certainly an interesting coincidence."

"Come on, Tom. Colonial Oil has branches all over the country not to mention all over the world. They must have fifty-thousand employees—and twice that many ex-employees. You've been away from your old desk too long, and reading too many books in your fiction department. Sometimes an accident is just an accident."

"You're right." There was no sense in arguing the point. Joe hadn't come up against the Golden Guys' network and didn't know how they operated. "Just fax that stuff to me when you get a chance. Thanks for helping me out."

"Hey, no problem."

"Stop by the shop when you get a chance. I've got an autographed copy of Lou West's *Coach!* for you."

"That's great! You can bet I won't keep it on my desk. One of these guys might pinch it."

Within a minute the phone rang and the fax light flashed. Tom read the printout but found nothing that Joe had not already told him. Where had Juan Valdez been going with his daughter at five-thirty in the morning? And why? There was no mention of luggage in the car, so they hadn't intended a long trip.

Tom turned back to the autopsy report. No sign of drugs or alcohol in either body. But there was something else. He had been so focused on Valdez, he hadn't asked Joe about the man's daughter. She had been four and a half months pregnant. Had Valdez known?

The back of Tom's neck prickled. Was that why they were in the car at that hour? Were they on the way to a doctor? To an abortion clinic?

Or had Valdez been interrupted on a mission of revenge?

Tom put the papers in his desk drawer and locked up the store for the day.

But the questions followed him home and haunted him for the rest of the evening. The problem was that Valdez had taken the answers with him.

CHAPTER 17

EXPANDING ON Beth's belief that one could learn more about what is really going on in the nation and the world by reading the business section of the *Times* rather than its front page, Tom bought the *Wall Street Journal, Crain's, Forbes,* and *Businessweek* on his way to work the next day.

Reading between the lines, he found the pages of the publications strewn with the carcasses of corporate officers, employees, and corporations that had been victims of the voracious appetites of the Golden Guys. Tony Portman, through some financial sleight of hand, had just beat out an arch rival, Richard Pomfrey, and won the contract to develop a new civic center in Maryland. Neal Bernard, up in his Nantucket lair, was reaping megabucks from the bankruptcies he had helped to create with leveraged buyouts in the '90s that soured in the new century. And now he and Robert Michaelson were helping their good buddy Nicholas Hammond III, the CEO of the private-equity firm Hammond Enterprises, launch a hostile takeover of Fletcher Bowman's publishing conglomerate. Bowman, from his corporate headquarters at the *Baltimore Sentinel,* was launching a vicious counterattack on the Golden Guys, collectively and individually, in all his publications.

The men behind any one of the many names he had come across had ample reason to hate one or more of the Golden Guys and to seek revenge. But Fletcher Bowman's name seemed to lead the rest. The man was an egomaniac whose eccentric behavior had been reported with glee on the *Post's* Page Six for years, and without need for exaggeration. He was known for hard drinking and fast living, and was not above taking a physical poke, as well as one in the press, at anyone who offended him. An excuse for a talk with Fletcher Bowman would have to be found. Tom was scheduled to report to Foster in the afternoon. Perhaps, between the two of them, they could think up something to gain him entrée.

The phone rang just as Tom was about to lock up the shop at lunchtime. In a hurry to get to midtown and his meeting with Foster, Tom decided to let the answering machine kick in. But when he heard Nora Malcolm announcing herself, he rushed back and picked up the receiver.

"You sound breathless," she said. "Were you on top of a ladder, dusting off first editions?"

"Nothing like that. Book dust is not only healthy, it's also aesthetic and adds to the charm and price of first editions. I was on my way out to lunch and rushed back from the door."

Actually, he wasn't at all out of condition. His rapid heartbeat had nothing to do with the short sprint from the door.

"Then I won't keep you. I was just returning your call. Sorry I couldn't get back to you before this. What can I do for you?"

Another man, one with more charm or expertise, might have been able to come up with a witty answer that would get a laugh and make an impression. But Tom was out of practice. In fact, he had never really been *in* practice. He had met Beth when they were both very young, before he'd had the time to polish up a line, and though he could never understand it, he would forever be grateful that she had loved and accepted him just the way he was.

"I wanted to take you up on your offer of help with information on the Golden Guys. Blair Whitney has been reminding me that he has a deadline to meet."

She laughed. "Don't we all? I'd really like to help you out, but I'm not going to be in my office for the rest of the week."

His disappointment was far out of proportion to her news. "Will you be working out of town?"

"Philadelphia tomorrow. After that we'll be shooting locally for a while."

"You're going to have to take time out to eat, then. How about meeting for dinner Thursday or Friday?"

"Friday I can't, but Thursday might be good—if we could make it early. I have a meeting at eight."

"Where's the meeting?"

"Upper East Side—in the Seventies."

His mind raced as he tried to think of a suitable place. Nothing radically expensive—he didn't want her to think he was trying for a date and wanted to impress her. But he didn't want schlock, either. Maybe it would be best to let her pick the place.

"I don't know too many places that far uptown. Do you have a favorite in that neighborhood?"

"Not really. And there's no need for you to travel that far up, Do you know La Mangeoire on Second Avenue?"

His heart dipped. It was one of Beth's favorites. He had never been there without her.

"It's in the Fifties…" Nora prompted.

He gave himself a mental shake. "Sure, I know it," he said in his most cheerful voice. "Great French food—just off Fifty-third."

"That's the place. It's not all that far from where I'm going afterward. Would six be too early for you?"

"No, six is fine. I'll see you then."

He hung up and headed for the door, his step light, almost carefree.

SINCE FOSTER WAS seeing Tom on his break between morning hospital rounds and office hours, he had suggested that, to save time, they meet at a Karl's Kajun Kitchens near the NYU Medical Center. It was, of course, only a flimsy excuse to indulge Foster's fast-food craving, but Tom didn't mind because it would get him back to his shop that much sooner.

"So," Foster said around a mouthful of shrimp jambalaya, "have you got a suspect?"

"Are you kidding? Almost every one of these guys' business contacts has reason to hate them."

"Oh, come on now."

"Don't give me that wide-eyed look. Surely you know that when it comes to dealing with outsiders, it's no holds barred. Most of your friends would sell their own grandmothers if they could find a way to turn it into a tax write-off. Your pals are on the up and up only with one another, and I'm not so sure they're trustworthy even then. My problem's not in finding suspects. It's in narrowing them down."

"And how far have you gotten with that?"

"Several can be eliminated because of time and opportunity. But, of course, that doesn't mean that there isn't some kind of conspiracy and they aren't working together in some way."

"That seems to me to be highly unlikely." Foster eyed the slices of hot pork sausage that Tom had extracted from his black-eyed peas and pushed to the side of his plate. "Are you eating those?" While Tom shook his head, Foster shot his fork into them with the expertise of a striking rattlesnake.

"Seems unlikely to me too, but stranger things have happened, and I think we should keep it in mind."

"Okay, we'll keep it in mind. But who are you thinking about in the real world?"

"Vittorio Capperrelli is still high on the list."

"Speaking as a physician, it's my theory that muscle-bound guys spend so much time developing their biceps to compensate for the fact that they're cowards at heart."

"Luckily, you specialize in urology rather than psychiatry. As an ex-cop, I can tell you from experience that guys with a lot of muscles frequently get a charge out of using them. Capperrelli stays on the list. He certainly was on the scene when Portman got hit, and there's no reason why he couldn't have been in the other places too. My only reservation is the self-control he showed in not beating the victims to a pulp while he was at it. On the other hand, he might have been smart enough to realize that beatings could be traced to him more easily than castrations."

"Okay. Who else?"

"Lou West."

"Are you kidding? He loves us like his own kids. The Golden Guys made his reputation." But Foster's laugh sounded forced.

"That's not the way I heard it."

"I told you, there's nothing to that story. Besides, if Lou wanted revenge, he'd have taken it years ago, out on the football field. The guys don't want you bothering Lou." His eyes narrowed. "Have you been talking to him?"

Something in Foster's gaze put Tom on his guard. It was the same look his mother used to level at him when she asked him a question she knew the answer to and expected him to tell her a lie. But how could Foster know that he had met with Lou West yesterday? Had Lou contacted Foster or one of the others? Somehow, Tom doubted it.

"Why shouldn't I talk to Lou West? Are you afraid he'll tell me something you don't want me to know?"

"Of course not. He's an old man whose health has become precarious. We just don't want you disturbing him."

Tom stood up. "That's very touching, but it goes against our agreement. I told you from the beginning that I must have a free hand if you want me to find who's behind this. If you're changing the rules, we can forget about the deal."

Foster waved away Tom's objections. "Sit down and finish your lunch. No one's changing the rules. You'd just be wasting your time with Lou. Surely there are more likely suspects."

"One guy I think I should look into sooner rather than later is Fletcher Bowman."

"Isn't he in Maryland?"

"This is the age of the corporate jet. And he's really got it in for your pals. Three of them in particular—Bernard, Michaelson, and Hammond, who have been spearheading a hostile takeover of his conglomerate. Bernard and Michaelson have already been hit, and Hammond could be next on the list. I need an excuse to get in to see him. Can you set me up as an emissary from Hammond?"

"That shouldn't be a problem."

"I'll need to see Hammond first, to get my story straight."

"No problem there, either." Foster took out his cell phone and pressed a number. He listened a moment, made a face, and said "shit" under his breath. His voice was calm and friendly as he recorded his message. "Hey, Nick. It's Al. Give me a call, will you? We need to set something up." Next, he pocketed his phone, gulped down the rest of his Coke, and stood up. "I'll call you when I hear from him."

At the corner of Thirty-fourth Street and Park Avenue, Foster stopped to buy a giant pretzel with a lot of mustard from a pushcart vendor. Then he hailed a cab. "Do you want me to have Nick set it up for any particular day?"

"The sooner the better."

Tom caught a glimpse of Foster munching away on his pretzel as the taxi took off.

At ten to six Foster called the store. "Nick can see you in his office Thursday at four," he said. "Setting up something with Bowman will take a little time. The guy took off for Europe a couple of days ago, probably trying to shore up his holdings there. He won't be back till sometime next week."

From the background came the grumble of a male voice, which became more muffled as Foster put his hand over the mouthpiece of the phone and replied. Finally Foster came back on: "Tony's here. He was my last patient of the day. He wants to talk to you."

Portman must have grabbed the phone from Foster, for his voice came over the line immediately. "I thought you were such a hotshot," he roared. "How come you don't have this thing wrapped up by now?"

"How come you don't have that civic center in Maryland built yet? Don't hassle me, Portman. I'm working under your rules— alone and discreetly. If you want fast, you and your buddies can spill your guts to the cops and let them put a dozen men on the job."

"Okay, you've made your point. Just don't waste time and money by sitting around waiting for this Baltimore wild-goose chase to come through."

"I never chase wild geese, and you guys are getting far more than your money's worth on this. What I'm beginning to wonder is whether it's worth it to me. Now put Al back on before I think that one through and come up with an answer you won't like."

There was a pause while another muffled, angry conversation took place at the other end. Then Foster said in soothing tones: "Come on, Tom, don't take offense. We all have confidence in you. You know Tony. He just gets a little antsy sometimes. He's that way with everyone, but we pay no attention to it because we know that underneath all that bluster he's really a great guy."

"Sure. To know him is to love him. Let's cut the bullshit,

SECRET AGENDA | 173

Al," he added as the electronic bell signaled that someone was walking through the door. "Just give me Hammond's address. I've got a customer to take care of."

NICHOLAS HAMMOND III ruled Hammond Enterprises from its impressive corporate headquarters on the fourth and fifth floors of the Woolworth building in downtown Manhattan. Upon entering, Tom paused for a moment to admire the magnificent art deco lobby, the light reflecting back from its high rose-and-black marble arches in warm, golden tones. As he showed his ID to the guards and passed through the metal detectors, he reflected that the Woolworth empire of five-and-dime stores that financed this building had been as ephemeral as the multitude of small, second-hand bookstores on Fourth Avenue in Manhattan.

In contrast to the 1920s splendor of the building that housed them, the offices of Hammond Enterprises had the appearance of having been designed by a time traveler from the twenty-second century. The walls were stark white and the carpeting was sky blue, giving the impression of a world turned upside down. In keeping with the pristine yet topsy-turvy atmosphere, the furniture was all sharp curves and smooth angles rather than the other way around, and it was either white or Lucite perched on steel frames, evoking the impression that the visitor had come upon it when it was in the midst of materializing or disappearing.

Perhaps it was no accident that the young woman who sat at the long white reception desk was a platinum blonde in a crisp white blouse. Since the huge canvases mounted on the walls depicted only the palest of gray or beige geometric forms on a white background, the only flash of color in the room appeared to be her large gold hoop earrings, long blood-red fingernails, and matching red lips. She stretched the lips into a bright smile and asked, "May I help you?"

"I'm Tom Berenson. I have an appointment with Mr. Hammond."

Still smiling, she picked up her white telephone and announced his presence to the person on the other end. She then told Tom to make himself comfortable.

That was easier said than done. He chose the least lethal-looking piece of furniture—a sloping S- or perhaps backward Z-shaped Lucite chair, and slid into it, hoping that when the time came he would be able to extricate himself gracefully. The tables held no magazines to help visitors while away the time as they cooled their heels.

Having performed her duty toward him, the receptionist turned to the white computer on her desk and resumed typing. Her desk provided her with a long, wide workspace, but contained no pens, no pencils, no container of paper clips. A bookman, Tom found the total absence of paper disconcerting, and he couldn't resist asking, "Don't you ever have to write something down?"

For a moment she looked blank, as if he had asked her a question she couldn't connect with, one on the level of "Do you travel by horse and buggy?"

He made a writing motion with his hand. "Don't you ever write things down?" he repeated, then gestured toward the phone. "Telephone messages, things like that. I don't see any paper on your desk."

She laughed. "No one needs paper here, except for printouts, of course. We pass messages along through e-mail and instant messaging." She didn't have to add that anyone who wasn't set up to operate his entire life that way was pretty pathetic; her expression said it for her. Tom nodded and left it at that. He didn't ask what doodlers did when they were on the phone. No doubt she would have told him that they made computer designs.

Because she was wearing a short hot-pink sweater dress that glowed like neon against the stark background, Tom saw the young woman approaching the double doors to the interior offices long before she stepped through them. About eighteen, she had a mane of dark hair that was fashionably messy and frizzy. "Mr. Berenson?" she asked through glossy lips that matched her dress, which clung to her voluptuous figure as if it had been knitted directly onto it at birth. "I'm LuAnne. Mr. Hammond can see you now. Follow me, please."

He wondered how many men had resisted saying it would be a pleasure.

Hammond had removed his jacket and tie and was working out on a Nordic skiing machine in a corner of his office that had been set up as a mini gym. He worked hard to maintain his football-player build, and, except for some thickening around the waist and belly, had been moderately successful.

Though they had been introduced at the reunion, the two men had not had an opportunity to talk there. But, perhaps for the benefit of his escort, who hovered in the doorway, Hammond greeted Tom like a long-lost buddy. "Tom! How're ya doing? Come on in!" He glanced at LuAnne. "Thanks, uh...."

"LuAnne."

"Right. LuAnne. We have a lot of catching up to do, so see to it that we're not disturbed. Okay?" He winked and then smacked his lips as the door closed behind her. "New girl on the staff. One of these days I'm going to get me a piece of that cute little ass."

"It might come with an ugly sexual-harassment suit attached to it."

"Are you kidding? My girls all love me. I take good care of them, and in more ways than one." He nodded in the direction of an Exercycle and some barbells. "Grab yourself a piece of equipment and we'll try to get you in shape while we talk."

"Thanks, but I take care of that at the Y." As Tom sat down in an upholstered chair, he noticed that the furniture in Hammond's office was much more comfortable than that in the reception area and the outer offices he had passed through.

Hammond shrugged and speeded up his skiing. "Me, I never lose an opportunity to work out. Keeps the juices flowing."

"That's my mission too—to keep your juices flowing. You know what's been going on with your buddies. You may well be next on the list."

The eyes Hammond turned on Tom were those of the ruthless businessman. They must surely strike terror in the hearts of competitors when he moved in for the kill. "Not if you do your job right." His voice was as icy as his gaze. "I'm not a make-believe hero like Doug McGrath. These muscles"—he flexed his biceps for emphasis—"are *real*. Anything happens to me, you're dead meat, man. Remember that."

"And here's something to put in *your* memory bank. I'm an

ex-cop with a lot of friends both on the right side of the law and the wrong side. Some of them are so violent that you couldn't even dream them up in your nightmares. If anything happened to me, they'd come looking for the person responsible. It's amazing, the accidents that can befall men in high places, both figuratively and literally."

For a moment their eyes remained locked. Then Hammond hopped off the skier and picked up a barbell. "Not to worry," he said affably, as though Tom had been merely reassuring him. "That bastard won't get within ten feet of me. And if he does, I'll cut *his* cock off." After five presses, he set down the barbell and leaped onto his Exercycle like Doug McGrath onto a horse in a film. "So, what do you want to know?"

"A list of your enemies would be helpful."

"Don't have any."

"Of course not. This is being done by a big Golden Guys fan."

Hammond's face hardened. "It's being done by a nut case. Look, Doug's not to be compared to the rest of us. He's always been a muscle-bound schmuck, so he's probably made lots of enemies along the way. But guys like Tony and Neal and me—we're straight shooters. We play by the rules. There's nothing we do to anybody out there when we're making a deal that they wouldn't have done to us first, if they'd had the brains or the chance. Of course, we're too smart to ever give them that chance. But we're respected for that, not hated."

"And Fletcher Bowman respects you too?"

"Fletcher Bowman's a putz who doesn't know how to protect his right flank."

"That may be so, but he's a dangerous putz. He's been known to beat up guys who offend him. He's stayed out of jail only because his victims are too scared of him or of publicity to press charges. He's more than capable of being behind all this. I want to talk to him when he gets back from Europe. Al Foster said you could fill me in on what's going on with this takeover deal and get an appointment for me with him."

"It's a takeover deal like all takeover deals. It's the best thing that ever happened to him, and the bastard should be on his knees thanking me instead of fighting me. His stockholders will make a killing, and so will he. I'll get together some of the figures for you, and I'll send you down as my emissary to put the screws on." He gave a mean smile. "As an ex-cop, that should come easy to you. Who knows? You get him to knuckle under, I'll make it worth your while."

"Once I'm in the door, I'm going to be concentrating on my business, not yours. Just get me inside." Tom stood up. There was nothing more to be said or learned here.

"Bowman will be back on Wednesday. I'll arrange for you to see him Thursday morning."

"How can you be sure he'll be able to fit me into his schedule?"

"He'll fit you in, even if he has to scratch George W. Bush, who owes him almost as many favors as the five justices who elected him. Leave your address with the kid with that cute little ass. I'll have some papers sent over that you can deliver to him." Hammond climbed off the bike and walked to the door with Tom.

"What if someone gets hit before Bowman comes back?"

"It could save me a trip to Baltimore. By the way, have you ever slept with Ilsa Grant?"

"Why do you ask that?"

"Why do you think? She could be the link. She's married to a jealous Latin lover with an overdose of machismo. All the other victims have slept with her."

"So have half the guys in the insider's appendix to Celebrity Service."

"And are you included in that half?"

He made a nostalgic smile. "Not recently. It happened years ago. It was either while she was married to her first husband or maybe in the interval between him and her second. I don't remember. I don't remember much about the sex, either. Mainly because it was far from memorable. She looks great when you see her being humped on the wide screen, but in real life she's a lousy lay. In fact, I think she probably has a stand-in—or, more accurately, a lie-in—for the nude scenes. Her tits are nothing to write home about. At any rate, Capperrelli wasn't even on the scene when the two of us were getting it on."

"That wouldn't necessarily keep him from wanting to exact revenge if he found out about it."

"Revenge for what? Had he expected a virgin?" Hammond glanced over at his gym. "I could take care of him in a minute."

"Good. Then there's nothing to worry about if he's our man."

DOWN IN THE STREET, limousines were pulled up to the curb, waiting to transport the executives who moved and shook Wall Street and the world with the mere touch of their smartphone. It was not yet five o'clock, but the narrow sidewalks were already crowded with swift-walking men and women, middle managers who could leave their clerks and secretaries behind to close up shop.

Caught up in their midst, Tom hurried along with them, wondering what he could do till six o'clock. There was not enough time to go back to Brooklyn, yet there was over an hour to kill before he would be meeting Nora. It had been raining earlier, but there was a break in the clouds. He considered heading for Trinity Church and taking a stroll through its ancient, historic graveyard, but that was something to be done in a quiet moment, not with the rush-hour crowd and traffic bustling around on all sides. Instead he walked over to City Hall station and took the Number 6 local uptown.

There was standing room only in the train, but it was not yet jammed. Tom grabbed on to a pole, took his paperback from his pocket and began to read. It was about four stops later that he started to get a prickly sensation on the back of his neck, an uncomfortable feeling that he was being watched.

Pretending he was trying to read the station signs through the scratched-up windows, he turned and looked around. The other passengers were lost in their newspapers or gadgets, or gazing into space, or dozing.

He went back to his own reading, but the back of his neck still prickled. Either he had developed an overactive imagination, or his cop's intuition was kicking in again.

CHAPTER 18

INTUITION OR imagination, Tom decided that the best course of action would be to exit from the train at the last possible moment. He had intended to get off at Fifty-first Street, but instead exited at Grand Central, one of the city's busiest stations. He waited until the boarding passengers had pushed their way inside, then, as the doors were closing, he elbowed his way through and leaped beyond them. Of course, since this was New York City, several other passengers disembarked the same way, through other doors. Still, it seemed unlikely that his pursuer, if he had one, would have had the opportunity to join them.

He ran up the stairs, feeling exhilarated. By the time he reached the surface, he had convinced himself that if he were being watched at all, it was only one of those everyday New York incidents, with danger, perhaps, but no personal malice.

To kill some time, he walked up to Fifth Avenue and sat down on one of the benches by a mermaid fountain in Rockefeller Plaza. On his left were three middle-aged men, tourists from Japan, or businessmen on a break, animatedly consulting their guidebooks and one another. To his right sat an impeccably dressed and made-up woman of about seventy, a Saks Fifth Avenue shopping bag at her feet, loudly describing what must have been its contents to the person on the other end of her cell phone. Tom reached into his pocket for his paperback. He had been rereading his well-worn copy of Viktor Frankl's *Man's Search for Meaning*, but he found he couldn't concentrate on it now. It wasn't the high-decibel conversations on either side of him that were distracting him. His mind was so preoccupied with the meeting to come that he was barely aware of his surroundings.

Finally, he gave up and headed for the restaurant. Even walking slowly, he arrived ten minutes early. He paused for a moment at the entrance, remembering the last time he had been there with Beth. It had been on an anniversary. Before the cancer struck. Or, at least, before they had known it had struck. They had been so happy back then, full of love and laughter, sure of their future.

With a sigh, he reached for the door. Better to go in with happy memories on his mind, rather than sad ones. He had forgotten how warm and cheerful the restaurant was. Its yellow stucco walls hung with bright paintings of the French countryside and its hanging planters overflowing with fresh flowers made walking inside feel like slipping through a time warp and winding up in a country inn on a sunny day in Provence.

He had made a reservation, but at that hour there was still a choice of tables available, and he asked to be shown to one within sight of the door. That way, he could watch for Nora and wave to her as she came in, sparing her embarrassment if she failed to recognize him immediately from afar.

Now, why had that thought occurred to him? He certainly remembered what she looked like. He could still recall her in detail, from her short-cropped blond hair to her long, slim, tanned legs as she had dashed gracefully across the tennis court. But, then, Nora was a strikingly attractive woman. And he was just average, an inch over six feet, with medium brown hair that was not quite as thick as it used to be and beginning to gray at the temples. Beth had always said he was handsome, but she had seen him through the distorting eyes of love. To her he had remained the dynamic young man she had given her heart to. Affection had eradicated from her view the lines that his years as a cop had etched upon his face, softened the hardness they had brought to his eyes. Nora would observe him through the sharp eyes of a journalist.

But why should that matter to him?

He ordered a glass of pinot noir, and as soon as the waiter turned away he ran his hand over his hair, resisting the impulse to go to the rest room and comb it. A business meeting—that's all this was.

Trying to be casual, he sipped his wine and looked around the room instead of keeping his eyes fixed on the entrance. But more and more his gaze was drawn to the door. He was surprised at the disappointment he felt every time it opened and the face he expected didn't appear. Even more surprising was his stab of excitement when Nora did walk in, right on the dot of six.

She spotted him immediately, smiled, and raised her hand in recognition. He stood up while she took off her raincoat and checked it along with her umbrella. He wondered whether he should walk around the table and hold out her chair, then decided against it. Though she was a woman who valued her independence, he doubted that she would be offended by such a gesture. What he feared was that she would be amused by it.

"Hi," she said, reaching out to shake his hand. "Looks like we timed it right. The place isn't bursting at its seams yet."

Her hand was warm, and soft, but her grip was firm. He released it reluctantly and resumed his seat as she slipped into hers.

"Been here long?"

He gestured toward his wineglass. "I'm only three sips ahead of you."

"We'll have to remedy that." She turned to their waitress and asked for a Dubonnet. He wished she hadn't. Beth had always been partial to Dubonnet. He pushed the thought from his mind and tried to concentrate on what Nora was saying—something amusing about her shoot that day. He laughed and relaxed, and by the time her glass was set before her, it didn't hurt to see her lift it to her lips.

"Cheers," she said.

"Cheers." He lifted his glass too. She had very pretty lips, full, but not too full, and colored a glossy pink that matched the flowers on the silk scarf she wore draped over the shoulders of her periwinkle knit top. The color of the top came close to matching her eyes.

"It feels good to relax after chasing around all day." She sighed and leaned back in her chair. "I suppose, owning a bookstore, you're blessed with work that's more anchored down than mine."

"But not necessarily less frenetic, especially at holidaytime.

And dealing with the public brings its own frustrations all year round." He told her a few of the classic cases and soon had her laughing.

"You make it sound like fun." She gave him a friendly, half-curious, half-measuring look. "Somehow, if I didn't know what you do for a living, I wouldn't guess that you owned a bookstore. You don't really look the type."

"What type do I look?"

She shrugged and tilted her head to the left, still studying him. "More the man of action," she said at last.

He laughed. "You're putting me on. I'm not the outdoorsy, muscle-bound, mountain-climbing type."

"No, that's not what I mean. It's not your build that sends that message, though it certainly seems made for climbing mountains and chopping down trees, if that's your definition of a man of action. It's something in your eyes...a kind of restless determination that makes you look like a man who wants to get out and do things, change things...."

It was difficult to keep his gaze from sliding away from hers so that she could not continue to read in his eyes what he did not want her to know. There was a moment when he did want her to know everything about him, a moment when he almost told her that he used to be a cop. But as strong as that temptation was, he knew it wouldn't be wise, for her sake as well as his. Telling her about his past would only lead to telling her about the part it played in his present work. That knowledge could place her in danger. And so he smiled and let the moment pass, putting the first secret between them.

"Sorry to disappoint you, but I'm just a bookman."

She returned his smile. "Not 'just,' I'm sure. It's something fine and admirable to be. A friend of mine used to say that she wanted to open a bookstore when she retired. She always made it sound like the next best thing to paradise."

"Used to? What made her change her mind?"

"Nothing. She died long before retirement age had a chance to creep up on her. But, on the brighter side, at least she didn't have to settle for the next best thing."

"I'm sorry."

Nora nodded, her eyes bright. "Me too." She took a sip of her drink, forced a smile, and reached for the menu. "Enough gloominess. Let's talk food. What's your favorite here?"

"I have several. Today I'm going for the filet of salmon with pesto."

"Excellent choice. I always tell myself that one of these days I'm going to order something else, but I can never resist the Provençale shepherd's pie. If I promise to be good and not bring up gloomy subjects again, will you share a wickedly high-calorie chocolate dessert with me?"

"You've got a deal."

They talked and laughed through soup and salad, finding that they agreed on major aspects of politics and literature and life, and disagreed amicably on minor ones.

During a congenial lull in conversation halfway through the entrée, Nora said, "I hope this doesn't cancel out my dessert, but didn't you want to ask me some questions about Beta Alpha Beta Phi's finest cohort since its establishment, or so they say they are?"

He laughed. "Your dessert's safe, but I don't know if your appetite is."

"It would take more than the likes of the Golden Guys to turn me off chocolate. What do you want to know?"

"The general facts and statistics are easy enough to come by, but Blair wants some intimate information to humanize his book—interesting anecdotes, past and present. They can be amusing, heartwarming, even sad."

"Heartwarming isn't an adjective that can readily be applied to events in the lives of these men. I suppose if you looked hard enough, you could find incidents where they actually paused to pat a puppy on the head. Of course, it would probably turn out that the puppy belonged to someone they were trying to manipulate into a billion-dollar deal."

"It doesn't have to be heartwarming, just something that would give an insight into what makes them tick."

"That's a tall order. We can rarely discover that about ourselves or the people we're closest to, no less virtual strangers."

"It's usually easier to make educated guesses about strangers."

"Easier maybe, but just as unreliable."

"Anyway, we seem to have wandered off the subject. Blair doesn't intend to draw conclusions, he just wants the material. The guys haven't been forthcoming with me. They rarely work me into their busy schedules, and when they do, it's for only a few minutes. Blair's book will be a scholarly work, and it's doubtful that their being in it will reap any kind of profit for them. On the other hand, your documentary will be great PR for them and should help to keep the big bucks rolling in. I'm sure they're a lot more open with you."

She nodded. "It's amazing what looking into a camcorder or camera will bring forth. Reality TV and YouTube have turned us into a nation of hams. I'm sure they are more open with me, but that doesn't necessarily mean that they're also more truthful."

"But you check their stories out, don't you?"

"When it's something that I think needs verification, I have my staff check it out. You're welcome to go down to my office and have a look at our files, but I doubt that you'll come up with anything illuminating. Mostly, you'll probably find the same hard facts and statistics you already have."

"Thanks. I appreciate that. Who knows? I may find some facts and figures I haven't been able to get hold of." He leaned back to let the waiter put down two forks and the dark chocolate cake with Tahitian vanilla ice cream that Nora had ordered for dessert. "As I mentioned, these guys haven't exactly been bending over backward to give their fellow Beta Alpha help with his book. Maybe they'd be more forthcoming if I were a member of their exclusive club."

"Personally, I'm glad you're not a Beta Alpha. I wouldn't be enjoying this meal so much if you were. And I'd be on the road to getting fat."

"Why?"

She handed him one of the forks. "Because, if that were the case, I wouldn't share my chocolate treat with the likes of you."

He laughed as he cut off a small corner of the cake. "Then I'm glad I'm just a hardworking guy from Brooklyn."

"Me too."

For a moment their eyes held. There was an odd sensation in the center of his chest. It was as if the warmth of her smile had begun to melt the lump of ice that had been lodged there since Beth was torn from his life.

Did Nora sense it? Or did she feel it too? Perhaps that was why she pulled her gaze away and began concentrating on the cake. He couldn't take his eyes from her lips as she raised the fork to her mouth.

"You're obviously not a fan," he said. "How come you're spending your time doing a documentary on them?"

"Who says you have to love your subject to do a documentary? It came along when I was between projects and had a tuition bill due. The Golden Guys want it as a showcase for their buddy Lyle Wayne, and their companies have put up a lot of the funding. But I made it clear from the beginning that it wouldn't be a total puff piece. A good journalist can always find a way to work in the truth. That's the fun of it. Besides, there is some genuine gold among the Golden Guys. Most of them contribute to a favorite charity or two, so even if it is just for PR purposes, they put some of their money to good use. And then, they actually have a winner of the Nobel Prize and a man who ministers to the poor."

"And Al Foster. He seems like a decent sort."

"The best that can be said for him is that he probably isn't any greedier than most doctors."

"But he gives his patients good care."

"If they or their insurance companies can afford it. I know that he won't treat poor people on Medicaid."

"Be fair. He probably never gets the chance. How many Medicaid patients do you think wander into his Park Avenue office?"

"At least one—the person I sent there as a test case. The man said it was an emergency and he was in great pain. But these days, the first question doctors have their assistants ask is not, 'Where does it hurt?' but, 'What's your insurance?' As soon as they heard that the poor guy had no health insurance, they told him to try the emergency room at Bellevue." Her eyes twinkled. "And I have it all on tape. The guy had a hidden camera."

Tom shook his head. "I've certainly had enough experience with doctors, so that doesn't really surprise me. Still, I'm a little disappointed in Al. I rather like him."

"So do I. Compared to his friends, he's an angel of mercy. You have to remember that these days healing is a doctor's business, not his mission in life. Foster behaves like the businessman he is. Who else do you like?"

"I haven't talked to them all yet, but the ones I've met come over as too self-centered and ruthless for my taste. You obviously know them better. Who do you like?"

"That's easy. Arnold Simon is head and shoulders above the others. He seems to have wandered in from another century. It's certainly hard to believe that in this day and age there exists an American businessman who could walk away from all that money and power to devote himself to helping the downtrodden, but he did. He's one of the few genuinely good people I've come across in my work...in my life. And he's a really nice guy too, not sanctimonious or heavy-handed when he talks about his work. He doesn't try to proselytize and, by current standards, he doesn't use strong-arm tactics to get donations. Of course, if you're around him too long, you begin to feel a little inadequate." She shook her head and smiled. "Have you met him?"

"Just briefly, at the reunion. I haven't had chance for a one-on-one talk. I'm going to call and try to meet him Monday."

"You're in for a disappointment. He's off on a fund-raising trip and won't be back till the end of next week. When you do see him, be prepared to do it on the run. He doesn't like to sit still. He'll probably haul you off to one of his centers for AIDS patients, or addicts, or pregnant teenagers, or the homeless. And if you're smart, you'll leave most of your money home, because without his even asking, you're going to find yourself handing over every cent you have on you. Denise was so impressed when we taped him that she signed on as a volunteer."

"How about you?"

She shrugged and looked a little sheepish. "I'd like to say that I was strong enough to resist, but I did promise to drop in occasionally now, and more often when I've wrapped up this project. In the meantime, I wrote him a whopping big check."

"I'm looking forward to meeting him, but I'll profit by your example and leave my checkbook behind. How about my credit card?"

"That too. But bring your notebook. He'll certainly have

plenty of stories to tell, though they may not be the kind Blair Whitney is interested in for his book. Still, Arnold keeps in close touch with his fraternity brothers, so he may be able to fill you in with some anecdotes about them. Most of them seem to regard him as a royal pain, by the way."

"That figures. Who else do you like?"

"Arnold's a hard act to follow, but if one can get beyond all his brilliance, Jason Gilbert is a nice guy when he warms up a bit."

"I got the impression that he's kind of an outsider, not completely accepted by his brother Beta Alphas."

"So did I."

"Any idea why?"

"I'd like to say it's because they're overawed by and maybe jealous of his brilliance. But, aside from Doug McGrath, who seems to have been kicked in the head by a horse, they're a pretty brainy crew. I think his circumcision gets in the way."

"Then why did they let him into their exclusive fraternity in the first place?"

"I can think of only one reason. They must have needed a token Jew, and he seemed the least offensive candidate—brilliant, good-looking, and a decent football player too. They took him into their clubhouse, but they never really took him into their club."

"You'd think the years, and the Nobel Prize, might have brought them around."

"Are you kidding? We're talking about old-line WASPs here. In some of them, anti-Semitism is almost genetic. They're experts at camouflaging it with a coating of genteel civility. A lot of people don't pick up on it."

"But you did."

"I've got double antennae: I'm a trained journalist, and my husband was a Jew. Sid could spot a bigot a mile away. But he was good at reading the character of all people." She looked at Tom carefully. "You seem to have the same ability to read people. What do you attribute it to?"

He caught himself just as he was about to attribute it to his years on the police force. "Must be all those psychology books I read in between waiting for customers."

"Must be," she said. But she studied him as though she suspected it was a great deal more. As their waiter approached with a coffee pot, she glanced at her watch and turned down the refill. "It's getting late," she said. "I really have to be going."

Tom asked the waiter to bring their bill. While they were waiting, he told Nora that he would be going to Baltimore next week to look over an estate-sale library. "I thought I'd take Stephanie with me and we'd take a look at Hopkins. Do you think your daughter might have some free time to show us around?"

"When will you be there?"

"My appointment's for Thursday morning, so I thought we'd get there sometime Wednesday. We could make it earlier or later, according to your daughter's schedule."

"I'll check with Leslie and let you know."

The waiter returned with their bill, and Nora reached for her purse. Tom motioned her to put it away, saying, "This was a business meeting, remember? It's on my expense account."

"I have one too,"

"But it was my business meeting. When you have to pick my brain, we'll use your expense account."

She laughed. "Deal." She picked up one of the cake crumbs that remained on the plate, popped it into her mouth, then licked her fingers and her lips. "Thank you...and Blair Whitney."

The check room had filled up with raincoats and umbrellas since their arrival, and Tom watched as the woman behind the counter ferreted through the hangers for his number. As she reached for his trench coat, the sleeve of a nearby raincoat caught his cop's eye. There was a faint streak of paint or whitewash from the cuff almost up to the elbow. The man he had noticed in the bookstore the other day had been wearing a coat just like it.

As he slipped into his coat, Tom retreated a few steps and glanced casually around the dining room. Anyone intent on watching him would have chosen a table where he could keep him in sight. There were several men eating alone or waiting (or pretending to be waiting) for someone to join them. Since Tom hadn't had a good look at the face of the man in the bookstore, all but two, a young African-American and a bald man of about seventy, could have been the fellow he'd seen before.

And, of course, there was always the possibility that his imagination was working overtime again. In a city of millions, thousands of men wore blue trench coats, and no doubt many of them had a stain on one sleeve....

"Is anything the matter? Did you forget something?" Nora broke in on his thoughts.

Tom gave himself a mental shake, and forced a laugh. "As a matter of fact I did. I was trying to remember what I promised to pick up for Stephanie on my way home. It will come back to me," he added, opening the door.

There was the chilly promise of fall in the breeze, and it ruffled Nora's hair and brought an intriguing sparkle to her eyes. "I'm going to taxi up to Seventy-second Street," she said. "Can I drop you off somewhere?"

He wished he could say yes and prolong their time together, but they both knew that Brooklyn lay in the opposite direction.

"Thanks, but the subway's only a few blocks from here. The exercise will do me good. I'll walk you over to Sixth Avenue. You'll probably have a better chance for a cab there."

"No need," she said, rushing to the curb. "Here comes one now."

His heart sank as she waved it down. But she didn't climb in immediately. Instead, she stood there with her hand on the door handle.

"Thanks again," she said.

"Thank *you*."

"I'll call my office first thing in the morning and tell them to expect you and to give you all the help you need." She opened the door, yet remained standing there.

He wanted to ask to see her again, but the words seemed lodged in his throat. He hadn't felt so awkward around a female since he was fourteen and scared stiff his voice would break in the middle of asking Phyllis Rabinowitz if she'd like a slice of pizza.

"I—we barely scratched the surface in there. If I can't find all I need in your files, can we do it again?" There. That sounded casual enough. Or did it?

She smiled, as if those were the words she had been waiting for. "We can do it again even if you do find all you need in my files. I don't know about you, but that was the most relaxing meal I've had in ages. I really owe you one for that—and for being such a good sport and pretending not to notice that I ate most of the cake. How about letting me take you to dinner Saturday night?" She made a face. "That's kind of short notice. How about the Saturday after that?"

"No. This Saturday is fine." He would have backed out of an invitation to dine at Buckingham Palace if he'd had one.

"Hey, lady, are you taking root out there?" the cab driver demanded. "I gotta be back in the garage sometime this century."

Nora rolled her eyes. "I'll call you tomorrow about the time and place." She gave Tom a brief wave as she climbed into the cab. The driver zoomed away from the curb, no doubt determined to cut off any chance for further conversation.

Tom stood on the sidewalk, watching the taxi get lost in traffic, feeling a little lost himself. As he headed toward the subway, though, his step was lightened by the thought of speaking to Nora again tomorrow and being with her Saturday evening.

By the time he reached the subway, he was feeling happier than he had in years. He had forgotten what it was like, that delicious mixture of elation and anticipation. He was still savoring it as the train doors closed behind him. But it drained away as he took a seat across from an old man dozing over a copy of the *Daily News*. The man was overdressed for the season, wearing a wool knit cap and a dark-blue parka. The color of the parka reminded Tom of the navy-blue trench coat he had seen in the restaurant.

Slowly he turned and looked over the other passengers. There were some blue trench coats, but none with a noticeable white streak on its sleeve. Somehow, that didn't set his mind at ease.

CHAPTER 19

"YOU GOT A FRIEND with a drinking problem?" Max asked the next morning before Tom left for the shop.

"Not that I'm aware of. Why?"

"Because after you left the store yesterday, some guy with maybe a phony Italian accent called and wanted to speak to you. He insisted he was Vittorio Capperrelli, the guy with all the muscles, and that he was calling an insurance company. I couldn't get rid of the nut until I agreed to take down his number and ask you to call him back."

Tom took the slip of paper and put it into his pocket. "Thanks, Max."

"Don't tell me it was Capperrelli?"

"I met him at Portman's. Maybe he wants to buy a book."

"From an insurance company?" Max gave him a level look. "What's going on, Tom? This is more than just doing some simple research for a professor on the West Coast, isn't it? My guess is that it has something to do with Portman, and that smells bad to me. I don't care how rich they are or how many financial and society columnists write about them, guys like Portman are the scum of the earth. They play rough and dirty. Nothing's worth getting involved with them. If it's money you need, I've got my mutual funds and my IRAs...."

Tom lay a reassuring hand on Max's arm. "Not to worry. Everything is under control. It's a simple matter that'll be cleared up in a week or two, and will be well worth the time I have to put into it."

"If it's so simple, why don't you tell me what it's really about?"

"Because I can't. And I know you can understand and respect that. I really appreciate your pinch-hitting for me at the shop while Phil's away so I can take care of this. He'll be back and able to take over for me a couple of days next week when I have to go out of town, but can you close up for me Saturday night?"

"You know that's no problem. But can't you at least give me a hint where you'll be going?"

"Saturday's related, yet not related." Tom felt a smile creeping up on his face. "I'm having dinner with the woman I met with last night. She's the one who's shooting the documentary about Portman and his fraternity brothers. Yesterday was a business meeting, to get some information from her. Saturday...." He shrugged, still grinning.

Max grinned too. "Hey, that's great. It's about time. Is she going to be on that trip you're taking?"

"We're just having a friendly dinner tomorrow night. That's all. The trip's to Baltimore, and if she doesn't have any tests scheduled, I thought I'd take Stephanie with me so she can get a look at Johns Hopkins."

"Well, that's good news." Max looked relieved.

"Why? Because you'll be glad to have the place to yourself for a couple of days?"

"No. Because if you're taking Stephanie, it must mean that there's no danger involved in what you're doing."

"That's what I've been trying to tell you," Tom said, and wished it were true as he left for the store.

VITTORIO CAPPERRELLI DID his best to sound mysterious when Tom returned his call. The matter was urgent, and he could not discuss it on the phone. He was on his way out to make a commercial. If Tom would meet him at the advertising agency's studio about eleven-thirty, he should be finished and they could talk then. "Why do you work from a bookstore and not your insurance company?" he asked. "The man who answered the phone yesterday said the number you gave me is a bookstore."

"I'm a consultant," Tom said. "Like most industries, insurance companies are cutting down on regular employees and outsourcing office jobs to India and the Philippines, and hiring mostly outside consultants like me for investigations that have to be done here. I opened the bookstore thinking I'd need it to make a living, but my old bosses keep me so busy I spend hardly any time here. You would have reached me more easily if you had called my cell phone. I left that number with you and your wife too."

"Cell phone!" Capperrelli yelled the words as if they were a curse in Verdi's *Otello*. "I won't have one—and I won't make a call on one. Don't you know they could cause cancer of the brain? You should throw yours in the nearest garbage can."

Tom knew better than to argue with a health fanatic about a crackpot theory. "I'll take that under advisement," he said. "In the meantime, if you have any doubts about me, you can call Tony Portman. Or I'll give you the number of the guy I work for at the insurance company. He's a friend of Tony's."

"No, no. That isn't necessary. Before you came to see us, Tony told me to cooperate with you. I know how he does business, and he wouldn't have sent anyone he hadn't checked out. I'll see you at eleven-thirty."

Since Max did his literacy volunteer work Friday mornings, Tom had no choice but to lock up early for lunch. The studio was in NoHo, in a loft in a building on Bond Street. A century and a half ago, the street had been an elegant thoroughfare where society men and women could be close to the fine stores and entertainment centers on Lafayette Street and Broadway. For decades, forgotten by time and the city whose economy they had once served so well, its stately buildings had stood weatherworn and in disrepair, huddled over the same cobblestones that had once supported the carriages of the well-to-do. Now, rediscovered in the real estate boom, many of its buildings were being turned into co-ops and condos that sold for a million dollars and up.

The building Tom entered had not yet been taken over for renovation. At least on the outside and in its vestibule. A shaky and hesitant elevator delivered him to the third floor, but when he stepped out, he was back in the twenty-first century—or maybe ahead in the twenty-second. A young woman was shouting into a phone, apparently negotiating the price of props. Her tight, low-cut jeans showed off her navel ring, and her clinging T-shirt announced to the world that I TRIED BEING GOOD, BUT I GOT BORED.

"Okay.... Yeah, sure. I'll believe it when I see it.... Just get it here by three. And remember, no moth holes!" She slammed down the receiver and looked up at Tom. "The son of a bitch drives a hard bargain, but he *does* have the best gorillas in town. You here for the Hang-in-There shoot?"

"No. Vittorio Capperrelli asked me to meet him here. What's Hang-in-There?"

"Don't you ever watch the evening news? It's some kind of new denture-adhesive shit." She put her head to one side and examined him more closely. "Yeah, I should have realized you're not the type."

That was a relief. His spirits had sunk at the realization that he looked old enough to this young woman to be mistaken for a spokesperson for denture adhesive.

Then she rose from her desk with shake of her head and a silly-me smile. "I must be slipping. I see now that you're too old. Like in the ads for wrinkle cream, the client wants the models to be young and sexy."

So much for lifted spirits. He decided not to intensify his ego's decline by asking if the stuffed gorilla had a pivotal role in the Hang-in-There commercial. The answer was probably yes.

The young woman led him through a maze of doors and corridors to a studio with a set that duplicated a state-of-the-art home workout center. There, Vittorio Capperrelli, in matching blue head and wrist sweatbands, white gym shorts, and a low-cut yellow athletic shirt that provided a wide view of his massive hairy chest, was having his gleaming body resprayed with canned sweat.

"It rolls right off the goddamn oil, Terry," the sprayer was complaining.

"That's okay," a woman with a clipboard told him. "Sweat's supposed to roll off. As long as there's enough there for us to see it while we reshoot this last line."

"I have been sprayed with enough water to grow an olive orchard back in Italy," Vittorio grumbled. "I have said that last line twenty-five times, Theresa. How many more times must we do this?"

"Twenty-six will be a charm," she soothed him. "We'll choose the best one when we're editing. Bill, give him one more spritz down the front of his shirt so it sticks better to that gorgeous chest. Great. That's just right."

Bill stood back, head to one side, to scrutinize his master-piece. He adjusted a few strands of hair over Vittorio's headband, and then, satisfied, stepped off the set.

A finger to her lips, Tom's escort indicated that he should stand quietly and out of the way on the cable-strewn floor near one of the monitors. She then left the area on tiptoe. When Tom turned his eyes back to the set, he saw that Vittorio now held a huge dumbbell aloft in his right hand while his left hand extended a juicer toward the cameras.

"Okay. Quiet, everybody," Terry ordered, and a countdown began both verbally and on the monitor near Tom.

Vittorio's mouth stretched into a beefcake smile. "The Mini-Jet Juicer," he intoned in a voice that seemed an octave deeper than his natural baritone. "Now you can keep fit and juice-up on the job—just like me!"

The crew and technicians burst into applause.

"Gorgeous, Vic baby!" Terry cried, and she blew him a kiss. "Perfecto! You got it just the way they want it."

"No more takes?" he asked.

"No more takes," she promised. "You can go home now and spend all that beautiful money Mini-Jet's paying you and your agent."

A thin young woman in jeans and a NYU sweatshirt relieved him of the juicer and the weight, which she stuck under one arm while she bent to remove a hidden microphone. She said some-thing to him, and he nodded, looked in Tom's direction, and, wiping his face on a towel, walked over to join him.

Tom was watching in fascination as the young woman added the barbell to the collection of equipment she was nonchalantly carrying off the set.

Vittorio laughed. "Plastic," he explained. "Theresa says they need it for insurance purposes, so I won't sue the client if I get hurt." He took a deep breath, swelling his chest to magnificent proportions. "As if *I* could get hurt lifting weights! I think they are afraid that if they ask me to do too many takes, I will get angry and throw the weights at them. They were nearly right." He threw the towel around his neck. "Come. You can wait in one of the offices while I shower and get rid of this ridiculous layer of oil. Then we'll have lunch and talk."

He dropped Tom off in a cramped cubicle that was packed with what appeared to be a collection of standard props. Behind a desk was a low chair that tilted slightly to the right. After testing it, Tom sat down gingerly, reminding himself not to get too comfortable and lean back. Atop one of the piles of paper on the desk was a recent copy of *Variety,* and he began to skim through it.

By the time Vittorio appeared in the doorway, wearing dark glasses, a leather jacket, and form-fitting Ralph Lauren jeans, Tom had learned more about show biz and show biz people than he'd need to know if he were a guest on one of the morning shows on television. Most interesting had been a short article about Doug McGrath's temporary retirement from movies and TV to work as a special consultant to the Citizens' Task Force on Family Values, whose honorary chairman was Senator Lyle Wayne. The article was accompanied by a photograph of the grinning McGrath in a cowboy hat.

"I am ready," Vittorio announced. "The amenities here leave much to be desired, but at least now I no longer smell like a Caesar salad. Come. I know where we can get a great lunch."

Since they were so close to Little Italy, Tom assumed they would head in that direction and Vittorio would introduce him to an out-of-the-way, little-known trattoria where he would experience the calamari of a lifetime. Vittorio, however, headed west to Broadway in a quick march and halted before a combination grocery-deli.

"They have the best and freshest salad bar in the city," he announced, opening the door with a flourish.

Inside, when Tom paused to read the sandwich list above the deli counter, Vittorio took his arm and guided him instead to the salad bar. "Fresh vegetables. That is what you need. Pure food makes pure bodies." He thrust a large plastic container at Tom. "Fill it to the brim!"

Since he had no objection to salad, and it was a lot easier than insisting on a sandwich and then enduring a lecture, Tom complied.

For himself, Vittorio filled two huge containers. He also bought a liter of San Pellegrino mineral water with which to wash it all down, explaining, "I do not trust any juice that I do not create myself."

Though the establishment provided tables and chairs for its patrons, Vittorio refused to eat there. "Too many people around," he said. "We must go where we will not be closed in and overheard."

They toted their plastic shopping bags up West Third Street to Washington Square Park. There, Vittorio carefully surveyed the area for a bench they would have to themselves. He chose one that was a distance from the fountain.

"Good," he said, settling down and removing one of his plastic containers from the bag. "Here we should be safe."

"What makes you think we're in danger?" Tom asked.

"Danger? Who said such a thing?" Vittorio puffed out his chest. "There is no such thing as danger when I am around. No one dares try to harm Vittorio Capperrelli or what belongs to him. No, what I meant was that here we are safe from busybodies who might try to overhear the important matters we must discuss."

"And what are those matters?" Tom struggled to open the top of his salad container, but it wouldn't budge.

Vittorio reached over, pinched the container on the sides, and the top sprang up. "Where are your carrot sticks?" he demanded. "You must have them for your vitamin A."

"They're probably on the bottom. Now, you were saying...?"

But Vittorio's stern gaze was now fixed on a group of young women, probably NYU students, who were strolling by. Most were dressed in tights and denim jackets, a few in jeans so tight they seemed painted on. "The little whores," he said. "Back in my village in Italy, the priest would have given them penance for dressing to inflame men. Their fathers would have beat them or locked them in the house."

"It's the style." Tom rooted out a carrot stick and waved it triumphantly. "Fat or thin, tall or short, young or old—women all over the Western world dress that way. Even your own beautiful wife."

"That's different. She has explained it to me. She is a professional woman. It is part of her work to maintain her image. Besides, she is a married woman, and she has me to protect her. But these girls do not do it for their art or profession. They do it to arouse the beast in a man."

"I think you read far too much into it. They do it because it's the current fashion. My wife always said women dress to be like and to impress other women, not men. Besides, we men are in control of our own lives. Those who behave like beasts are responsible for their actions. To argue otherwise is to say that we're not as smart or as mature as women. Do you believe that?"

"Of course not! We are the stronger sex—in brains as well as body."

Beth and Stephanie would have to forgive him, but he was not about to open that can of worms. "In that case, there's nothing to worry about, is there? And the law is right. The man who attacks or rapes a woman is the one to be punished, not her."

A fierce look came over Vittorio's face. "The law is too easy! Any man who dirties and defiles a good woman deserves more than jail. He has ruined her for life. So should he be ruined also. He should have his balls cut off and thrown to the dogs!" He bit savagely into a carrot stick. "You must forgive me," he went on, suddenly calmer. "My wife says that I sometimes get—how do you call it? — carried off. That is not what we are here to discuss, is it? What I want to talk to you about is the night of August twenty-seventh." Vittorio glanced around for eavesdroppers. "Since our last meeting, I have been thinking about poor Tony and that negotiable bond. Just how valuable is it?"

"I'm not at liberty to reveal the exact amount."

"Why not?"

"There are legal and technical reasons, some involving reinsurance with Lloyd's of London."

"Lloyd's is an excellent company. They once insured me when I made an Italian movie in which I was a circus strongman who was so vain of his strength that it became his ambition in life to straighten out the Leaning Tower of Pisa with his muscles alone. Then, in the movie, the Virgin Mary appeared to me in a dream and told me to use my strength to help the poor in the slums of Naples, because it was God's will that the Leaning Tower has been leaning all these years."

"Sounds like a great film," Tom said.

Vittorio made a charming smile. "Naturally, I would not want to ask you to break the law. But surely you could tell me if the bond was in the seven-figure range?"

Tom was at a loss to see where this was leading, but he followed along anyway. "There's no ethical problem in answering such a vague, general question. Especially when I'm sure the answer will go no further." Vittorio's emphatic nod indicated that he could be counted on to be the soul of discretion. "Then I can tell you in confidence that the bond very definitely was somewhere in the seven-figure range."

"Just as I thought." Vittorio speared some of his salad and transferred it to his mouth. In his massive hand, the white plastic fork looked like a tiny implement from a child's tea service. "It has been my observation that here in America, as in Italy, there is something called a finder's fee. Somebody who helps you come into a big sum of money is entitled to a nice, fat portion of it."

"Do you have information about the whereabouts of the negotiable bond?"

"It is possible. But I don't see why I should give it to you and your company for nothing. After all, insurance companies and their executives and directors make big sums, but when hardworking athletes like me suffer an injury that can end our careers, they try to avoid their legal responsibilities and pay us off in peanuts, as you say here.

"Ilsa's friend Millicent Stewart, who used to dance with the American Ballet and is now married to a New Jersey congressman, was made a director of Empire United. She gets ten thousand dollars and a banquet at the Waldorf four times a year merely for attending a meeting and saying yes to a few proposals that are put before her by the officers of the corporation and which she knows nothing about. I also happen to know that Tony Portman's friend

Senator Lyle Wayne got twelve percent of the sale price for an insurance-office site in his state."

Tom saw where this was leading, and since there was no negotiable bond, he decided that he could be equally generous. "If your information leads to the recovery of the bond and a conviction, then it will certainly be worth twelve percent of the sum involved," he said.

"I want it in writing."

"Are you sure? Everything that's in writing at the insurance company will go into a dozen computers, and it will all be reported to the IRS."

Vittorio thought that over a moment, then shook his head. "It is nice of you to tell me that, but if I don't have some written proof, how do I know that I will not be cheated?"

"My boss ordered me to report directly to Tony Portman, and Tony has told me to use my own discretion in the course of my investigation, to stop at nothing, this side of the law of course, to get the bond back. My word here is the same as Tony Portman's handshake."

That seemed acceptable to Vittorio, who, evidently, had never been on the opposite end of a business deal with Portman. Or perhaps he had, because after his nod, he turned a level gaze on Tom and warned: "I shall hold you both personally responsible the moment the arrest is made."

Tom nodded his understanding and acceptance of terms. He assumed that Vittorio was drawing out the pause that followed in order to heighten the drama of the moment. But when Vittorio finally spoke, drawing himself up, expanding his chest, and jabbing his little white fork in Tom's direction for emphasis, he appeared to be changing the subject entirely.

"The Reverend Arnold Simon," he said.

"I beg your pardon?"

"The Reverend Arnold Simon," Vittorio repeated.

"What about him?"

"What do you mean, 'What about him'? He is the man who took the bond."

"That's impossible. Arnold Simon is to America what Mother Teresa was to Europe and Asia."

Vittorio shook with rage. "How dare you speak of Mother Teresa in the same breath as Arnold Simon! She was a Catholic, a saint."

"All right. We've made our agreement. Tell me what you know about Simon."

"He was making a pest of himself at the party. He kept asking everyone for money. He even asked me, and I am not a business-man or one of his Golden Boy friends. It was the very first time we'd ever met. Unlike his friends, he is not a gentleman. I was appalled by his bad taste."

"What was the money to be used for?"

"He tried to make me feel responsible for all of the poor and homeless in New York—in the entire country. He said the money was for his charities, but who can tell for sure? Just yesterday the *Post* had a story about a charity for children with AIDS that was organized by two doctors who once worked as top officials for the Federal government. They collected over two million dollars but gave only fifty thousand to the sick and dying. They told the reporter that if it had not been for them, even that fifty thousand dollars would not have been collected."

"That certainly sounds like the reasoning of top government officials. But I'm not sure what it has to do with Arnold Simon."

"He's as greedy as them all. He probably skims off for himself most of what he collects. Anyway, I finally got away from him, and a little while later I saw Tony rushing over to him. Tony looked very angry about something, and I was sure that he was furious about Simon putting the touch on all his guests, who might now be afraid to attend his next party despite the free food and drinks. Whatever people say about Tony, and some people say a lot of things, you have to give him credit for doing more than his share for charity. But he wasn't spon-soring a fund-raiser that night. That night, with the help of my beautiful wife, he was selling apartments and suites in his new condos."

"Did Portman and Simon argue? What did they say to each other?"

"I was too far away to hear what they were saying, but it was obvious that Tony was talking to Simon in a way that I would never talk to a man of God, even of another religion." Vittorio nodded his head for emphasis.

"And that's it?"

"That is definitely not it. Later on, Tony went out through the French windows. I thought he was going to the beach, maybe to gaze at the stars and constellations as I often do. Well, not five seconds later, the Reverend Arnold Simon went out after him."

"About what time was this?"

"I've been thinking hard about that, and I would say it was sometime around eleven o'clock. Simon was talking to one of the television women, probably asking her for money, but suddenly he rushed away after Tony. I'm sure she was glad to get rid of him." Vittorio nodded knowingly. "Somehow, after that, Simon managed to get that bond away from Tony. I'm as sure of that as I am that Michelangelo painted the Sistine Chapel." His expression dared Tom to contradict his version of the theft.

"Why didn't you tell me all this the day I met with you and your wife?"

He shrugged his massive shoulders. "I had forgotten it. But I have been thinking about your problem ever since, and the memory came back."

"And how do you think Arnold Simon managed to steal the bond without Tony's knowledge?"

He shrugged. "Maybe some of those lowlifes he is always helping showed their gratitude by teaching him how to pick pockets. He has the bond. I am sure of it. Your next step should be to visit him. Take my advice and make it soon. I read or heard somewhere that he is going to personally conduct some mission to feed the hungry all over Africa."

"What if he intends to use Tony's bond for his good work there?"

He shook his head sharply. "That still wouldn't make it right. It's Tony's bond."

And your twelve percent, Tom thought. "I'll look into it carefully, of course," he said, "but I must tell you that I think it's most unlikely that Arnold Simon had anything to do with the theft."

Finished with his salads, Vittorio closed the containers and returned them to the bag, took the last swig of his mineral water, and stood up. "You will discover that I am right. Now I must go."

Tom joined him as he walked virtuously to the waste bin.

"You will keep in touch?" Vittorio asked as they tossed in their garbage.

"If I have any news."

"You will. Remember—twelve percent. And tell your insurance company that I want it in cash. I am also available if they need someone fresh and strong on their board of directors." He flexed his biceps. "Mention that it would be very good for their image to have me, a human Rock of Gibraltar."

"I'll pass the word along."

Tom watched Vittorio as he strode from the park. Why had the man made up such a wild story? One explanation, of course, was greed. He believed there was a bond, and he wanted to get his hands on some of the money. In that case, it was possible that he had seen Simon leave the room around eleven o'clock and thought that he might be the thief. Or, he might want to throw suspicion on Simon because he knew that, aside from the hired help, Simon was the only one at the party poor enough to stoop to illegal theft for cash. The others stole millions legally, with the help of creative accounting and tax lawyers.

And then there was the other, darker possibility: Perhaps Vittorio Capperrelli was the castrator. He would know then that it wasn't a stolen bond Portman was searching for. He would want to put Tom off the scent by tossing a solid suspect in his path. Pretending he believed the bond story would be a clever way to do it. He might even know that Arnold Simon would be out of town for a while so that Tom wouldn't have a chance to check out the story immediately.

Tom started toward the subway. To learn Vittorio Capperrelli's whereabouts when the other victims were hit moved up on his list of priorities. He already knew that New York had been the Capperrellis' home base for most of the year. They also had homes in Beverly Hills and Naples, but the one in California was being renovated and they had been in Italy for only six weeks, from the middle of February through the end of March. Vittorio certainly was on the scene that night in Montauk when Portman was attacked. And it would have been easy enough for him to stage hit-and-runs on Michaelson and McGrath.

But what about Neal Bernard? Nantucket wasn't exactly just around the corner. Still, no place was inaccessible when one had the money to charter a plane. Vittorio could have flown in and out in a matter of hours. Or he could have rented a boat. A versatile sportsman, he probably had his own boat.

But all that was true for any number of suspects. Tom shook his head, remembering what he had said to Nicholas Hammond about Fletcher Bowman and corporate jets.

THERE WAS A MESSAGE from Nora on the machine when Tom got back to the store. Could they meet tomorrow at eight at Rockefeller Plaza? She would be away from her phones most of the day today and tomorrow, but he could leave a message on her machine confirming or setting up a different time and place. Or reach her on her cell phone, if he preferred. She gave him the number.

Disappointed that he had missed a chance to talk with her, but not wanting to interrupt her in the middle of something by dialing her cell phone, he called her answering machine and confirmed.

It was a quiet afternoon, and in between customers he updated his on-line mail-order catalog. Except for socks and underwear, he hadn't bought any clothes since Beth died, and at four he had a sudden impulse to close early and go back into the city to look for something fresh to wear tomorrow night. He laughed at himself, remembering how Stephanie always moaned that she had nothing to wear when she got ready for a date. But he locked up the store, headed for Montague Street, and took the R train to the Rector Street station and Syms.

It was a few years since his previous shopping expedition, and he was astounded at the price tags, even with their discounts. But the tan jacket of a cotton-and-silk weave looked great, felt comfortable, and a Syms "educator" assured him it was a perfect fit. He added a pair of brown slacks, a blue and gold silk tie, and both a white and a maize oxford shirt to the pile he brought over to the cashier. As steep as it was, the total price would make hardly a dent in the advance he had collected.

He was on a high as he turned to leave with his purchases. Then he spotted the customer at the tie counter a few yards up the aisle. The man was in a sports jacket, not a navy-blue trench coat, and a crushed-brim khaki hat obscured part of his face, but there was no mistaking that he averted his gaze when Tom turned toward him.

There was also no mistaking that he looked very much like one of the customers in La Mangeoire last night.

Tom considered walking over to the guy and starting a conversation about the ties or great bargains of the past. But at that moment his cell phone went off.

It was Ilsa Grant. She was obviously trying to sound casual, but he could hear the tension that underlined her words. She needed to see him. Could they meet soon?

"I'm in the city right now," he said. "I can be at your apartment in a half hour or less."

"No, not there." He could hear traffic in the background. Either she was using a cell phone Capperrelli didn't know about or she was calling from a public phone. "There's a coffee shop on Forty-fourth, off Sixth. Can you meet me there in a few minutes? I don't have much time."

"It will take me more than a few minutes to get that far uptown. Maybe we should make it another time."

"No, now. I don't know when I can get away again."

"Okay. I'll get there as fast as I can."

As he returned the phone to his pocket, he looked back at the tie display. The man in the khaki hat was nowhere in sight.

CHAPTER 20

Tom joined the rush-hour crowd funneling through the narrow stairway down to the Rector Street station. His Metro card got temperamental, telling him to SWIPE AGAIN AT THIS TURNSTILE. It took two more swipes, during which he missed a train and infuriated the straphangers behind him awaiting access to the turnstile, the trains, and, ultimately, home and the pleasures or pressures of the weekend.

The one positive aspect of rush hour was that the subway trains ran frequently, sometimes. This was one of those times. Tom squeezed himself into the R train that pulled in almost immediately after the N he had missed. Fifteen minutes later he was joining the throng pushing out though the doors at Times Square while another pack of passengers was pushing in through them.

As he entered the coffee shop and glanced around, Tom thought he had arrived before Ilsa but then noticed the woman in a back booth, a hand raised just to her shoulder, wriggling her fingers at him. In a denim jacket, a blue beret, dark glasses, and very little makeup, Ilsa Grant was indistinguishable from most of the thirty-something New York women Tom had just been seeing on the train and in the street. In fact, she was not nearly as attractive as many of them. Marveling at the advantages of makeup, lighting, and public relations, he made his way to the table where Ilsa was nursing a cup of coffee.

"I was afraid you might not recognize me in this disguise, but I didn't want to be hounded for autographs." She nodded at the large black shopping bag he was sliding before him onto the banquette opposite her. "Shopping?"

He caught the amusement in her voice as she eyed the Syms educated consumer slogan. "Not all of us can afford Gucci's and Saks. Black coffee, please," he told the waitress who had followed him to the table. He turned back to Ilsa. "I don't think you wanted to meet me to chat about my great buys."

"Oh, I was just wondering how your investigation is coming along." She said it casually, like a line from a movie script.

"I could have told you that on the phone."

"I thought you wouldn't want to talk about it over the phone."

He wanted to tell her to cut the crap, but he wasn't a cop interviewing a reluctant witness anymore. "Maybe," he suggested, "you're the one who doesn't want to talk on the phone. Have you remembered something about that night that you want to tell me?"

"Enjoy." The waitress put down his coffee and refilled Ilsa's cup.

"Is that it?" he prompted as the waitress walked away.

"No, I—" She concentrated on stirring in some SweetN' Low. "What did Vic tell you?" She was trying to sound as if she was just making idle conversation.

"You were there. You heard what he told me."

She gave her best coquettish laugh. "Now you're playing games with me. You know I'm talking about today. I know you saw him."

"Did he tell you?"

"No, but I heard him setting up a meeting with you on the phone."

"We had lunch."

"Rabbit food, I'm sure. One of these days, maybe on Easter Sunday, he's going to wake up with big ears and a tail. What did he tell you?"

"That I should eat more carrot sticks."

Suddenly the play-acting disappeared. "Please. I really need to know. If he wanted to meet with you, it must be because he saw something that night. What did he see?"

"Are you afraid that he saw you steal the bond?"

"Of course not! I've never stolen anything in my life!"

Long experience had taught Tom that sometimes silence is the best response. He took a sip of his coffee and leaned back.

"What did he see?"

"Did you see him leave the party that night?"

"No. But if he wanted to talk to you alone, it has to be because he saw something." She reached across the table and touched his hand. Her voice turned sultry. "I promise not to tell anyone else. Just between the two of us, what did he see?"

"Why don't you tell me what he saw?"

She pulled her hand back. "How should I know?" Not all her training as an actress could hide the nervous anxiety in her laugh.

"I think you know very well what he saw. Do you want to tell me?" He wished he could read her eyes behind those damn glasses.

She leaned toward him. "Was a bond really stolen? Or did Tony Portman send you just to make trouble between us?"

"Why would Tony do a thing like that?"

"Because he's a bastard. That's why."

"A bond really was stolen. And I think you have Tony all wrong. He's not the kind of guy who would deliberately make trouble between a husband and wife."

She gave a very unladylike snort.

"Is there any reason why you would think he'd do such a thing?"

She shrugged and picked up her cup, obviously trying to get back into her casual mode. But the cup trembled a bit as she brought it to her lips for a dainty sip and then set it down again. "Look, it's nothing, really. But Tony and I had a little tiff that evening, around that time. Silly business. About how he wants me to dress for the ads."

"So you were with him, or just leaving him, when the bond was stolen, and you saw what happened."

She shook her head. "No. I didn't see anything."

"Come on. We wouldn't be here unless you saw something or someone. Was it your husband?"

"No, no! You don't understand! It's not what I saw—it's what Vic might have seen." She made a dismissive little laugh. "After Tony and I had that little squabble, I rushed back to the party and went directly into the ladies' lounge to straighten up a bit."

"Straighten up? Sounds more like a tussle than a squabble."

This time she tried for a giggle. "'Straighten up'? Did I say, 'straighten up'? I meant *freshen up*. You know what it's like on the beach. The wind was blowing. I had some sand in my hair and on my dress. I wanted to be sure that the mist from the ocean hadn't messed my makeup."

Tom nodded that he knew how it was. He let the pause drag out.

"Well?" she burst out. "For God's sake, will you please tell me! Did he see me?"

"If he did, he didn't tell me. Why haven't you asked him yourself? Surely, there's nothing strange about a woman coming in from a stroll on the beach and going into the restroom to comb her hair."

"You don't know Vic. He can find something strange in the simplest things I do. He gets something in his head, and he goes crazy with jealousy. Now he's got it in his head that there may be something between Tony and me. There's no way I can convince him otherwise." If she had started to sob, Tom would have labeled it as phony, but the slow tears that began to trickle out from under her dark glasses seemed genuine. "My fans think we're the perfect couple, but I'm not sure how long I can take it."

"There's no reason why you should take it. You're a famous actress. An independent, self-supporting woman."

"Self-supporting! Multi-supporting is more like it." She reached into a pocket for a tissue, took off her glasses, and wiped her eyes. "Do you know how many people I support? There's my agent, my financial manager and financial adviser, my publicist, my hairdresser, my secretary—" Quickly, she put her glasses back on, but Tom had already seen the bruise under her right eye that makeup couldn't cover entirely.

"The hell with them all if you're not happy."

"Easy for you to say. You've never had a taste of being on top. The future hadn't been looking too great for me after I had been turned down for a spin-off of *Sex in the City,* but then along came the offer to be spokeswoman for Portman Condos in the Clouds. That sparked some interest. A cable network is exploring the possibility of a morning show for Vic and me. That should start landing me good roles again. No way can I leave him now."

The waitress, who either had perfect timing or had waited discreetly till Ilsa had dried her tears, came over. "Anything else, folks?" When they shook their heads, she put down the check. "Have a great evening."

Tom picked up the check and fished out three dollars for a tip.

"That's pretty extravagant for two little cups of coffee," Ilsa observed.

He had read somewhere that rich people are the worst tippers. From the working class himself, he knew how hard servers worked, often for less than minimum wage, and how much they depended on tips. He preferred to err on the side of generosity. "Consider it rent for the table," he said. "She'd have made a lot more if we'd ordered a meal."

Ilsa preceded him to the cashier and waited while he paid. "Be a dear and get me a cab," she said as they walked outside.

At the curb, they eyed the long line of traffic dotted with occupied taxis. "You still haven't told me what Vic wanted to talk to you about," she reminded him.

"He thinks he knows who took the bond."

"Really? Who?"

"Can't say till I've checked it out."

They returned to their taxi watch. "There's one!" Ilsa cried out in glee, pointing way down the street to a taxi stalled in traffic, its occupant exiting in frustration.

Tom gave a shrill whistle. "By the way," he asked as the taxi started toward them, "did you see anyone when you were on your way to...freshen up that night?"

She thought a second. "On my way in, I saw the preacher guy— I can't think of his name."

"Arnold Simon. Was he on his way out?"

"No, he was near the door, talking with Senator Wayne. I think he was trying to get some money out of him. That guy gives the hard sell for his mission to everybody he meets or even passes on the street. One of these days I expect to see him in the boutique on Madison Avenue where I buy my bras."

Tom opened the taxi door and she climbed in. "Guess he was still at it when you came out of the ladies'."

She shrugged. "Probably, but it must have been with someone else. Wayne was standing there, surrounded by a bunch of other people. He called me over. I can't stand the guy, but he's got great connections. Some of his billionaire contributors may be latent Howard Hugheses, dying to produce movies. Even Wayne himself. You never know about people, do you? They're full of surprises."

"Right." Tom closed the door.

For a moment, he stood there, watching the taxi inch its way back into traffic, remembering the bruise under Ilsa's eye. *People are full of surprises,* she had said. It was a lesson he had learned early in life, as a man and as a cop. He had also learned that all too often those surprises are very nasty ones.

CHAPTER 21

TOM BEGAN to fidget as he waited for Nora Saturday evening. He felt a little foolish in his new clothes, rather like a kid on the first day of school. He watched the tourists strolling and the native New Yorkers hurrying through Rockefeller Plaza. Most men seemed to be tieless. Maybe he should have gone for a more casual look—an open collar or a turtleneck. Of course, several men were in suits, with women dressed to kill at their sides. Maybe he should have sprung for a new suit instead of the sports jacket.

And maybe he should have invested his money in a shrink instead of new clothes. He gave himself a mental shake and turned his attention to more important matters, like searching the crowd for the face of the man he had spotted at Syms yesterday. The guy was either doing a good job of staying out of sight or he wasn't around tonight.

A touch on his shoulder make him whirl round.

Nora stepped back. "Hi," she said, smiling apologetically. "Sorry. I didn't mean to startle you."

"Just my New York City street nerves taking over for a moment. You're early."

She laughed. "And you're even earlier."

"That's because I had a lot to look forward to. What's your excuse?"

Her eyes never left his. "The same. And it's not an excuse."

He had been hoping she would say something like that.

"I probably should have picked a meeting place closer to Brooklyn," she said, "but this is the first landmark that came to mind, and we can get anywhere from here. Besides, I have to admit that it has always been a favorite spot of mine. It's so New York, with its mixture of expensive shops, elegant fountains and plants, and that marvelous statue of Prometheus overlooking the restaurant. When the Japanese owned Rockefeller Center in the Nineties, I was afraid I'd wake up one day to find it radically changed."

"You mean, mini rock gardens substituted for the exotic plants and a gigantic samurai exchanged for Prometheus?"

She looked down on the statue that for more than half a century had stared blindly at the wilting tourists who spent high sums for the dubious pleasure of dining before him al fresco in the hot, humid New York summers, and at the colorful ice skaters who, in the cold, damp winters, glided past him like exotic fishes slipping round and round an enormous bowl. "That last might have been an improvement. But I'd have missed the old boy. You know, when I was a little girl, I thought that was not fire but a bunch of bananas he held in his hand."

"Not such a bad guess when you consider that he's overlooking a fancy restaurant in spring and summer. When I was a kid, I recognized that he was holding fire, but I thought it was to light the chef's barbecue."

"Speaking of barbeque, where and what would you like to eat?"

"If you're not starving, why don't we discuss it over a drink? Rubbing shoulders with all these tourists has brought out the New York chauvinist in me. Let's go across the street to the Rainbow Room, where we can look out over the city lights." The idea had just occurred to him, but he thought it was a good one.

She did too. Her face lit up as she said, "That sounds like fun! I haven't been there in ages."

They headed for the NBC building, where they took a crowded elevator to the sixty-sixth floor. The conversations around them were in German, French, and Japanese, and in English softened by Southern accents or Midwestern twangs.

"This might not have been such a good idea," Tom whispered. "There may be a long wait."

"Not to worry," Nora assured him. "I'll bet that most of these people, especially the ones from abroad, are big spenders and here for dinner."

She was right. Except for one party of three, all the others had dinner reservations and where whisked away. Within five minutes, Tom and Nora were led to a little marble table near a window that overlooked the lights of Manhattan, straight out to the East River, with its magnificent bridges. "Oh, ye of little faith!" she said as she seated herself on the chair the maître d' held out for her.

This time she ordered a gin and tonic. Tom asked for J&B on the rocks.

"So tell me," she said when their drinks were served, her eyes sparkling mischievously in the candlelight, "did you really think Prometheus was holding fire for a barbecue when you were a little boy?"

"Actually, no," he admitted. "But I was at a loss about the symbolism. I thought the guy was a lunatic to hold fire in his hand."

"You weren't far from wrong. Considering the price he had to pay, he was a lunatic to give it to mankind, wasn't he?"

"Mankind has paid a price too. Forever after, we've been able to see the faces of the monsters that lurk in all the dark and scary corners of our world."

"But we created most of those monsters, and isn't identifying them the first step toward conquering them?"

"I wish that were so, but so far in our sad and shameful history it hasn't been. The front pages of our newspapers bear witness to that every day. So do some of your documentaries."

"Don't blame the messenger. There's something to be said for putting a spotlight on our problems and our villains. It sometimes leads to a cure."

"You're much too idealistic. It doesn't happen nearly often enough."

She gave a little shrug of agreement. "Notoriety or punishment for the villains, then."

"Again, not often enough."

"Well, we can't win them all," she conceded with a smile, "but even you will have to admit that in the few cases where it does happen, it's delicious."

He laughed. "Ah, what have we here? A bloodthirsty idealist."

She laughed too, but she shook her head as she reached for her drink. "I'm afraid you're only half right."

He could have kicked himself. "Hey," he said softly, reaching across the little table to touch her hand. "I was only kidding. I didn't mean to offend you. I really admire your work, and the high purpose behind it."

Her eyes met his, and they held surprise and perhaps pleasure at the intensity of his apology. She turned her hand over and curled her fingers around his, squeezing gently. "Don't look so sad and guilty. No offense taken," she assured him. "Haven't you heard that we journalists are a thick-skinned bunch?"

She looked so beautiful, her eyes shining, her face glowing in the soft candlelight. And her hand felt so warm and good beneath his. It was a moment before he found his voice. He made an effort to keep it light. "I'll have to keep that in mind. Still, under all that professionalism of yours, I can sense a lot of the idealist and even catch a glimpse of the little girl who thought Prometheus was a glorified grocer."

Embarrassed by the compliment, she laughed and withdrew her hand. "I'm afraid that little girl faded fast once she was exposed to the harsh lifework of a journalist."

"I don't believe that for a minute." Deprived of her brief touch, his hand felt oddly cold and awkward.

"Oh?" There was a teasing challenge in her voice. "And what about the little boy who worried about a statue's burned hand? Is he still as wide-eyed somewhere inside you?"

No, he had faded fast too, exposed to the harsh lifework of a cop. Tom sighed. "I see your point. I'll have to admit that I miss him sometimes, though."

"Me too. There was a poem I read in school when I was a kid. Sometimes it comes back to haunt me. It's about childhood memories, and the poet ends it describing the trees in his backyard and how tall they were, so tall that he used to think their tops rested against the sky. 'It was a childish ignorance,' he wrote, 'But now 'tis little joy—'"

The lines awakened warm memories of long-ago English classes back in Cunningham Junior High School. "'To know I'm farther off from heav'n/ Than when I was a boy,'" Tom finished with her.

"You know it too!"

"Required reading back in Mrs. Griffin's Honors English class. Along with Keats and Shelley and Byron and Shakespeare—to name a few. It's stuck with me too. Thomas Hood had the common touch. He was able, as the kids say today, to hit you where you live."

"You even remember his name." She sighed. "I think my daughter went all the way through school here in New York, and they were good schools too, without reading a single poem. And she still hasn't been exposed to poetry, even in college. I think it's an elective there, an elective that most kids avoid like the plague."

"Stephanie's in the same boat. No doubt she and her friends think rap is what poetry's all about. I have to admit that it has been a long time since I've read a book of poetry, though. How about you? When was the last time you checked one out of the library?"

"Touché. But tonight when I get home, I'll turn over a new leaf—both figuratively and literally. I'll dust off my old college anthology and plunge in. And the next time Leslie comes home, I'll offer to lend it to her."

"Do you think she'll take you up on it?"

"Sure. Right after she finishes teaching your daughter the minuet."

Both were in the mood for Italian food, and they took a taxi down to Bellavitae in Greenwich Village. The maître d' greeted Nora with the warmth merited by a familiar patron, and showed them to a cozy table near a wall lined with jars and flasks of presumably exotic olive oils and vinegars. "This is my home turf," she confided as they perused their menus. "I live only a few blocks away. There are lots of great restaurants around, but this is so rustic and homey that it's one of my favorites. I come here when I want to spoil myself. We'll have to come back in the summer when, on fine days, they open the doors so you can eat and watch the world pass by, like on the Via Veneto. It's a treat."

To Tom the treat was her casual reference to their seeing each other in the future, long after their projects would be wrapped up. He became so engrossed in that pleasant thought that, though he asked her for her recommendations, he hardly heard her glowing descriptions of the appetizers and entrées.

When their waiter reappeared, Tom followed Nora's lead and ordered the Crostini Poverella to start, followed by the salmon special. It was an excellent choice, as was the bottle of Brunello she chose to go with it.

Perhaps it was the delicious food. Perhaps it was the good wine. But by the end of the meal, Tom found he had relaxed and opened up with Nora more than with anyone since Beth had slipped from his life. He said nothing, of course, about his years as a cop, but by the time they had been presented with their bill, he had shared memories of his childhood and college years in Brooklyn, his work in the store, his life with Beth and Stephanie and Max.

Though Nora had made it clear that the Golden Guys would be paying, Tom still felt awkward about letting her pick up the tab. He didn't know the rules of the new world order for men and women, and he felt like a fish out of water. The evening had really been a social one and he felt obliged to point out that they hadn't once discussed their Golden Guy projects.

"Yes, I know." She looked up from the credit-card slip, a wicked twinkle in her eyes. "Isn't that delightful?"

Out on the street they discovered that the temperature had dropped considerably since they entered the restaurant. They both turned up their collars against the chill.

"What train do you usually take?" Nora asked.

"The four or the five," Tom told her, "but I'll see you home first."

"Thanks, but there's no need. I live only a few blocks from here, and I always walk it. The streets in this neighborhood are alive with people at night. Especially on weekends."

"Yes, but what kind of people?" Tom nodded toward the couple who had just passed—a tattooed young woman with purple hair and her leather-and-steel-clad companion.

Nora laughed. "Weird maybe, but harmless. Really, there's no danger. I'll be fine. I can take care of myself." Her voice was gentle but firm.

"I know you can, but humor me. I'll feel a lot better if you'll let me walk with you."

"All right. You really are old-fashioned, aren't you?"

"So my daughter keeps telling me."

With a smile and a shake of her head, she turned and steered their steps toward University Place. Whether it was to protect them from the chill or to keep Tom from holding one of them, she tucked her hands into her pockets. He did the same with his own, relieved that the decision, if not the temptation, had been averted.

As they walked, they talked animatedly about their daughters—the joy they took in the girls, the girls' dreams and aspirations, and their own dreams and hopes for them. By the time Nora paused before a brownstone on East Thirteenth Street between Fifth Avenue and University Place, another warm bond had been forged between them.

"Here we are," she said, "safe and sound."

"So we are," Tom agreed. She looked beautiful in the pool of light from the street lamp. "Thanks for humoring me. And thanks for spending the evening with me. I really enjoyed it."

"So did I." She regarded him seriously for a moment, as though weighing something in her mind. Then she seemed to come to a decision. "Would you like to come up for a cup of coffee? I have a folder with some notes I keep when I'm working on a project. They're sketchy and pretty general, but you can look them over. If nothing else, it will put the seal of legitimacy on our tab."

"Thanks. I'd like that."

He followed her up the stoop and into an ornate, high-ceilinged vestibule that was lit by a crystal chandelier and dominated by an elegant, curved mahogany staircase.

"This is a very impressive place," he said.

"Yes, isn't it? It has a rather morbid history, though. When I rented my apartment, the journalist in me couldn't resist digging it out. The house was built by Alexander Humphrey, a nineteenth-century New England merchant who amassed a fortune in making, of all things, candlewicks and candle snuffers. He set up Miranda Taylor, his New York mistress, here, probably so he wouldn't be lonely on business trips." They started up the carpeted stairs. "It seems, however, that *she* liked to give balls to stave off her own loneliness while *he* was away."

"Good for her."

"Not really. On a surprise visit, Alexander found her in the arms of one of her handsome party guests, and they weren't dancing a waltz. The other man was kicked down the stairs and was lucky to get out of the building alive. Miranda, according to Humphrey, was so filled with remorse that she shot herself through the heart with his dueling pistol, an heirloom that had once belonged to Alexander Hamilton, a distant relative for whom our guy was named." Nora inserted a key into the lock of a door on the second landing.

"Sounds fishy to me," Tom observed.

"And probably to all the upright gentlemen on the coroner's jury too. But, gentlemen to the last, they protected their own and ruled the death a suicide. I'm sure they never questioned the rightness of their verdict. Women were considered expendable back then, and death was thought to be just punishment for those who strayed. Unfortunately, it still is in too many parts of the world today. Even for women who are raped. As for Humphrey, those men on the jury were probably grateful to him for giving them a legal precedent they could use to keep their own mistresses in line." She had opened two locks and now slipped a key into the third.

"I suppose some kind of justice was meted out somewhere along the line. If he made his fortune in candlewicks, no doubt he lost it there too when society moved on to better lighting technology," Tom said.

"Unfortunately, that didn't happen until after old Alexander had gone to a fat and comfortable death. Making kids suffer for the sins of their fathers has always seemed to me to be rather sadistic and unfair. But—who knows? — maybe Alexander made his own hell and carried it inside him. Let's hope so, anyway."

She thrust open the door with a little flourish. "Whatever one thinks of the man, he certainly knew how to pick architects. And, of course, so did a subsequent owner who had the building redesigned into apartments. Voilà."

They had entered a foyer that led into large living room with a high ceiling and a huge window that overlooked one of those delightful city surprises, an enclosed courtyard garden. Plants, obviously well loved and nurtured, flourished on the windowsill and on the glass table with shelves set before it. Tall bookcases lined two walls, and the rest of the furnishings were an eclectic mixture of modern and antique, tastefully chosen with an eye toward warmth and comfort. On the walls not occupied by bookcases hung framed prints, a mixture of Impressionist and early Chinese art. Delicate Chinese vases and dishes were displayed between some of the books and on the tables in the room.

"Make yourself comfortable," Nora said as she hung up their coats. She then went off into an adjoining room, and returned with a manila folder. She laughed when she saw him examining the contents of one of her bookcases.

"Busman's holiday?"

"You've got quite a collection here. I like the variety. By the way, if you're ever interested in selling this first edition of *Some Tame Gazelle,* I'd like to make you an offer."

"Not on your life. That's one of my special treasures. I picked it up for a quarter at a church sale some years ago. Are you a Barbara Pym fan too?"

"She's one of my favorites, even though the men in her books are always unworthy of the excellent women who love them. But I guess most of us are." He slipped the volume back on the shelf.

"What I love about her books is that there seems to be no problem in life that can't be made a little bit better by a good, strong cup of tea. Speaking of which...." She handed him the folder. "I'll make some coffee. Unless you'd rather have something else."

"How about tea—in honor of Barbara?"

She looked rather pleased. "Good idea. I'll be back in a minute."

Tom sat down on the sofa and looked through the folder she had given him. She was right. Aside from her shooting schedule, which had no bearing on his investigation, the short biographical notes added nothing to what he already knew about Tony Portman and his friends.

In a few minutes Nora was back, carrying a tray laden with cups, saucers, sugar bowl, pitcher, a plate of cookies, and a teapot. "I thought we should do it up right—in honor of Ms. Pym."

Having set down her tray on the cocktail table in front of the sofa, she sat down and began to pour. "I hope you like your tea strong. In this house, there's none of that namby-pamby stuff we Americans try to pass off as tea. This is Taylors and Harrogate's Darjeeling—the real thing."

"I can take it," he assured her. He took the cup and raised it toward the bookcase. "To the immortal Ms. Pym."

"Hear, hear." She took a sip from her cup, then nodded toward the folder. "Anything helpful?"

"Not really. I have higher hopes for what you have in your office. I'll get there sometime this coming week. I see you have more shots scheduled with Lyle Wayne."

She made a face. "He's coming back to town the week after next to make some speeches. Denise is going to love that."

"I take it she's not a big fan."

"Neither am I, but I've lived longer, and have seen his kind of politician come and go. They're dangerous when they come, and they leave a lot of damage behind when they go. But the good news is that eventually they all do go, and the country survives them. Denise is too young and idealistic to realize that."

"It may be more realism than idealism," Tom suggested. "Do you really think that, once in absolute control of the government, they'll go gentle into the night?"

"Who knows what can happen in the next election? Bush and Cheney now need Wayne to be a spokesman for their policies in the Senate, but do you really think they're going to let him waltz off with the nomination? I'm sure George, not to mention his parents, wants to pass the crown to brother Jeb. And then there's John McCain and all those ultra-religious guys who predict the end of the planet if they're not nominated and elected the next time round. But those guys are going to self-destruct in the primaries."

"Sounds to me like you're the idealist, not Denise."

"We're talking labels here. I doubt that there's a single label that would fit you or me or Denise. Maybe it's her youth, but she does have a harder time stomaching these so-called 'golden' guys than I do. Wayne in particular. Of course the fact that she's African-American and so much of his verbiage is covert if not overt prejudice doesn't help. Sometimes I'm afraid she's going to throw the camcorder at him when he uses one of his insidious buzz words that the morons in his base love."

"Maybe your equipment would be safer if you hired a different assistant for this project."

She laughed. "I was indulging in hyperbole. I never have to worry about Denise's behavior. On the job, she's always a total professional. TV journalism could use a lot more like her."

"How long has she been with you?"

"Seven years, if you count the summer internships she put in while she was in college. We've grown very close—she's like a second daughter. In fact, she and Leslie are close friends, and we all spend a lot of time together. It's nice. Sid and I had wanted a bigger family, but it just never happened. Now I've accomplished it the easy way. How does your Stephanie feel about being an only child?"

"A little lonely sometimes, I think, but she's never really said anything to me. Beth and I had wanted more children too. There were four miscarriages after Stephanie was born."

"I'm sorry." Nora's voice was soft. "That must have been very hard on Beth."

Tom nodded, old, hurtful memories suddenly rushing back. He looked away from the compassion he saw on Nora's face, and, determined to change the subject to something less personal, spoke about the first thing his eyes came to rest on—a Chinese watercolor of cats sleeping in a garden. "I see you're a Sinophile," he said lightly.

"Ancient China was Sid's passion. Of course, he got me interested in it too. It's a fascinating civilization and culture. So rich and beautiful, and at the same time so dark and cruel. We visited many times, and not long before he died, we spent a couple of years there filming a documentary. For him, that documentary was the fulfillment of a lifelong dream." Her eyes misted. "You have no idea how much it means to me that we were able to complete it."

Beth had always wanted to see England, but the year of the trip was the year she became so ill, and they wound up having to cancel it. So much for trying to change the subject to something less personal.

"I think I have a very good idea how much it means," he said, his voice husky. He put down his cup, but shook his head when Nora extended the teapot. "I really should be going. It's almost midnight."

Their eyes held for a moment, and Nora seemed to be on the verge of saying something. Tom thought she might be going to protest that it wasn't all that late. But she didn't. With a smile and a nod, she put the teapot back on the tray.

"Is tomorrow a workday for you?" she asked at the door.

"Weekends are our busiest time, especially now, the beginning of fall with the opening of schools and colleges. Then we go into the holiday season. I have extra help on weekends, though, so some Sundays I take off. On others, I come in late and leave early. It gives me a little time to unwind."

"I'm planning to do a little unwinding myself tomorrow," she said. "For once, Denise and I don't have a Sunday shoot scheduled or have to use the day for traveling to get to a Monday location. In a neighborhood newsletter I saw a mention of a kite-flying competition in Central Park tomorrow. It sounded like fun, and I thought I'd take it in. Would you like to join me?"

"Do I have to bring a kite?"

"Not unless you're dying to fly one. I intend to relax on the grass and be a spectator."

He laughed. "What a relief. That's more my speed too."

They agreed to meet at one o'clock near the entrance at Fifth Avenue and Seventy-ninth Street.

"Till then," Nora said.

She was standing close to him, one hand on the doorknob, her eyes meeting his in a clear, warm gaze. He could easily have reached out and touched her...kissed her. And he wanted to. For the first time since he had last held Beth in his arms, he wanted to hold another woman. The temptation was so strong it turned into a physical pain. Yet, unsure how she would react, and even of how he himself would react, he held back.

And then the moment passed. With a smile, she turned her attention to unlocking and opening the door.

"See you tomorrow," he said as he left.

"Tomorrow," she repeated softly, and closed the door behind him.

Down in the street, he turned up his collar against the sudden chill, but it was an automatic, not a necessary, reaction. Wrapped in the echo and warm promise of that *tomorrow,* he headed home, forgetting to look behind him.

CHAPTER 22

DESPITE HIS not arriving home till nearly one a.m., Tom awoke at eight-thirty the next morning to the sounds of Max trying to be quiet as he had a quick cup of coffee before leaving to buy the Sunday papers. He lay in bed awhile, warmed by the memories of last night and the pleasant anticipation of the day to come. It had been a long time since waking up had felt so good.

By the time Tom had showered, shaved, and dressed, Max still had not returned, which was unusual. Tom set the table and poured a cup of coffee for himself. He had almost finished drinking it, and Stephanie had emerged sleepy-eyed from her room, when there was the sound of Max's key in the lock. He came in with a plastic shopping bag and the newspapers, his cheeks a little rosier than usual.

"Is everything okay?" Tom asked, relieving him of the shopping bag, which he handed to Stephanie.

"Sure. What shouldn't be okay?"

Tom shrugged. "Nothing. It's just that you were gone a little longer than usual."

"Oh, that." Max hung up his jacket. "I ran into Gloria yesterday and she told me that she'd hurt her ankle, so I volunteered to pick up her *Times* this morning. When I dropped it off, she insisted I stay for a cup of coffee. Naturally, I didn't want to hurt her feelings."

"Of course not, Grandpa." Stephanie and Tom exchanged a smile.

"So how was her coffee?" Tom asked.

"Not as good as mine, but a lot better than yours, and it's

time to change the subject." Max handed Stephanie the comics and feature section from *Newsday,* gave Tom the news section of the *Times,* and took its magazine section for himself. While Tom poured the coffee, Stephanie placed the rolls, muffins and doughnuts from the bakery on a serving platter.

"Grandpa, I think they made a mistake," Stephanie said. "There are only two jelly doughnuts."

"No mistake," Max said casually, sitting down. "I gave mine to Gloria. I thought it would cheer her up." He opened the magazine and studied the table of contents. "No cracks, please."

"Grandpa! Who'd make a crack about a nice gesture like that? I'm sure it really did cheer up Mrs. Alexander. Jelly doughnuts always make me feel good. You can have half of mine."

Max looked up and smiled. "Thanks, but there's no need. It's time I cut down on the calories, anyway."

Gertrude wandered out and sat down, looking at Max expectantly. "Sorry, kid. Not this week," Max told her. Not taking his word for it, she leaped up on a kitchen counter for a better view of the table. Then, satisfied that lox was not being served behind her back, she jumped down and returned to Stephanie's room for her midmorning snooze.

The three at the table ate and read in silence, but Tom was aware of the glances Max and Stephanie were sending his way. Ignoring them, he kept his eyes, if not his mind, on the newspaper in front of him.

Finally, Max cleared his throat and asked, supercasually, "So, how did it go last night?"

Tom looked up to find two pairs of eyes glued to him. "Last night?" he asked, as though he had no idea what Max was talking about.

"New jacket, new tie, new pants—*that* last night."

"Oh, right. We had a very nice time." He returned to his newspaper.

"Come on, Dad!" Stephanie said, exasperated. "Where did you *go?* What did you *do?*"

"Isn't that what you call the third degree when you get it from your grandfather and me?"

"That's different."

"Oh, I see. Well, in that case.... We had a drink in the Rainbow Room, and then we went down to the Village and had dinner at an Italian place."

Stephanie and Max exchanged a look.

"And *that* took until one o'clock in the morning?" Stephanie asked.

"Who said it was one o'clock in the morning?" Tom asked, trying for Stephanie's wide-eyed look. "I thought you both were sound asleep when I came in."

"We were," Max assured him. "Gertrude told us."

"The little snitch."

"She was just doing her job," Stephanie pointed out. "Anyway, what matters is did you have fun?"

"Yes, we did have fun. In fact, I'm seeing her again today. We're going to watch a kite-flying contest in Central Park."

"Hot."

Max teased, "The Rainbow Room one day, kite flying the next. Sounds serious to me."

"Oh, I don't know." Tom reached for his doughnut on the pastry plate. "I haven't sacrificed a jelly doughnut yet."

Later, following Stephanie's suggestion, Tom stopped off at a deli and had a lunch packed—corned beef and pastrami on rye, pickles, coleslaw, and a bag of potato chips.

It was a beautiful day, with just a teasing bite of early fall in the air. The breeze was gentle yet determined and promised to give the kites all the support they would need to soar high and far. Tom's spirits were soaring too as he left the subway and headed for the park.

Wearing jeans, a denim jacket, and a pair of beat-up Reeboks, Nora was seated on a bench outside the entrance. She was so absorbed in the book-review section of the *Times* that she was unaware of Tom's approach.

"Hi," he said. "Have you been waiting long?"

"Ages and ages," she informed him with a smile. "I was determined to be here before you this time." She slipped the magazine into her oversized shoulder bag, stood up, and took a deep breath. "It's such a nice day even the New York air smells good. I hope you're ready for a hike. Before I left this morning, I found the flyer and discovered that I was wrong about the location. It's almost a mile from here. Sorry."

"I'm not. It's a great day for walking. Besides, I brought us some lunch, so we can work up an appetite."

They started off across the park, falling into an easy gait and easy conversation. A rainy summer had provided the trees with lush leaves that were now turning red and gold, and the grass beneath their feet was still thick and green. All around them New Yorkers were enjoying their slice of country in the city. Some were sprawled on the ground, engrossed in the Sunday papers; others were walking hand in hand. Children were running, shouting, playing. Dogs were chasing balls and sticks.

They turned off onto a main path, and, beyond a rise in the distance, the sky became a mass of dancing, jumping colors, as if a convention of odd-shaped tropical flying creatures was about to be called to order.

Nora stopped short. "Oh, will you look at that!" she exclaimed, catching her breath. She reached into her satchel, pulled out a camera, and took a photograph. "Busman's holiday," she said. "I hope you don't mind."

"Not at all. I'm sorry I didn't think to bring mine."

"I'll e-mail you the best ones," she promised, and put the camera to her eye for another shot.

In a few minutes they were in the midst of the kite fliers, who were as diverse and as colorful as the shapes and tails at the other end of their strings. Nora's face lit up. "This is a photographer's heaven," she said. "Would you mind very much if I concentrate on pictures rather than conversation as we wander through the crowd?"

"No problem. Let me have the book review, and I'll make myself comfortable over there." He indicated an oak tree.

"Sure you don't mind?"

"Just come back when you get hungry. Do you want me to hold your bag for you?"

She hesitated a moment, then handed it over. "Thanks."

"Now I know you'll come back," he said.

She gave him a slow smile, then headed into the crowd. The thought of that smile warmed him as he strolled over to the oak. It had told him that he didn't need her purse to ensure her return.

About an hour later, when he was halfway through a review of the latest revelation of corporate fraud, a shadow fell over the page and he looked up to see Nora smiling down on him. She plopped down beside him and leaned back against the tree. "What culinary wonders do you have in that mysterious bag?"

"Corned beef and pastrami. I hope you like deli."

"Are you kidding? I'd be chased out of New York if I didn't." She reached for one of the sandwiches and bit into it with great relish. "Um." She half closed her eyes. "Delicious. I must have died and gone to pastrami heaven."

"The doctors insist that's exactly what will happen to us if we eat too much of this stuff."

"Ah, but what a way to go." She glanced at the page he was reading. "I read that review before you came. Sounds like a fascinating book, but it hardly scratches the surface of what Denise's research has turned up about the Golden Guys alone. Lyle Wayne pushed through legislation that gave them license for corporate rape and pillage, and of course his friends Bob Michaelson and Nick Hammond saw to it that he got a big piece of the pie they were cutting up. Now he, they, and Tony Portman are making out like bandits while less well-connected guys like Bernie Evers are taking the fall and going to jail." She brushed some crumbs from her lap. "I suppose we shouldn't be surprised that they've walked away unscathed by the scandals and are cleaning up in legal and consulting fees, buying up the shells of companies left behind and reorganizing them for Beta bucks. And that pun was definitely intended. If these guys fell into a sewer, they would come up with the lost chord, which they would then sell for a million pounds to the organist at St. Paul's Cathedral in London. They're untouchable."

Tom knew otherwise, but, of course, couldn't say so. He recalled what Vittorio Capperrelli had said about Arnold Simon arguing with Portman at Montauk and later following him outside, and now saw a chance to check out the story.

"There's always Arnold Simon," he said. "He seems to be the self-appointed conscience of the group. I'm sure he's taken them to task for all their excesses."

"Fat lot of good it seems to have done."

"You never can tell. Someone mentioned seeing Simon really coming down on Portman at the Montauk shindig. Maybe it was about some of his corporate slight of hand. Were you near enough to take it in?"

"No. And I seriously doubt that it actually happened. I can't imagine Arnold delivering a public scolding. It's not his style to embarrass people in front of others. Though, of course, he wouldn't neglect a gentle reprimand if he had someone off to himself. Maybe that's what the person you spoke to saw."

"Could be. Did Simon mention it to you when you spoke with him that evening?"

"Actually, I can't recall talking with him at all that night, except to say hello and to get him in a couple of shots with some of the other men."

So much for Capperrelli's story, Tom thought. The ball was back in the macho Italian's court now. Ominously so.

"Why?" Nora asked.

"Why what?"

"Why the interest in what Arnold Simon said or didn't say?"

"It's not so much an interest in what he said as it is in what makes these guys tick. I've never been around so many men like them at one time. They're a mystery to me."

"They're a mystery to everyone who's decent, but they're really not so hard to figure out. It's never occurred to them that it was by a simple accident of birth that they were born to wealth and privilege. They figure they're a special class and they deserve it, and they conduct their lives accordingly." She reached for a can of soda and popped it open. "How did you know that I like cream soda with deli?"

"Because you told me Sid was Jewish. We Jews know that there's only one right way to wash down deli—with cream soda. I figured Sid would have shared such important information with you."

She laughed. "Along with his mother's secret for making fluffy matzo balls."

"Which is...?"

"A secret. My lips are sealed forever. Though, if you're very good, I may make them for you someday."

"It won't be easy, but I'll try."

After sharing their crumbs with the pigeons that had been waiting impatiently, they disposed of their trash and set out across the park. They paused to listen to a flutist playing Vivaldi and a guitarist singing a medley of Beatles songs. Nora snapped a few photos, capturing the performances forever on camera, giving the entertainers a touch of the immortality they had not yet and perhaps never would achieve on stage.

At Bethesda Fountain, Tom relaxed while Nora took candid shots of parents and children sailing toy boats, playing, and feeding the birds and squirrels. He sat on a bench, enjoying the late-afternoon sun, his legs stretched out before him. Idly, his eyes wandered from Nora to her subjects to the other Sunday strollers and occupants of nearby benches.

His gaze came to a sudden stop at a bench on the other side of the fountain. A man in chinos and a Mets jacket and cap sat there casually reading a tabloid. The cap and the newspaper obscured his face, as they were intended to do, but there was no escaping the trained eye of an ex-cop. It was the same guy he had spotted in the restaurant and in Syms.

The hair on the back of Tom's neck bristled. His first impulse was rush the guy and make him reveal the name and motive of his employer. That, of course, was impossible right now. How could he explain it to Nora?

He wished he had his gun with him. He hated the weapon, and its purpose, and had been glad when he retired from the force to be rid of the obligation to carry it at all times. He kept it locked in the safe at the store.

A waste bin stood near the bench where the guy in the Mets cap sat, still reading though he had yet to turn a page. Tom wandered over to it, tossed in a tissue, and remained there a little longer, gazing at the fountain. Then, in a sudden but smooth move, he turned, took two quick steps, and sat down beside the man, who was burly, but he'd taken on bigger guys. Obviously taken by surprise, the guy started to shift to his right. Tom closed the gap and grabbed his arm.

"Don't even think of getting up. You've been following me. Why?"

The guy shook his head as if he had never heard of anything so fantastic. "I don't know what you're talking about. I've never seen you before in my life. I'm here in the park enjoying the last of the good weather, like everybody else."

"Sure, you are. And you were in the bookstore on Fifth Avenue when I was there, browsing, just like everybody else. And in La Mangeoire when I was there, eating, just like everybody else. And in Syms when I was there, shopping, just like everybody else. And those are the places where I've actually seen you. I won't bother with the places and times I've been aware of your presence. Who's paying you?"

"I told you. I don't know what you're talking about. You can't be a cop."

"Nowadays, there are all sorts of cops. More than you know. Slowly, so I can see where your hand is and what it's doing at all times, take out your wallet."

When the man hesitated, Tom tightened his grip. "I have a gun with me, and I wouldn't be asked a lot of questions if I used it." He lifted his hand. "Take out your wallet, open it and hand it to me. Smile, like you're about to show me pictures of your adorable kids. Now."

Smiling too, Tom took the wallet, which the man had opened to some family photos, and flipped back to the identification cards. The guy's name was Richard Fulton, he lived in Lindenhurst on Long Island, and his blood type was A positive. He was allergic to penicillin. The credit cards in the wallet bore the same name. There was no work ID card.

"You're a long way from home, just to get a little fresh air. I'd have thought the air was a lot fresher out on the Island."

Fulton shrugged. "I grew up in the Bronx. I like city air. In fact, I thrive on it. Which accounts for why you may have seen me around before."

"Right." Tom closed the wallet but held on to it. "What other ID do you have with you?"

"None."

It was probably a lie, but Tom couldn't conduct a body search in public. "Not even your Denning and Pankhurst ID?" The slight flicker of Fulton's eyes told him he was right.

"Who are Denning and Pankhurst?" Fulton tried for a tone of innocent bewilderment. He was a lousy actor, a bad flaw in a detective, public or private.

"The founders of the worldwide detective agency you work for. Your memory seems to be as poor as your tailing ability, so I doubt that you'll be with the company much longer." Tom handed him back his wallet. "Now get on your cell phone and tell your bosses to inform their client that the cover has been blown. No more tails. No more spying. Tell them I don't intend to chat with the next guy I spot. I'm an ex-cop with a lot of friends on the force. I can shoot first, and you can be sure that I'll be asked very few questions later."

Fulton made a point of not hurrying away, but he didn't look back, either.

Tom watched his retreat. Tomorrow, he would call Joe Henley and have him check out his hunch, just to be sure. It was becoming more and more obvious that he had put himself in the middle of a very dangerous game.

"Friend of yours?"

He had been so lost in thought that he hadn't noticed Nora's return. He gave a nonchalant shrug. "Not really. Former customer. He lives out on the Island now." He didn't like having to lie, so he changed the subject. "Do you have enough pictures for a coffee-table book yet?"

She smiled as she considered the possibility. "*Sunday in Central Park*. Not a bad idea. How many copies can the publisher put your shop down for?"

"At least a dozen. More if the author promises an autographing session."

"Sounds like a good deal." She sat down beside him and stretched out her legs. "So, what would you like to do next? It's your turn to choose a point of interest."

"It's almost five. The sun will be gone soon. We should start making our way out of the park. Would you like to see a movie?"

"There's nothing that I'm itching to see. The reviews I've read lately make everything sound either too stupid or too violent for my taste. Or a combination of both."

"I know what you mean. Okay, so a movie's out, the museums

are closing, and it will soon be evening. That doesn't leave us a lot of options. Are you hungry yet? We could go someplace for an early supper." He didn't really like that idea. He wasn't ready for the day to wind down and end.

She pursed her lips, thinking about it.

"How about South Street Seaport?" he suggested. "We could walk around there for a while, then find somewhere to eat."

"South Street Seaport?" She laughed and patted her camera. "You really are a glutton for punishment. My feet are telling me we've done enough hiking for one day. How about going back to my place? We can relax for a while, and when we get hungry we can go out for a pizza or I can fix us some eggs."

"Sounds good to me," he said. Actually, it sounded great to him.

"MAKE YOURSELF COMFORTABLE," Nora said as she hung up their jackets. "I'll be back in a minute." She disappeared down the hall, and Tom sat down on the sofa and started to glance through her copy of *The Village Voice*.

Minutes later Nora was back, her hair combed, her face bright. "If you'd like to freshen up," she said, "it's the second door on the left."

When Tom returned to the living room, Mozart's Clarinet Concerto was playing on the stereo and a bottle of chardonnay and two wineglasses were on the coffee table. Nora filled the glasses and handed one to him.

"Cheers," They said, touched glasses and drank.

They sat down on the sofa, and Nora removed her shoes and curled up her legs. "That was a very nice afternoon," she said with a sigh of contentment.

"I enjoyed it too. Those kites were quite a sight. I don't think I've ever seen so many at one time."

"Sorry I left you on your own so much. Next time I promise to leave my camera home."

"No need. That would probably be like leaving your right arm behind. The world is full of photo opportunities. I understand."

She studied his face a moment. "You really do mean that, don't you? You're a very nice guy, do you know that?"

"It's easy to be a nice guy around you." He thought he would get lost in her eyes. His heart began to pound, and the temptation to pull her close was so strong he could almost taste her lips. What was holding him back? Memories?

"I think you really mean that too." She moved a little closer and reached up to touch his cheek.

He moved his own hand up and covered hers. Her gaze never wavered from his.

And then there was nothing holding him back.

Slowly, so slowly it seemed to take an eternity of delicious anticipation, he brought his lips to meet hers. The kiss was whisper-soft at first, tasting, testing. Then her arms crept up around his neck, and he pulled her close, closer, closer still. So close he could feel the exquisite softness of her breasts pressing against his chest. His heart was racing, his head spinning. He wanted to hold her this way forever, lost in a kiss that knew no past, no future, only this moment.

But, of course, it had to end. As if by a prearranged signal, they began to ease their lips away.

Nora leaned back a little, one hand on his shoulder, the other warm and lingering on the back of his neck. "Where did a nice guy like you learn to kiss like that?" Her voice was even huskier than usual.

"Must be that you bring out the best in me."

And then he pulled her close again, and they were lost in another kiss. And another....

Tom wasn't quite sure how it happened. Had he eased Nora down on the sofa, or had she pulled him down? But soon he became conscious that they were reclining, her head on the sofa arm, one leg curled under her, the other on the floor. His right arm was jammed between the sofa back and her side, and his left knee was pressing against the rug.

Nora burst into laughter. "I think we just turned into a human pretzel." She ran her hand through his hair. "I don't know about you, but I know that if I continue this way, I'll never be able to walk in the morning. There's a big, comfortable bed in the other room. Why don't we make the most of it?"

With a mixture of concentration and laughter, they managed

to extricate themselves and get to their feet. Then Nora took his hand and led him into her bedroom.

Half of the large, airy room had been converted into a study. Against the far wall was a bookcase crammed with books, and near it stood a worktable that was strewn with camera equipment, film, photos, and slides. Against the opposite wall was a desk on which a computer was set up amid what looked like neatly disorganized piles of notes and charts. Closer to the door was the bedroom furniture—bed, night tables, bureau, and dresser—all crafted of cherry wood in a warm and welcoming Queen Anne style. On both night tables, above piles of books and magazines, stood what were either original or excellent copies of Tiffany lamps. A large, sad-eyed Gund beagle was propped on the pillows of the queen-sized bed.

Nora picked up the toy dog and patted its head. "Meet Bartleby," she said.

"As in Melville?"

She made room for the dog on a night table and gave its head another pat. "I can't be sure he actually read the story of poor Bartleby the scrivener, but that's what he told me his name was. My staff gave him to me to cheer me up when I was ill a while ago. Funny how a sad-eyed toy can make you smile, isn't it?"

He nodded. "My daughter has a whole menagerie."

"We never outgrow them, or the need to cuddle them once in a while." As she removed the bedspread, he reached out to help her. "I sometimes think that if boys were allowed to grow up with stuffed toys instead of Terminator games and G.I. Joes and plastic AK-47s, this would be a much better world to live in."

"Certainly safer," he agreed, bringing his end of the spread over to hers.

She took it from him, folded it once more in the middle, and brought it over to the worktable.

Watching her, Tom felt awkward as she walked back toward him. Somehow, in the heat of the moment, out on the couch, everything had seemed so right, so inevitable. Now....

She was standing close to him again, and his heart began to pound once more. She reached out and touched his cheek. "I hate to bring up such a mundane subject," she said. "But...do you have something?"

He must have looked blank, for she quickly became more specific: "A condom."

God, what an idiot he was! Of course, a condom! His sex life was a thing of the past. He and Beth had never had to worry about AIDS or unwanted pregnancy.

"Sorry," he said. "It's not the kind of thing I stuff in my pocket every day, along with my wallet and my keys."

A slow, soft smile lit her face. "That's nice to know." She nodded toward the door. "If you go into the bathroom, you'll find a package in the medicine cabinet."

It took a while to find the Trojans, which were on the top shelf behind a bottle of Maalox. The package had never been opened, and Tom wasn't sure why that made him feel good, but it did.

Back in the bedroom, he was relieved to see that Nora was neither naked nor in bed. She had removed her clothes and was wearing a long, silky blue kimono. Her back to the door, she was standing at the window looking out into the little garden. Then she released the blind and turned.

His breath caught at the sight of her. The blue silk caressed her breasts, hinting at the delicate rounded tips of her nipples. Tied at the waist, the kimono fell in soft folds to the floor, parting just enough as she walked toward him to give an intriguing glimpse of her smooth white thigh. She was holding a glass of wine, and she paused at the dresser to pick up another, which she handed to him.

"Cheers again," she whispered.

"Cheers," he echoed.

Not in a long time had he been intimate with a woman, a warm and beautiful woman, and he was afraid of appearing awkward, overeager, gauche. He and Beth had been so in love, and so used to each other. What if he couldn't perform with another woman?

Nora sensed his hesitancy, and said, "Want to talk?"

"It's been a long time for me, Nora. You're so lovely. So special. God, I want you! For all those years, there was only Beth. Just the two of us. She was all I ever wanted. All I ever needed. And now I'm—" He shook his head.

"I understand. Really, I do. But I think you expect too much of yourself. I hope that doesn't mean you'll expect too much of me. I'm far from the perfect lover. We both have a lot of memories between us." She began to unbutton his shirt. "But that doesn't mean that we shouldn't make a few of our own...."

His hands moved up to her shoulders and slipped the kimono from them. The beauty of her creamy breasts left him breathless. She reached down and untied the bow at her waist, letting the kimono fall to the floor in a shimmering blue puddle of silk. Her beauty made his eyes sting, and he trembled with the white-hot pain of desire.

Together, they removed his clothes. And then they were lying on her bed, wrapped in each other's arms.

"Just hold me," she whispered. "For a little while, just hold me close."

Though his heart was pounding, he lay still, his arms around her, feeling the soft, delicious wonder of the length of her body, the warmth of her flesh pressed against his. He rested his cheek on her silky hair and breathed in her perfume. The scent was flowery and delicate, reminding him of spring days and fresh meadows and all the hopeful promises of his long-ago youth.

Slowly, he turned his head until his lips met the smoothness of her cheek. Then softly, gently he began to kiss her, moving his lips from her cheek, to her neck, to her breasts. Slowly, tenderly, he moved his hands, caressing her.

"Yes," she whispered. "Yes...."

And then her hands, her lips began to move over him too....

Later, after the long-stoked embers of desire had been consumed in a roaring burst of passion, they dozed in each other's arms. His chest was moist with her silent tears, and his eyelids and cheeks with his own. He didn't know why she had wept, and he wouldn't invade her privacy by asking. He couldn't be sure why he too had cried. Perhaps it was both the sadness at finally letting go of the past and the joy at being able at last to look to the future. He knew only that he felt at peace, and that Nora felt oh so right and wonderful in his arms.

CHAPTER 23

TOM CALLED Nora as soon as he opened the store the next morning. When there was no answer on her home phone, he didn't leave a message but tried her cell phone. Probably in a meeting or out on a shoot, she didn't pick up. He could have kicked himself. He should have left a message on her home phone. But what if she wasn't going home tonight? What if she was out of town? Would she think he hadn't called? In his sudden anxiety, it never occurred to him that she would call her home phone for any messages.

"Hi," he began when the beep came through. "I just wanted to say hello and to tell you how much…. Oh, hell, I'm not very good at this. I—"

"You're fine at it," Nora's voice suddenly broke through. "You're very good at a lot of things. Sorry I didn't pick up right away. I'm just leaving a meeting. The phone was on vibrate."

She was speaking softly, so he realized there were other people around. He spoke softly too, though he was alone. "Thank you for yesterday. Everything about it was terrific. It was…." How could he possibly tell her what it had meant to him?

"I know," she helped him out. "For me too."

"When can I see you again? Are you free for lunch? For dinner?"

She hesitated. "Not today." There was another pause. "Look—I have to run. I'll call you."

"Okay. 'Bye."

He thought she said good-bye too before ending the call, but he couldn't be sure.

The store phone rang. It was a woman who had seen the tiny ad he occasionally ran in *The New Yorker.* She was looking for a copy of Milton Shapiro's *Jackie Robinson of the Brooklyn Dodgers* for her husband's baseball collection. He told her she had come to the right place and he had a few of the Archway paperbacks and a couple of the hardcover later printings. He also had a mint-condition 1957 Messner first edition. She went for a 1966 library edition for ten bucks. He put it down as a good, but not great, marriage.

It turned out to be a busy morning, but in between reordering stock and taking care of walk-in customers, he got in a call to Joe Henley. When he was about halfway through the tomato and provolone sandwich Max had packed for him, Joe called back.

"I've got a line on your boy. You were right: Richard Fulton is employed by Denning and Pankhurst. He was hired about three months ago. Before that, he was a bouncer at Bertie's, a hot new club on Delancey Street. Evidently he got in trouble for bouncing rowdy customers a little too hard. No one ever brought charges, but the place had to drop him."

"Before he dropped someone on his head, no doubt. Does he have a record?"

"No. D and P wouldn't have hired him if he did. You know that. It's a so-called high-class agency. That's not to say that his strong-arm background wouldn't have been a plus to them. Also in his favor, this guy had some earlier experience in hotel security in a few places in Connecticut. I checked them out too. Seems he never got into serious trouble, but always left 'under mutual agreement.'"

"A real sweetheart."

"What are you getting yourself into, Tom? First, it's information about a fatal accident in New Hampshire. Now it's background on a thug who works for D and P. What the hell does all this have to do with running a bookstore?"

"I'm just checking out a couple of things for some friends."

"Sounds like they could be dangerous friends."

"You have an overactive imagination. Thanks for the info. When Commissioner Kelly's memoir is published, I'll get you an autographed copy. In the meantime, when are you coming out to Brooklyn for one of Max's chili dinners?"

"Last time I had Max's chili, it nearly blew off the top of my head. How about you and me taking Max out for a pizza one of these days? It's safer."

"Sounds good. I'll check with him and get back to you. Thanks again for your help."

"Anytime, buddy. And I'm available for more than just help with information. Remember that."

"You bet." It was always a comfort to remember that he had friends who were good with a gun. The next order of business was to call Foster. He didn't bother with a greeting or small talk when Foster's voice came over the line. "Get your goddamn tail off me, or I'm off this fricken case!"

"What are you talking about?" Foster was all innocence.

"Denning and Pankhurst, your buddies' private eyes, the boys they hire for their dirty work. I've warned off the guy they had tailing me. His name's Richard Fulton and he lives in Lindenhurst. You want his height, weight, and health insurer?"

Foster gave a phony little laugh. "I have no idea what you're talking about. If you've been followed, then someone else must have hired the detective."

"Sure, a little old lady who didn't like the ending of *The Da Vinci Code*. Cut the crap, Foster. We both know it's your guys. Tell them to lay off. I didn't survive all those years bringing in scum-of-the-earth crooks and murderers by not watching my back. The next sleazy trick you guys try to pull will be your last." He slammed down the phone.

At the same instant, the chime that announced the entrance of a customer went off. Tom looked up and saw LuAnne from Neal Hammond's office in the doorway. She clutched a manila envelope to her bosom as if it were her only covering and she was afraid someone might wrest it from her. There was a chill in the air today, and he wondered if she was cold in her miniskirt and short denim jacket.

"Hi," he said. "Did your boss send that for me?"

She extended the envelope. "He said to be sure to get all the papers signed."

Tom smiled, unfastened the clasp, and made a show of glancing at the contents. "Looks like everything's in order. Would you like a cup of coffee or tea?"

"No, thanks. But a Diet Coke would be good."

He retrieved one from the small refrigerator in the storage room.

LuAnne shook her head at the Ingram mug he had picked up at the last BookExpo, popped the top, and pressed her pink-glossed lips to the can. "Can I ask you something?" she said between sips. "How come Mr. Hammond wants *you* to deliver these papers? Are you a lawyer or something?"

"Just a friend doing a favor."

She looked skeptical. "A friend? You don't really look like one of his friends."

"You're right. I'm more of an acquaintance. But we do have a mutual friend, and, since I have to be in the area tomorrow, I said I'd do your boss this favor."

If she wasn't convinced, she was polite enough not to say so. Tom glanced out the display window, expecting to see a company car and driver parked or double-parked outside. There was no sign of one.

"Where did your driver park?" he asked.

She looked blank.

"Didn't you come in a company car? Or did they send you in a taxi?"

She laughed. "I took the subway. I don't rate a company car or taxi."

"I'd think you would for such an important errand. Who does rate?"

"Oh, management and...."

"And...?"

"Some of the other girls."

It didn't take a degree from GMU's prestigious School of Business Administration, to figure out how some of LuAnne's female co-workers had earned their company-car privileges. Even in her trendy clothes and makeup, LuAnne didn't look like she could be more than eighteen or nineteen. Just a few years older than his Stephanie. He hoped she wasn't looking forward to gaining those company-car privileges.

"Thanks for the soda." She put the can down on the cash-register counter and ran her tongue over her upper lip. "Gotta go now."

He walked her to the door. "Thanks for bringing the material. Do you know your way back to the subway?"

"Yeah." She sighed, perhaps thinking of how much nicer it would be to ride in a chauffeured car.

"Stick with the subway," he advised. "It may sometimes be crowded and have delays. But the only thing it costs you is your two-dollar fare. Free rides in fancy cars often come at a very high price."

For a second, she looked startled. Then she nodded and started down the street. He had read in her eyes that she knew what he was talking about. What he couldn't read there was whether she agreed.

IT WAS A BUSY afternoon, too busy for him to spend much time wondering why he didn't ditch the case. But he knew why. It wasn't just keeping Portman out of the neighborhood. It was more than that. Much more. It was Nora. They had met because he was supposed to be working on a Golden Guys project. That link gave him excuses to speak with her, be with her. He didn't feel secure enough yet to believe he could hold on to her if that link were broken. Not even after last night.

When the phone rang just before closing, he thought it might be Foster with more denials, and he tensed, preparing to deal with his lies. But it was Nora. In an instant, the tension slid away, replaced by a delicious rush of anticipation.

"Sorry if I was a little abrupt this morning," she said. "I was in the middle of things. People all around."

"Sure. I understand."

"I forgot to tell you that Leslie called this morning. She's figured out how she can juggle her schedule. She'd love to show you and your daughter around Hopkins. I gave her your cell phone number. Here's hers. Give her a call when you get to Baltimore."

He jotted down the number. "We're not leaving till Wednesday. I hope I can see you before we go."

"I—" She hesitated. "When will you be back?"

"Probably Thursday evening. I haven't checked flight schedules yet."

"I'll be in Pennsylvania Wednesday and Thursday for more shooting at GMU, and tomorrow's totally booked."

He thought she sounded disappointed. "This weekend, then? Though that sounds a long way off to me."

"To me too." There was another pause. "Those plans I had for this evening—they were canceled. Would you like to come over for dinner? Nothing fancy. An omelet, a salad…."

He would have been on his way for bread and water. "Sounds great. What time?"

"Oh, seven-thirty—eight. That will give me time to get home and get things started."

"See you then. I'll bring the wine."

"MUST BE SERIOUS," Max said when Tom walked into the kitchen where he was adding the finishing touches to his chicken-and-pasta casserole. "Two showers and shaves in one day."

Tom tried for a casual shrug. "I don't know her long enough for 'serious.' But it feels good."

"Then go with the feeling…wherever it leads."

There were times when Tom almost felt that Max was his father, not Beth's. This wasn't one of them. "Max, you know I loved Beth. It's just—"

"It's just that Beth has been gone a long time now." Max wiped his hand on his apron, then put it on Tom's shoulder. "I loved her too. We both always will. I loved my Sylvia. God knows she was the light of my life, and she always will be. But we're here, and they're gone. Forever. I'm a lot older than you are, and I can tell you that forever is a hell of a long time even when you may have only a few years galloping away before you. Memories aren't enough to fill the time and that stabbing ache in our gut. If you've found someone you can share with, who can ease that ache, then don't agonize but enjoy. And now, please get out of my kitchen before I put you to work and make you late for your date, or whatever it's called these days."

On his way to the subway, Tom stopped into Montague Wine and Spirits. He didn't want to go for something too expensive, which might be taken as pretentious or even a slight on the simple meal they were to share. After consultation with a guy in his twenties wearing Ralph Lauren jeans and carrying a camel-colored Gucci messenger bag over his shoulder, he purchased a bottle of Yellow Tail chardonnay. It was, his adviser, who obviously knew his burgundies from his zinfandels, assured him, "one of the new Australian budget wines that have been getting so much good press."

Evidently it was a good choice, for Nora seemed pleased when she took it out of the bag. "Mmm," she said. "Australian. They do great things with their grapes. I'll pop this in the fridge for a few minutes. Make yourself comfortable. I have just a couple of things to finish up, and, no, you can't help," she added as he started to protest. "Go sit down and relax. Everything will be ready before you know it."

In the living room, he strolled around, unable to resist looking at the contents of the many bookcases. Here and there he pulled out a volume and examined it. He had always believed that book collections revealed a great deal about not just the tastes but also the character and lives of their owners. Years ago, he had actually broken a case when, in his suspect's study, he had noticed a shelf devoted to exotic flora, some poisonous. He longed to know more about Nora, but the collection was so wide-ranging and eclectic that it told him nothing he had not already discerned: she was as bright as she was beautiful, with a curious mind and an admirable thirst for knowledge. Several of the shelves were two rows deep. On many of them, books were lying, spine out, on top of the vertical occupants. There were, of course, many books on subjects that Nora had made documentaries about, but there were also contemporary fiction and nonfiction, the classics, history, philosophy, science, religion. There were shelves of books about China, even some very old ones in Chinese.

"Still on a busman's holiday, I see." Nora had walked in with the bottle of wine and two glasses.

"Always. It's an occupational disease. If you ever decide to give up documentaries, you have enough stock to start your own bookstore."

"Not a chance. I like to move around too much." Nora put down the wine and walked over to join him. "This is what happens when two people who love to read and hate to throw things out get married." She took the old medical book he was holding. "One of these days I suppose I should weed out some of these books, but so many of them were Sid's. I know it's silly, but I can't bear to part with them."

Tom nodded toward the book. "Was he interested in medicine?"

She patted the book as she found a place for it atop several other medical tomes. "What wasn't he interested in! I never met anyone with a mind like his, so hungry for knowledge. His parents wanted him to be a doctor, but he knew it would be too confining. He wanted to study, to learn, and he wanted to travel. Happily, we were able to combine the two and make a decent living."

"You have quite a few books in Chinese. Are they collectors' items or could he actually read them?"

"Both. He was a linguist. Spoke and read several languages. Chinese he spoke like a native, which was one of the reasons we got around the country with such ease. It was also an advantage when we visited a restaurant here in Chinatown." She sighed and headed for the cocktail table where she had put down the wine and the glasses. "I wish you could have known him. You would have been great friends, I'm sure of it."

He made the usual sounds of agreement as he followed her, but he wasn't at all sure that they would have been great friends. Certainly not if he met Sid now. Not after last night with Nora. Of course, last night with Nora wouldn't have happened if Sid were still around. Or Beth. Oh, hell. He could use that drink.

Nora had already uncorked the bottle and was pouring the wine. "I was testing a new gadget. Sorry to deprive you of your display of a traditional manly skill." She flexed her arm. "We independent women have to learn to do many things on our own. Opening a wine bottle is high on the list—just above changing a flat tire." She raised her glass. "To good wine and pleasant company."

It wasn't the toast he would have made. He had intended to say *To us,* and he was about to add it, but something in her eyes held him back. "Good wine and pleasant company," he echoed, touching his glass to hers.

She made a terrific omelet. The secret, she revealed, was a dash of *herbs de Provence* and a generous sprinkling of feta cheese. They were still in the pleasant stage of discovery that comes at the beginning of a relationship, and yet, though Nora talked easily about her work and her politics, she was a very private person and said little about herself. Tom longed to know more, but he didn't want to prod her, realizing that she would expect him to reciprocate with details about himself. That was something he couldn't do. Not yet. Later, when his work for Foster was finished, there would be time for all that. There was something hopeful and comforting in thoughts about *after* and *later.* For too long the future had stretched out before him as an interminable gray and barren path along which he had to struggle alone.

They took their coffee into the living room, where Nora put on a Satie CD. "This album is called *After the Rain*," she said. "Wouldn't it be nice if all rains were so gentle and refreshing?" She sat down on the sofa, but not as close to Tom as he would have liked. "God! I wish I was down in New Orleans right now and doing a documentary about the devastation caused by Katrina. But I'm stuck up here with a project about millionaires who will use their government connections to make a profit out of it." She sighed. "I've promised Denise that we'll go down there as soon as we wrap up here."

"Is her family down there? Were they affected by the hurricane?"

"She grew up there, but her parents are dead. Her two sisters have lived in Chicago for years. But she has a couple of cousins in New Orleans. She was worried about them until she learned that they had gotten out safely and were staying with other relatives in North Carolina. But there's the grandmother and mother of a friend of hers who haven't been heard from since the hurricane struck. She's furious about what has been going on and can't wait to get down there with our cameras. The money from this Golden Guys project will give us a good start." She leaned back and smiled. "Isn't that a delicious irony?"

She herself looked delicious, sitting there with her feet tucked under her, her head tilted back. Tom started to move closer, but she straightened up and reached for her coffee cup. Had she done that deliberately, or just not noticed his shift in position? He picked up his cup too.

"How much longer will you be tied up with the project?"

"A couple more weeks should do it, thank God. We're dividing up some of the work to get it over quickly. That's why I'm off to GMU this week to get some more background shots and to finish an interview with Jason Gilbert. He was not exactly in the best condition last time we talked. I'm hoping he can stay off the booze this time around. Denise will wrap up Nick Hammond while I'm there. Then we have to get Lyle Wayne to fit us into his schedule. That will be either before or after we're set to tape him on a visit to one of Arnold Simon's charities, a residence for abused women in lower Manhattan." She laughed. "Wayne doesn't want to do it, but Arnold shamed him into it by inviting him when I was taping them both together at the anniversary reception. He looked ready to choke Arnold when I turned off the tape. By the way, how's *your* project coming along?"

"Not as fast as I'd like, because I have a business to run, which takes up most of my time. I have an appointment with Simon early next week. That's one meeting I'm looking forward to."

"You'll like him. He's really the best of this bunch. Just be sure he remembers the appointment. He's always running around from one good deed to another. It's hard to keep track of him."

"Thanks for the tip. I'll remind him well in advance." He put down his cup and moved a little closer to her.

"More coffee?"

He shook his head and took the hand that was reaching toward the coffeepot.

She turned to face him, but he couldn't read the message in her eyes. He only knew that it wasn't the one he hoped to see there. "I wish you wouldn't look at me like that," she said softly.

"Why?" he asked through the cold band of disappointment that began to close around his throat.

"Because—" She hesitated, searching for the right words. "Because— Oh, hell." She sighed and shook her head. "Because I like it too much!" In the next instant, she was in his arms.

Making love was even more exciting and satisfying than it had been last night. This time, there was no embarrassment as they made their way into her bedroom. No nervousness as they hastily slipped out of their clothes and he eased her down onto the bed. No tension as he gazed at her gorgeous body, the flesh glowing like gold-flecked snow in the soft lamplight. There was only the sweet, hot thrill of desire as she reached up and pulled his head down, burying it between her soft, warm, welcoming breasts.

Later, they dozed in each other's arms. He was awakened by the gentle touch of her fingers making soft circles in the hair on his chest. He clasped her hand, brought it to his lips and kissed it. She was leaning on her elbow, looking down at him. "Time for you to go home," she said softly, but she didn't take her hand away.

"Really?"

"Really." He heard the reluctance in her voice. She sighed and withdrew her hand. "Really," she repeated, a trifle more firmly, getting up and slipping on her robe. "We both have work tomorrow. And you have a daughter to go home to. You don't want to set a bad example."

He laughed and reached for his clothes. He was aware of her watching him as he dressed. Beth used to watch him too, assuring him that a woman found as much pleasure in the sight of her lover's body as he found in hers. That was difficult to believe, but Beth never lied to him, so it must have been true, though certainly on a much lower scale of wonder. A woman's body was a treasure trove of pleasure, made up of an intriguing, delectable combination of mystery and delight. A man's body was straight and plain and held no secrets. Beth had laughed when he said that, and told him that he didn't have a clue. Now, as he felt Nora's gaze on him, he hoped Beth had been right, and that he was being watched with pleasure. He was glad that he had continued to jog and work out after he left the force. He didn't kid himself that he was in as great a shape as twenty years ago, but he knew he looked a lot better than many guys his age. He hoped that was what Nora was thinking as she watched him. He wished that her beautiful eyes weren't so unreadable.

They held hands as they walked to the door. She seemed to melt into his arms when he kissed her, but when his lips moved along her cheek to her ear and he whispered, "When can I see you again?" he felt her stiffen.

"It's a busy week," she said. "You're off to Baltimore. I'm off to Pennsylvania."

"What about Friday night? Or Saturday? Or both?"

She shook her head. "I'm going to be tied up for a long while. There are the last of the interviews, and then, in between, all the editing that has to be done. I'm really in a rush to be finished with this damn project."

"But you have to take time out to eat, to sleep. We could—"

She was shaking her head again. "No, we couldn't." Her voice was soft but firm.

The constriction in his chest was the same as the tensing he had felt years before when he and Beth visited her doctors and he knew damn well that the news would not be good. "This isn't about your schedule. What are you trying to tell me?"

"What I should have told you this morning, but couldn't bring myself to say over the phone. Then I meant to tell you this evening, over dinner, but once you were here—well, I just couldn't. Oh, damn. This is so hard." She touched his cheek, then slipped out of his arms. "This isn't about you. It's about me. Last night, tonight—they were wonderful. Too wonderful. But I can't—I just can't go on with it."

The pain in her eyes seemed to reflect the ache in his heart. "I know what you're trying to say. I feel torn too. We both have a lot of memories to deal with, but that's what they are—memories. The past is the past. It's over. We're here. We're now."

"The past is never past. It's always part of here and now. It's what makes us what we are."

"But it doesn't prevent us from changing, from going on with our lives. Beth and Sid will always be a part of us. That doesn't mean we can't be part of each other."

"I'm not sure that's true for me. I'm not sure I was meant to be part—a serious part—of another man's life. That's why I think we should stop now. I don't want to hurt you."

"And do you think this doesn't hurt?" She turned her face away, but he turned it back toward him. "Look, what's happening between us is something good. Maybe it's happening too fast for you. Maybe we should take it a little slower. But we shouldn't run away from it. It deserves a chance. We deserve a chance."

"I don't want you to be hurt," she repeated, but he could see that she was weakening. She didn't resist when he pulled her back into his arms.

"I'm a big boy," he whispered. "I can take care of myself."

"That's what all big boys think." She smiled and shook her head, and ran a hand through his hair.

"You'll find I'm right about a lot more than that."

Their lips came together sweetly, tenderly, in a kiss that seemed filled more with promise than regret. The memory of it kept him warm all the way home. That, and the vision of her standing there in the dim hall, her silky kimono clinging to her soft curves, shimmering in the dimness, her eyes so filled with longing and sadness as she tried to tell him how she felt. She had looked so vulnerable. He had never thought of her that way before. He wondered if she would ever let him see her that way again.

CHAPTER 24

IT WAS A busy afternoon and, hoping to leave early to get everything arranged for the trip tomorrow, Tom had asked Phil Howard to come in at three. He was at the computer, entering a special order, when Phil arrived, followed almost immediately by a walk-in who was not one of their regular customers. Tom saw Phil ask if he could help her, and turned back to the computer while they conferred. When he had completed the order and looked up again, he found the woman standing at the counter, obviously waiting to speak to him.

"Hi," he said. "Can I help you?"

She was a tall, attractive African-American of about sixty. Though she stood erect, there was a subtle, weary slant to her shoulders, and her eyes held a sadness that seemed there to stay.

"I hope so." Her voice was soft, cultured, with just the slightest hint of a long-ago Southern accent. "The other gentleman said you're Tom Berenson."

Tom nodded and looked at the business card she held out to him. It was his.

"I found this in my husband's wallet. It seemed so strange. We've been going to the same bookstore near our town for years. Did he order some books from you?"

Tom studied the woman's face. She didn't look like the sneaky type who riffled a man's private spaces when he was out of the house. But, then, who did? Did she think her husband was hiding a secret passion for porn? He didn't sell porn, but, of course, she couldn't know that. And without a court order, he would never give out information about customers and their purchases and interests.

"What's his name?"

"Oh, yes. Of course. James Rutherford."

It didn't ring an immediate bell.

"He worked for President and Mrs. Colbert at GMU," she added.

Ah! Rutherford, the Colbert's butler. Tom remembered giving the man his card in what he had been sure was a vain hope for some relevant gossip about the college days of the Golden Guys. "Yes, I remember now. We met a couple of weeks ago. Mrs. Rutherford, did you say *worked?*"

The sadness in her eyes deepened. "James died on the nineteenth."

"I'm so sorry. Had he been ill?"

There was a flash of anger in her eyes. "Nothing like that. It was a hit-and-run accident."

A chill went up Tom's spine. "Hit and run! Have the police found the driver?"

"No, and I'm not holding my breath." She extended the card. "Look, Mr. Berenson, I don't want you to think I'm a nosy wife, snooping in my husband's things. It's just that I found your card in his wallet when they gave it to me at the hospital. James was the most meticulous and organized person I've ever known, and sometimes it drove me a little crazy. But he never kept anything without a reason. After the funeral, our son brought me back here to stay with him and his family for a while. I brought James's wallet with me. Maybe it sounds silly, but I just needed to have something of his to hold on to till I get back to our own home."

"That doesn't sound silly. I know exactly what you mean. Only too well."

Their eyes held for a moment, and then she glanced at the card. "Have you any idea how he got it and why he kept it?"

"I gave it to him. As for why he kept it...." He stepped out from behind the counter. "I was about to leave for the day as you came in. Why don't we go someplace where we can talk? I live nearby. Would you like to come up for a cup of coffee? Or would you feel better if we went to a restaurant?"

"Let's go to your place," she said. "I always feel more comfortable at a kitchen table."

By the time they were settled across from each other with mugs of coffee and slices of Entenmann's crumb cake, they were Edith and Tom, and Tom had learned that Edith and James had met over forty years ago, when she was a clerk in the bursar's office and he was on the GMU janitorial staff. In the beginning, they had both taken advantage of GMU's discount rates for staff and studied at night, hoping to earn their college degrees.

"But we were young and in love and couldn't wait to get married," Edith said, her eyes filled with memories. "And then when our babies came, James said it wasn't fair that I had to give everything up to stay home with them. He dropped his studies so that he could be home at night to take care of the children and I could go to school. Eventually I earned my teaching degree. By that time, James was the chief custodian's assistant, he'd educated himself, and he preferred to spend his free time with me and the children. I suppose if he'd stayed on, he would have been chief custodian someday, but he caught the eye of Dr. Paul Fielding when he came in as president of the college, and Dr. Fielding asked him to run his household and oversee all the president's functions. It was a great opportunity, and he did it so well that every president who followed kept him on." She took a sip of coffee, then fixed her eyes on Tom. "James loved to read, but up till now, our library, the GMU library, and our local bookstore always provided every book he could possibly want. That's why I don't understand why he had your card."

"He had it because I gave it to him when we met. It was the Sunday before he died." Tom explained that he had been at Morris for the Golden Guys weekend, that he was helping with research on them for a book about fraternities, and that he had given Rutherford his card in case he recalled any anecdotes about them that he would like to pass on.

"Then I'm surprised that he kept it. James wouldn't have gossiped about anyone at the college."

"I wasn't after gossip, just some memories of the guys' halcyon days, maybe some high-spirited pranks. You know, the sort of 'all in good fun' stories that lighten up an academic book that might otherwise be dry."

"Those boys never did anything 'in good fun.' They were

bad news back then, and they're worse news today. There are exceptions, of course—Jason Gilbert and Arnold Simon. I don't know why Jason wanted to join and stay in their fraternity. It was obvious they would never let him, a man of the Jewish faith, be a real part of their 'in' group. But he's a brilliant man who has made great scientific discoveries that will benefit the world, and the fraternity is very happy to bask in the glow from his light now. And Arnold Simon is truly a man whose good works are making the world a better place. As busy as he is, he took time out to preach at my James's funeral. As for the rest of them, they never even acknowledged James's passing, though word was sent out to all the alumni. It's typical of them, though. They have never outgrown their arrogance and megalomania. They were born thinking this country, including everything and everyone in it, is their private property." She shook her head. "No, James would have had no charming anecdotes to share with you."

Tom nodded. "Well, maybe some not-so-charming ones, then?"

"He would never do that. James never told tales out of school."

Tom didn't point out that neither did dead men. "So maybe it was just an accident that he kept my card."

"Not my James. If he kept that card, it was for a reason. Tom, why are you involved with these men? I mean, *really* why are you involved with them?"

"I told you, I'm helping a college professor out on the Coast do research for a book on college fraternities."

She gave him a level look, no doubt the same one she focused on students who claimed the dog ate their homework. "I don't think you're the type to be associated with these men for something so unimportant. I've been around a long time, and I can read people well. James was the same way. Because of where we come from, we had to be. I don't have to tell you that for black people it's a matter of survival. We'd done well and moved up, relatively speaking, but old habits die hard."

The subtext was clear. She could spot a cop a mile away. Smiling, he shook his head and spread his hands. "Sorry, but with me, what you see is what you get."

"Whatever you say." She smiled too, but she obviously wasn't

convinced. She took a sip of coffee. "Don't dig too deep in looking for your anecdotes. You're dealing with dangerous people.
There are things about their past at Morris that they wouldn't
want anyone to know."

"They haven't put me on warning."

"Maybe they think you're too smart to need it."

"They know that if I come across anything embarrassing, I
won't pass it on."

"We're not talking about embarrassing here—we're talking
about lethal."

"Now you're exaggerating."

"I wish I were. But I'm a plain-spoken woman. When these
men were in school, they wrecked lives without a thought. Girls
were left with their reputations in tatters, and guys who got in
their way didn't last long at GMU."

"Kids are resilient. I'm sure they could all start over."

"Not everyone lived to start over."

"You mean Lou West's son."

She nodded.

When she didn't elaborate, he added, "I've heard about that,
but it was an accident. An unfortunate initiation rite that went
awry."

"I'm sure that's what they told you."

"What's the real story?"

She hesitated awhile, then said, "No one talks about it
anymore, but maybe you should know, if only to keep you from
asking the wrong person about it. Mike West was a sweet kid, but
he wasn't really college material. I don't mean that he was slow,
but GMU is a tough school, and Mike wasn't as bright as most
students have to be to get in, unless they're great athletes or the
children or relatives of alumni or politicians or benefactors. Of
course, as the son of the school's best-ever football coach, there
was no question about admittance. Mike was no athlete, though,
and there was no way he could make the team. But Lou saw to it
that his star players asked his boy to join Beta Alpha Beta Phi. Your
Golden Guy friends had no choice but to invite Mike, but they
didn't like him and they didn't like being dictated to. They picked
a cold, wet November night for his initiation, got him stinkin'

drunk, then sent him out in his underwear and bare feet on an impossibly long paper trail they had set up earlier. Then they all went to bed. Mike was found the next morning, half frozen and drowned in a puddle. No one's ever been sure whether he passed out from the liquor and fell into the puddle, or whether when he fell into the puddle he passed out from the liquor. That's just a minor detail on the way to the inevitable, tragic end."

"Surely there was an uproar, an investigation."

"What investigation? The word was that Mike had had too many drinks and then died in a hiking accident. As for the underwear— Well, college kids do crazy things. They think they're indestructible. I'm sure you're familiar with William Hazlitt and his essays. He said that 'no young man believes he will ever die.'"

"And Lou West went along with that?"

"Those boys all had powerful parents. They could have seen to it that he never worked again."

"What about his wife?"

"That's really sad. Mrs. West wound up in an institution a few years later. As far as I know, she's still there. It isn't easy to lose a child under any circumstances. But under circumstances like those...." She shook her head.

They sat in silence for a while. Then Edith pushed her chair back. "I really should be going. My son and daughter-in-law will worry if they get home from work and I'm not there. They mean well, but I'd really rather be back home, working things through in the place where James and I had built our life."

"I know what you mean. I felt the same way when Beth died."

Tom stood up too, and walked her to the door, where she turned to him. "I'm sorry for your loss, but it's good to talk with someone who understands."

"I spoke with your husband for only a little while, but he struck me as a fine, a remarkable man. I'm sorry that I'll never have a chance to know him better. I'm also sorry that I wasn't able to help you discover why he kept my card."

"He must have liked you too. That's probably why he kept it. Maybe he planned to warn you about the people you're involved with. In a way, he just did." She put her hand on his arm. "Get finished with your work as soon as possible. And, until you do, watch your back. That would have been his advice to you."

He stood by the door after she left. Had James Rutherford needed that same warning? Was he dead because he had forgotten to watch his back?

CHAPTER 25

S INCE THE Golden Guys were paying, Tom had reserved first-class seats on the flight to Baltimore. Stephanie was as wide-eyed as having to leave home at six-thirty a.m. for the nine o'clock flight would allow. "Wow," she said as she settled into the cushions and stretched out her legs. "So this is what it feels like to be a gazillionaire. How come you didn't tell me you won the lottery?"

"Sorry to disappoint you, but I just used up some frequent flyer miles that were about to expire."

"So I should forget about the yacht and the castle?"

"'Fraid so. But not about breakfast—it comes with the seats. And it may even be lox and bagels."

Breakfast did not include lox and bagels, but she made the best of it, then slept the rest of the way to Baltimore.

When they spoke the night before, Leslie had suggested that she meet Tom and Stephanie in the lobby of the Intercontinental Harbor Court where they would be staying. "Less of a hassle than trying to figure out someplace on campus," she said. "Just call me when you're in a taxi and on your way to the hotel."

Even if she hadn't been the only one in the lobby in a blue Hopkins sweatshirt, it would not have been hard to identify Leslie. She was as tall and lithe as her mother, and though her hair was longer and darker, it framed a face that seemed to be a picture of how Nora must have looked when she was a co-ed. Only the color of the eyes was different. Leslie's were dark brown, no doubt like her dad's.

After checking in, Tom took the girls to lunch at an off-campus fish-fry place that Leslie assured them had the best crab cakes on the East Coast. It was packed with kids from Hopkins, and Leslie seemed to know half of them. Apart from waves and greetings, though, she kept her attention on Stephanie, and by the time their orders came, the two girls were talking like old friends. Tom looked at all the students surrounding them—some laughing, others in earnest discussions—and suddenly he began to feel an outsider, an over-the-hill, lonely outsider. This was a world Stephanie would soon be entering, if not at Hopkins then at another college. And he would have to let go of her hand and allow her to enter it alone. It wasn't his letting go of her hand that he minded so much. It was her letting go of his. She would be fine. But how would he fare?

Then Leslie laughed, and she looked and sounded so much like her mother that it brought him back to himself. He had a lot of life to be lived yet.

They spent the afternoon touring the Homewood campus. Established in 1876, Hopkins was still a freshman compared to GMU, which had opened its doors more than a hundred years earlier, but Tom found the Hopkins campus, with its red and white Federalist buildings, warmer and more welcoming. GMU was a hodgepodge of historic halls and gleaming modern high-risers; Hopkins restricted its new buildings to the same Georgian style and so exuded more of a preserved sense of history.

After a stop at the Visitors' Center, they took the mandatory stroll through the campus. Autumn had already left its mark on many of the trees, adding even more color to the gardens. Leslie explained that after the freshman year, most of the students opted to live off-campus, but with the help of a current freshman friend she showed them the dorms. Then they headed for the Eisenhower library, where Tom would have enjoyed losing himself in its miles of books, but Leslie tore him away with the announcement that the next stop on the tour would be The Hut, the reading room in historic Gilman Hall, the oldest academic building on campus.

Stephanie smiled as they strolled around the huge, sunlit room. "If I come here, I know where you'll want to hang out when you visit," she teased Tom.

"I hope you do decide to come," Leslie said. "It's really a great school. They make you work hard, but, hey, that's what it's all about. And, socially, a big plus is that the guys still outnumber us."

"I'm not exactly overjoyed to hear that," Tom said.

"Spoken like a true dad. But it really is an advantage when it comes to Saturday night. It probably won't last much longer. Though women were admitted to the graduate schools almost from the beginning, it wasn't until 1970 that we got in as under-graduates. Seems like every year there are more of us."

They ended the tour with a stop at the Homewood House Museum with its magnificent period rooms. They agreed that Gertrude would love to curl up by the fireplace in the drawing room and Tom with a book in the library. Leslie and Stephanie much preferred the rolling lawn in front of the building where students were spread out, reading, talking, studying, listening to iPods, working on their laptops. In their jeans, jogging shoes, and sweatshirts, they created an appealing if anachronistic picture in front of that stately Georgian building. Tom sensed that Stepha-nie was picturing herself among them, and it pleased him to think that if she did decide on Hopkins, Leslie would be there to guide her through the first year.

The shadows were lengthening and the first chill breeze of evening was coming in from the harbor. Leslie suggested that they go to her apartment to freshen up before dinner. "Got to admit this was Mom's idea," she told Tom as she led the way. "She didn't want you to freak out when you heard about the apartment thing." She took out her cell phone and dialed. "Parent-type male on the way!" she announced to whoever picked up on the other end.

She and her friends lived on the second floor of a boxy, gray-stone walkup on East 30th Street, just a few minutes' walk from the campus. It reminded Tom of some of the streets in Cobble Hill back in Brooklyn. The halls were clean but the walls shook with rock music from behind every door.

"Fair warning," Leslie said as she unlocked one of those doors. "We're not exactly into decorating and housekeeping, but we did pick up a bit this morning in honor of your visit."

"Not necessary, but I'm impressed," Tom said. And he was. Books and papers scattered on tabletops and shelves, a few sweatshirts and unidentifiable garments slung over chair backs— all in all, it was a look of casual, comfortable chaos. Stephanie's eyes widened in pleasure as she looked around, and Tom sensed that she was anticipating the day when she might be living in just such a place.

A pretty redhead in distressed jeans and a SAVE THE PLANET T-shirt emerged from one of the back rooms, and Leslie introduced her as Madison from Chicago.

"You're going to love it here," Madison assured Stephanie as though there were no other college on earth that was worth her consideration. And then she hurried off to the library.

The rest of the apartment shared by the four girls consisted of two bedrooms with posters of rock stars on all the walls, a cramped bathroom with a schedule of shower times taped to the door, and an eat-in-kitchen stocked, Tom was pleased to see, with more cans of soda than of beer. After the grand tour, Leslie handed out Cokes and they settled in the living room to relax and decide where to have dinner. Tom was thinking small and quiet, but he saw how Stephanie's eyes lit up when Leslie described the Rusty Scupper, with its great view of the inner harbor, and he dug out his cell phone to make a reservation for six o'clock, requesting a table near a window, as Leslie suggested.

It turned out to be a great choice. The restaurant was bigger than Tom had expected, but the tables were far enough apart to offer privacy. And the view of the harbor, with the lights of the skyline reflected in the bay, was spectacular.

Tom raised his glass of chardonnay to Leslie. "Here's to you. You're a great guide, and a human Google on everything from faculty to food. Thanks for taking time out to show us around."

"I loved it, and loved meeting you both." Leslie touched her glass of iced tea to Stephanie's Coke and to Tom's wine. "I'm still not clear on how you and my mom met," she said to him. "She told me you're working on parallel projects, or something...."

"I'm doing some research for a guy out on the Coast who's writing a history of fraternities. He wants a little more information on the men in Beta Alpha Beta Phi back in the early eighties, and your mom is doing a documentary on some of them."

Leslie made a face. "Yeah, the so-called 'Golden Guys.' Yuk. I don't know what my mom sees in them."

"Maybe just a way toward getting some of that 'gold' so she can keep you here."

"I'm sure you're right. Actually, I should probably be grateful to them for more than that. The job came when Mom was way down, and it helped her get herself together again. I was getting worried about her."

"What happened?"

"My Aunt Ronnie died. Mom took it really hard. We both did."

Tom sighed. "Losing someone close is tough. Stephie and I know all about that. Your mom never mentioned her sister to me."

"Ronnie wasn't really her sister, but they were so close that she might as well have been. They knew each other like forever. She was pretty much a loner. I think Mom and I were practically all she had. She was really great, you know? Sweet and funny. But then there were what she called her black zones. Times when she just sort of fell apart. Mom was usually able to get her the help she needed to bring her out of it. But not that last time. Mom was away when Ronnie took all those pills. It was the first time she had done anything like that. Or at least the first time that I know of. Anyway, by the time Mom got back, nothing could be done. She kind of blames herself for that. I guess I should have called Ronnie more while Mom was away too...."

Tom thought of the many suicides—some atrociously messy, others as clean as a pin—that he had investigated when he was a cop. Could the perpetrators know how selfish that final act was? What emotional havoc it would bring into the lives of those left behind? "No one," he said, "is responsible for how other adults choose to live their lives—or to end them. Not ever."

"Yeah. I know that. Still...." Leslie looked away and toyed with her napkin. When she looked up again, she was smiling. "Anyway, that seems a long time ago now. Everything's great again with Mom, and that's what matters. So I can't hate those greedy creeps she's documenting too much. Besides, they got us all together too. So Mom has a new friend"—she turned to Stephanie—"and so do I. It would be terrific if you decide to come here."

Tom thought so too, but he didn't say anything. That would be up to Stephanie. He leaned back to let the waiter serve the appetizers that Leslie had suggested they share: artichoke and crab dip over pita chips and fried popcorn shrimp served with an "out-of-this-world remoulade."

"What was your favorite part of the tour?" he asked Stephanie.

She rolled her eyes heavenward as she bit into one of the shrimp. "At the moment, this!"

"There's lots more to see, and not just on campus," Leslie said. "How long are you going to be here tomorrow? I don't have a class till four, so that would give us plenty of time."

"I have a business appointment that will take up the morning, and our return flight is at five, which means we have to be at the airport before four. That doesn't leave us much free time."

"That's lots of time. Stephanie and I can go ourselves. I'll show her the city and some of the places where we like to hang out."

Tom hesitated. He wasn't sure about two young girls wandering around in a strange city all by themselves. Of course, Leslie was nineteen and the city wasn't strange to her....

"Maybe we can take in the aquarium too," Leslie pressed on.

"Come on, Dad!" Stephanie said. "It would be a lot more fun than sitting in the hotel room and reading till you get back."

"Okay, but you have to be back at the hotel by three the latest."

"No problem," Leslie assured him.

The two girls spent the rest of the meal planning their itinerary, which sounded to Tom like one that would take a few weeks to cover rather than a few hours. But he relaxed and enjoyed his rockfish *piccata* while they chattered away. His gaze drifted out over the harbor, to the boat lights and their gleaming ripples in the dark water, then over to the bright city skyline on the shore. Next, a sign blinking on and off above one of the tallest buildings caught his eye: The Portman Palace. It was an unpleasant reminder of the real reason for this trip. As delicious as his dinner was, his appetite suddenly drained away.

CHAPTER 26

NICHOLAS HAMMOND leaned back in his leather chair and watched the tall black chick pack up her equipment. As she leaned down, her breasts moved forward, revealing an enticing scoop of mocha décolletage. Now, that was some equipment he would like to get his hands on. He was glad her boss hadn't been able to hang around. She just came to help set things up, then had to rush off because she was going to GMU to get some nighttime atmosphere and to talk with that schmuck Jason Gilbert. She was okay, but a little long in the tooth for him. If he wanted sexy and forty, he could go home to his wife.

"Sorry we had to set this up so late," he said, making an elaborate gesture of looking at his Cartier Pasha.

She shrugged. "No problem."

She didn't bother to look at him as she replied. Since he had spent most of the interview working out on his ski machine and with his barbells, he would have thought she wouldn't be able to take her eyes off his terrific build. But she just kept on packing.

He stood up and stretched, showing his biceps and flat belly. "It's nearly seven-thirty. You must be hungry. How about dinner?"

This time she did look up. He hoped she got an eyeful. She made a polite, regretful smile. "Thanks, but I can't. Sorry."

He raised an eyebrow. "I was thinking of the Bull and Bear. Best steaks in New York." What he was really thinking about was the hotel suite he kept upstairs at the Waldorf for just such occasions. A couple of bottles of Grand-Puy-Lacoste with the steaks, and then....

She shook her head, her smile a little tighter. "Can't."

"Maybe another time."

"Maybe." It came out sounding like a definite No. She zipped up her carrying case.

The arrogant bitch. Did she know who she was talking to? Now it was a real challenge. And there was still the couch in his office.

"A drink, then. I make a great martini." The bar was near the door to his office, and he stationed himself in front of it. She would have to walk around him to get out.

She sighed, and put down the carrying case. "All right, but wine, not a martini. Do you have pinot noir?"

Damn. Compared to his martinis, wine was like soda pop. Well, he would get her to drink a couple of glasses. "You name it, I've got it." He bent down, looked through the wine rack, pulled out a bottle. "El Molino 2002," he said, pouring out two glasses.

There was a slight shrug of one shoulder and the hint of a polite smile, which told him she couldn't care less about the provenance of a wine.

He carried the glasses over to the long, leather couch and held one out to her. Not until she was standing next to him did he become fully aware of how tall she was. Those gorgeous legs seemed to go on forever until the tops of her thighs disappeared into her miniskirt. He couldn't wait to get between them.

When she took her glass, he raised his. "To you and your project, Diane."

"Denise," she corrected him.

Oh, shit. He made what he was sure was a beguiling smile. "I must have been thinking of the goddess. You remind me of her."

Her laugh was charming and self-deprecating. "Of what she represented or how she looked?"

"Both, of course." He sat down and patted the space beside him, inviting her to do likewise.

She glanced around, but the chairs were all on the other side of the room. On purpose. She sat down but didn't lean back.

"So...does your boss always make you work so late?"

"It's the nature of the job, but you were the one who set the time for your interview," she reminded him.

Right. Well, he'd work around that one. "True, but your boss could have let you go home and done this herself. If you worked for me, I'd see to it that your hours were better. And I'd double your salary, whatever it is."

"And what would I be doing for so much money?"

He moved a little closer. "You could be my special assistant."

"Helping you buy companies, milk them dry, or break them up and resell them?"

"It's called 'maximum utilization' on Wall Street, and I can't think of a better way to make an honest living. But if you didn't like that, I'd find something else for you to do."

"I'm sure you would." She gave him a level look that said she knew exactly what he was talking about. "But I like what I'm doing now."

"I could buy your boss's company, and then you'd both be working for me."

"I doubt that you'd be interested in such a small business. But if you did buy it, I'm sure Nora would just go off and start another company. And I'd go along with her." She put her glass down on the cocktail table in front of the couch.

He laughed. "Just kidding." How could he get the conversation off this dead-end track? He had thought she would be delighted to work for him for a huge salary. And very happy to show her gratitude. After all, as gorgeous as she was, she was black, and how many such opportunities could she have? He reached out to pick up her glass, his hand oh-so-accidentally brushing her thigh. That tempting, brown-sugar thigh. He handed the glass to her. "Drink up. You spent the last hour interviewing me. Now it's your turn. Tell me about yourself."

She took a sip. "Not much to tell. You already know what I do for a living."

"But I want to know all about *you*." He moved closer, his voice as soft as a feather in her ear. "The real you."

"No, you don't." There was laughter in her eyes, which offended him more than scorn would have. "We both know exactly what you want. But you can't have it."

For a moment their eyes held. How dare she laugh at him! He felt like pushing her down on the couch and taking her right there. It might be fun, but he knew she was the type to fight back and it would be ugly. And there was that damn documentary to think about. He had to protect his image in that. And there would be hell to pay with Tony if he screwed things up.

She took another sip from her glass, put it down, and stood up. "I really do have to go now."

He watched those exquisite long legs take her across the room as she headed for her equipment. He got to the door before she did. "Are you sure you want to go? I could give you an evening you'd never forget."

"I'm sure you think so, but I have to go. People are waiting for me."

He doubted it. "Call them. That's what cell phones are for."

She shook her head and started past him.

"It's dark out there. Everyone's gone home. I'll walk you to the elevator." Maybe he could change her mind on the way.

"Not necessary. I can find my way. Thanks for the drink."

"You deserve a lot more than a drink after all your hard work." He kept his voice at its low and seductive best. "Come on, Diane...."

"Denise."

Shit. He had done it again. "I know your name." The lie came out in a warm whisper. He put his hands on her shoulders and tried to bring his face close to hers. "But to me you'll always be that beautiful goddess."

"That's too bad. Maybe you should Google her before you invoke her." With a smile, she shrugged her way out of his grasp. "Good night. We'll call if we need to retape anything." She didn't bother to hurry as she made her way through the deserted office.

The bitch. It was her loss. If she thought he was going to follow her and beg, or stand there and pant after that gorgeous ass as she exited, she had another think coming. He slammed the door, turned to the bar and poured himself a double Dewar's Signature. Then another. Who the hell did she think she was, turning him down? And what did she mean, Google *Diane?* He took another drink and headed to the computer on his desk.

What was she talking about? What had *he* been talking about? There was no fucken goddess Diane. Oh, there she was. Diana. Oh, shit. She was protector of virgins. He thought all those goddesses loved to jump in and out of bed with mortals. Venus. That was the one he must have meant. But Venus didn't sound anything like...what was her name again?...Delores? No, Denise. On the other hand, it did sound like Vanessa. The beautiful, voluptuous Vanessa. He fumbled in his pocket for his cell phone, then took another drink while he waited for her to answer.

Hi, this is Vanessa. You can't possibly know how sorry I am to miss your call. Leave a message, and I'll get back to you as soon as I can. Wait for the—

"Hello—" Her breathless voice came on just as he was about to click off.

"Where were you?"

"On my way out the door. I had to dig the phone out of my purse."

"Wherever...whoever—cancel it. Meet me at the Bull and Bear in fifteen minutes."

"I can't, Nick. I can't just drop everything when you call."

"Sure, you can. Fifteen minutes." She loved the suite at the Waldorf.

"Make it twenty if you want me to wear that garter belt you love."

He smiled and licked his lips. "Twenty, then. But not a minute longer."

"Patience, baby. Didn't your mama tell you good things are worth waiting for?"

"Tell that to my dick." It was already tingling in anticipation. He put the phone in his pocket, finished his drink, and put on his jacket.

He walked through the deserted office, a king strolling through his darkened domain. Far off on the left, someone had left on a desk lamp. He thought of going over to turn it off, but his gait wasn't quite steady. Best just to keep walking straight for the exit and the elevators. He made a mental note of the desk. Whoever sat there would regret his negligence in the morning. He hoped, though, that it was that cute kid with the great tits. They would work out a way for him to forgive her....

When he got to the double doors leading to the elevator corridor, he paused. He desperately needed to take a piss. He turned to go back to his office and his private john. And he thought of something better than that long walk. The men's room for the staff was just to his right. That made more sense in his condition.

Heading toward it, he thought about Vanessa and that black lace belt with those long, satin garters. How he loved getting her out of that delicious contraption....

He was unaware of footsteps behind him. But he became quickly aware of the black-clad arm gripping his neck in a choke hold.

"What the hell—" He could scarcely gasp out the words. He tried to raise his hands to dislodge the arm, but the grip was like iron and he was woozy from the drinks and fast running out of breath.

"Take my watch. Wallet. Back pocket. Don't hurt me. What's your price?"

"Shut up. This is one deal you can't pull off." The harsh, whispered words whistled in his ear, sending a chill knifing through him. "Good night, Nick."

The arm tightened, his knees buckled. And then everything went as black as the arm clutching his throat.

CHAPTER 27

AS AGREED the night before, Leslie was at the hotel at eight o'clock the next morning. She laughed when she saw that Stephanie was wearing the SAVE THE WHALES sweatshirt Tom had brought back for her from Nantucket. "Now we really have to work in the aquarium," she said. "I have the same shirt. I got it when Mom and I went whale-watching. If I'd known that's what you were wearing, I'd have worn mine too. Oh, well." She grabbed Stephanie's hand. "Come on. I know a terrific place for breakfast."

"Back here by three!" Tom called after them.

"We'll be here!" Leslie assured him over her shoulder.

Tom was still smiling as he fastened his tie. He wished he were going with the girls. They were in for a much more pleasant day than he was. He shrugged into his jacket and headed for a quick breakfast at Espresso Etc. in the lobby.

While he ate, he thumbed through a copy of the *Baltimore Monitor,* Bowman's tabloid. Since it could give Rupert Murdoch's *New York Post* a run for its money in the right-wing-slant department, only a small streamer at the bottom of the front page took note of a Texas grand jury's indictment of Tom DeLay. Next to a thumbnail photo of the Speaker of the House, it announced: SLAMMED! "THE HAMMER" INDICTED FOR CONSPIRING TO VIOLATE ELECTION LAWS *See page10.* The rest of the front page screamed: STAR TURN FOR BALTIMORE! CITY TO HIGHLIGHT NEW "STAR SPANGLED" TRAIL. Inside, the first two pages of the paper were devoted to a spread detailing legislation introduced in Congress to establish a "Star Spangled Banner National Historic Trail," commemorating the War of 1812. Only passing mention was given to the fact that Virginia and the District of Columbia would also be included on the trail. The local, national and international news were all reported with an eye on any possible sensational angle. The lead editorial was devoted to a defense of Tom DeLay. Tom tossed the paper into a waste bin on his way out.

FLETCHER BOWMAN OVERSAW his media empire from the top floor of the Bowman Building, a mediocre glass-and-steel skyscraper built in the late 1950s. After staring at his photo ID, an armed security guard stationed inside its double glass doors announced Tom on his cell phone, and then told him to take the elevator to the penthouse floor. There, he was stopped by another armed guard, who also asked to see a photo ID. He, too, made a call, then unlocked a door and indicated the direction Tom was to follow. The walls were covered with larger-than-life blowups of news photos of Fletcher Bowman shaking hands with and towering over domestic and foreign statesmen and celebrities, past and present.

As Tom neared the executive suite, a woman of about fifty with short-cropped brown hair emerged. "Mr. Berenson?" She extended her hand. "I'm Joanna Fieldston, Mr. Bowman's assistant. I didn't know where to contact you. I called Hammond Enterprises first thing this morning, but the woman I spoke to didn't know your cell phone number or where you're staying. I'm afraid Mr. Bowman isn't here."

"Where is he?"

She shrugged. "I had to leave early yesterday. When I came in this morning, I found a note on my desk. He said he had to go out of town but would be back around noon. I was to reschedule his morning appointments...."

Tom tried not to show his annoyance. It wasn't this woman's fault. "I have a plane to catch this afternoon. I have to be back at my hotel by three to pick up my daughter."

"I know you're in from New York, so I didn't reschedule anyone else yet. I'm giving you priority. Can you make it at twelve-forty-five? Unless he has some unforeseen delays, he's sure to be at his desk by then. He's always very precise about the time."

"I hope you're right. I'll see you later."

Down in the lobby, Tom took out his cell phone and called Nick Hammond's office. He was told that Hammond hadn't come in to work yet. He was about to ask when he was expected when another call came in. "I'll call back later," he said, switching to the incoming call. It was Foster.

"Goddam it, Tom, where are you?"

"You know where I am. In Baltimore to see Bowman."

"Well, get the hell back here. Nick just walked into my office. He was hit last night. So Bowman obviously isn't our man."

"Not necessarily. Two minutes ago, I had to reschedule our appointment. Bowman left town unexpectedly yesterday and won't be back till noon. Maybe he was in New York. Let me talk to Hammond."

There was a mumbled exchange on the other end, and then Hammond's voice came over the phone:

"Fuck you, Berenson! I'm going to get you for this. If you were here on the job, this wouldn't have happened."

"I am on the job. That's why you guys sent me to Baltimore, remember? You hired me as a detective, not as a bodyguard. I told you to get protection. But you're all so damn macho you think you can take care of yourselves. Where did it happen?"

"At my office."

"Your office? Then surely you saw him. Or someone else did."

"No. It was after hours. I was alone. It was outside the john."

"How did he get into your private john without your seeing him?"

"Not my john, the staff's men's room. I was on my way out. I had to take a piss and didn't want to go all the way back to my office. I wish to hell now that I had. Oh, jeez! What am I going to do? How can I live this way?"

"Calm down. I'm sure your friend Al Foster will come up with a cure sometime soon."

"Yeah. After he finds a way to prevent prostate cancer. Oh, God!" He sounded like he was about to burst into tears.

"What time were you attacked?"

"Around eight. Maybe later."

"What were you doing there alone so late?"

"I stayed to be taped for the documentary."

"Was Nora Malcolm there? Maybe she got something on tape."

"No, she wasn't there. She just helped set up and then had to leave. She was going to GMU. Her assistant did the taping."

"Maybe she got something."

"Not unless the guy was hiding under my desk. The whole interview was in my office. She packed up everything and left when it was over. She didn't stop for any more footage. I watched her walk to the elevators. What a great ass! Oh, jeez!" His voice cracked. "Al, you gotta help me! It can't be over forever!"

Tom could hear Foster saying soothing things in the background.

"You'll talk to Al later. Right now you're talking to me. What time did Denise leave?"

"Who?"

"Denise. The woman who was interviewing you."

"Oh, yeah. Sevenish."

"And you left right after her?"

"No. I stayed on."

"Why?"

"Had some drinks."

"How long and how many?"

"How the hell should I know? I was furious at that unsociable black bitch. Half a drink and she was out the door. Wouldn't let me touch her. Arrogant bitch. Who does she think she is? I even offered her—"

"Spare me the details. When did you leave?"

"Eightish, I guess. I got pretty pissed. Called a great girl I know and told her to meet me at the Bull and Bear. Then I headed out and went to take that goddam pee."

"Tell me about the attacker."

"He came out of nowhere. Shit. If only I'd gone back to my office! If only—"

"Life is full of *if only's*. Did you get a look at him?"

"How could I? He came up from behind and grabbed my

throat in a chokehold. He was huge, though. That I know. Otherwise, I'd have been able to take him on. All I saw was that black sleeve and glove."

"What did he say?"

"Nothing."

"Nothing? Think. He must have said something."

"Maybe…. Yeah, he did say something, but I can't remember. He whispered. I was trying to fight him off…"

"Weren't there any cleaning people around?"

"They don't come on till after midnight."

"Why so late?"

"It's an arrangement we have with the contractor."

"Are they illegals?"

"I can't be bothered with such details. I know for a fact that some of the high and mighty in Washington have similar arrangements."

"Okay. What happened then?"

"I woke up on the floor. It was close to ten. I took a cab to the Waldorf."

"Why didn't you go directly to Al Foster? Surely you must have realized what had happened to you."

"I hoped it was just a mugging. Besides, I had a date waiting for me. But when I got to the Bull and Bear, I was told that she had left. Vanessa has a lot of virtues, if you know what I mean, but patience isn't one of them. I took a cab to her place. She was mad as hell till I told her I'd been mugged. We had a couple of drinks, then went to bed. But I couldn't get it up. She thought it was the drinks. I hoped it was. But this morning I couldn't get it up again. She was very understanding, said it was probably stress from the mugging. I hate it when bitches try to be understanding! When I was getting dressed, I found the note in my pocket."

"What does it say?"

"You know what it said: *You're not the man you thought you were.* I tore it up and flushed it down the crapper."

"You should have saved it for me."

"Why? So you could gloat?"

"Call your building's security office. Tell them you want a

copy of the tape of the people who came in and out of the building yesterday."

"They'll ask me why!"

"If they do, just say that you had a security breach that you want to check out but keep private."

Tom heard Foster's voice in the background, saying something about "a waiting room full of patients."

"Tell your patients to go fuck themselves or go home," Hammond told him. "*I'm* the only one you have to take care of right now."

"We're done for now," Tom said. "Let Al do whatever he can for you. We'll talk when I get back. Be sure to get that security tape."

FLETCHER BOWMAN DIDN'T bother to stand up or shake hands when Joanna Fieldston ushered Tom into his office. He was a big man who dwarfed even the mega-size executive desk he sat behind.

"You can tell Neil Hammond and his friends to go to hell," he said as Joanna closed the door behind her.

Though he wasn't invited to do so, Tom sat down in the visitor's chair closest to the desk and deliberately took a moment to lean back and make himself comfortable.

"I thought maybe that was what you went to New York to do in person yesterday."

Bowman's cheeks flushed with anger. The look on his face was pure menace as he leaned across the desk. "What are you, some kind of goddam detective? What makes you think I was in New York?"

Tom shrugged. "Just makes sense, with all that's going on."

"Doesn't make a shit's worth of sense to me. Your pals make me want to puke. I have no desire to see them, except to see them dead. I wasn't in New York." The brief flash of surprise that had come to his eyes before the glare chased it away told Tom he was lying about New York, not about seeing Hammond and his friends dead.

"That's too bad, because then they could have given you these papers to sign and saved me a trip." Tom reached into his briefcase and took out the large envelope he had been given to deliver. Bowman didn't extend his hand for it. Tom put it on his desk.

"You their lawyer?"

"No, just a messenger."

"Then give them this message: They can go fuck themselves. They'll never get their filthy hands on my company."

"From what I read in the *Wall Street Journal,* your back is up against the wall. You don't have much choice in the matter, unless you consider being taken over by Hammond or by Rupert Murdoch a choice."

His face turned crimson. "Murdoch! I wipe my ass with the *New York Post.* He wants to own the whole fucken world. But he'll never add Bowman Media to his belt. And neither will Nick Hammond and his pals." His lips stretched into a slow, nasty smile.

Tom nodded toward the envelope on Bowman's desk. "That's not what those papers say."

Bowman picked up the thick envelope and tore it in half as though it were a piece of tissue paper. Tom noted that the knuckles on his right hand looked raw.

"Tell Nick Hammond to shove it. As of last night, it's over."

"I talked to Nick a little while ago. He didn't tell me that it's over."

"Some guys just don't know when to give up. He and his pals will soon find out that no one messes with me. It's over. If they don't know it yet, they'll know it soon. So get your ass out of here before I call security and have them throw it out."

Tom took his time standing up. "Nasty bruise on your hand. Did you have an accident?"

Bowman smiled slowly and blew on his knuckles like a cowboy blowing smoke off his six-shooter. "That's what the other guy must be wishing. You should see his shiner."

Maybe I will, Tom thought as he walked out the door.

IN NEED OF some cleansing fresh air, Tom walked over to the harbor, sat down on a bench, and gazed out at the water. Once again he asked himself what he was doing, getting involved with these greedy, malicious men. Hadn't he had enough of the underbelly of humanity when he was a cop? But he knew what he was doing. He was taking advantage of an opportunity to keep Portman's mall away from his neighborhood and also to earn enough to send Stephanie to a college like Hopkins or any other expensive college she might choose. Besides, he had to admit that the puzzle intrigued him. It felt good to have all his cop's instincts back in working order. And then there was Nora. If he hadn't taken this on, he would never have met her, never have cut through the dark fog of grief shrouding him since he lost Beth. He would be glad to get back to New York. Even if he couldn't see Nora tonight, at least it would be comforting to know they were in the same city.

He pulled out his cell phone and called Stephanie.

"Hey, Dad."

"Where are you?"

"I was going to ask you the same thing. Leslie and I are back at the hotel, waiting for you. It's twenty to three."

Twenty to three! How long had he been sitting on that bench? "I'm on my way. Is your bag packed?"

"Packed and by the door, next to yours."

"See you in a few minutes."

He found Stephanie and Leslie on the sofa in the suite, drinking Cokes and listening to Stephanie's Pearl Jam CD.

"You missed a great day," Stephanie called out over the clamor.

"I'm sure it was more fun than mine," Tom told her, collecting their bags. "Did you cover everything on your list?"

"Just about," Leslie said, following Stephanie out the door. "We saved a couple of things for your next trip, which I'm hoping will be soon."

"Sounds good. Maybe we can tag along with your mom the next time she comes."

"Great. She can't get here often because of her schedule, but I'm sure she'd like that. Sometimes I think being on campus makes her a little sad. It's where she and my dad met."

"I know she's happy that you're here, though, and we are too. I can't thank you enough for all the time you spent with us."

"I loved it." She hugged Stephanie. "Call me."

On the flight home, Stephanie talked animatedly about the places she and Leslie had visited.

"With all that running around, did you take time out to eat?" Tom asked.

"Of course we did! We had lunch at a great Chinese place Leslie knows. Real tiny and out of the way. The food was terrific, but strange, and nothing like what we get in Brooklyn. Leslie says it's authentic and un-Americanized, like in most restaurants. I guess she should know. She lived in China for a couple of years while her folks were making documentaries there. She didn't get to see much, though. They left her in Beijing with a tutor while they traveled around."

"Sounds like she's had an interesting life. Do you feel deprived, not having been left with a tutor in Beijing?"

Stephanie laughed. "I'd much rather have been left with one in Paris. After lunch, we went to the aquarium. It's fantastic. I love the one we have in Coney Island, but you could fit three of them inside the one in Baltimore. It has a rainforest, and..."

Tom's mind began to wander. He enjoyed hearing about her day, but couldn't help wondering whether the girls had talked about him and Nora, and if so, what had been said. Suddenly, he felt like a teenager himself, and couldn't bring himself to ask.

"So, what did you talk about while covering all that territory?" he said finally.

"Oh, this and that. By the way, in case you're interested, Leslie said she thinks her mom likes you a lot."

"'Thinks'?"

"Evidently that's big praise from her mom. Leslie says she doesn't talk much about personal things. Like someone else I know." She gave Tom a long look, smiled, and popped on her earphones.

Tom leaned back in his seat. "...likes you a lot." The words had a nice ring. They warmed him all the way back to New York.

CHAPTER 28

MAX SERVED his skillet lasagna wearing the Hopkins sweat-shirt that Tom and Stephanie had brought back for him. As they ate, Stephanie told him all about the campus and the places she and Leslie had visited in Baltimore. When, during clean-up, Tom announced that he was going out for a while, Max and Stephanie exchanged knowing glances. They thought he was going to see Nora, and he didn't correct them. But when he got outside, he called Al Foster.

"I'm back. Where's Hammond? I want to see him."

"I'm with him at his place. If you want to talk to him, you'd better get here fast. He's called his pilot and has him getting his plane ready. He wants to go to his place in Bermuda."

"Did he get the building's security tape?"

"Yeah. He had it delivered here."

"I'm on my way. Don't let Hammond out till I get there."

"That could be easier said than done."

"Just do it."

Twenty minutes later he was in the mirrored lobby of Neil Hammond's Park Avenue condominium. When he asked to be announced, the doorman said, "I'm sorry, sir, but Mr. Hammond left on a trip a few minutes ago."

Tom refrained from cursing. "Please ring the apartment anyway. A mutual friend is waiting there to meet me."

The doorman dialed, listened, and hung up. "No answer, sir. A gentleman left with Mr. Hammond. Maybe that's the person you had in mind."

This time Tom did curse. "No offense," he said to the

doorman. "That's for the guy who left, not for you." He took out his cell phone and dialed Al Foster.

"Hello?" Foster sounded like his mouth was full.

"Where the hell are you?"

"I'm in the McDonald's on Seventy-second Street. Thought I'd have a bite while I waited for you."

"Where's Hammond?"

"Halfway to his airport. Look, despite what happened to him, the rest of him is hale and hardy. There was no way I could stop him."

Foster had finished his Big Mac and was halfway through his fries when Tom arrived. He turned the container toward Tom. "Join me?"

"No, thanks. I just had dinner."

"That never stops me."

"So I've noticed. How do you eat so much junk and manage to stay thin?"

"It's all in the genes. I was born with a great metabolism."

"Too bad. If you were fat, maybe you could have sat on Hammond and held him down till I arrived."

"What good would it have done? You spoke with him this morning. He told you all he remembered then."

"I wanted to see him. Did he have a black eye?"

Foster looked incredulous. "No."

"Any bruising?"

"No. The symptoms were the same as all the other guys'. Just those two tiny incisions and a puncture wound. Why do you think he'd be different?"

"Because Fletcher Bowman had bruised knuckles, and I suspect he was in New York last night."

"Do you think he's our man?"

"I wish he were. It would put an end to all this. But it's not his m.o. If he intended to do physical harm to your friends, he'd just beat the shit out of them. He's done it to lots of guys who have gotten in his way. I've checked him out, though, and he's never gotten physically violent with high-level business competitors. He prefers sliming them in his tabloids. Besides, unless he has been able to create elaborate cover-ups, which is not impossible, he really was out of the country when McGrath was hit. Still, I'm not eliminating him till I see the security tapes and do some more checking."

Foster pushed across the floor a shopping bag he had stashed under the table. "Be prepared to be bored out of your skull. Nick and I watched for a while. They're grainy. Everyone starts looking alike."

"Takes a practiced eye. You have to know what you're looking for."

"Maybe." Foster shrugged. "There's a big problem, though. Seems the camera in one of the elevators malfunctioned in the middle of the day and it wasn't caught and corrected till this morning."

"Damn. Was it a malfunction or did someone tamper with it?"

"The guy who delivered the stuff said they'd been having trouble with that camera on and off for weeks. They've asked for a new one, but the building's owners are dragging their feet."

"So billionaire landlords penny-pinch the same as slumlords in Brooklyn and the Bronx."

"I think it's in their genes. We're still waiting to get a replacement for the torn carpeting in my condo which cost a fortune."

Tom picked up the bag and got to his feet. "Let's hope our guy took an elevator with a working camera."

"And that you'll be able to recognize him." Foster gave Tom a level look. "Tony's getting real antsy. We all are."

"Then maybe it's time you went to the police. They have immediate access to all kinds of privileged information and could put a lot more men on the case."

"You know that's not a possibility."

"In that case, you'll just have to be patient. In the meantime, tell your pals to get bodyguards and to watch their backs. You should too."

Foster looked so surprised at the idea that he dropped the French fry he was about to pop into his mouth back into the container. Apparently it had never occurred to him that he, too, could be a victim.

FOSTER HAD BEEN right. The security tapes were as dull as an all-night session with a tax manual. Assuming that the castrator wouldn't be spending the entire day just hanging around, Tom began the search with tapes time-stamped in the late afternoon. He got a surprise in the Number Three elevator going down at four-forty-seven: There was Arnold Simon chatting with a man wearing a yarmulke and another man wearing the collar of a Roman Catholic priest. Tom couldn't see the other men's faces clearly, but he thought it was possible that the Jew was Rabbi Samuel Rosenberg, who had a Modern Orthodox congregation in Midwood and taught ritual at Yeshiva University. Tom had consulted him once about a case in Williamsburg. He wished now he could lip read better. He reversed the tape and saw the men boarding the elevator together on the fifteenth floor. They all exited together on the main floor, still talking.

Had Simon returned later and taken an elevator to the fourth floor, where Hammond had his offices? There was no trace of him at a later time. But, of course, there was that damn elevator with the malfunctioning camera. Could Simon have lucked out and taken that one both up and down? It seemed unlikely. The entire idea of Simon as the villain seemed unlikely, but over the years, Tom had arrested too many men who had hoped their good works would prevent them from being suspected of their criminal acts. Tomorrow, he was scheduled to have lunch with Simon. He would find out how the minister had spent Wednesday evening, and what he and the other clergymen had been doing on the fifteenth floor.

The rest of the tapes held no surprises or revelations. He spotted Nora and Denise arriving at five-forty-nine; Nora leaving at two minutes to six; Denise, at six fifty-six; Hammond staggering into the elevator at nine-fourteen. There were no other familiar faces among the few who were coming and going at that hour. Some were obviously cleaning staff; others, people who had worked overtime. None of them got on or off at the fourth floor. He would have them checked out, of course, but he doubted the castrator would be among them. Obviously, the guy had gotten lucky and taken the elevator with the bum camera. Or maybe he had managed to knock out the camera, which seemed the more likely scenario. Or maybe he used the fire-exit stairs. It was only the fourth floor, and the guy clearly was in good condition.

Tom turned off the TV in his bedroom and put the tapes back into the shopping bag. It was nearly midnight. Way too late to call Nora. Yet he longed to hear her voice. Its soothing sound was the only thing that could ease the sweet, fierce ache of missing her. It was a delicious feeling, one he had never expected to enjoy again.

Maybe, like him, she was up and working late. Maybe she missed him too. He held his cell phone, trying to decide. Then, as if by a will of its own, his finger speed-dialed her home number.

It rang four times before the answering machine kicked in. She was out. His stomach contracted, sending the bitter taste of disappointment up through his throat. Should he leave a message or just hang up? What kind of message could he leave at this hour?

But before he could make up his mind, her beautiful, husky, sleepy voice came through. "Hello…who is this?"

"Hi. It's me, Tom. I—"

"What time is it?"

"After midnight. I know it's unforgivable to be calling at this hour, but I thought you might be working late."

"I usually am," she yawned. "But I haven't been sleeping well. Took a pill tonight and went to bed early."

"Sorry." He could visualize her sitting on the edge of her bed, her hair tousled, her eyes still a little dreamy from sleep. Was she wearing her silky, blue kimono? Was she wearing anything under it?

"Don't be. I was hoping to hear from you." She sounded more awake now. "Leslie called, and I know she had a great time with you. How did Stephanie like Hopkins?"

"I think she moved it to the top of her list. It's a very impressive school. Speaking of impressive, Leslie is terrific. She went out of her way to show us around and to take Stephanie under her wing. She's a beautiful girl, both inside and out. Just like her mom."

"Thanks, but I'm responsible for only half her genes. I think she gets all the good ones from her dad. Every time I look at her, I see him. There are times when she'll say something or a certain expression will flit across her face and…." Her voice trailed off into a poignant sigh.

He looked over at the photo of Stephanie and Beth on his dresser. More and more, Stephanie resembled her mother—same eyes, same nose, same determined chin. And then there were her smiles, her frowns, and all those little mannerisms and expressions. They weren't copied. They were innate. "I know what you mean. I have the same thing with Stephanie. It hurts, but it's a good kind of hurt."

"Do you think it will always hurt?"

"I don't know."

For a moment, they both got lost in memories. Then Nora seemed to give herself a mental shake. "Sorry. I didn't mean to go all maudlin on you. It's not like me."

He thought of how she liked to preserve her cool, efficient image, and he tried to help her. "It's probably the late hour, combined with that sleeping pill. What was keeping you awake?"

She sighed. "This damn project. It's taking longer than it should. I want to wrap it up and get on to more important things. Denise and I are itching to get down to New Orleans, but these guys won't cooperate. I was supposed to interview Jason Gilbert the other night, but he wasn't there. Then Denise's interview with Hammond didn't turn out right. The egomaniac was jumping up and down on all his exercise equipment and came out looking like an idiotic aging jock, which, of course, is what he is. I think he may have made a pass at Denise, too, because she doesn't want to go back to re-shoot. I was ready to do it myself, but I couldn't get through to Hammond. Al Foster finally returned my call and said Hammond was taking off for Bermuda and no one knows when he'll be back. If he thinks I'm going to go chasing after him down there, he—" She stopped herself and took a breath. "Oops. Sorry. I'm venting. Let's talk about something more pleasant. How did the business part of your trip go?"

For a second he was nonplussed. Had she discovered the real reason why he was involved with these guys? Then he remembered that he had told her he was going to Baltimore to look over the library in an estate sale and that while he was there, he and Stephanie would check out Hopkins. It was another lie he had put between them, and he hated it. Nora was so open and aboveboard with him. She deserved better. Somehow, when he finally solved this damn case and could put it behind him, he would find a way to tell her the truth.

"Tom?"

"Oh, sorry. Guess I'm half asleep. Unfortunately, the sale turned out to be a waste of time. The only worthwhile books were collectors' items that I couldn't afford, and as for the rest, there was nothing of real interest to my customers. I don't need to invest in more stock to gather dust in the back room. No, the best part of the trip was the time I spent with the girls. It was fun watching them together. They took to each other right from the start. As if they'd known and liked each other for years."

"Yes, I know." Was it drowsiness that made her voice even more husky, or, like him, was she thinking of how it had been between the two of them from the start? When she added softly, "I'm glad," he felt sure she was.

"I'm glad too," he said. "About so many things."

"Yes," was all she said, but it was enough to let him know her thoughts were at one with his. The silence that followed was a soft, reflective one. Finally, she said, "It's late, Tom, and I have a full schedule tomorrow."

"Can you fit me in for dinner?"

"Sorry. I've got a dinner meeting. I'm trying to raise money for my next project."

"Maybe I could drop over later, then."

"I'm not sure when the meeting will be over."

"Call me."

She hesitated.

"Do you know there's a Barbara Pym cookbook, and I just acquired a copy?"

She laughed. "You really do know the way to a girl's heart, don't you? Okay. It will probably be late, but I'll call you."

He didn't realize he had been holding his breath until it came out in a happy rush.

CHAPTER 29

T OM PAUSED in the doorway to watch Arnold Simon ladling out stew in a soup kitchen in Bedford-Stuyvesant. There were three other servers, two women and a man, and they all smiled and said a few cheerful words to each person who extended a bowl. But Simon went further. He addressed everyone in his line by name and chatted intently with him or her for a while. His line moved slowly, but everyone left it with much more nourishment than a bowl of stew.

"I'm Louise. May I help you?" The voice came from a gray-haired African-American woman wearing an apron over her sweat shirt and jeans. She had left her position at a table of bread, rolls and bagels to greet Tom.

He shook the hand she held out to him. "I'm Tom. I'm here to see the Reverend Simon."

She smiled. "Aren't we all!"

"Actually, we have a lunch date."

Her smile and gesture took in the entire room. "Then you're obviously in the right place."

Tom looked from the tables crowded with diners to Arnold Simon, who was still busy offering counsel and comfort food. "I was supposed to meet him here and then we'd go on to someplace else." He shrugged and smiled. "Maybe he forgot."

"Arnold never forgets anyone or anything," Louise assured him.

"Tom!"

They turned to see Simon looking their way and gesturing them over to him with his ladle.

Louise patted Tom's back to send him on his way, then went over to a table and began chatting with the diners.

"Glad you could make it," Simon said. "Pick up a bowl and enjoy our four-star stew."

"Looks delicious, but I was hoping to take you to lunch some-place where we can talk uninterrupted. I doubt that's possible if we stay here."

Simon nodded as he took off his apron. "I doubt it too, but first let me show you around."

Tom knew it would be useless to protest. Besides, he had heard so much about Simon's good works that he was curious to see one project close-up. The soup kitchen was in a two-story storefront. Three-quarters of the main floor was devoted to the dining area. The walls were painted an airy sky-blue and deco-rated with huge reproductions of sunny, joyful Impressionist art. There were Renoir's "Luncheon of the Boating Party" and "The Swing"; Monet's "Springtime" and a couple of his water-lily stud-ies; Van Gogh's sunflowers and irises; and several of Gauguin's Tahitian scenes with at least minimally clad beauties. The tables were round and covered with colorful plastic cloths, and at the center of each one stood a vase with bright artificial flowers.

"What do you think of our dining room?" Simon asked.

"I have to admit that when I first walked in, I thought I had come to the wrong address. This looks more like a neighborhood restaurant than my idea of a soup kitchen."

"That's because everyone, including most people who set them up, has the wrong idea of a soup kitchen. The people who come here have lives filled with hardship, tragedy, adversity. We try to make our facilities a place where they can find a little respite from that. Eating should be a pleasant experience."

"I agree, but there are some who might say you make it too pleasant and encourage freeloading."

His eyes hardened. "Like my friend Lyle Wayne and his bud-dies inside Congress and out. Yes, they like the poor to grovel. Well, I'd like to take Lyle and all his pals and make them live for a month without their wallets and bank accounts and charge cards. Make them live on the street not knowing where their next nickel is coming from. Let's see how they'd enjoy groveling for a meal when their bellies are empty." He looked around. "There isn't a person in here who wouldn't prefer to be self-sufficient. There's no need to push their noses in it. In the afternoon we get mostly the unemployed and senior citizens who have to choose between paying their rent and buying medicine and eating. In the evening, we get families. Most of them are working poor who just can't stretch their budgets to take care of all the needs of their families, especially their sick kids who are thrown off health insurance because they have so-called pre-existing conditions. This may be the only place where they can escape from their troubles for a few precious moments."

He opened a door at the back of the dining area. "Let me show you the kitchen." The equipment wasn't new, but it was spotless and gleaming. "The cooking, cleanup, and shopping are all done by volunteers, and many of the people who come here for meals are among them, or return to be among them when they get their lives together."

Next, they walked up to the second floor, which was devoted to office and community space. A man of about fifty was typing at one of the computers that were set up on a long table. Simon rested a hand on his shoulder. "How's it going, Bob?"

"It's getting a little easier. Angela's coming to help me when school's out."

"Did you eat?"

Bob shook his head. "I want to get some time in before Angela gets here. Show her I've made a little progress."

"Food in your belly helps feed your mind. Go downstairs and see Louise. She'll fill up a plate for you."

Bob hesitated, looking at the computer screen.

"Put it on hibernate. You've signed up for it till four, haven't you? Then, go on. You'll still have time to study before Angela gets here. You wouldn't want your belly growling while you're working together, would you?"

"You're right, Reverend. Thanks."

Simon shook his head as he watched Bob walk over to the stairs. "From the day he dropped out of school at sixteen, that man worked in the factory of a giant pharmaceutical company in Queens. Two years ago, the company shut down without notice and moved all manufacturing to China. Bob hasn't been able to find work since. He's trying to get his GED, but he's dyslexic, which complicates things. We're helping him all we can, and he's making progress."

"Is Angela his daughter?"

"No. His wife took the kids and moved back with her folks in Ohio about a year ago. Angela is a teenage volunteer. She's terrific with him. I'm trying to find scholarship money for her. She'd make a wonderful teacher, but there's no way her mom, who's bringing up four kids on her own, can afford to send her to college."

On the other side of the room, a corner had been set up for children. There were kid-size chairs and tables, toys and books. Nearby there were shelves with books and magazines for adults. Computer manuals, inspirational self-help, resume-preparation guides—all were well worn and dog-eared.

"I understand you're in the book business." Simon spoke from over his shoulder. "We could always use some more. It's hard to keep current."

Tom took the not-so-subtle hint. "I'll send over a carton. How about I add a few westerns and romances? All work, et cetera."

"Sounds good."

"Why not come back with me now and pick them out? Then we can eat someplace in my neighborhood."

"Where's that?"

"Brooklyn Heights."

Simon shook his head. "That's a world away from here."

"A taxi could get us there in minutes."

Simon laughed. "If you could find one in this neighborhood. There's a pizza place a few blocks away. We'll go there. Come on. Having spurned our four-star stew, you must be hungry, and I don't want to be away too long."

On the stairs, they passed a few of the people who had eaten and were now on their way up for time at the computers. Simon had a word of encouragement for each one.

The pizza store was only about three blocks away, but it took a while to get there. Simon appeared to know almost everyone on the street, and they were all eager to stop him and chat. He had a good word and helpful advice for every one of them.

And then he spotted two teenagers smoking pot in an alley. He was on them in a flash. "Get that garbage out of your mouth! Are a couple of puffs worth risking time in jail?"

Tom held his breath. Simon still had his football physique, but the kids were a lot younger and over six feet. He expected them to pull a gun or a knife. Or at the very least to tell Simon to fuck off. Instead, they dropped their joints and merely looked on while Simon ground them to dust under his heel.

"Why aren't you in school?"

"Come on, Rev. You know why. School sucks." The boy who spoke looked a little older, a little more self-assured than his friend.

"Not as much as jail sucks. You think you're going to be sixteen all your life? No way. Where will you be when you're twenty-five? Thirty-five? Sixty?"

"Shit. Everyone knows we don't got those kind of years, Rev."

"Not in this hood," his friend added.

"Not in this hood the way you two are going. Trouble isn't a profession. It's a destination—to jail or to the grave. You're smarter than that. Your lives are worth more than that." Simon pulled a notebook and ballpoint from his pocket and handed it to the more talkative boy, but his gaze took in both of them. "Write down your full names and addresses. And don't try to shit me, because I'll find them out. You know I will."

He looked at the pad when the boys handed it back. He flipped to a new page, wrote something down, tore out the page and handed it to the older boy. "Okay, DeVon. Do you and Randolph know where my center is?"

The boys nodded.

"Get there. *Now.* Give that to Ms. Louise. She'll give you some real food to eat and show you what to do to help with the cleanup. Then she'll take you upstairs and get you started on studying for your GED's. I expect to see you there every day from now till you earn those diplomas. Then we're going to get you into college or find you a steady job. Probably both."

"Yeah, sure," DeVon grumbled under his breath. "At Harvard University and then Chase Bank."

"Yeah, definitely. I don't give up on guys I believe in, and I believe in you. It's time you started believing in yourselves. Go on, now. I expect to see you at the center when I get back, and every day from now on. If you don't show up, I have guys twice your size who'll be out looking for you."

"Jesus," Randolph said, but the boys had already started off in the direction of the center.

"Don't bring him into the conversation until you're ready to bring him into your life!" Simon called after them. "Till then, it's just us, and I'm not as easygoing and forgiving as he is. Stand up straight. Let's see some pride in your steps."

The boys paused for a second, and Tom fully expected to see them give Simon the finger and run off in another direction.

"Go on!" Simon sounded like a drill sergeant. "And pull up your pants! You aren't rap singers on top of the charts."

They hiked up their jeans and headed for the center. Simon looked after them a moment, then turned and began to walk in what Tom hoped was the direction of the pizza place.

"Will they really show up?" Tom asked, falling into step beside him.

"The kids in this neighborhood know that once I get hold of them, I don't give up. I just wish I could get to more of them. Those two want to be helped. Despite their swagger, I could see it in their eyes."

"So they'll keep coming back."

"Once they make that first trip through the door, there's a strong probability that they'll keep coming. We have to fight a lot of negative outside influence and peer pressure, but every time they come back, the chances of their completing the program increase. It's not just studying and helping out around the center. We get them involved in community projects and in helping one another. It builds up their pride and self-confidence. And I also have a powerful secret weapon."

"Which is?"

"Louise. A few years ago, she lost her only child to a stray bullet when two drug dealers were shooting it out. A beautiful, bright girl just fifteen years old. Now every kid who walks through our doors becomes Louise's kid. She's determined to get them the life her daughter was robbed of. A lot of the kids don't give a damn about me, but they don't want to disappoint Louise. And recently a new volunteer came on board who's terrific with the kids. Denise Jackson. Maybe you remember her. She was there with her boss at the reunion, working on that ridiculous documentary."

"Sure, I remember Denise. What's she doing with the kids?"

"She's teaching them how to use various devices, getting them to make a documentary of their own about their neighborhood, the trouble spots, the things that need changing. To get in on the project, they have to keep up with their studies."

"Sounds terrific."

"It is, and she is. She's a great role model for the girls, and I think the guys all have crushes on her. She knows where they're coming from. She was born poor, but, unlike a lot of the kids she works with, she had a father who was determined to get the family out of poverty. He struggled and saved and finally managed to open a little restaurant that did so well that he was able to open a few more and send her off to college. Unfortunately, he lost it all not long ago. It was too much for him, and he took his own life. He was all she had, and the loss devastated her. She says working with the kids here helps her cope with her depression."

"Who'd have thought? She seems to be so positive and focused."

"Most people have a side they hide from the world. As a man who spends his life with books and literature, I'm sure you know that."

"Right." Tom didn't add that he knew it even better as a man who had spent so many years as a cop.

The pizza parlor was mostly takeout, but there were a couple of tables in the back. Before they ordered their calzone and salads, Simon had a long talk with the owner, checking on every member of his family, following up on the help that Simon had gotten for the man's Alzheimer-stricken father-in-law, and whether he'd finally gotten his daughter to leave her abusive boyfriend and seek counsel at one of Simon's women's shelters, and offering to counsel his brother when he got out on parole.

When they were at last sitting at their table, Simon shook his head. "Nick has a lot on his plate besides pizza and pasta."

"Seems to me you have even more."

"Ah, but I choose to take on other people's troubles. They don't choose the troubles that are visited on them."

"You certainly do a lot to help them through the hard times."

Simon sighed. "Not nearly enough. There's never enough time, enough volunteers, enough money to do all that has to be done. And I can reach only tiny corners of the world. I need all the help I can get." He gave Tom a meaningful look. "You know, there's nothing like the satisfaction you get from helping others. How about coming down the center and helping out? You could work with the teenagers, get them interested in books and reading, help them find out what kind of jobs or careers they're suited for. Look at all Denise is accomplishing. In just a few hours a week you could do so much good. You—"

Tom held up his hand to stop Simon before he felt like a complete heel for turning him down. "Wish I could, but I'm already overcommitted. I have to work long hours at my shop to keep it from going under. I have to look after a teenage daughter and an aging father-in-law whose health isn't the greatest. And now, to earn money for my daughter's college tuition, I've taken on the job of helping Blair Whitney gather information for his book." He saw that Simon was not about to give up. Before the minister could speak again, Tom reached for his checkbook. "I really don't have any time to spare right now, but maybe I can help out a little this way."

As Tom wrote, and Simon looked aloof from worldly things and goods, he remembered Nora's warning to leave his checkbook home when he met with Simon. He smiled to himself. They would have a laugh over this when he told her about it this evening.

"Thank you." Simon placed the check in an inside pocket and gave his jacket a little satisfied pat. "You're most kind."

For a change, Tom felt pleased that he had taken on Portman's job. At least it enabled him to be generous. "And I won't forget the books I promised you," he assured Simon, though he was sure there was no way Simon would let him forget.

The two men leaned back to allow Nick to place their salads and calzone on the table. "Enjoy," he commanded. "There's plenty more where this come from."

"Best calzone in Brooklyn," Simon assured Tom as he took a bite.

Tom thought it was just an exaggerated compliment to please Nick, who beamed as he turned to go back to the counter, but his first bite confirmed Simon's pronouncement. He hoped everything else the minister said would prove equally true. And then he said casually, "I thought I saw you on Broadway near the Woolworth Building on Wednesday evening. It must have been around eight or nine o'clock. I was too far away to be sure."

Simon shook his head. "Couldn't have been me. I was at our drug rehab center in Jamaica Wednesday evening. Funny, though. I was in that very building earlier with Rabbi Sam Rosenberg and Father Ed O'Connor. We were trying to convince Ronald Townsend to replace the community center that's in a dilapidated building he bought in Crown Heights with a new and better one when he knocks it down and builds his next fancy luxury condominium."

"And were you successful?"

"On the first trip? Never."

"But you'll keep trying."

"First comes the quiet, diplomatic approach. Then come the noisy demonstrations."

"Even those don't work some of the time."

"Most of the time," Simon corrected him. "But we have to keep trying. It shows the public how important these things are."

"What about your friend Tony Portman? Maybe you can get him to put up a community center in the area. It would build good will for him."

Simon's eyes hardened. "Tony Portman's not a friend, just a fraternity brother, which I'm sure he'd rather forget. Like the other brothers in our year, he's not interested in building good will. Only in accumulating money and power."

"But he's contributed to your causes, hasn't he?"

"Sure. But only enough to shut me up and get rid of me. I'd never get him to take on a project like this."

"Maybe I'm sounding like the minister here, but surely you can't know that unless you first try."

"What makes you think I haven't? I'm talking from experience.

Believe me, if I walked into Tony's office with Jesus Christ himself by my side and asked him to build a community center or any other project where he wouldn't make a huge profit, he'd throw me out. And tell me to take 'the greedy Jew' with me."

Tom thought it best to smile as though Simon was making a joke, but he could see in his eyes that he wasn't. He may have preached love of one's fellow man, but it was obvious that there wasn't much love in his heart for Tony Portman.

Simon's face softened. "Not to worry. We'll get our center in the end. We'll just have to go out and raise the funds for it. It means working longer and harder, but I'm used to that. I have to admit I even like it. If doing God's work was easy, it wouldn't be called *work*, would it?" He took a satisfied bite of his calzone. "Now tell me about yourself."

It wasn't just a polite conversation changer. Simon was obviously genuinely interested. Tom sensed he couldn't just dismiss it with a "nothing much to tell." So he kept it as brief as possible, telling a little about losing Beth, and how he and Stephanie and Max were building a life together. He ended, "Stephanie will soon be off to college, which is why I took the job of helping Blair Whitney with his project. I can use the extra money toward her tuition."

"Blair is a good man. He's one of my contributors, and I've heard he devotes time to running writing programs for prisoners out there. How do you know him?"

Tom reached for his coffee cup to avoid Simon's gaze. "He ordered some books from my website, and we began corresponding through e-mail. When he needed some help, he thought of me. So that's why I'm here." He reached into his pocket and took out his notebook. "What kind of interesting anecdotes can you tell me about your fraternity years? Great plays on the football field. Good deeds...."

"Good deeds—the Golden Guys? You've got to be kidding."

"High jinks, then. Nights on the town. Incidents that will add a little color to Blair's book."

"I'm the wrong guy to come to for that. I don't look back on those years with rose-colored glasses. I'm sure Tony and Doug and the rest of the guys will have plenty of stories for you, though not all of them may be printable."

Tom laughed. "I got a few from them that I'm sure Blair will clean up before they go into the book, but he'd appreciate something from you, a man of God and not a wheeler dealer like the others. How about a football memory? A great pass you made, or something the coach said that inspired you for all time."

"Lou West wasn't much of an inspirational guy. Just believed in winning at any price. He's had a hard life, though, and I'm glad to see that his book is a big success. I ran into him Wednesday when I was on my way back from the meeting with Townsend. We stopped for coffee. Had a good talk. He's a very bitter man. I have to keep in better touch with him. He needs help."

So Lou West was near Hammond's office not long before Hammond was hit. That was news. "I thought he was away on his book tour."

"That seems to be winding down. He said he's here for a few weeks, working as a consultant on a new program for ESPN."

"Is that where their offices are?"

Simon shrugged. "Who knows? Lou didn't say why he was in the area. It's a busy part of town. You said that you were there later too. And when Lou and I left the restaurant, we ran into Vittorio Capperrelli. He's a strange guy. He greeted Lou like a long-lost brother, but he looked like he'd seen a ghost when I held out my hand and reminded him that we'd met at a big party Tony Portman had thrown back in August. He seemed relieved when I said I had to be going. I think he had somehow gotten wind of Lou's ESPN project and hoped to get in on it. Maybe it's the clerical collar. It has that effect on some people."

"Not on your fraternity brothers. I'm sure they were happy to see you at the reunion."

"Probably because they figured I wouldn't hit on them for contributions there. They always make a good show of welcoming me on public occasions. Having a clergyman among their number is almost as good press as having a Nobel laureate unless he's a leftist or atheist. But I think that even more than they detest Jason Gilbert for being a Jew, they disdain me for being one of them and rejecting the life of greed and privilege and power they believe they're all entitled to."

"Looks to me like you're getting more out of life than they are."

"I didn't make the change to get more out of life. That would just be another kind of greed."

"Then why did you do it?" Tom couldn't resist asking the question that had been in the back of his mind since the first time he saw Simon among his peers. "Forgive me for asking, but I've met many types of people over my lifetime, yet never someone like you. Did you have an epiphany? Suddenly hear God call out to you?"

Simon's smile was the kind that is turned on a child who has asked a taboo question.

"Sorry. I didn't mean to get personal."

"No problem." Simon dismissed the apology with a wave of his hand. "The truth is, epiphanies are damn hard to come by. God didn't call out to me, Tom. I called out to God. Sometimes a bad conscience can lead to good things." He shook his head. "That's why I told you I'm the wrong guy to come to for amusing anecdotes about the good old days at GMU. You're probably thinking of me as a younger version of the man I am now. Back then, I was as much of a hell raiser as the other guys. Maybe I was a little more studious, but like most kids, I wanted to be popular and to belong. If I had any qualms, I kept them to myself, and they usually disappeared in the flood of booze we consumed. We harassed professors we thought were too tough and classmates who rubbed us the wrong way.

"The first time the booze cure didn't work was when we rigged the engine in old Professor Grinwald's car. The guy had his grandson with him when it went out of control. The kid went through the windshield, was in a coma for a couple of days, and then needed plastic surgery on his face. We were scared out of our skulls for about a week, but, though Grinwald probably had his suspicions, nothing was traced to us and it was put down as an accident. Then there were the girls. They'd lure ones they considered social climbers to the fraternity house, get them drunk and have at them. The guys always said the girls were so drunk they were willing, but I had my doubts. I had sisters, though, so I stayed away whenever one of those parties was planned. Unfortunately,

I did witness one in our junior year. I didn't take part, but there was no way I could leave without the guys making life hell for me afterward. That time, it was two girls." He shuddered. "I can still hear their screams. The guys raped them, then just threw them out like so much garbage."

"Did they report it?"

"Are you kidding? Girls didn't do that back in those days. At least not at GMU. I understand that too many of them don't do it these days, either." Simon shook his head. "I can't remember their names if I ever knew them in the first place, and I no longer remember what they looked like. But I can still hear their screams. It's those screams, and the look on the face of Lou West's son as he begged for at least one of us to come with him when we forced him out into the cold and rain, drunk and half naked, on a paper chase we knew he could never complete, that I could never get out of my mind." He made a fist. "I can still hear myself laughing at him even when I knew in my heart that I should have turned my back on my brothers and gone with him." He sighed and shook his head. "Those memories haunted me and finally hounded me into the ministry. Those and so many other memories of damaging, disgusting things we chalked up as fun. I can't ask any of the victims for forgiveness, but I'm trying to work my way through to some kind of redemption."

"Seems to me you must be well on your way to it."

"That's not for any of us to judge. And I certainly can't get there until I've made my brothers see how wrong they have been. But they're not interested."

"Somehow that doesn't surprise me. They look to me like men who'll never change."

"That's where you're wrong. They have changed." Simon's eyes grew dark with anger. "Their venality has intensified. Every one of them is three, four times the miscreant he was when we were young. And now they do ten times the harm they did back then. They let nothing and no one get in the way of their greed for money and power. Their paths are strewn with wrecked lives and careers and hopes. And when I try to get through to them, they laugh and try to turn me away with a contribution." His face reddened. "But they're finding out that their money can't buy me off. They'll never be rid of me until they face up to their wrongs and change."

"And how do you plan to go about that?" Tom asked carefully.

"I've got my ways." There was none of the benevolence of Jesus toward sinners in Simon's eyes, only the fire of an Old Testament prophet.

A chill went up Tom's spine. "Tony Portman, for example. How do you plan to get through to him?"

"I'll get to Tony. I'll get to them all. But right now I'm concentrating on Lyle Wayne." He spit out the senator's name as though it was something spoiled and unexpected in his calzone. "One would hope that the very activity of running for office, of having to be out among the public, would make him aware of and sensitive to the needs of the people. But, no. He's the same arrogant, self-satisfied, nincompoop he always was—only more so. And he has the audacity to think he has been chosen by Destiny to become president of our great country. And nothing or no one can stop him."

"It's happened before," Tom said.

"Once is enough."

"I doubt that Wayne will be running anytime soon. The Republicans are sure to nominate McCain to run in 2008. After the dirty tricks Bush pulled on him, they're bound to give the man his turn. They owe him that."

"Since when has that counted for anything?" Simon shook his head. "No. I know what Lyle and his buddies have planned for 2008. I was there, in on it, part of it, when they plotted it way back when we were all a bunch of drunken sophomores. Everything they've done since then has been working toward that goal. I turned my back on it when I walked away from the so-called good life, but it's what drives those men. Every one of them."

Tom remembered the secret meeting in Nantucket that Jason Gilbert had told him about. Were these guys really planning to take over the country? *President* Lyle Wayne? He'd make even Bush look good. "Excuse me for saying this, Reverend, but Lyle Wayne is a putz, as we say here in Brooklyn. He's greedy and ruthless and ignorant of the real needs of the country and the people. Whatever they planned long ago, surely these men have changed their minds. They wouldn't want him in the White House."

Simon looked at Tom as though he were not too bright himself. "It's precisely *because* he is a putz that they want him there. The country, the world will be their exclusive territory. They'll be pulling Wayne's strings. This will be the final step on their march toward a corporate takeover of the country."

"Wayne will have to be nominated first, then elected."

"From what I hear, they're working on it. They're getting all the pieces into place. They've got it all figured out. What they haven't figured on is me." He raised his hand and called over to Nick for the check.

"On the house, Rev," Nick called back.

"No way. I teach the kids that they have to pay their way on earth and that only God's love is on the house."

Tom grabbed the check before Nick could hand it to Simon. "Expense account," he explained. "This is on Blair."

"Doesn't seem fair," Simon said as they left the restaurant. "I didn't give you anything Blair can use in his book."

"You're a man of honor. Knowing Blair paid for the lunch may help you to think of something." He reached in his pocket for his card. "When you do, give me a call."

Simon looked at the card. "Beth's Book Nook. Nice name. That reminds me. When you send those books, I'd appreciate it if you'd add a few for the kids, little ones through teens."

"I'd intended to." They stopped and shook hands at the subway entrance to the A train. "What did you mean before when you said that when it came to the Golden Guys' plans for Senator Wayne, they hadn't figured on you?" he asked casually.

Simon's eyes hardened. "I meant that I'm going to get to him first, before they get him set to run. I'm going to take that arrogant son of privilege and make him see all the misery around him. Then, when they get him where they want him, he'll be where I want him too. I'll be at him day and night, making sure he takes care of the people who need it most."

"Admirable, but isn't it a bit naive?"

"Deep inside everyone is a little kernel of good that gives him or her the capacity to change. I haven't found it in my other fraternity brothers yet, but I'll never give up looking for it, no matter how much it gets under their skin. I'm determined to find it in Lyle before it's too late. In fact, I'm starting tomorrow. Lyle's coming in for the weekend. He's scheduled to address a Heritage Foundation breakfast at the Waldorf Sunday morning. He's agreed to accompany me on my nightly rounds tomorrow. I know he's just doing it to get me off his back, but I'll open his eyes all right. We're meeting in the Bowery, then going on to my women's shelter not far from there, and then off to our drug rehab halfway house on Avenue A. And I told him to come alone. I don't want any of his snooty entourage following us and whispering snide remarks in his ear. He agreed to let Denise Jackson and her boss, Nora Malcolm, accompany us and tape the tour."

"Impressive, but I don't think one night will change him."

"Neither do I. But I'm not stopping there. I've got three years before the next election. One way or another, he'll be a changed man by then."

It wasn't the words but the look on Simon's face that flashed across Tom's mind all the way back to Brooklyn Heights. He couldn't decide whether it reminded him of Carl Heinrich Bloch's painting of Jesus preaching on the Mount—or of Gustave Doré's drawing of Moses hurling down the Ten Commandments at the reluctant Jews.

CHAPTER 30

I T WAS TEN-THIRTY-FIVE when Tom's cell phone went off. He had been sitting in the living room, willing it to ring, yet he jumped when the call came through. With a rush of pleasure and relief, he saw it was Nora. He had feared she had forgotten her promise last night.

"Did I wake you?"

"It's Friday night, the evening's barely begun. How did your dinner meeting go?"

"Too long, obviously. But I did get a promise for some funding. Not as much as I'd like, but it will encourage others to get on board. I hope. How has your evening been going?"

"Stephanie's out with her friends, and Max and I have been having such a high old time watching a re-run of *The Big Sleep* that Max fell asleep even before Lauren Bacall made her entrance."

"Great movie. I've probably seen it a dozen times, but I've never been able to figure it out."

"That's the beauty of it. Every time you see it, it's a challenge. If you like, I can come over and give my interpretation of the plot."

She laughed. "That would spoil it for me. I like the challenge. One of these days, I'll figure it out for myself. In the meantime, I'll just enjoy watching Bogart." She hesitated, then added, "As for coming over, maybe we should skip this evening. It's getting late."

"Not that late. I can grab a cab and be there in twenty minutes. Don't forget, I'm bringing Miss Pym. Put the kettle on, and we'll solve all the world's problems with a cup of tea."

"All right," she gave in. "Earl Grey or Darjeeling?"

"You choose. See you soon."

Max's look of concern when Tom woke him to say he was on his way out, quickly turned to one of pleasure when he learned it was to see Nora. He got up and started for the kitchen. "Enjoy yourself. And don't worry. I'll make myself a strong cup of coffee so I'll only be pretending to be asleep when Stephie gets home."

As Tom had expected, traffic was fairly light, and it was just a little after eleven when he rang Nora's bell. She had used the intervening time to make herself comfortable, and she padded to the door in bare feet, jeans and an I ♥NEW YORK T-shirt. Her face was scrubbed and her hair still damp from a quick shower.

"You look like a teenager," Tom said, and patted down a wayward curl.

She gave him a quick kiss. "Wish I felt like one. Then I'd be full of energy and not so pooped."

He hoped that didn't mean she would want him to leave soon.

Off in the kitchen, the kettle began to screech. "Go sit down," Nora said. "I'll bring in the tea."

On the table in front of the sofa, a tray was set up with cups and a plate of Lorna Doones. Tom put the little cookbook beside it and settled down to wait. In a moment Nora came in with an elegant pink-and-gold teapot.

"We have to let this brew for a few minutes," she said. As she set it down, she spotted the book. Her face lit up with delight. "Small and compact, just like her novels. Thank you, Tom!"

She curled up beside him and opened the book. "I hope it has her recipe for marmalade. Her characters were always making marmalade."

"'Fraid not. But there is one for plum jam, and fairy cakes."

"Fairy cakes! The name has always enchanted me." She leafed through the book. "Here they are…yum. I'm going to have to make them sometime. Oh, and rock buns! And Victoria sandwich cake, just like all her characters ate."

"Or at least hoped to eat. Sometimes, just as they were disappointed in love, they were disappointed at tea," Tom reminded her.

"True, but her readers never are." She continued leafing

through the book. "Oh, dear. What's this? 'Rabbit with Forcemeat Balls.' I think I'll pass on that one."

"I didn't say that every recipe was a winner."

She laughed. "But the book is a treasure. Thank you again." She put it down and kissed his cheek, then reached for the teapot. "We'd better drink this before it stews."

As she handed him his cup, she glanced at the plate of cookies. "I'm afraid these Lorna Doones will be pretty disappointing after reading about scones and rock buns and steamed apple pudding."

Tom took one and dunked it into his tea. "They're delicious," he assured her. "And we have plenty of time ahead of us to try all the tea-time recipes."

She smiled, but quickly turned away to fill her own cup. Tom understood how she felt, but he wished she wasn't still so skittish when he talked about the future.

Obviously, it was time to change the subject. "I had lunch with Arnold Simon today. He's quite a guy."

"He is indeed. Did you follow my advice and leave your checkbook home?"

"No, and I'm glad I didn't. I saw his soup kitchen and community center in Bedford-Stuyvesant, and I'm happy to support his work. I'll be supplying him with books for the center too."

"That's just the beginning. Next, he'll have you volunteering your time."

"Is that the voice of experience talking?"

She nodded. "When I'm in town, I try to work in a couple of hours a week at his women's shelter."

"He didn't mention that to me. He did say that Denise is a big help with the teenagers at the Brooklyn community center."

"She's really enthusiastic about what she's doing there. He's lucky to have her. So am I."

"Simon told me a little about her. He said that her father worked hard to lift the family out of poverty, but that eventually he lost everything and committed suicide. That must have been really tough on her."

"It was, and it hit her hard. For a while, I thought I might lose her, but when we had to go back to re-shoot some footage for our whale documentary, getting out there on the ocean and close to those beautiful creatures helped pull her out of her depression and make peace with her loss."

"I'm sure being with you helped too."

She gave a deprecating shrug. "I hope so."

"What happened? Simon didn't seem to have the details. He just said her father opened a couple of successful restaurants and then suddenly lost everything. He must have had business savvy if he was able to start from nothing and then expand and be able to send a kid through college. Did he have a drinking or gambling problem?"

"He had a being-too-successful problem."

"He overextended?"

"No. He caught the attention of the of Wall Street vultures. The poor guy had dreams of turning the business into a small Southern franchise, but the private-equity guys in New York spotted him and had bigger ideas. They swooped down on him and, as I understand it, on the ruse of helping him recapitalize, they hoodwinked him into signing papers that later forced him out and left him broke. It was too much for him. He went into a deep depression and hanged himself."

"The bastards. Surely they could have kept him in the picture or given him compensation. You read in the papers all time of successful start-ups that are bought for multi-millions."

"You're thinking of the dot-coms and their like, enterprises that are already making millions. The Big Guys couldn't be absolutely sure Kajun Kitchens would be the huge success it turned into, so why bother to compensate the originator and take him along with them? What F. Scott Fitzgerald said about the rich goes double for the Wall Street elite. They think that everyone who isn't in their tax bracket and a fan of Ayn Rand is less than human and expendable. They never give a second thought to the wrecked lives and dreams they leave in their wake."

Tom thought of Portman and his pals. "Someday it may come back to haunt them."

"Fat chance," Nora said. "You've been hanging out in the fairytale section of your store too long. Men like this never change.

They keep going and growing, and in the wrong direction. Just look at our so-called Golden Guys." She made a face and reached for a Lorna Doone. "I can't wait till this project is over. The money is good, but I've had enough."

"Me too." Tom took her in his arms. She smelled of soap and Artemisia, and tasted like cookies and tea. It was a wholesome, intoxicating combination that swept away for the moment all thought of the ugly, greedy side of life they had been talking about.

Suddenly, she stiffened in his arms. "Damn! I'm getting a spasm in my right calf. Up! I've got to get up and walk it off."

He moved away, and she jumped up. "Sorry," she said as she paced. "It's those damned high-heeled boots. I knew I'd be sorry if I wore them all evening, but you've got to look your best when you're trying to get money for a project." She stood still for a moment and pinched her upper lip. Slowly, she relaxed. "Ah," she sighed. "That always works."

"No kidding. I'll have to try it the next time I get a spasm in my thigh."

"Forget it. Don't ask me why, but it works only for the calf. You've got to walk through the ankle, toe, and thigh spasms. Unless you have some magnesium tablets handy." She laughed. "Will you listen to us? Two minutes ago we were making love, and now we're trading spasm cures. How come this never happens in the movies?"

He pulled her close. "Because they're fiction, and we're flesh and blood."

"Flesh and blood that shouldn't be thrashing around on a narrow sofa like a couple of kids when there's a nice, big bed nearby." Her breath was warm and moist against his ear, like secret kisses traveling into his pounding bloodstream.

In the bedroom, she shed the sweatpants and T-shirt, then lay naked on the bed, watching him disrobe.

"Spasms all gone?" he asked, tossing the last of his clothes on a chair.

"In my leg," she said huskily, holding out her arms to him.

Perhaps because it was so late that they were too tired to be inhibited, or perhaps because they were at last starting to sense each other's unvoiced needs and secret places, their lovemaking took them to new and dizzying heights.

Later, as they lay in that dozy twilight time when hearts and breath slow down to normal, Tom reveled in the feel of her head on his chest. He reached out to stroke her hair. "I think I treasure this quiet time with you almost as much as what comes before it," he whispered.

He took her silence as agreement.

Slowly, his fingers trailed from her silky hair down to the soft flesh of her cheek. It was damp. "You're crying."

She shook her head and pulled away.

He could have kicked himself for breaking the spell. "What's wrong?"

"Nothing." She was sitting up now, her back straight, the soft glow from a streetlight filtering through the window and outlining the beautiful curve of her breasts.

He sat up too. "It must be something. Did I say something, do something wrong?"

She shook her head and turned to him. "Everything's right. Maybe too right." She reached out and touched his cheek. "I can't get used to it."

He pressed her hand closer, wishing he could read her eyes in the dimness. "Give it time. We both know we have to give it time."

She sighed and nodded, then gently pulled her hand away and got to her feet. "I guess I'm just overtired. It's very late. Time you started home."

"Tomorrow night?" he asked when she walked him to the door.

She shook her head. "Tomorrow night Denise and I are following Arnold Simon on his rounds. Senator Wayne will come along."

"So he told me."

"I can't imagine that he'll really show, but I do want to get Simon and his good works on tape for the documentary."

"We could get together afterward, like tonight."

"I don't think so. It will probably be really late."

"It's never too late to call me."

She smiled and kissed him.

It wasn't until he was halfway home that he realized that she hadn't said yes.

CHAPTER 31

"MAN, YOU SURE you want to get off here?" the driver asked. He had just pulled up his taxi at a dark and deserted corner on the Bowery. "For a fifty, I can take you to a lot safer place where you can get ass galore. Gorgeous, clean whores with tits out to here. And clean shit to sniff too."

The presumptuous son of a bitch. But Lyle Wayne kept his temper as he handed the cabbie his fare. Even in his Armani jeans, Gucci T-shirt, and Chanel mirror sunglasses, he might be recognized if he called attention to himself. He pulled down the Yankees cap he had bought earlier in the day from a street vendor in midtown. "I'm meeting someone." He lowered his voice to disguise it.

"Yeah. Whatever you say." The driver took the twenty-dollar bill from Wayne. The meter read fifteen-eighty. "You want change?"

"You bet." He handed back to the driver the two dimes and a dollar.

"Thanks, sport. You'll need a lot more than what's left in your hand if you're looking for a blow job."

The driver sped from the curb the second the door slammed shut, but Wayne saw his extended middle finger. "Same to you, you son of a bitch!" he called out, but the cab had disappeared around a corner. The thought of having to cozy up to creeps like that when he ran for president in a couple of years made him want to puke. Never mind. Thanks to his army of advisers, he knew exactly how to press all these idiots' buttons as if they were robots to get them to vote the right way. And once in office, he would fix them so they would never know what hit them, and still they would keep voting the same way over and over again. The dumb asses. There had to be a better way to win elections, a way without having to kiss up to the so-called "people." What the hell did they know? Tony and the guys were working on it. Once he was in office, they would set it all in motion. As Tony said, the less he knew about it at this stage, the better.

He smelled the guy before he saw him. "Help a feller get a drink?"

"Shove off."

The man staggered closer, put a filthy hand on Wayne's shoulder. "Come on. You got money. You won't miss a couple of bucks."

The guy was too drunk to be a threat. Wayne shrugged off the hand. "Get out of here—or you're going to need an ambulance more than a drink."

"Take it easy, man. Forget it. No harm in asking." The drunk shuffled off, mumbling, "Go to hell, you stingy son of a bitch. If you're down here to get pussy, I hope you get AIDS."

Wayne glanced around uneasily. Where the hell was Arnie? The next drunk or junkie might not be so docile. He walked over and stood close to a building, hoping to make himself less visible. The stench of urine was disgusting, but preferable to standing out in the open. He raised a hand to look at his Movado, then remembered that Simon had advised him not to wear jewelry or carry a lot of cash.

A couple of crackheads, their vacant eyes fixed on an invisible horizon, walked by in slow motion, shoulder to shoulder, propping each other up.

Come on, Arnie! He strained to see into the distance, but there was no sign of the tall, lanky guy. Damn. He could think of a dozen if not a hundred better ways to spend a Saturday night than prowling along the Bowery to observe life's losers. How long had he been here? Well, he'd had it. He had been out of his head to say he would come. It was just that he knew he would never get Arnie off his back if he didn't agree to it. He pulled out his cell phone and checked the time. He had been on this godforsaken street for nearly a half hour! He dialed the minister's number.

For a moment, it seemed he would be bounced to voice mail, then Arnold Simon's voice came on. "Lyle?" He seemed to be shouting over noise in the background.

"Arnie, where the hell are you? I've been standing in the Bowery so long that I'm beginning to feel like a vagrant. And I sure as hell could use a drink."

"Sorry, Lyle. I got an emergency call on my way to you. Just stay put. I'll be there in a little while."

"The hell I'll stay put. I'm getting out of here."

"I'll be there before you know it. You can get started without me. Put Nora Malcolm on. She knows the places I want to take you. Let me speak to her."

"She's not here."

"That can't be. She and Denise were supposed to be set up and waiting for you. Maybe you're on the wrong street."

"I'm on the right street. I called Malcolm and told her not to come. I must have been out of my head when I let you talk me into having her along. I can't take a chance on my contributors seeing me do this. It would make me look like a fricking bleeding-heart liberal."

"It would make you look like a hero—a compassionate conservative."

"I'm already a compassionate conservative. I'm co-sponsor of an amendment to an energy bill that will pay Blackwater to go to New Orleans to protect property. I'm outta here, Arnie."

"And how are you going to leave? Have you seen any cabs cruising by? You probably had a hard time finding one that would take you to the neighborhood. I'll be there in a little while, and I'll take you back to your hotel after we've finished the tour you promised to take."

"You forget the business I'm in, Arnie. It's built on broken promises."

"Come on, you can't break a promise to a fraternity brother. I'm on my way. Look, if you're uncomfortable where you are, we'll skip the Bowery mission and start with the women's shelter. It's in Shinbone Alley. Get over to Lafayette Street and walk north to Great Jones Street. When you get to Jones Alley, take the turn and walk along it till you come to Shinbone."

"What the hell kind of name is that?"

"An old one. You're in one of the oldest parts of the city, and that's one of the oldest streets. Real estate was cheap there when we opened up. Wait inside the shelter. I'll be there in no time."

"You'd better be. I'm not hanging around long."

"Wait inside the shelter. They'll take care of you till I get there. You owe me this, Lyle. Don't get cold feet now."

"I never chicken out on anyone or anything," he lied, and clicked off. He couldn't believe Arnie would stoop to reminding him that Beta Alpha Beta Phi's never broke promises to one another. It was a sacred obligation among the Golden Guys, and he would never break it with the others. But Arnie wasn't really one of them. Not anymore. He was a goddam man of God, for chrissake. Forgiveness was his stock-in-trade.

Wayne strained his eyes, but Arnold was right. There were no taxis in sight. In fact, there was very little traffic at all. He looked at the cell phone, warm in his hand. He could call one of his assistants to come get him. But no way did he want anyone picking him up in this outfit in this weird part of the city. Even if he swore them to secrecy, it would be common knowledge, blown way out of proportion, before a week was out. Everyone in the Beltway gossiped like a drunken old hag.

He turned his attention back to the sidewalk. A tall figure all in black was approaching. Or at least the gloom made him look like he was dressed in black. Was it Arnie? No, it couldn't be. If Arnie had been that close when they were speaking, he would have said so.

The figure slipped into a doorway. Had he gone into the building or was he just hovering there?

A speeding Lexus suddenly appeared from a side street and pulled up with a screech halfway down the next block. A guy built like a football player appeared from the shadows and walked over. He bent down and extended something through the window. When he withdrew his hand, he paused for a moment to count what was in it. Then he gave a nod and the Lexus sped off. He turned and looked in Wayne's direction.

Jesus! Did he see me? Does he think I'm a cop? Wayne pressed himself tighter against the building. Sweat made his T-shirt stick to him.

But the pusher pocketed his take and then receded into the shadows to wait for his next customer. Wayne didn't want to be around for the next buy. He knew he couldn't count on remaining invisible.

Slowly, clinging to the building, he began making his way toward the corner. With his eyes fixed on the doorway on the next block where the pusher had taken cover, he couldn't see the figure he had observed earlier emerge from the doorway halfway down the block behind him.

Once around the corner, he felt more confident. Maybe he would spot a cab on Lafayette Street. If he did, he would take it. But there was no cab, and he turned in on Jones Street and then Jones Alley as Simon had instructed. He couldn't believe such a dark, narrow street existed in a city like New York. He felt as if he had slipped into a time warp. Shinbone Alley still had its ancient cobblestones, brought over by the Dutch. The buildings looked antediluvian too, dark and huddled together as though fearing a second coming of the Flood. The alley appeared to be a cul-de-sac, and at the end he saw a dim glimmer. That must be the shelter. It sure as hell was hard to find. If Arnie wanted to hide the women inside it from their abusers, he had picked the perfect place. Not that such women needed protection. Half of them were probably prostitutes, and the other half lowlifes not much better. These bitches always asked for it, egging a guy on. They got no more than they deserved. Most of them probably even liked it.

He liked a little rough stuff himself. Made things more interesting. Unfortunately, his wife didn't go for it. Too much of a goddamn Southern belle and Daughter of the Confederacy, but she and the kids looked great on his campaign posters. Never mind. He had found plenty of high-grade whores who were happy to indulge him for a price, and he never left bruises where they would show. There were a couple of them he liked to engage for a night when he was here in New York. Maybe after he got finished with Arnie.... Just thinking about it made his penis come to life.

He took out his phone, dialed Cheri, and got only her answering gizmo.

"This is Cheri, and I can tell you're as hot as I am," came her sultry message. "You know the routine, don't you, honey?"

"Hi, it's Bruiser," he said, using the name she had suggested after their first encounter. "I'm in town tonight and thought we could resume what we did last time. Ring me back."

He knew he couldn't count on hearing from her. After all, it was Saturday night and the town was full of johns, both foreign and domestic. Still, he had that awful, delicious ache that only a good whore could cure....

Maybe Serena. She wasn't so serene last time, though. Said he overdid it and should take her off his list. But that was a while back. Surely, she had forgotten. Or maybe if he offered a bonus....

She answered, but her first words were, "I told you not to call me again."

"Come on, baby. That was a one-shot last time. You're so sexy I got a little overexcited. It won't happen again."

"That's what you said the time before that."

"But this time I mean it, and I'm willing to double your fee."

"I needed stitches last time. You know how much that cost me out of pocket? I can't get health insurance because my asthma is a pre-existing condition. Which is not what happens in England, according to my clients from over there."

"You should have called me. I'd have paid for the stitches. I'll pay for them tonight. You still at the cozy apartment on East Sixty-fifth? I'm in the middle of something right now, but I'll come over when I'm finished."

"Forget it. And don't call me again until you've gotten a decent health-care bill through Congress, one that takes care of all the needs of working women like me and makes pre-existing conditions illegal."

He laughed. "You're kidding, right?"

"I've never been more serious. Shove off! Or, rather, go jerk off!"

The bitch! Who did she think she was talking to? He was a United States senator. Soon, he would be president. No woman could talk to him like that and get away with it. He tried calling her back, but she wouldn't pick up.

Goddamn whore. Monday morning he would phone George

Hanover of the real estate lobby. George would make some calls, and that bitch would be thrown out of her fancy apartment before the end of the day.

He slipped the phone back into his pocket and continued toward the lights. No. Calling George was good, but it wasn't enough. After he was through with all this crap with Arnie, he would go over to Serena's place. She would let him in. She wouldn't want to make a fuss the neighbors might hear. And once inside that fancy soundproof apartment, he would let her have it. He'd beat her till she knew who she was and who he was. And she would finally beg to be forgiven for her arrogance. And then he'd fuck her. God, would he fuck her! Just thinking about it gave him a hard on.

Smiling in anticipation, he paused a moment in the shadows to pat his fly. "Down, boy," he said. "Plenty of time for that later."

"Wrong. Time just ran out."

The whisper was harsh and so close to his ear that he could feel its warmth. He tried to turn, but an iron arm had him in a hammerlock, and he could feel the prick of a knife at his throat. He wanted to run. He wanted to lash out at the attacker. But the hammerlock paralyzed him and he was frozen with fright. Not so frozen that he couldn't croak out as he pissed himself, "Do you know who I am?"

"You bet, senator."

And then everything went as black as the deserted alley around him.

CHAPTER 32

"SATURDAY NIGHT and you're home?" It was a question, not an observation.

Tom looked up from his laptop, where he had been checking on Lou West's schedule. "Nora's working tonight. What about you? Got cold feet about asking Mrs. Alexander out?"

Max shrugged sheepishly. "I guess we're both a little skittish about dating, or whatever it's called these days. At our age, we take things slowly. But I did ask her to join us for dinner *Erev* Rosh Hashanah. Seems she usually spends the holidays with her daughter in Philadelphia, but this year her daughter and her family are going down to Florida to be with the husband's folks. Gloria was invited, but she thought they deserved the time alone. His folks don't get to see the grandkids as often as she does. I've also arranged for her to come to services with us. She's excited about it. She's never been to a temple that has a woman rabbi. I thought maybe you'd like to invite your friend too."

"Thanks, Max, but Nora's not Jewish."

"So? Even if it's just another Monday night to her, she still has to eat. And once she tastes my chicken soup and matzo balls... who knows?"

Tom laughed. "I'll think about it." He turned back to the computer. "For now, I have to concentrate on this stuff."

"Something for the store, or for that other project?"

"The other project."

"I wish you were finished with that damn thing. Your dealing with those people makes me nervous."

"No need to be. It's just a simple research job."

"I know. You've told me." Max didn't sound convinced, but he turned and left the room. A moment later Tom heard him turn on the TV.

According to the official website for *Coach!* Lou West was the featured speaker at a dinner being held at the Roosevelt Hotel to raise funds for college football scholarships. The speech would be followed by book signings, of course. So he was still here in the city. Tom decided to reach him tomorrow to find out just what he had been doing in the neighborhood when Hammond was attacked. The website had a photo of him at a book signing in White Plains that day, but it wasn't clear about the time.

Next, he went to the GMU website in search of information on the professor whose grandson was injured in the rigged car Simon had told him about. No Professor Grinwald was listed on the current staff. The man had either retired, died, or moved on to another university. Not knowing his first name made a Google search unhelpful. Maybe the accident had been reported in the local papers. Unfortunately he didn't have a date, but he opted for the Golden Guys' sophomore year. By then they would have overcome any freshman fear of being apprehended, if such a possibility had ever crossed their arrogant minds. It took a while, but at last he found a short article in the March 18, 1977, edition of *The Philadelphia Enquirer.* It reported that Professor Nathan B. Grinwald of Gouverneur Morris University had been in an accident the day before when his brakes failed on a stretch of icy road. The professor had sustained a broken arm, but his grandson, twelve-year-old Reginald Phillip Grinwald, had been thrown through the windshield and was in a coma and in critical condition at St. Agnes Hospital.

Now he could Google again, and it turned out that Nathan Grinwald had been a Shakespeare scholar, the author of many learned papers on such world-shattering subjects, if only to fellow scholars, as Shakespeare's use of gerunds and participles; the secret and profound meaning of the stage direction, "Exeunt, Pursued by a bear," in *A Winter's Tale;* and whether Shakespeare's references to food and eating may have indicated that he had digestive problems, especially with venison and suet puddings. Grinwald died in 1994 of a heart attack at the age of eighty.

Among his survivors the obituary listed Reginald Grinwald, his grandson.

What was Reginald Grinwald doing now? And where was he? If his grandfather had suspected that Portman and his pals were involved in the accident, had he passed that information on to Reginald?

But Reginald Grinwald didn't show up in Tom's Google search. Nor did Reginald Phillip Grinwald or Reginald P. Grinwald. What if the kid had hated the name Reginald? Maybe he dropped it and was using initials. No. That didn't work, either. Maybe a switch. And that was it. Or was it? At any rate, there was a listing for Phillip R. Grinwald, a surgical oncologist at Mount Sinai Hospital in New York City.

A search of the hospital's staff listings on its website showed that the dates worked out. Dr. Grinwald had earned his Bachelor of Science degree from Brandeis University in 1987, and had been graduated from the medical school of the University of California, Berkeley, in 1991. He interned at UCFS Medical Center at Mount Zion in San Francisco, then did his residency at New York's Mount Sinai Hospital, where he had been affiliated since 1995, and on the teaching staff since 2001.

Brandeis, Mount Zion, and Mount Sinai. Was it possible that the Grinwalds were Jewish? If so, anti-Semitism may well have contributed to the sabotaging of the professor's car. Of course, it could turn out that Dr. Phillip R. Grinwald was not the boy who had nearly been killed in the accident, but that seemed unlikely. Too many things fell into place, including the double *l*'s in his first name.

Feeling the surge of excitement he used to get when he came up with a new lead, Tom wrote down all the contact information. There was nothing he could do on the weekend, but he would get to Grinwald first thing Monday morning. As a surgeon, Grinwald would certainly have the skill to perform the quick procedure. Did he also have the strength to overcome these guys, and could he be placed at the out-of-town attacks? Certainly, it would have been easy for him to keep track of their comings and goings both out of town and here in New York. The activities of all these guys were covered thoroughly in the business section of the *Times* and in the *Wall Street Journal*. And Lyle Wayne often appeared on the front pages.

As for Wayne, he was in the city this weekend. Tom looked at his watch. Wayne was now probably in the middle of Arnold Simon's tour. Simon and Nora and Denise would be with him, so he was safe from assault for the time being. But what about afterward? What if Grinwald, or whoever the castrator was, was following them, and waiting for when they would all go their separate ways and Wayne would be alone? The attacker couldn't have known about the tour, but he could have been following Wayne from the moment he left his hotel.

Tom jotted down the addresses of the tour stops Simon had told him about. Then he grabbed a jacket and his car keys. He had to meet the group before the tour was over and get Wayne safely back to his hotel.

"Where are you off to?" Max had awakened from his doze in front of the TV.

"I have to meet someone."

Max smiled. "Nora?"

"Yes." It wasn't really a lie. She would be there, taping the tour. "I'll be late."

The smile broadened. "Don't forget to ask her to dinner Monday," Max called after him.

THAT DAY, FOR the first time in months, Tom had found a parking space on his own block. And now he had to give it up. He tried not to think about his bad luck as he climbed into his Chevy. A Lexus had been hovering from the second he approached his car, and it zipped into the gap the moment he pulled away from the curb.

To avoid the usually heavy traffic on the Brooklyn Bridge, he took the tunnel into Manhattan, but afterward the going was slow, especially on the narrow downtown streets. If they had started the tour on the Bowery, as Simon had planned, Tom was sure they would be at the women's shelter by now, and he headed in that direction. Knowing there would be no room to leave his car in the narrow Jones Alley, or the even narrower Shinbone Alley beyond it, he began searching for parking spots as soon as he hit Lafayette Street. Amazingly, just as that Lexus had lucked into his departure in Brooklyn, he spotted a Jeep about to pull away from the curb. He slipped into the spot, then hurried off to Great Jones Street.

The lighting dimmed considerably when he turned into the narrow Jones Alley. The cobblestones and huddle of early nineteenth century buildings made him feel he had wandered into a novel by Dickens. At any moment he expected to bump into Bill Sikes or Daniel Quilp, but the alley was deserted, as was the even dimmer and narrower Shinbone Alley that broke off from it. He started toward the building at the end, which he was sure was the shelter. His eyes fixed on the lighted windows, he nearly tripped over the drunk sprawled on the broken sidewalk. He wondered if he should try to rouse the man or just walk around him and let him sleep it off. Then it struck him that there was not even the slightest stench of alcohol.

He bent down and found himself looking into the unconscious face of Senator Lyle Wayne.

Tom shot up and whipped around, straining to see into the darkness. He had known how dark these alleyways were. Why hadn't he thought to bring along the flashlight he kept in his glove compartment? Damn it, when had he stopped thinking like a cop?

There was no movement in the shadows. Whoever did this had probably long since fled.

Down by his feet, Lyle Wayne stirred and groaned.

Tom bent down to help him up.

"Get away from me, you son of a bitch!" Wayne cried, shrinking back.

"It's okay, senator." Tom got a grip under Wayne's arms and started to haul him to his feet. "Whoever attacked you is gone."

"Then who the hell are you?"

"I'm Tom Berenson. We met at the reunion, remember?"

It was unclear whether the shake of Wayne's head meant yes or no. "What the hell are you doing here?"

"I came down to see you safely back to your hotel."

"Well, you're goddam fucken too late."

"Obviously. But I thought you were in good hands with the Reverend Simon. Where is he?"

"Burning in hell, I hope. He never showed. When I talked to him, he said he was on his way and I should meet him at the shelter. Said it would be safer there for me than hanging around on the street. Shithead preacher! What the hell does he know? He probably thinks fricking angels are all around to protect us."

Tom had Wayne almost to his feet when Wayne's knees buckled. The man was a dead weight, and Tom struggled to haul him up again. "Where are the two women who were going to videotape your tour?"

"I called them before I came and told them to stay the hell away. And I'm damn glad I did. All I'd need is for this to be on tape. It would be the end of me."

"If they were here, they might have protected you."

"Two women? You've got to be crazy."

Tom had Wayne on his feet now, but he kept his hands on the man's shoulders to hold him steady. "Can you walk? My car is a couple of blocks away. We need to get out of here."

Wayne shrugged off Tom's hands. "Of course I can walk." But as they started out of the alley, he paused and bent over for a second. "Jesus. I think the guy kicked me in the groin."

"I think he did more than that," Tom said, and he gave Wayne his arm for support.

CHAPTER 33

O N THE WAY to his car, Tom tried to get Foster on his cell phone. He was bounced to voice mail. "Call me back. It's an emergency. I'm bringing Lyle Wayne to your place."

Next, he tried Foster's home phone. The teenager who answered said her father wasn't there, and, no, she didn't know where he was. Her bored voice said she couldn't care less.

"Try to get him on his cell phone," Tom said, opening his car door. Maybe Foster would respond more quickly to a call from his daughter. "Tell him that Tom Berenson is coming over with Lyle Wayne. While you're at it, you can tell your doorman to expect me. Just say I'm bringing a friend. Don't mention the senator's name."

"Whatever."

Tom clicked off, knowing that was the best he was going to get out of the kid.

Still dazed from the attack, Wayne needed help getting into the car. Tom buckled him up, secured his own seat belt, and pulled away from the curb.

"Tell me all you remember about the attack."

"I don't remember anything. I was walking along that goddamn alley. I thought it was deserted, but suddenly this guy jumped out of nowhere and grabbed me from behind."

"Did you see his face?"

"I told you, he jumped me from behind. I tried to fight him off, but he was huge, big as a wrestler, and strong, with muscles like iron. Had me in a hammerlock. I thought he was going to choke me to death."

"Did he say anything?"

"No." The slight hesitation that preceded the word told Tom it was a lie.

"Are you sure? Try to remember."

"No. Not a word."

Tom gave up and explored another angle. "When you spoke with Arnold Simon, did he tell you where he was?"

"No. He just said he got tied up on his way, that he'd be with me in a little while. Said I should wait at the shelter. I'll kill the son of a bitch when I see him. This is all his fault."

"Did he say what held him up?"

"No, but he was shouting over a lot of noise in the background."

At the next red light, Tom called the minister.

"Nice to hear from you, Tom. What's on your mind?"

"Senator Wayne."

"Did you want to talk to him? I'm on my way to meet him right now. He's waiting for me at the women's shelter in Shinbone Alley. You could meet us there."

"Where are you, reverend?" The light changed and Tom took his foot off the brake.

"I'm a few blocks away. Just got out of the subway at Bleecker Street."

"The senator isn't at the shelter."

He could hear Simon's sigh. "So he decided not to wait for me, after all."

"He intended to wait for you, but he got mugged on the way to the shelter."

"Are you sure? How do you know this?"

"Because I found him." Aware that Simon had never been told about the castrations, Tom added, "I was on my way down to the shelter myself. I remembered that you'd told me about the tour when we met, and I thought I might get a chance to talk with the senator for Blair Whitney's book. He's a hard man to get hold of. I found him unconscious in Shinbone Alley."

"That's terrible! Where are you now? In St. Vincent's emergency room? Or Beekman Downtown?"

"Neither. He doesn't want the press to get on to this. I'm driving him to Al Foster's place."

"Makes sense. I'll meet you there."

"I don't think that would be a good idea. He's pretty riled up. He blames you for this. Says it wouldn't have happened if you had met him on time."

"But it couldn't be helped. He'll understand when I explain. There was a near riot about squatters' rights in Tompkins Square Park. A friend on the City Council asked me to stop off to help settle it, and then— Let me talk to Lyle."

"I don't think that's a good idea."

"I need to talk to him," Simon insisted.

Tom extended the phone to Wayne, who grabbed it so violently that Tom had to hold tight to the steering wheel to keep the car from swerving.

"Arnold, you goddam bastard! This is all your fault. I'm going to get you for this! I'll see to it that every fricken project of yours is shut down. I'll—"

Tom grabbed the phone from him. "As I said, reverend, this is not the time to talk with the senator."

"But I—"

A car zoomed out from behind to cut him off with an illegal left turn. Tom jammed on the brake, screeching into a swerve. "Sorry, but it's not the time to talk with me, either. I've got to get the senator to Al Foster's place." Tom tossed the phone into the glove compartment.

"I don't want to go to Foster's. Take me back to my hotel."

"I can't do that. Foster's got to check you. You know what's been happening. First Bernard, then Michaelson, Portman, McGrath. Just this week Hammond was hit. Now you."

"Not me. No one would dare do that to me. It was just a run-of-the-mill mugging."

"Really? What did he take? You've still got your watch on. And that ring on your pinky doesn't look like something you bought in a ninety-nine-cents store. Check for your wallet."

Wayne grimaced with pain as he squirmed to get his hand into the right-hand pocket of his tight jeans. When he pulled out his wallet, a folded piece of paper tumbled onto the seat. He opened the wallet and looked into it.

"Money all there?"

Wayne nodded.

"What about credit cards?"

They were there too.

Wayne jammed the wallet back into his pocket.

"What's on the paper?"

"What paper?"

"The one that fell out of your pocket when you reached for your wallet."

Wayne picked up the paper and slowly unfolded it. "Jesus Christ!" His face beet red, he shredded the paper in a fury and threw the pieces out the window.

"Damn it! Why did you do that? I needed to see it."

"Nobody can see it now. That's how it should be."

"What did it say? If you want my help, you have to tell me." But Tom already knew the answer.

"'You're not the man you thought you were.'" Wayne slammed his fist down on the seat. "Turn this car around! Take me to the airport. I want to go back to Washington."

"First, Al Foster has to see you."

"Well, I don't want to see *him*. He's nothing more than an ass-licker and a hanger-on. I don't know how the hell he ever got into Beta Alpha Beta Phi in the first place. He's the grandson of a goddamn illiterate Latvian butcher, for God's sake."

"A Latvian butcher who started what has grown into the biggest food-distribution conglomerate in the world."

"Once a dumb-ass butcher always a dumb-ass butcher. Al's not like the rest of us, and he knows it. Our families go way back, and we've made our money the real way, the American way, through real estate and banking and Wall Street. My family has been one of the biggest landholders in South Carolina since 1697."

And one of the biggest slaveholders too, but Tom kept that observation to himself. "Whatever his origins, Al Foster is always listed as one of the top urologists in the country by *USA Today*."

"He probably bribes them. I want to see my own guy in Washington. All the guys I live with on C Street go to him. He's gotten every one of us out of jams when we've picked up crap we don't want to pass on to our wives or current girlfriends. He's a Jew, but he's a great urologist, and not as greedy as the rest of them."

The way he said *Jew* made Tom's blood freeze. He wanted to stop the car and throw the anti-Semite out into the gutter where he belonged. But he kept his eyes on the road and his hands clenched on the steering wheel. "How nice for you and your friends that he's not as greedy as the rest of us."

"Oops. Sorry." Wayne shrugged, obviously not sorry at all. "Didn't know you were one of them."

"Yeah, I'm 'one of them.'"

"Don't be so goddamn touchy. It's just talk, that's all." Wayne sighed in frustration. "Jeez, you people are as bad as the nig—the blacks. Everyone's got to be so damn careful what they say around you."

"Must be a great burden. Let's cut the crap and get back to the note. What did it look like?"

"How the hell should I remember what it looked like?"

"Was it handwritten? Cut and pasted? Typed?"

"Typed."

So it must have looked just like the others. Having it wouldn't have helped.

"I meant what I said before. Turn around. I want to go back to Washington and see Dr. Goldstein."

"You'll be seen at the airport. The press will want to know why you're running out on your talk at the Waldorf tomorrow."

"The hell with the press. I don't owe those bastards any explanations."

"They'll be happy to dig them up on their own."

"Shit."

"You got it." They were getting close to Foster's building. "We're almost there. Keep your eye out for a parking spot."

Like a sulky kid, Wayne closed his eyes.

"Not to worry," Tom said. "Looks like the Parking Fairy, if such a creature exists, is hovering nearby. There's one, and we're only about half a block from Foster's building."

The doorman nodded to Tom, announced him on the intercom, and waved him through. It was a while before Foster's daughter opened the door. She was holding a cell phone to an ear pierced with hoop earrings all the way up to its top, and she neither paused in her conversation nor glanced at the two men as she let them in.

"Did you get your father on his cell?" Tom called after her as she started away from them.

She shrugged a shoulder and continued on her way, laughing and chatting.

"Stop right there." It was his cop's voice, and the words were out of his mouth before he even knew he was going to say them. He was sick of these people. Sick of the case.

The girl stiffened, but she stopped and turned. She was about Stephanie's age, but definitely a different species of teenager. She was wearing tight, low-slung distressed jeans that looked like they came out of a dumpster but had probably set Foster back a couple of hundred bucks. A bright gold ring pierced the navel that was exposed beneath her snug, short black top. Her hair was dyed with streaks of magenta and azure, and her brown eyes would have been pretty if all the heavy makeup surrounding them wasn't a distraction.

"I'm on the phone." Her nostrils flared with annoyance.

"Then get off it for a minute. We're your father's guests in your father's home. Give me the courtesy of an answer to my question. Did you talk to your father?"

For a second it was a battle of wills, but the cop's authority in Tom's eyes won out.

"Hang on," she said into the phone, then took it from her ear. "No," she said to Tom. "I left him your message, okay?"

"And you have no idea where he is?"

"How should I know? Maybe he's out with one of his whores." Her voice was tough, but he saw the vulnerability in her eyes.

"Anyone else home?"

"Just me, and I'm going to be history in five minutes. Okay? Are we through?"

"What's your name?"

"Madison. I said, 'Are we through?'"

"Yes, we're through. Thank you, Madison."

"Right," Madison said into the phone. "Ten minutes. See you." She put the phone into her pocket and brushed past Tom. "I'm outta here."

"Does your father know where you're going?"

She gave Tom the finger, and slammed the door behind her.

"Little bitch," Wayne said. "But she's got a great ass. Kids like her are real troublemakers. They should be put in convents and not let out till they're eighteen and no longer jail bait."

"Maybe you should introduce a bill in Congress." Tom led the way into the living room, went over to the bar, and poured Wayne a Johnnie Walker Blue. He could have used something himself, but the thought of drinking with Senator Lyle Wayne disgusted him.

He was reaching for his cell phone to try Foster again when it began to ring.

It was Foster. "Where are you?" he said.

"I was about to ask you the same question. I'm at your place with the senator. Where are you?"

"I'm in a cab on my way home. I'll be there in a few minutes. I just got your message. I had my phone off all evening."

"What happened to the old rule of doctors always being within reach in case of an emergency with a patient?"

"It went the way of all the stupid old rules. That's what we have answering services for. If there's an emergency, there are plenty of residents available to take care of it. That's how they learn."

"I'll have to remember not to get sick on weekends."

"Or holidays." There was a crackling on the line just before Foster hung up. No doubt he was munching potato chips.

Tom was handing Wayne another scotch when he heard Foster's key in the door.

"Where the hell have you been?" Wayne demanded as Foster walked into the room.

"At the Edison hotel. I'm on *New York* magazine's panel of fast-food experts." Foster beamed with pride. "We were meeting to decide who makes the best French fries in the city. But we're sworn to secrecy until *New York* breaks the story, so don't ask me who won."

"Who the goddamn hell cares? Look what's happened to me. Fuck French fries. You should have been here, Al!"

"Being here wouldn't have changed a thing. You shouldn't have been wherever the hell you were. And you shouldn't have been there alone."

"I wasn't supposed to be alone. I was supposed to be with Arnie, but he didn't show up."

"Where was he?"

"Out saving the goddamn world."

"He told me he got tied up trying to stop a riot in Tompkins Square Park," Tom filled in.

"Shit. And how did you get to Lyle? Did he call you?"

"No. I found him lying in the street. Simon had told me about his tour for the senator, so I thought he'd be safe with the reverend and the women who would be taping the event, and he'd be surrounded by the people the reverend was taking him to see. But it occurred to me that he might need protection going back to his hotel, so I went down to join him."

"Too late."

"Obviously."

"Where were the girls with the camcorders and stuff? Did they run away to save their own asses when he was attacked?"

How Nora would have bristled at that *girls*. "The women weren't there."

"I told them not to come," Wayne said. "I didn't want to be taped looking like some bleeding-heart liberal. It could be used against me in the presidential primaries." He jumped to his feet. "Why are we standing around here talking? Do something, Al! Help me. Maybe he didn't go through with it this time. Maybe he realized who he was dealing with. Maybe he just gave me a kick. I don't care how rich the other guys are. Compared to me, they're just schmucks. I'm a United States senator. No one can do something like that to me. He was probably just trying to scare me. Well, I can't be scared!" His voice cracked on the last word.

"Sure, Lyle. Maybe you're right. Come into the other room. Let's have a look." Foster reached into his pocket, pulled out a folded piece of paper, and handed it to Tom. "The tests were blind, but that's a list of the places that supplied the fries," he said over his shoulder as he led the senator out of the room. "Salt was okay but ketchup wasn't allowed. Look it over." He licked his lips. "It was a real blast. Next year, we're doing pizza. I can't wait."

Without a glance, Tom tossed the paper on the coffee table. He looked around the room while he waited. He had been here before, but he still didn't feel comfortable. The design was Swedish modern. The furniture was white and black, the sharp angles of one piece set off by the curves of another. There were white vertical blinds on the windows, but no curtains or drapes, and the only art on the stark white walls was a huge frameless canvas that was divided vertically, three-quarters of it white and the other quarter dove gray. It was signed, but Tom wasn't interested enough to walk over to see the name of the artist. No doubt the room had appeared in the pages of *Architectural Digest,* but it left him cold. Not one piece of furniture in it, not even a vase or a lamp, looked as if it had been picked with loving care by two people who wanted to make a home together. And where was the bookcase? Where were the books? Not a single volume or magazine was in sight.

"*No!*" The blood-curdling cry came from the other room. "You're wrong! You're just a goddamn quack. What do you know? Let me out of here. I want Dr. Goldstein!"

"Give me a hand, Tom!"

Tom rushed down the hall and found Foster trying to hold Lyle Wayne down. The senator looked pathetic and diminished, lying on a king-sized bed, his jeans and bright-red bikini jockey shorts down around his knees.

"Let me up! Let me out of here!"

"Do you want the whole world to know what happened to you?"

"Goldstein can fix it. He can fix everything."

"No one can fix it. Not even your precious Goldstein who, according to the grapevine, is light years behind the times. But I'm working on it. If there's a way to fix it, I'll find it. Till then, and even after then, you don't want anyone to know what's happened to you. Hold him, Tom."

Tom gripped Wayne's shoulders while Foster reached into his medical bag. But by then, the fight had gone out of the senator.

"What's that?" Wayne asked when Foster approached with a hypodermic needle.

"Just a mild sedative. It will help you relax. Make you feel better."

"I'll never feel better," Wayne said, but he didn't fight the injection. "Oh, God! I'll never be the same again! Who'll sleep with me now? Who'll want to vote for me now?" He began to weep.

"Come on," Foster said. "Pull yourself together. Act like a Golden Guy. We'll start testosterone treatments right away, to keep you from getting any visible changes. No outsiders will ever know about it."

"What about him?" Wayne pointed at Tom.

"He'll never talk. He's as good as one of us now."

The thought was revolting, but when Foster added, "Right, Berenson?" Tom nodded.

"But the bastard who did this, he might talk."

"He hasn't talked yet about your buddies," Tom said. "It's unlikely he'll start now. He knows it could lead us to him."

Wayne seemed to be about to say something more, but the effort was too much. His eyelids began to droop.

"The sedative's starting to take effect," Foster said. "I'll keep him here tonight. Tomorrow, I'll pump him up with Prozac. He has to make that Heritage Foundation talk about privatizing Social Security and Medicare. No one will be able to tell from his appearance that anything happened."

Tom looked down at the sleeping senator. Foster was right. The man's appearance was unchanged. It was the attacker's usual m.o. He did his dirty work and then left. He could have beaten his victims either before or after they were unconscious, leaving them with an embarrassing black eye or broken nose, but he chose not to. Why? In crimes of revenge, the perpetrator usually couldn't stop himself once he had initiated the attack.

Silently, he ran through his list of suspects. Could Lou West or Vittorio Capperrelli have been able to resist throwing some punches? Fletcher Bowman was notorious for blackening his enemies' eyes, and he still hadn't been able to pin down Bowman's whereabouts when Hammond was hit. Tom himself had witnessed Jason Gilbert duking it out with Doug McGrath. Could any of these men have had the self-control to resist pummeling the victims? Gilbert, maybe, but he wasn't that strong a suspect. Hadn't he been too drunk to come back and attack McGrath later? Or had he been pretending to be that drunk?

Who else would have such self-control?

And then it hit him: Arnold Simon, the man of God. *Vengeance is mine...saith the Lord.* Maybe Simon had decided to help the Lord along. Surely, he would have the self-possession to exact the punishment he thought appropriate and go not one step further. He had to find Simon and check out his alibi.

"You don't need me here," he said to Foster, and turned to leave.

"Where are you off to?"

"To retrace the senator's footsteps, check out the scene. The attacker's been at this a long while now and may be getting sloppy. That's often the pattern."

"Did you tell Tony what happened?" Foster called after him.

"That's your job."

Tom heard Foster's "Shit!" as he closed the door.

CHAPTER 34

PREFERRING TO surprise him, Tom didn't call Arnold Simon but went directly to the shelter. The gray-haired woman who came to the door eyed him suspiciously, no doubt presuming he was an angry husband in search of his wife. She was tall and broad, and looked as though she could easily take on overly insistent thugs.

"I was invited to meet the reverend here earlier," he said. "I got held up in traffic behind a big accident."

"Oh, you must be the man he was going to take on a tour. He was very mysterious about it. We thought you were a celebrity." Her face softened and she looked disappointed.

Tom smiled. "No, just a prospective donor."

She brightened. "That's even better." She stood aside to let him in. "I'm afraid Reverend Simon isn't here, but I could show you around. I'm Phoebe Collins, the night supervisor. Ours is one of the best shelters for abused women in the city. We—"

"I'm sorry to interrupt, Ms. Collins, but Reverend Simon has filled me in on your good work here. I'm on a tight schedule, and I really need to speak with him now to finalize my participation. When did he leave?"

"Oh, he didn't come. He phoned to say that you wouldn't be able to make it, so he was going to take care of some other work he had to do."

"What time was that?"

She shrugged. "I don't know, maybe a couple of hours ago. I guess when you called to tell him of your delay, he thought you were canceling."

"Obviously we got our signals crossed. Did he say where he was, or where he was going?"

"No. You know the reverend. He's always off helping someone. It's a big city, and filled with troubled people."

"That's for sure. I'll call him on his cell phone and try to set up another appointment. Thanks for your help."

"You're most welcome. You know, sometimes the reverend gets so involved with what he's doing that he doesn't answer his cell. But he'll be here tomorrow morning at ten to conduct a service for our ladies. I know he'll be very happy to see you then. We all will."

"Thanks. I'll keep it in mind."

PHOEBE WAS RIGHT. Simon was either too involved to answer his phone or was deliberately ignoring selected callers. "I need to see you tonight about what happened to Senator Wayne," Tom said when the message tone went off. "Please call me back."

He drove over to Tompkins Square Park in the East Village. Strewn with broken boxes, crates, clothing, and remnants of makeshift tents and protest signs, it looked like a hurricane had just struck. Cops were all over, checking under packing crates for stragglers, keeping out people who where trying to sneak back in. A news van from Cablevision's Channel One was pulling away, and a woman and two men were packing up equipment and putting it into a van with the CBS logo.

Tom walked over to a rosy-cheeked cop who was returning to his post near the Slocum Fountain after bringing a bedraggled woman with two children over to someone who was probably a social worker. The guy's badge identified him as part of the Ninth Precinct. He looked like a kid. Were cops getting younger, Tom wondered, or was it just that he was getting older?

"Hi, I'm Tom Berenson. I used to be a lieutenant with Homicide until a bullet put a stop to it. Looks like all hell broke loose here. What's going on?"

"It started out with a demonstration to help the homeless,

but then a fight broke out between a couple of squatters. It ran through the crowd like wildfire. Everybody was bashing everybody, maybe instigated by people with a political agenda. There was blood everywhere. Ten people were taken to the hospital. One of them was just a little kid who got trampled."

"You guys obviously did a great job restoring order. When did the fighting start?"

The cop shrugged. "Can't be sure. We were called in about seven-thirty, so it started sometime before that. We got some help from the guys in the Seventh, so we had things pretty well settled down within about an hour. Captain says the mayor wants us to stick around and make sure no one comes back to start trouble again. Bloomberg must be blowing his top. The media was all over the place. They're going to make this into a worse calamity than New Orleans."

"Funny how things work out," Tom said. "I was supposed to meet a friend of mine here by the fountain at eight. I got detained, and I haven't been able to get him on his cell phone. I hope he wasn't hurt. Maybe you saw him."

"I didn't see all the people the ambulances carried away."

"Hopefully he wasn't one of them. He's a minister—Arnold Simon. He was probably wearing his clerical collar."

The cop's face brightened. "Oh, the Rev. Yeah, he was here. He's terrific with people. Broke up a lot of fights."

"That's just like him. I'll bet he was here till the bitter end."

"Actually, no. At least, I don't think so. I saw him on his phone kind of early on. And then he took off. I mean, I think he took off, because I didn't see him after that. Could be he was just at the other end of the park, though most of the action was right here. Anyway, you're in luck, because he's back around here someplace. I spotted him a little while ago walking with a man and woman and two kids. Probably taking them to the homeless shelter on Avenue C."

"Thanks. I'll see if I can find him there. Is Jack Franklin still your captain?"

"Yeah."

"Tell him I said hello."

SIMON WASN'T AT the shelter, but the security guard on duty said that he had been there a short time before. "We're busting at the seams. He pushed and pushed until they agreed to squeeze in the woman and two kids he had with him, but not the guy. The two of them left maybe five minutes ago."

"Any idea where they were going?"

"Nobody tells me nothing. But you can ask Roz. She runs the place." He nodded toward a harried-looking woman on the other side of the lobby who was trying to settle an accelerating squabble between two agitated residents.

"She's got her hands full. If they just left, maybe I can catch up to them on the street. Thanks for your help."

"No problem."

Tom was halfway out the door when the guard called after him: "If you don't see them, you might want to head for East Ninth Street. There are a couple of squats there. I know the Rev doesn't like them, but 'Any port...,' as they say."

As soon as he turned the corner onto Avenue C, Tom spotted the abandoned graffiti-sprayed brownstone. When built back before the turn of the last century, it had no doubt been an elegant small apartment house for upwardly mobile clerks working downtown on Wall Street. Now its windows were broken and boarded, and the cherubs that had been carved above the lintel were covered in grime, as if the devil had kidnapped them and they had been singed on their escape from his hell to this one. Once, debonair men in their bowler hats and starched collars and refined women in their Gibson Girl skirts and high Cathedral boots had climbed the steep stoop. Now the steps were filled with litter and stained with urine.

Knowing that the door would be bolted, Tom didn't mount the front steps. Instead, he descended the stairs leading down to the old service entrance. The locks on the door and the iron grilling protecting it had long ago been jimmied, and he gained access with ease. Inside, he was surrounded by darkness and a stench of dust, mold, and excrement that was so profound he could feel its weight as well as smell it. He paused for a moment to give his eyes a chance to adjust, and reached for a tissue to protect his nose from the stink.

But his hand never made it to his pocket.

"Who the hell are you?" The voice was deep and as menacing as the arm that came out of the darkness, crushing his neck in a hammerlock.

As strong as the arm was, Tom sensed that he was taller than its owner and he was certain that he was better trained. Also, there was no weapon. No knife at his throat or gun to his back. A black belt in judo, he could easily toss the guy over and get the upper hand, but he thought it wiser to hold off that course of action and try a more peaceful approach first.

"I'm here as a friend."

The grip didn't loosen. "If any of us in this rotten place had friends who looked like you, we wouldn't be here. We'd have jobs and help for our families. And you sure as hell don't look like you need a place to squat."

"I'm a friend of Reverend Simon. I work with him. I was told I might find him here."

"What do you want him for?" The arm began to relax a bit.

"Someone close to him has been seriously hurt. I was sent to get the reverend for him. It's an emergency."

"Mister, you don't know from emergency. The life of every man in this hole is a goddam emergency."

The arm relaxed and dropped away, and Tom turned to look at his assailant. He was a little shorter than Tom had estimated, but in better days he must have had a powerful build. Now, malnutrition had left him thin but wiry. It was difficult to estimate his age. Worry or time had grayed his long, thinning hair, and the bitterness and despair that haunted his eyes had etched deep lines on his gaunt face. He could have been anywhere from forty-five to sixty-five.

"The Rev's upstairs. I'll take you to him."

"I can go myself if you have to stand guard here."

The man shook his head. "If I come with you, they'll know you're okay. Otherwise, they may think you sneaked by me—or worse."

"How long have you been here?" Tom asked as they made their way through the debris to the stairs that led to the main floor.

"Going on a year. To you it probably looks like one of the circles of hell, but after sleeping in cartons on the street and under bridges for a couple of years it seems closer to heaven, especially when winter hits."

"What landed you on the streets?"

"Not booze, if that's what you think. That came first, after I got back from 'Nam—the booze and drugs. My folks pulled me out of it. I finished college, found a job, got married and had a kid. For years I thought I had it made. The whole American dream shit. Ever hear of a company called Appleton-Fennimore?"

"Doesn't ring a bell."

"No matter. It was family owned, went back over a hundred years. Started by two brothers-in-law. We made the best office furnishings in the country. I was in the accounting department. We were so goddam good at what we did that the big shots on Wall Street noticed us. Said we were undervalued. Hammond Enterprises, a private-equity firm, bought the company out from under us. Then the spiral began. First the downsizing, then the sell-offs, then the flipping of the company from one private-equity guy to another. Know how that works?"

"Can't say that I do," Tom said, wanting the man to continue.

"It's like a game of hot potato, except the potato was pure gold for these sons of bitches. Every time they flipped it, the guys doing the flipping made millions in profits on the millions in debt the guy it was flipped to took out to buy it. Not to mention all the millions that went to the bankers and lawyers involved in the sale. Last I heard, it had been flipped seven, maybe eight times, and had filed for bankruptcy, and was over a billion dollars in debt. A billion dollars! Bye-bye, Appleton-Fennimore. Hello, some other poor schmuck of a low-flying successful company. Nobody stays below the radar with these bastards for long. They're vampires, vultures, black widow spiders. They suck the guts out of a company that has been the lifeblood of guys like me for generations and spit it and all of us out on the slag heap of their greed."

They were halfway to the top of the stairs, and the man was getting winded, more from emotion than exertion, Tom suspected. "It's a lousy deal," he said. "When did you get hit?"

"A few months on, in the first downsizing. In the beginning

it wasn't too bad. I had a month's severance, my unemployment check, and Cobra for my health insurance. I thought I'd get another job in a matter of weeks. But when you're over fifty and have spent your working life with one firm, employers think you're over the hill and they interpret your dedication to the company as laziness not loyalty. Not all the references in the world can save you from that kind of label. I kept trying even harder after the health insurance ran out. Then the unemployment dried up and the savings went. My wife's job didn't come close to paying the mortgage. We lost the house. We lost the car. Then my wife took off with the kids. I can't blame her. There was nothing to hang around for. I was a dead weight around her neck."

"Things could turn around." Tom knew the words were pathetic, even ridiculous, given the circumstances, but he felt he had to say something and giving vent to his true feelings would not have been helpful.

"You're a friend of the Rev's, all right. You sound just like him." The man swung open the door at the top of the stairs. "Problem is, you both live in a dream world. In the real world for guys like me, life is shit and then you die. We just have to work out the right time for the dying part." He thrust Tom ahead of him. "There he is. I got to get back to my post.

"This guy's okay—he's here for the Rev," he called out to the men standing around Arnold Simon in the vestibule.

About ten men in shabby jeans and T-shirts surrounded the minister. Most were middle-aged, a few older, but the eyes they turned on Tom held the weariness, not the wisdom, of advanced and defeated old age.

"Tom!" Arnold Simon looked up from the notebook he had been writing in. He looked surprised but not displeased. "How did you find me?"

"It wasn't hard. I just looked for people you'd be helping."

Even the men encircling Simon managed to smile with him.

"Lyle sent me. He's asking for you."

"Lyle. Oh, yes. How is he doing?" Like Tom, Simon knew better than to give the senator's full name in front of these men, victims of the anti-labor legislation associated with him.

"Not too well."

"I should go to him." He turned to the men. "I have your information. I'll start making calls on Monday. It may take time, but I'm going to get you all out of here. You deserve better than this. I'll see to it that you get it."

The men didn't look convinced, but they were polite enough not to say so.

"I know what you're thinking, but ask around. You'll find I'm a man of my word."

"You're in good hands," Tom said, opening the door that led down to the basement. "No one can stop the reverend when he gets going. He's able to leap tall bureaucracies in a single bound."

"Oh, I don't know about that," Simon said with a laugh. "Sometimes it takes two bounds. After all, I'm not Superman."

Downstairs, Simon shook hands with the man on guard. "Thanks, Roger, for helping me convince the others to let the man I brought with me stay. I couldn't have done it on my own."

"Sure you could, reverend. I just made it go a little faster."

"Have you been keeping off the booze?"

"Can't afford it."

"That's not the answer I'm looking for."

Roger shrugged. "I can't make promises, Rev. Not to you. Not to myself. But I can tell you that I try. Lately, when I manage to scrape up a couple of bucks on the street, I buy some food for me and the guys. I know the booze is no escape. When I wake up, I've got the same problems, plus one hell of a headache."

"Promises are easy. Trying is what counts. Every day, try a little harder. I'll be back Monday or Tuesday to let you know how things are going."

"The guys and I will try to get the place cleaned up a bit for you."

"Better that you clean it up for yourselves."

Out on the street, Tom took a deep breath, hoping to wash the stench of the building from his lungs. There would be no way to wipe from memory the abject poverty and despair he had seen inside.

"You mustn't judge them," Simon said. "They're all good men and most of them have been brought down by circumstances out of their control."

"I don't judge them. I judge the greedy, power-hungry bastards who control those circumstances."

"Even their judgment should be left to God."

"Then I'm giving God a head start."

Simon sighed, but, to Tom's relief, he didn't pursue a religious argument. Instead, he asked, "How's Lyle?"

"He's resting comfortably. He wasn't hurt seriously. No bruises or broken bones."

"That's a relief. Is he back at his hotel?"

"He's staying with Al Foster."

"I'll go to him now."

"Not a good idea. That's why I'm here, to make sure you don't do that. He blames you for what happened."

"But that's ridiculous. I was unavoidably held up. If we'd been together, we might have both been mugged. If Lyle won't see me, I'll go back to the park. They may still need my help. Thanks for coming down here to let me know how he's doing."

Tom nodded, but he wasn't ready to accept the dismissal. He needed more answers. "My car's not far from there. I'll walk you over."

"That's nice. I'll enjoy the company. How's the research coming along?"

"I still have Senator Wayne to interview. Of course, there was no chance of that tonight."

"Of course. But Blair is lucky to have someone as dedicated as you working with him, and coming out late at night to get a chance to interview Lyle. Turns out Lyle was lucky too."

Was that sarcasm? Tom wondered. Or was it fishing? Did Simon suspect that he had a deeper purpose for being around his fraternity brothers? Or was it just a compliment from a minister who had no idea what was going on around him?

"Unfortunately, not as lucky as he would have been if you or I had turned up a little earlier. He said that when he called you, you told him that you were on your way. If you had taken a cab, you'd have been there way before him."

"I'm on a very limited budget. I never take cabs."

Or admit to it. A taxi would have had him on the scene before Wayne arrived. Even the subway should have had him there. Maybe it had.

"It's only a couple of stops on the subway, but you said you just got out of it when I called you from my car. Was the train delayed?" He kept the question casual, just something asked out of idle curiosity.

"No. I intended to get there as quickly as possible, but I got sidetracked. Some of the rioting had spilled over into the streets, and I stopped to break up a fight in front of a Korean vegetable store on Avenue B. It took a while, but, happily, no one was seriously hurt."

"Except the senator."

Simon looked startled. "You said he wasn't seriously hurt."

"That's Dr. Foster's opinion. The senator thinks otherwise."

Simon smiled knowingly. "Lyle would. But I suspect his pride was hurt more than anything else. Still, a little suffering might be good for him."

"How so?"

"It might wake him up to the suffering all around him."

"It's been my experience that men like Lyle Wayne never wake up to the suffering around them."

Simon gave him a penetrating look. "You speak like someone who has lived far beyond the confines of a bookstore."

"Perhaps it's books that taught me that."

They paused as they reached one of the entrances to the park.

"It's late," Tom said. "Why don't you let me drive you home?"

Simon shook his head. "There's still work to be done." He looked up at the sky. "Wish there was less of a haze. People tend to behave better when the sky is filled with stars and the moon is bright."

"Even without the haze, there wouldn't be much moon. We're at the end phase."

"Are you a star-gazer?"

"No—a Jew. New moon is coming Monday evening, and with it our new year."

"Of course. Rosh Hashanah. You know, I've always liked the idea of your Yom Kippur, with its concentration on getting forgiveness from God for your sins."

"God can forgive us only for our sins against Him. For sins

against everyone else, we have to ask for and earn forgiveness directly from those we have hurt or offended."

"Not an easy task."

"No one ever said being a Jew was easy."

"History has certainly proved that to be true." Simon held out his hand. "Thank you for coming down here to tell me about Lyle."

There was blood on the shirtsleeve that extended beyond his jacket. "How did that happen?" Tom asked.

Simon looked surprised to see the stain. "Who knows? Somewhere along the line of the night's adventures. Good night. And a happy new year to you and your loved ones."

"Thanks."

But it wasn't the holiday wish Tom thought about as he drove back to Brooklyn. It was the bloodstain and the minister's hope that Lyle Wayne's attack would prove to be a lesson for him.

Just how many "adventures" had the Reverend Arnold Simon had that night?

CHAPTER 35

THOUGH HIS hours were only ten to four on Sunday, Tom went to the shop at nine to unpack a recent Ingram delivery and restock some shelves. It took less time than he had expected, and he sat down at the computer to look at the news online.

All three papers reported the riot on the front page. The *Times* gave it a wide-angle picture and the second lead under the headline, PROTEST LEADS TO RIOT IN TOMPKINS SQUARE PARK, plus a thoughtful analysis article about the plight of the homeless. The *Daily News* screamed, HOMELESS HELL, above a picture of the melee. The *Post* bellowed BRAINLESS BASH IN TOMPKINS over a close-up of bloodied rioters. All three stories put the start of the riot at around seven p.m., and the *Times* and the *News* both mentioned that the Reverend Arnold Simon had helped bring it to an end without significant casualties. Neither noted how long he had been on the scene, however.

On the way home last night, Tom had driven along Avenue B. The street was littered and there were some taped-up store-front windows behind the iron gratings. One was a greengrocery, but the store could have been in that condition for days if not longer. The *Times* story reported that the rioting had spilled out into the nearby streets, and that windows were broken, and that shopkeepers had closed up and locked their gates to prevent looting. It didn't mention Arnold Simon's being on hand to cool things down outside of the park. Nor did the *Post* and the *News*.

Then one of the photos accompanying the runover in the *News* caught Tom's eye. It showed an angry crowd in front of a grocery, and a tall man in a black suit separating a Korean man, obviously the owner, and a young black man who appeared to be shouting at him. The caption identified only the street, Avenue B, but it didn't name anyone in the picture. The man in the black suit had his back to the camera, but he was certainly tall enough and broad enough to be Arnold Simon. There was no way of ascertaining what time that altercation took place, or if the man shown was definitely the minister, but the photograph certainly made Arnold Simon's excuse for not being nearby when Wayne was attacked even more plausible.

If not Simon, then who? Instantly, Tom's mind jumped to Phillip Grinwald, the surgical oncologist who could well be the grandson of the late Professor Nathan Grinwald. His practice was here in New York City. Surely he lived nearby. Could he be seeking revenge for the accident that nearly cost him his life so many years ago?

A tapping on the door caught Tom's attention. Ten to ten. He opened the door for Phil Howard.

"I have to leave soon," Tom told him. "Max can't come in today, but I arranged for Jack Wilson to give you a hand. He'll get here around noon."

Phil closed his umbrella and put it in the stand next to the door. "With this weather, I don't expect a lot of customers, but I'll be glad for the company. Maybe we'll be able to get the remainder tables organized."

Back at the counter, Tom phoned Joe Henley on his cell. "Are you on duty or off?" he asked when Joe answered.

"Off. First Sunday in ages, and wouldn't you know it would rain? What's up?"

"I was hoping you could get some information for me. Is Mike Farley on? I'll give him a call."

"Mike's on leave. His wife just had another kid—a boy. What do you need?"

"The home address of a doctor affiliated with Mount Sinai."

"Has Max taken a turn for the worse?"

"Nothing like that. I need to contact him for this project I'm working on, and time's running out. I can't wait weeks to get an appointment at his office. Can you give me the name of someone I can call?"

"Tell me who it is, and I'll take care of it for you. There's a new kid who's great on research. I'll call him. He'd ask you questions. Me, he'll just get the info."

"The name's Phillip R. Grinwald—Phillip with two *l*'s. I'm hoping he doesn't commute from the suburbs."

While he waited for Joe's call, Tom sorted through and packed some orders that had come in over the Internet. It was nearly noon, and he had just finished gift-wrapping a signed third printing of *A Tree Grows in Brooklyn,* which had brought in a nice five hundred and fifty dollars, when Joe called back.

"You're in luck—no suburbs. The guy lives in Riverdale, the Hudson Hill area. Pretty fancy."

"He's a surgeon. He can afford it and more," Tom said, writing down the address and phone number. "Thanks, Joe. That's another one I owe you."

"You can pay up right now. You're a word guy. This *Times* puzzle is driving me nuts. What's a five-letter word for 'cowboy raiment,' ending in *s?* And don't tell me 'boots' or 'jeans'—they don't work."

"Chaps."

"Jeez! Why didn't I think of that? Your debt is paid."

"Much too easy. You're going to have to think of something else."

"Well, you could make it stop raining so that I can toss the puzzle and play a round of golf."

"I think I'm going to have to stick with 'chaps.'"

"Probably for the best. The course must be too soggy to play today anyway. Tell me, when is this project of yours going to be done? I've never liked the smell of it."

"Grinwald could well be my last interview. And don't worry about me. I can take care of myself."

"Words written on too many tombstones for my taste."

A kid answered the phone at the Grinwald home, and Tom asked to speak with her daddy. It took so long that Tom began to wonder if the child had delivered his request, but finally a male voice came over the line.

"Hi," Tom said. "I'm Tom Berenson. Blair Whitney at Stanford University probably got in touch with you about me."

"No, he didn't, and I don't think I know him."

"He's writing a history of GMU in the Seventies and Eighties, and I'm helping him with some of the research on the faculty. We'd like to get more details and anecdotes about your grandfather for the book. I'm going to be in your neighborhood today, and I was wondering if I could drop by and talk to you, maybe pick up a photo or two. It won't take much time, and it would be a big help to Blair, who's in a deadline crunch. I'm surprised he wasn't in touch with you. He told me he'd call. I guess it slipped his mind."

"There were no messages here that I'm aware of, but, as you can tell by the young lady who answered the phone, sometimes messages get lost."

The voice was pleasant, not suspicious, which was a relief. Even more of a relief was the fact that Grinwald had not denied having a grandfather who had been on the GMU faculty.

"So would it be okay if I dropped over today? I can be there in about an hour. I can give you Blair's number, if you'd like to call him."

"Not necessary, but I'm in a bit of a deadline crunch myself. I'm going to be taking a couple of days off, and I'm trying to catch up on a pile of paperwork. Could we put this off for another day?"

"I wish we could, but I have to be up in Boston tomorrow, and then I'm flying back to the Coast. And we really want to have your grandfather in the book. I promise not to take up much of your time."

"All right." Grinwald sighed. "I wouldn't want Granddad left out. Make it around three-thirty or four, closer to four…. Sorry, but what's your name again?"

"Tom Berenson. Thanks a lot. This is a big help. I'll see you later, and if you have a chance, try to dig up some photos."

He had hoped to knock off the interview with Grinwald earlier, but now Tom looked upon the extra time as a bonus of an hour or two he could spend with Nora.

"Hi," he said when she answered her cell phone. "How about brunch? You pick the place, and I'll meet you there in a half hour."

"Wish I could." She sounded disappointed. "Unfortunately, Tony Portman just called. He insists on a meeting this afternoon, and I'm rushing around, getting together some samples for him to see and figures to go over. These guys give me a royal pain. They want everything and everyone at their beck and call. Maybe we can make it later, but I have no idea how long this meeting will run. I'll be glad to see the end of these creeps and this project."

Which would probably be coming sooner than she suspected, but Tom didn't tell her that. "I'll be happy to be done with my business with them too," he said. "I have things I have to take care of later in the day, and I'm not sure how long it will take. Why don't I give you a call when I get back? Hopefully, you'll be free by then too."

"Sounds good."

"By the way," he cut in before she could click off, "how did it go last night with Senator Wayne?" He had thought she might find it strange if he didn't ask.

"It didn't. The son of a bitch phoned me at the last minute and ordered me to stay away. Said he didn't want any kind of record of his slumming. Denise and I were halfway there, but I couldn't talk him out of it. We had to turn back. Denise is young, and she had a party to go to. Actually, I thought of calling you, but I knew I was too angry to be good company. I went home, had a glass of wine, and went to bed early. I woke up this morning feeling rested and great—until Tony called. Got to run now. Talk to you later."

Tom slipped the phone into his pocket and picked up his laptop. Jack Wilson had arrived, and he and Phil were busy at the remainder tables when Tom left the store. On his way to his car he bought a copy of the *Daily News,* but a closer examination of the photo taken in front of the greengrocery provided no new details. The man separating the two antagonists remained obscured. Maybe the shopkeeper would be able to identify him.

Traffic was heavy and parking seemed impossible, but he finally found a spot on East 11th Street. The shops on Avenue B were open for business, their windows taped and awaiting glaziers. This was the only sign of last night's riot. The man behind the cash register at Kim's Fruits & Vegetables was obviously the man in the photograph. Tom selected a bunch of bananas, and as they were being rung up, he took the copy of the *News* from under his arm, opened it to the picture, and tried to look like he had just made a happy discovery. "Hey, I think you're famous," he said. "Isn't this you?"

The grocer smiled and nodded.

"Looks like there was a lot of excitement here last night," Tom pressed on. "Who's the man who helped you settle things down?" He pointed to the black-suited figure in the photo.

The grocer looked confused.

A young man who was arranging oranges in a neat pyramid turned around. "Sorry, Dad's English isn't too good. But, yes, that's him in the picture. Wish I'd been here to help him out."

"He seems to have done all right. Ask him if he knows who this is. From the back, he looks like a friend of mine, but I can't be sure."

The father shook his head in answer to the son's question in Korean.

Tom gestured toward his own neck. "Ask him if he was wearing a clerical collar. My friend's a minister."

This time, the father nodded and smiled.

Tom smiled too. "I figured it had to be Arnie," he said to the young man. "Reverend Arnold Simon. Maybe you know him. He always turns up when people are in trouble."

This time the son shook his head, but added, "I've heard of him, though. Whoever it was, I'm glad he was here to keep Dad from getting hurt—or doing something stupid. Dad has a hot temper, and not speaking much English doesn't help in bad situations."

"Arnie has a way of calming things down. I don't think the man ever sleeps. What time did all this take place?"

"Search me. I was uptown with friends and didn't get home till after midnight. By then it was all over but the cleanup. Dad usually closes between seven and eight. As for last night, who knows?"

Tom was afraid the young man was going to leave it at that, and he didn't want to raise suspicion by pushing for a definite time. But then the son turned to his father and said something in Korean. The older man answered him with a few words and a shrug. Then added a few more words.

"All he says is it was before closing. He wants to know why you asked." The son looked like he wanted to know too.

"Just curious." Tom picked up his bag of bananas. "I'm glad no one got hurt and not much damage was done. Tell your dad I think he's much better looking than his picture."

The son laughed. "He'll be happy to hear that. And when you talk to your friend, tell him thanks for us."

"You got it." He left the store feeling only half satisfied. He could be fairly sure that it was Arnold Simon in the photograph, but the time frame remained problematic.

After a quick late lunch at a coffee shop on Avenue A, he got into his car and headed for Riverdale. It was already close to four, so there was no chance of annoying Grinwald by arriving too early.

Even in the rain the Tudor house at the end of the long, curving gravel driveway looked stately yet welcoming. The leaves of the magnificent red oak that shaded its fieldstone entrance had already begun to slide into their brilliant vermillion welcome to autumn, their color defying the gloom of a gray and rainy day.

Happily, the two frolicking unicorns etched into the frosted glass of the mahogany door's tympanum appeared to be eluding the attention of the ferocious lion-head door knocker that hung below. Rather than reach for the lion's shiny brass ring, Tom pressed the small button on the doorframe and heard chimes ring out the first notes of Bach's "Sheep May Safely Graze."

A moment later the door was opened by an attractive brunette of about thirty-five wearing designer jeans, a turquoise Izod shirt, and a charming smile. "Mr. Berenson?" she asked.

"Yes. I have an appointment with your husband. Sorry I'm a little late, but the rain slowed down the traffic."

"Not to worry." She took his umbrella and put it in the brass stand near the door while he wiped his feet on the doormat. It would have been unthinkable to make tracks on the gleaming hardwood floor. She reached out to shake his hand. "I'm Sharon Grinwald. Phil's running late too. He's still deep in his paperwork, but he told me to show you right in. When it comes to scheduling, my husband seems to think he gets more hours in a day than everyone else, which means he's always behind. At his office, his staff keeps things in hand, but here at home...." She shrugged apologetically. "He said that your visit has something to do with his grandfather. He was really close to him, so I know he's looking forward to the break. Come."

She led the way through a French provincial dining room, knocked on a door at its far end, and opened it without waiting for an answer. "Mr. Berenson is here," she announced. "And I'm off to pick up the kids at Samantha's. See you later. Nice meeting you, Mr. Berenson," she added.

"You, too," Tom said, and meant it, but she had closed the door on his words and on her husband's, "Give Sam my love."

Phillip Grinwald was seated at an oversized cherry-wood desk covered with papers and folders. Behind him, French windows looked out on a beautifully landscaped garden that was surely a delightful distraction on sunny days. Bookcases on either side of the window were filled not only with what were obviously the mandatory medical volumes and journals but also an eclectic and beautifully bound selection of what, from a distance, appeared to be literary works, including several shelves devoted to Shakespeare-ana. When he stood up and reached over the desk to shake hands, Tom noted his athletic build and towering height. His strong arms, however, ended in the delicate, long-fingered hands of a surgeon.

"It's always a pleasure to meet someone who's interested in my grandfather." He nodded toward one of the two leather chairs facing his desk. "Please, sit down. Would you like something to drink? I'm sure Sharon left a pot of coffee in the kitchen, or maybe you'd prefer tea or soda?"

"No, thank you. I'm fine."

They exchanged pleasantries for a few moments, then Tom reached into his pocket for his notebook and pen. "Tell me about your grandfather. I understand that, among his other accomplishments, he was a highly respected authority on Shakespeare." He nodded toward the bookcase. "It looks like you share his love for the Bard, or is that your grandfather's collection?"

"The answer is 'both.' I share his love though not his vast knowledge, and the collection is his. He left it to me." He smiled lovingly at the tidy bookshelves. "He wrote quite a few of those books, and contributed to others. I can give you a list."

"Thanks, but we have that already from reference books. What we need are some human-interest stories."

Grinwald folded his hands behind his head and leaned back in his chair. "One of my favorite stories dates back to his undergraduate days. Seems he had thoughts of becoming an actor back then. He had the role of Osric in a student production of *Hamlet* and he put so much feeling into it that when he was doing that fawning bow, he lost his balance and fell flat on his face. The audience thought it was intentional and they loved it. Unfortunately, Granddad broke his nose and a tooth. That's when he decided he was better suited to taking a more academic approach to Shakespeare."

"Fortunately for all his students."

Grinwald pursed his lips and straightened up. "Maybe not all of them. I understand he had a reputation for being a bit of a martinet, especially in his later years. It's just that he wanted everyone to love and appreciate Shakespeare as much as he did, and it became harder and harder for him to suffer fools gladly. But I'm convinced that he was a gifted teacher. He certainly was with me, and many of his students, even some who went on to other fields, kept in touch with him through the years." He shook his head. "Damn! I didn't think of it before you came, but somewhere I have a box filled with letters that he saved from students. I found it among his things after he died, and I couldn't bring myself to throw it out. I'll look for it and send it to you, but I'll want it back."

"I'm not sure there will be time," Tom said, then added quickly when he saw Grinwald's disappointment, "but if you want to look through the letters yourself, you can always e-mail me some quotes. Of course, Blair is the one who has final say on what will go into the book. Sometimes there isn't room for everything he would like to include in his opus."

"I understand. I've contributed to enough medical journals to know all about the constraints of space." He reached for a folder on his desk. "I hope he'll be able to fit in a picture, though. I dug up a few good ones for you."

Tom took the folder and opened it. A man in his sixties with wispy white hair, a wide jaw, and surprisingly kind eyes looked back at him from the top of the pile. "He had very nice eyes," he said, starting to look through the other photos.

"Windows to the soul, my grandmother always told me. My favorite is the one of him fishing, but I expect your editor will go for the one in full academic regalia."

"Probably." Tom closed the folder and slipped it into his briefcase, feeling like a louse for misleading Grinwald about the nonexistent book. The ruse was particularly unpleasant because he rather liked the man and his wife. It was time he got down to the real purpose of the interview so he could eliminate Grinwald from his list of suspects. Or move him to the top.

"When I was doing my research, I learned that your grandfather was in a severe automobile accident. I think it was back in the early eighties. Maybe you were too young to have heard about it."

Grinwald's face clouded. "Not too young. I was there, in the car with him. I was in a coma for a while. I later learned that they thought they were going to lose me."

"That must have been a terrible burden for your grandfather."

"It was. He was never the same after that accident. He blamed himself for it, and no one could convince him that it wasn't his fault."

"What happened?"

"I don't remember much about the actual accident. Just that we were driving along, and suddenly the car spun out of control. Granddad said he should have kept it in better repair, but my grandmother had other ideas."

"That sounds ominous."

"It is." Grinwald picked up a letter opener and began toying with it. "If you're doing research on GMU, you've probably come across mention of its fraternities. There's one in particular, Beta Alpha Beta Phi...."

"Yes, I've come across it." Then Tom prodded when Grinwald's voice trailed off, "It's evidently the crème de la crème."

Grinwald looked up, his eyes dark with old anger. "Crap de la crap, would describe it better, at least back then. These guys came from big money, the so-called 'best' families, but they were pure shit. They thought they owned the world and could get away with anything. And evidently they did. They gave Granddad a hard time in class, and the accident happened soon after an exam most of them flunked though he had tried his best to prepare them for it. My grandmother never stopped believing that they rigged the car. My parents agreed with her."

"Didn't they report it?"

"Granddad wouldn't hear of it. As bad as those guys were, he couldn't believe they'd do such a thing. When the police examined what was left of the car, they said it was possible the brakes had been tampered with, but they couldn't be sure, so it was listed as an accident. Without Granddad's knowledge, Dad took the report and his suspicions to the authorities at GMU. That was the end of Dad. He worked in administration there, and he soon found himself out of a job. No other university would hire him, either. Eventually, he was taken on as an office manager for a retail chain. The pay was better, but he was never really happy. Granddad had lived so long in his ivory tower that he couldn't see the connection."

"Maybe there wasn't one."

"There was one, all right. More than one, a connection with every son of a bitch who had a hand in it." The knuckles turned white on the delicate surgeon's hand that was gripping the letter opener. "No doubt if the administrators gave it any credence, they thought that boys will be boys, and those creeps from their grand families would outgrow their murderous pranks. But narcissistic bastards like them never do. I know who they are, and I've been watching them over the years. They still think they can get away with murder, and they do."

"Murder?" Tom tried for an expression that he hoped conveyed only mild curiosity and skepticism.

"Oh, not the kind you're thinking of, with guns and knives. But they're poisoning our society with their selfish politics, and bleeding our economy dry with their hedge funds, subprime mortgages, private-equity buyouts, and mega real estate deals. Pretty soon the shit is going to hit the fan, and almost everybody in the country will be covered with it, but these guys will walk away unscathed."

"Surely, they alone can't bring everything tumbling down on us."

"They've got plenty of help. Just open the pages of *The Wall Street Journal*. It's packed with the names of the avaricious manipulators who are pulling the plug on us. But I'm only interested in the guys who wrecked my family. If there's any justice in this world, they will eventually pay for it, and in some cruel and horrible way."

A chill went through Tom. Grinwald's eyes held the same hate he had seen on the faces of men who willingly confessed to heinous crimes. Perhaps he had finally met his man, a fanatical surgeon with a motive. But what about opportunity? He couldn't sit here and quiz this man about where he had been on the days and nights in question. He would have to start inquiries, get in touch with Grinwald's staff.

Suddenly, Grinwald tossed down the letter opener. "Shit." He closed his eyes and took a deep breath. When he opened his eyes, he looked calmer. "Sorry. I didn't mean to run on like that." He made an ingratiating smile. "You're not going to put any of that in the book, are you?"

"Of course not. That's not what it's about."

Grinwald sighed. "I don't often lose it like that. I'm glad Sharon wasn't here. She says I have to let go of the past, and, of course, she's right. It's just that digging up those pictures and talking about Granddad brought it back. As for the rest"—he shook his head sheepishly—"I'm glad she didn't hear that, either. She calls it my flaming-liberal harangue. She's always afraid I'll go into one when her dad's around. He's a raging Republican. I usually manage to keep the lid on when we're together. Hey, if you're one of them, no offense, I hope. Some of my favorite patients happen to be Republicans, and boy, do they know how to take advantage of their benefits under Social Security and Medicare and Medicare prescriptions."

Tom wasn't about to commit himself one way or another, nor was he about to be taken in by the charm offensive. He merely smiled and said, "I'd better get going. Thanks for your time."

"You're most welcome. I'll walk you to the door."

The walking stick had been hidden behind the drapes. Grinwald swiveled in his chair, took it in his left hand, and pulled himself to his feet. When he came around the desk, Tom realized that beneath his slacks he probably wore a brace or other device on his right leg. Grinwald's gaze followed Tom's. "That's what Granddad blamed himself for. By the time he died, I think I proved to him that I never let it keep me from accomplishing the things that really matter. I'm so used to it, I'm not even aware of it." His laugh was brief. "Well, hardly ever."

They made their slow progress to the door, where Grinwald held out his hand. "Granddad was a good man and a fine scholar. I hope your colleague will do justice to him in the book."

"I'm sure he will."

The rain had turned to a misty drizzle, and Tom walked through it slowly, welcoming its soft, sleepy coolness. Inside his car, he saw that Phillip Grinwald was still standing at the open door. He raised his cane in his left hand and touched it to his forehead in a farewell salute. Tom returned his smile and made a little salute of his own. He was back to square one.

CHAPTER 36

*D*amn! Tom pounded his hand on the steering wheel. Traffic on the slick road had slowed to a crawl, but his impatience had nothing to do with the pace of the trip back. He was sick of the case. Sick of the Golden Guys and their opulent, depraved world. He wanted out. And he had thought he was so close to the answer. Phillip Grinwald had fit the profile of the perpetrator perfectly—until he limped around his desk.

If not Grinwald, then who? It had to be someone who was a victim of these men, or someone avenging a victim or victims. Lou West? Tom had phoned the Roosevelt Hotel when he got home last night. The fund raiser that West had been headlining started to break up at about eleven. Of course, that didn't mean that West had stayed till the end, or that he hadn't sneaked out earlier and then come back. And what about Vittorio Capperrelli? His wife seemed to have screwed with everyone in the group except Arnold Simon. And—who knows?—maybe with Simon too. And then there was Simon himself. Had he decided that vengeance was his, instead of the Lord's, for the sins of his fraternity brothers? Tom hated the thought of Simon's being the perpetrator, but he knew better than to let his personal feelings cloud his thinking. As a cop, he had put too many likable but vicious criminals behind bars. Until he could get a better handle on where Simon was and at exactly what time last night, Simon would have to remain a suspect.

Still, it was hard to think of the castrator being one of the Golden Guys. That would be like finding out that D'Artagnan was a spy on the payroll of Cardinal Richelieu. Then again, some Golden Guys were considered less golden than others. Jason

Gilbert said he was their token Jew and had never really been accepted. He certainly had the strength and the knowledge to carry out the attacks. Nora was scheduled to interview him on the night Hammond was hit, but she said he wasn't there. Was he in New York that night, and last night too? But Gilbert had been too drunk the night McGrath was hit to do anything but sleep it off. Or was he?

Was there anyone else who had been made to feel he wasn't as golden as his brothers?

Of course there was! Albert Foster.

Who was always conveniently around to tend to the victims? Foster. Who certainly knew how to perform the simple procedure? Foster. Despite his craze for fast foods, he had maintained his college football player's physique. Maybe he was always around to tend the victims because he created them. Early on, Gilbert had told him that the group had never fully accepted Foster, and Tom himself had heard several of them talking down to him. Tony Portman ordered him around like a lackey. Just last night, on the way to Foster's place and even while being tended by him, Lyle Wayne was bad-mouthing the doctor.

Was Foster finally acting on a resentment that had been building for twenty-five years? It wouldn't be unusual. There were killers behind bars, "quiet, nice guys," according their astonished neighbors, who had hidden their rage for decades before it erupted in violence and murder. Foster had simply chosen a different m.o., one closer to home for him.

Tom swerved into the next gas station, opened his laptop and Googled the Edison Hotel, after which he phoned its number. When he was finally transferred to the manager, he put on what he hoped was his most ingratiating voice.

"Hi, Tom Bryan of *Gourmet* magazine. Been hearing great things about the Edison. I'm writing an article on the growing popularity of fast foods, and it's just come to my attention that *New York* magazine held a panel at your place yesterday to judge the city's best French fries. Is that right?"

There was a slight hesitation at the other end. Then the manager laughed. "Yes. But, of course, even if I knew what the outcome was, I am not at liberty to tell you."

Tom laughed too. "Of course not. I never expected you to divulge the panel's findings. I just wanted to confirm that the great event was indeed held and also how long it took the panel to do its thing. We're going to press tomorrow, and I don't want to leave the French-fry event and the Edison out of the article."

"Oh, in that case.... I wasn't on duty yesterday, but I know the event was held here and ran a good couple of hours. Too long, according to some of our guests with more fastidious palettes, and who prefer the aroma of the international cuisine at our world-famous restaurant."

"Can you give me the exact time? It always looks more impressive to readers if we have that."

"Hang on. Let me check our bookings for that time frame." In a moment the man was back. "It was from five-thirty to eight."

"Hardly sounds long enough to test all the French fries in the city."

"I guess they had to be selective or else the competition would have gone on till Bastille Day." The manager laughed at his joke, such as it was. "Anyhow, that's the time the suite was rented for. The Judge Crater Society of Morningside Heights holds its monthly meetings here, and they had the suite from nine to eleven, so we needed the hour to get it cleared and set up for them. As you no doubt know, Judge Crater left for a Broadway show on the night of August 6, 1930, and was never seen again."

"I wouldn't have thought there would be enough people in a club with that name to need an entire suite."

"The name is misleading. They have members from all over the country. They're a very lively group."

"Not as lively as the judge was if he ran off to Havana with a stripper from Minsky's burlesque. Thanks for the information. If you give me your name, I'll have a copy of the magazine sent to you when the article comes out."

"It's Fred Konroy—that's Konroy with a *K*. And thanks."

Tom paused, as though jotting down the name, then said, "I thank *you* for helping me make my deadline. Have a great day now."

"You too."

Tom held his phone and gathered his thoughts. Wayne had

probably been struck sometime between eight-thirty and nine. Foster had implied that he had been at the contest until just before he came home last night, around ten. But the event had ended at eight o'clock. That gave Foster plenty of time to hit and run.

Tom dialed Foster's cell phone. "Are you home?" he asked when Foster picked up.

"Yeah."

"Good. Stay there. We have to talk. I'll be over in about a half hour."

"Do you have a lead?"

"Could be."

The rain had made the road slick, and an accident up ahead kept traffic at an infuriating slow-motion and start-stop pace. It was nearly eight by the time he reached Foster's neighborhood and found a parking space.

"I thought you'd be here an hour ago," Foster said at the door.

"So did I, but I got caught behind a huge pile-up."

"Hungry? I ordered from Kajun Kitchens while I was waiting, but it smelled so good that I got started without you." He led the way to a gleaming eat-in kitchen where he had set two places with plastic cutlery on one end of a marble-top table. He resumed his seat in front of a nearly empty Styrofoam container. Spread out next to it were several open medical journals. Obviously, he had been catching up on his reading while he ate. He nodded toward the unopened container at the other place setting. "Sit. Eat. Enjoy."

Garlic, onion, and a dozen spices he couldn't identify wafted up and tickled Tom's nose when he opened the container.

"Extra spicy Chicken Jambalaya," Foster identified the contents. "I had the shrimp version. I'd offer you a sample, but I've already polished off all the shrimp. Just some veggies left."

Tom pretended he didn't see the longing look Foster was casting toward his container. He pulled it closer and picked up the plastic fork. He was hungry, and the jambalaya was surprisingly delicious. He had no idea that fast food could be so good.

"So where were you that it took you so long to get here?" Foster asked.

"Up in Riverdale, talking to Dr. Phillip Grinwald. He's a surgeon at Mt. Sinai. Do you know him?"

Foster pursed his lips in thought, then shook his head. "Should I?"

"Probably. He's the grandson of your Shakespeare professor, Nathan Grinwald. I'm sure you remember him."

"Oh, sure, I remember *him*. What a bore! We called him 'Grim Grinwald.'"

"You did more than think up alliterative sobriquets for him. You sabotaged his car. Don't give me that innocent look. I went back and read the newspaper reports. The local cops may have been too ingenuous—or intimidated—to see the need for an investigation, but it's obvious to this cop that the brakes must have been cut."

Foster shrugged and made an ingratiating smile. "So what if we did? It was just a college prank. We were kids."

"Slashing someone's brakes isn't a prank, it's a crime. And as for being kids, you guys were old enough to vote and be in the Service. In the eyes of the law, you were men and fully responsible for your actions."

"So what are you going to do about it? Have us arrested? The statute of limitations has long since run out. Don't be such a nitpicker. It happened decades ago and no one was hurt."

"Tell that to the professor's grandson, who was in a coma for weeks."

"But he came out of it, didn't he?" A sudden realization lit up his eyes. "Is he the one? Is he doing this for revenge after all these years? How mean-spirited can a guy get?"

"That's what I thought at first, but you can forget it. The accident left the guy crippled. He has a brace on one leg and hobbles along with a cane."

"Shit. And he's a surgeon. He would have fit the bill perfectly."

"Yes. A surgeon would fit the bill perfectly."

"What the hell are you looking at me like that for?"

"I think you know."

Foster laughed nervously. "You're out of your mind if you think it's me. These guys are my brothers. We love each other. We stick together. We help each other."

Tom didn't answer or break his gaze. Let a man blather on long enough and he'll incriminate himself.

Foster picked up one of the journals and gestured with it to the others scattered nearby. "For chrissake, what do you think I've been doing here? I've been studying up, trying to find a cure for these guys. Would I be doing that if I'd been cutting them?"

"Makes a good cover. It would be a lot more convincing if you found something."

"I haven't yet, but I most certainly will!" He dropped the journal, rummaged through the pile and picked up another one. "There's a guy at Hopkins who's working on something that looks hopeful. It may take a couple of years, but it would be a real breakthrough if it works out. Seems there will be a big market for it." He picked up a copy of the *New England Journal of Medicine.* "A sharp increase in impotence is being reported around the country. Mostly among upper-income Caucasians between thirty-five and sixty who have always been sexually active if not overactive."

"And it's the same m.o.?"

"That's unclear. Could be, but most of the doctors seem clueless as to the cause. The way it happened to our guys could have slipped past me if it hadn't been that they thought they'd been mugged, and then found the note. Obviously, whoever's doing it to our guys—and it isn't me!—wants them to know they're being hit." He nodded toward the journals. "As for the cases that are being reported here, who knows? All possibilities are being looked into—pollution, a new virus or germ from Asia, allergies, drug interactions, magnetic waves from cell phones. The one thing clear is that there are as yet no magic little blue pills for these guys. We've got to find some other, more radical way to help them. At Hopkins, they're looking—"

Tom had had enough. "Where were you last night at eight-thirty?"

It was impossible to tell from Foster's expression whether the question had frightened or surprised him. Quickly, he regained his composure. "I was judging French fries at the Edison. You can check. Just between you and me, some of those entries could have used a lot of ketchup. They were so bland and mushy that I wouldn't be surprised if their makers didn't pay off the committee to be included in the contest."

"I did check with the hotel. Everyone was out of there by eight o'clock. That gave you plenty of time to get down to Shinbone Alley. Is that where you were at eight-thirty?"

"The hell it was. I told you, I'm not the one who's doing this!"

"So where were you? You didn't answer your cell phone and you didn't get back here till after ten."

"I'd rather not say."

"That's not an option."

"It's none of your business!"

"You've made it very much my business. But if you'd rather not tell me, maybe you'll tell Tony." Tom took out his cell phone.

Now there was real fear in Foster's eyes. "Put that damn thing away." He ran his hand through his hair. "This goes no further. I could get in a lot of trouble."

"I'm waiting.

"Okay. You know I'm going through a messy divorce. It's not enough that she has the house in Old Westbury, the bitch is trying to take me for every last cent too. Before she walked out, she swiped some papers that could ruin me, and she's holding them over my head so that I can't argue about the settlement. When my daughter came on Friday, she told me her mother was off to Paris for the weekend with her new toy boy. I stole the kid's keys and had copies made. After the panel, I hired a limo and went out to the house. I tore the place apart. The papers weren't there. Either the bitch stashed them someplace else or took them with her."

"Anybody see you there?"

"I sure as hell hope not." He took out his wallet and then removed a card. "But here's the number of the limo service. You can call them and check."

Tom did, and was informed that Foster had an account with the company. He had been picked up at the Edison yesterday at eight-ten p.m. and driven to 543 Pheasant Lane in Old Westbury, where he was dropped off at eight-forty-one. He was picked up again at nine-forty-five and returned to the city. Tom realized he was up against another brick wall, and wished he could throw the phone at it.

"So?" Foster asked.

"It appears to check out."

Foster grinned like a kid who had just convinced his teacher that the dog really had eaten his homework. "Hey," he said, an idea suddenly hitting him. "Maybe you can tail the bitch when she gets back, get something on her for me. I'll make it well worth your while."

"No way. This is my first and last case, and the sooner it's the last, the better."

Foster sighed in disappointment, then he brightened, his gaze shifting to the container in front of Tom. "You going to finish that?"

Tom pushed over the remains of his jambalaya, and Foster dove into it like a scavenger in an undeveloped country where foreign aid never trickled down. "I told you it wasn't me," he said through a mouthful, forgetting his digression. "It can't be one of us. There's no bond like a fraternity bond. You can't get into Beta Alpha Beta Phi without taking our loyalty oath."

"And learning a secret handshake too, no doubt. None of your buddies are men who take oaths seriously. They lie and cheat and break agreements every day to get what they want."

Foster waved a hand dismissively. "Yeah, but that's merely our American way. It's only for business and to get the better of other people who would do the same to us. We'd never do it to one another. And don't forget Arnie. He doesn't do it at all. Not ever. I don't think Arnie could tell a lie if you held a gun to his head."

"Even a saint could tell a lie if he thinks it's protecting a great act of retribution."

"What's that got to do with Arnie?"

"Maybe nothing, maybe a lot. He told me one of the reasons he became a minister is to atone for things that happened over the years at GMU. He seems intent on getting you guys to atone for them too. He mentioned the death of Lou West's son, the Grinwald incident, and rapes of co-eds. He said he wasn't in on the rapes but that he was haunted by a brutal double one he witnessed. Maybe he has given up on trying to get these guys to mend their ways. Maybe he has decided to mete out punishment that fits the crimes."

Foster shook his head. "Arnie's a gentle giant. He's been after our souls for years. Why would he suddenly change and go violent?"

"It's not unusual. People can simmer over past incidents for decades, and then something happens in the present to put them over the top. Maybe the publication of Lou West's book reminded him of the death of the coach's son." Tom thought it safer not to mention the fact that Simon also wanted to put an end to Golden Guys' plans to take over the country after the next election.

Foster considered this a moment, then nodded. "It's possible." Reluctance tinged his words. "Maybe he spotted the obituary of Renee Roberts. She was one of the girls who was raped the night Arnie was there. It was just a small piece in the *Times,* but it caught my eye. She'd gone on to be some kind of expert on education, and had written a couple of books. She committed suicide. The name certainly brought back some unpleasant memories."

"When was this?"

"The obituary?" Foster shrugged. "Quite a while ago. I'm sure it was months before Neal was hit. I'd forgotten about it till this minute. Forgotten about the rape, too, till I saw that obit. I wasn't in the frat house that night. When I got back, the guys were done and were hauling the two girls out. They always dumped them in front of their dorms. Arnie had come in a little before me. He was sitting there, looking totally grossed out. I have no idea who the other girl was. I knew Renee vaguely because she was in my art class. She was a homely, mousy little thing. I assume her friend was the same. I can't figure what they were doing at a Beta Alpha party, which always featured sex, booze and pot, and something stronger when we could get our hands on it. Go figure. Anyway, if that obit was going to push Arnie over the edge, I don't think he would have waited a couple of months to attack Neal. No, Arnie can't possibly be our guy." He pushed the Styrofoam carton back toward Tom. "Sure you don't want some more?"

Tom shook his head.

Relieved, Foster quickly snatched the carton back. "Funny, I keep thinking of Renee as a kid and forget that there were all those years in between. Like the rest of us, she must have been in her forties when she took her life. Wonder if she got better looking when she got older. Probably not. Once a mouse, always a mouse."

He reached into the carton, took the last piece of chicken and popped it into his mouth. He chewed contentedly, licked his fingers, then reluctantly shoved the empty carton away. "No one makes jambalaya like this. Of all Bob Michaelson's acquisitions, Karl's Kajun Kitchens is, if not the most profitable, certainly the tastiest."

"Did Michaelson's group take over Karl's Kajun Kitchens?"

"Sure did—him and Nick. Nothing good escapes their grasp. But if they hadn't been quick to grab it, some other Wall Street wizards would have. Like nature with vacuums, the buyout boys and top lawyers and investment bankers abhor an independent company that's bringing in big bucks. They all want a piece of it. And then the whole thing." He laughed. "Hey, you know, Karl's Kajun Kitchens belonged to a son of a bitch black guy named Aaron Jackson. He used the Karl because it sounded better. Bob told me Jackson put up a hell of a fight to hold on to it, and when he was finally forced to relinquish control, he refused to take his lumps in the proper spirit of American capitalism. He's from New Orleans. Maybe he's using voodoo to get even with Bob and his associates in the takeover. That doesn't sound fair, somehow."

"Who were his associates?"

"What? Have you gone 'round the bend? There's no way voodoo was involved."

"I know it isn't voodoo." He also knew that it couldn't be Jackson, because Jackson was dead. He kept that detail to himself. "Who among your buddies was in on this deal with Michaelson?"

"If you think Jackson is our guy, you can forget it. Bob said he's an old fart, and he was probably left too broke and broken after his fight with the big boys to do anything but creep back to his shack on the bayou, or wherever. Katrina probably washed away his shack with him in it."

"Still, did any of your fraternity brothers get a piece of this Cajun pie?"

"Probably all of them who got hit. There was Tony, for one. Through his real estate connections in New Orleans, he was the first to learn that Kajun Kitchens was a big comer. I'll bet he got himself a fat finder's fee in addition to getting in as an investor. Neal Bernard and his law firm handled all the legal work and strong-arming. Then there was—"

Foster broke off, his eyes widening. "Jesus! Jackson! That's the name of the black kid who's working on the documentary with Nora Malcolm. Maybe she's Jackson's daughter. Maybe she's carrying out a vendetta for him!"

The words hit Tom like a bolt of lightning that lit up the back corners of his mind. In a flash, everything started to fall into place. Denise actually was Jackson's daughter. Nora had told him that. She also said Denise had gone into a deep depression after her father died. Denise had been on the scene when Portman and McGrath were hit, and she had interviewed Hammond the night he was attacked. Could these all be coincidences? But then there were the hits on Bernard and Michaelson a few months before the others. Had she been around then too? He had to check, but he knew it would be dangerous to let Foster know he gave credence to the idea. He waved a hand dismissively. "That's crazy!"

"Why crazy? She was around, working on the documentary, when most of the guys were hit. For all we know, she was there when Neal and Bob got cut too." Excitement glowed in his eyes and spilled over into his voice as he rushed on. "Have you ever really looked at her? She's sexy as hell, but beyond that, she's *big!* Christ, she's built like an Amazon!"

"I hate to put a pin in your balloon, but she's from Chicago and her parents are teachers."

"How do you know?"

"She told me. And so did Nora Malcolm, her boss."

"So she lied to both of you." Foster jumped up from the table. "Why are you still sitting there? Go and do your thing. Find out all about her. I want to know everything. And I want to know tonight."

Tom got to his feet slowly. "I'm sure you've got it all wrong, but I'll check her out."

Foster was trembling in anticipation. "I'm right. You'll see. I can feel it!"

"Feelings are no substitute for facts. Just open the phonebook. There are pages of Jacksons."

"But only one of them was around when the last three guys were hit."

Tom headed toward the door, Foster close on his heels, rushing him, almost pushing him out. He paused on the threshold. "On the off chance that this doesn't turn out to be a wild-goose chase, as I'm sure it is, know this: I'll see to it that she's protected. You and Tony won't get your hands on her. She, or whoever else I find out has been doing this, will be turned over to the police. I've made that clear from the beginning. This is a criminal case. I know people who will be discreet."

"Yeah, sure." The look in Foster's eyes didn't match his words.

"I mean it, Al. You're—"

Foster slammed the door.

ONCE IN HIS car, Tom opened his laptop. He had the addresses and phone numbers of everyone present when Portman and McGrath were hit. Foster's words and actions hadn't fooled him. The doctor was going to try to get to Denise first. Or send one of Tony's goons after her.

He looked up the dates Neal Bernard and Bob Michaelson were hit. Then he dialed Denise's cell phone.

Four rings and then the message came on: "Hi. This is Denise. You know what to do. Talk to you soon. Bye."

"Denise, this is Tom Berenson. It's vitally important that I talk to you as soon as possible. Call me: 718-555-0312."

There was no land line listed for her. Like many young people, she evidently had only the cell phone. Next he drove to her apartment on Hudson Street in the West Village. There was no time to look for a parking space. He pulled up next to a Toyota and dashed up the stoop of the old brownstone that in another neighborhood might be considered a tenement but here in the gentrifying West Village no doubt passed as a desirable vintage habitation.

No one answered his blasts on Denise's downstairs doorbell. *Damn!*

Nora lived only a short distance from here. On his way down the steps he dialed her home number. She was out. *Shit!* In the car he tried her cell.

"Hi," she said, and the warmth of her voice calmed him a little. "I was going to call you, but it's been one hell of a day. Would you believe I've been fired? That's what the meeting with Tony Portman was about. They're pulling the plug on the documentary. He wants all the footage, all the notes. Everything concerned with it must sent to him. Immediately. Denise and I are in my office packing it all up. Frankly, I was sick of the project and I'm glad to be rid of it."

Tom tried to sound casual. "I know this sounds crazy and out of left field, but would you ask Denise where she was on May seventh."

"I don't have to ask her. I know. She was with me in Nantucket. We were putting the finishing touches on the whale documentary." Nora laughed. "Why is this date so important? Albert Foster just called to ask her the same question."

"Get her out of there!"

"Why? What's going on?"

"There's no time for explanations. Just trust me. Denise is in danger. Tell her not to go home. She should go to a friend's place or to a hotel. She's to tell no one where she's going. Not even you. And she's not to answer her cell phone unless the call is from me."

"Tom, this is crazy!"

"It only sounds crazy. The danger is very real. Get her out of there, Nora. You get out too, but leave the door open for me. I'm on my way. If there's a security guy in the lobby, tell him to let me in."

"Tom, I—"

"Don't argue. Get out of there. *Now!*"

CHAPTER 37

TOM HAD KNOWN all along that he would have to work fast to get the perpetrator into police custody and safe from the Golden Guys' vigilante justice. What he hadn't realized until that moment was that Foster, the sycophant who would do anything to ingratiate himself with his condescending brothers, had been chosen to exact their revenge. Like the Mafia, they were keeping everything in the family. It was why they had hired Tom to investigate rather than their favorite PI's at Denning and Pankhurst, where word was bound to leak out. That Foster already knew of Denise's presence in Nantucket on the night Michaelson was hit was bad news. It meant he was on his way to Nora's office to mete out his buddies' idea of justice. Tom was closer to West 23rd Street, though. That was the good news.

Or was it? He had no idea how long ago Foster had made his phone call.

He sped through caution lights and wove in and out of traffic, urgency turning him into the kind of horn-honking maniac he detested. When he spotted a parking space on West 22nd Street off Eighth Avenue, he grabbed it and ran the rest of the way. Not the sprinter he used to be, he paused a second to catch his breath in front of the gray nineteenth-century high rise where Nora had her office.

The door wouldn't open. Of course it wouldn't. It was Sunday, he reminded himself. He looked for and finally spotted a painted-over bell high up on the door frame, just below what looked like an ancient intercom. He pressed the bell, hard. When there was no immediate response, he pressed again. Longer, harder.

An angry voice yelled through the intercom: "Building's closed!"

"It's Tom Berenson." Tom tried to sound ingratiating. "I'm expected. Ms. Malcolm said she would tell you."

"Oh. Yeah. Hang on."

Tom waited, fidgeting, tempted to ring the bell again.

At last the door was opened by a thin, arthritic man well past retirement age, wearing an ill-fitting uniform in need of cleaning and repair. "Hell of a time for visitors," he said, locking the door behind Tom. "Fourth floor." He nodded toward the rickety elevator. "Any more of you coming?" He was obviously annoyed at having his rest disturbed. "I thought there was only going to be one guy. Her brother just went up."

A chill froze Tom's spine. Foster had beat him here after all.

"No. Just the two of us. I'll take the stairs."

He did so. Two at a time.

Off-hours lighting made the narrow, old-fashioned corridor look eerie, but it also intensified the sliver of brightness sliding out beneath Nora's door. Tom hurried toward it. Were Nora and Denise still there, or had they left before Foster's arrival?

He turned the knob slowly. Then, hoping to distract Foster from the women if they were inside, he opened the door and called out, "Hi, Nora!"

Foster was alone. He sat behind Nora's cluttered desk, a Glock semiautomatic aimed at Tom's chest.

Tom raised his eyebrows as though in surprise. "What are you doing here, and what the hell is the gun for?"

"You know the answer to both questions."

"I doubt it. Try me."

"I'm here for the same reason you are."

"To take Nora out for a drink? I'd be happy to make it a threesome, but you'd have to lose the gun." Tom started toward the desk.

"Very funny, and don't come any closer." Foster rose and came round the desk. "Hold your hands up." He felt under Tom's arms and reached into his pockets. "Where's your gun?"

"Never carry the nasty things since I no longer have to."

"No gun? What kind of a detective are you?"

"I'm not a detective anymore. I'm a bookman who was crazy enough to take on a private investigation."

"And a lousy job you've done of it too." Foster backed away and resumed his seat behind Nora's desk. "Sit down in that chair by the wall."

There was a half-filled packing carton on the chair. Tom considered throwing it at Foster, but doubted that his aim with the clumsy missile would be more accurate and faster than Foster's gun. He put the box on the floor.

"It's warm here. Okay to take off my jacket?" That would make it easier to tackle Foster if and when an opportunity came.

"Suit yourself." Foster smiled at his feeble pun.

Tom hung the jacket over the back of the chair and sat down. "Where's Denise?"

Tom shrugged. "Who knows? When I called, Nora said Denise had left. She didn't go home, because I stopped by her place and no one was there. You're barking up the wrong tree on this one. No way could she have done it."

"I checked. She was there when Neal got hit."

"So were thousands of tourists and hundreds of whales. Even you." It was a guess, but a lucky one.

Foster blanched, then quickly covered up. "I wasn't part of that exclusive party."

"Just as you haven't been part of a lot of things all through the years. Let's face it, Al. Just like in families, some fraternity brothers are closer than others. You've always been the one on the fringes, barely tolerated by your buddies until you're needed. Your blood isn't as blue as theirs. To them, you'll always be just the grandson of a fat hog butcher in a bloody apron. You're their gofer, their clean-up guy, their convenient schmuck. It finally got to you, didn't it? That's why you went to Nantucket. That's why you cut Michaelson."

"I didn't cut him. I thought they forgot to invite me. But when I got there, they were already out on the yacht."

"He wasn't hit on the yacht. He was hit on the beach. That was the beginning of your revenge for all those years of being left out."

"No! I went home. But Denise didn't. She was there the entire weekend."

"Out on a whale-watching boat. Do you think she swam to shore to get to Michaelson, then swam back?"

"I don't know how she got there, but she did it. She was there. She was or could have been present at all the attacks."

"So were you."

Foster smiled. "Not last night. You checked that out yourself."

"Come off it, Al. You're talking to a man who knows every angle of guys who think they can get away with anything and everything. You bought that alibi in advance, didn't you? I'll find out soon enough."

"No! She did it! And I'm going to see to it that she pays."

"Still doing your buddies' cleanup jobs, aren't you? All along, they told you that you'd have to silence the castrator, and then, probably, me too after I led you to whoever it was. But this isn't a cleanup job, is it? It's a cover-up job. You want to cover your own ass."

"She's the one! She did it!" Foster's face was red with rage. The gun trembled in his hand.

"Sure, she did. And before that she blew up the World Trade Center. Let's face it, you picked her because Tony and the others are getting impatient. You were looking for someone who'd be easy to deal with. Why didn't you choose one of the other suspects? Why not Vittorio Capperrelli or Lou West? Afraid they'd grab the gun and beat the shit out of you? No, you chose the easiest victim—a woman. With guys like you it's a pattern. Back in grade school, you probably blamed a little girl whenever you got in trouble."

Tom had pushed the right buttons. Suddenly Foster was a kid back in school, and caught out blaming a girl for something he had done. "Take that back!" he cried, just like a kid.

As Foster jumped up and ran around the desk in a rage, Tom jumped up too, prepared to wrestle the gun out of his hand. But at that moment, the door was flung open and Nora walked in.

"What the hell is going on here?" she demanded.

Both men froze, just a few feet apart.

Foster pointed the gun at Nora. "Where's Denise?"

Nora's eyes widened in surprise at the question. "I have no idea. She left here a while ago, on her way to a party somewhere."

"Get her on her cell phone. She'll answer when she sees it's you."

"I can't."

"What do you mean, you can't? Call her. *Now.*" Foster pointed the gun at her chest.

"Put that thing down." Nora sounded like a schoolteacher. "I can't call her because she doesn't have her cell phone with her. Remember when you called her earlier? She was in the middle of carrying a bunch of things to a packing box. After she spoke to you, she put the phone down and finished what she was doing. I found it after she left. I have it in my purse." Nora started to open her handbag.

"Don't open that thing!"

"Do you think I have a gun in here? I was going to show you Denise's phone." Her hand went back to the catch on her shoulder bag.

"Leave it!"

"Okay. But now it's your turn. This is my office. I have a right to know what's going on here. Why do you want Denise?"

Realizing that knowledge of the castrations would mark Nora for death, Tom jumped in before Foster could answer: "Al has become obsessed with Denise. He's afraid he'll lose his chance with her now that the documentary has been canceled. The whole idea has made him go round the bend."

"For that he needs a gun? You've got to be kidding! And what does that have to do with his wanting to know where she was back in May?"

"He's full of shit!" Foster said. "It has everything to do with where she was back in May. She—"

"Nora doesn't have to know!" Tom cut him off.

"Of course I have to know! Tell me!"

"Your assistant has been running around castrating my friends."

Nora's eyes widened, and then she laughed. "That's even more insane than your having the hots for her!" She turned to Tom. "He really has gone round the bend!"

"The hell I have! Denise Jackson has been getting revenge for her father's business failure."

"What do your friends have to do with it?"

"They put him out of business."

"You're crazy!"

"More desperate than crazy," Tom said. "He's the guilty one, and to cover his tracks, he wants to serve Denise up to his friends as the perpetrator. But he has to serve her up dead, so she won't talk."

He didn't add that both of them would have to be killed too, but Nora seemed to understand that. She paled and staggered back against the wall.

"Where is she?" Foster demanded.

"I don't know." Despite her pallor, her voice was firm.

"Of course you know. I've seen the two of you together. You're probably a couple of lesbians. She wouldn't go anywhere without telling you."

As Foster moved menacingly closer to Nora, Tom saw his chance. "Duck!" he shouted at her, and lunged for the gun.

Foster held on, and the two of them fell to the floor.

"Stop!" Nora cried. "You're going to get killed!"

Tom didn't know which one of them she was referring to. Probably both. And she could be right.

Neither of them was a kid, but as they fell to the floor, kicking and punching, Tom was the one who had the advantage. He was the one who was trained for situations like this. Foster, more adept with scalpels and forceps, had to struggle to protect himself with his left hand while he tried to hold onto the gun in his right. That made him a more dangerous opponent, not an easier one.

Over and over they rolled on the floor, knocking over the packing cartons, spilling their contents and rolling through them.

Finally Tom pinned him down, but the gun was wedged between them.

"Get off!" Foster grunted.

If he loosened his hold, Tom knew Foster would try to roll on top of him and they would be at it all over again. "Give me the gun."

"Get off me or I'll shoot."

"Then we'll both be dead. Give me the gun."

Somehow Foster managed to move his leg and to knee Tom in the groin.

Pain was a burning red flash behind Tom's eyes, but he held on. The movement shifted their balance, though, and they rolled to the side. As they did, Foster's right elbow hit the floor.

Tom's whole body shook with the explosion that followed. "Shit!"

Had Tom cried out the word? Or had Foster?

Tom felt the warmth of the blood saturating his shirt. He closed his eyes and waited for the pain. But the pain didn't come.

And then he felt Foster relax beneath him.

Slowly, he rolled Foster over on his back. Blood was spurting from his chest, but he was still breathing. Barely.

"Call 911!" he shouted to Nora.

"I already did."

She rushed over and pushed Tom aside. She tore open Foster's shirt and applied pressure to the wound with one hand. With the fingers of the other she closed his nostrils then leaned over to give him mouth-to-mouth resuscitation.

After a minute or two she stood up and shook her head. "He's gone. Tom, what was this all about? How are you involved?"

He shook his head and turned away from her pleas.

"Tom!"

He turned back and they stared at each other in a silence that was broken by the thunder of footsteps in the hall. "Forget everything you heard here," he said. "I'm an ex-cop. Let me handle this."

"Police!" The door burst open and four cops charged in, guns drawn.

"It's over," Tom told them. "I'm retired Lieutenant Detective Tom Berenson. You can check me out at Police Plaza downtown." He nodded toward the gun, which lay next to Foster's outstretched hand. "We fought over the Glock. Unfortunately, it went off before I could get it away from him."

One of the cops was already on his phone, reporting to the station. Another looked from Foster to Tom. "Who was he? A con you put away who got out and wanted revenge?"

"Nothing that simple. He was a Park Avenue doctor who went

berserk." Tom turned to the policeman who was putting away his phone. "Does Detective Jack Doyle still work out of your precinct?"

"I just spoke with him. He's on his way over."

"We worked together on a couple of cases some years ago," Tom said. "He's a good man. Let's get the basics over with and then wait till he gets here for the rest. No sense going over this ten times."

JACK DOYLE HAD gotten a little grayer and a little heavier around the middle, and his blue eyes were more world-weary from the depths of human savagery and despair they had been forced to examine over the years. It happened to the eyes of all good cops. It had happened to Tom too.

"Tom Berenson!" he said, a hint of an Irish sparkle coming into his eyes. "What the hell are you doing here?"

The story Tom told wasn't a complete lie, though it wasn't the complete truth, either. He was a friend of Nora Malcolm, who was doing a documentary about the men known as the Golden Guys, members of the elite Beta Alpha Beta Phi fraternity. They had graduated from GMU twenty-five years ago and Dr. Foster was one of their number. In accordance with the six-degrees-of-separation theory, Foster was also the doctor who was treating Tom's father-in-law. Foster was going through a messy third divorce, and becoming more and more paranoid about his wife and her lawyer, as sometimes happened. Knowing that Tom was a retired detective, he had even asked him to tail his wife, but Tom had turned him down. Still, once the connection had been made, Foster continued to call Tom and to rant about his personal problems. "Probably because I wasn't one of his circle," Tom said. "He must have thought he could spill his guts to me and it would never get back to anyone he knew."

This evening, Tom had called Nora suggesting they go out for a drink. She was working in her office, said she had to run out on an errand but would leave the door open for him and meet him here so she could finish up a few things before they left. She told the security guard that he was coming. When Tom arrived, the guard told him Nora's brother had gone up ahead of him. Knowing Nora didn't have a brother, Tom rushed upstairs, suspecting something was amiss. He found the office a mess— Tom pointed to the turned-over boxes—and Foster waiting for Nora, gun in hand. Foster had gotten it into his head that the documentary would make him look so rich his wife would sue him for even more of his money. He didn't believe Nora when she told him the project had been canceled that morning, which was the truth. She offered to give him the footage, but suddenly that wasn't enough. Foster got it into his head that Nora would go to his wife and reveal information about his wealth that was included in the documentary and as yet unknown to her lawyer. He thought the only way to stop her would be to kill both her and her assistant.

Tom continued: "And of course he'd have to kill me also. I tried to talk him out of it, but he just got wilder. I saw he was about to pull the trigger on Nora, and I jumped him. He was stronger than I expected, or maybe I'm just weaker than when I was still on the job. Just when I thought I had him, he kneed me, we rolled over and the gun went off. It was between us. At first, I thought I was the one who got shot. But his bullet took him."

Doyle turned to Nora, who corroborated Tom's explanation. He pointed at her bloodied blouse and hands. "How'd you get that?"

"I gave him CPR. Unfortunately, it didn't help."

"The guy was about to kill you, and you gave him first aid?"

Nora looked surprised at the question. "He was a human being. If I had saved him, he wouldn't have been in a position to hurt me anymore."

"No, not until he recuperated."

There were many more questions, and finally Doyle took their addresses and phone numbers and told Tom and Nora that they were free to go now but not to leave town until they heard from him. Before leaving, Tom took Doyle aside and said, "This guy has very powerful friends, on Wall Street and all the way up to the White House. They will all go berserk when the media gets hold of this."

"I've dealt with guys like them before. I can handle it."

"I know you can. All the same, watch your back."

"Point taken." Doyle pressed Tom's arm. "Now go home, wash up, and have a big drink. With Ms. Malcolm, I would suggest."

Nora was waiting at the door. She had taken a raincoat out of her closet and put it on over her soiled clothes. "Sorry I don't have anything that would fit you," she said, fastening her belt as they walked into the hall. "I also don't have a key to the men's room, but you can join me at the basins in the ladies'."

"Why not? After what we've been through, it will be like the feel-good segment at the end of a TV news show full of floods and massacres."

Inside, they scrubbed their hands and faces. Tom took wet paper towels and tried to get rid of some of the blood on his shirt, but the effort was futile.

Nora caught his eye in the mirror over the basins. "You owe me an explanation. A big explanation."

"I also owe you a drink. But I doubt I'd be welcome in even the sleaziest bar looking like this."

"Come back to my place."

"Later. I have to see someone first. Tony Portman."

In the lobby, the security guard was drinking coffee with a cop. "You okay, Ms. Malcolm?"

"I'm fine, Ralph."

"I hear a guy was killed in your office." He looked at Tom, then back at Nora. "Jesus! It was your brother!"

"Not my brother. I didn't know the man. He hated one of my documentaries. He came to get revenge. Lucky for me that my friend was there. He saved my life."

"God, I'm sorry, Ms. Malcolm! You told me you were expecting someone, and he said he was your brother. I—"

Nora put a comforting hand on his arm. "It's okay, Ralph. It's not your fault, and I'm going to make sure management knows that. Good night."

"Good night, and thank you."

"Poor guy," Nora said outside. "His wife has Alzheimer's, and his daughter's an alcoholic single mother. He really needs this job."

Tom took out his phone. "I'm going to call Denise and let her know the danger has passed for a while and she can go home.

I assume you were lying when you told Foster that she forgot her phone."

"Yes, and thank God he wouldn't let me open my purse. What are you going to tell her?"

"The version I told the police. And you stick to that one too."

Nora listened intently while Tom talked to Denise. "What did she say?" she asked afterward.

"Right now she was too relieved to ask many questions. I told her that you're exhausted and she shouldn't contact you tonight. But I'm sure that tomorrow she'll have plenty of questions for you. Let's go. I'll drive you home."

"I'll take a cab. Whatever it is you have to do, do it and get it over with. Then come to my place. I don't care what time it is. We have to talk."

"Yes, we have to talk."

Their eyes held for a moment. Then Nora turned and looked up the street. "Miracle of New York Miracles! Here comes a vacant one!" She gave a shrill, piercing whistle, and the taxi screeched to a halt beside them.

"Take care, Tom," she said. "Tony Portman is a nasty and dangerous guy."

It was the understatement of the year. She couldn't possibly know how nasty and dangerous he really was.

CHAPTER 38

"**I**T'S OVER," Tom told Tony Portman when he answered his phone. "I'll be at your place in a little while. Don't call any of your buddies, especially not Foster. Tell your doorman to expect me and let me in. I'm not exactly looking like an ad in *GQ*."

He clicked off, not giving Portman a chance to answer. Before pulling away from the curb, he checked out a few things on his laptop and then began to type. After copying the file onto a flash drive, he slipped the drive into an envelope and dropped it into the first mailbox he passed.

Entering the lobby of Portman's building, he held his laptop over his chest, a cover-up he dispensed with when he reached the door to Portman's penthouse.

The eyes of the stone-faced Boris widened for merely a second when he saw Tom's shirt, but he said nothing as he led him into the study where Portman was sitting behind an oversized mahogany desk.

"What the hell happened to you?"

"I told you, it's over. Some things have messier endings than others."

"So who is it?"

"First things first. I prefer to talk in the living room, where you won't be seated behind a desk with drawers that are hidden from me. I also prefer to talk in a clean shirt. We're about the same size. Please ask Boris to get one for me."

Portman nodded to Boris, who was still hovering in the doorway, then rose and came around the desk.

"After you," Tom said, and followed him into the living room. "I prefer white," he called after Boris.

"Get me a scotch," Portman told Boris when he came in with the shirt. "You want something?" he asked Tom.

Tom would have loved a drink, but he wanted to keep his head absolutely clear. "No, thanks." He turned his attention to buttoning the shirt and tucking it in. "It's a long drive home to Brooklyn and one likes to look respectable."

Portman took the drink from Boris. "So how long are you going to make me wait before you tell me?"

"Just till Boris makes himself scarce."

A nod from Portman, and Boris left the room.

Tom sat down on the sofa, rolled up his bloodied shirt and put it on his laptop. "The answer was in front of you guys all along: Foster."

Portman looked incredulous. "That spineless shit? You're out of your head. He does what we tell him to do. He's always been grateful to lick our asses."

"That's what you thought. I've seen it happen over and over again: The milquetoast, the patsy who takes everyone's shit and never seems to mind the humiliation. But he does. The resentment builds through the years until finally it boils over and he gets the revenge he's always dreamed of. Usually it's murder. You guys were lucky. Foster had powerful but less lethal tools at hand."

Portman shook his head, still skeptical.

"When you think about it, it's the obvious answer. He was on site for every attack. He—"

"You're wrong. He wasn't in Nantucket."

"That's what he wanted you to think, but he was there all right. He got wind of your get-together and was pissed that he was left out. He flew up, hoping to crash the party, but when he got there, you were all off partying on the yacht. He hung around, his resentment mounting, and then he attacked Bernard on the beach when you guys came back. He was on the next flight out to New York, ready to be surprised and shocked when Bernard came to him for help, as Foster knew he would. He had it all worked out: attack, and then observe the Hippocratic Oath and take care of the victim. Finally, he was to be the go-to guy when

I was brought in to investigate. It was the perfect cover—until tonight."

"That's bullshit." Portman waved a hand in dismissal. "Al doesn't have the guts to attack any of us, and he certainly doesn't have the brains to come up with such a plot."

"You're in deep denial, Tony. You and your friends think that anyone who doesn't come from your world can't possibly be as smart and as conniving as you are. You confuse lack of social status with lack of brains. It's a big mistake, and a very dangerous one, as five of you have found out."

"So it really is Al?"

Tom nodded.

"Then why the hell did it take you so long to figure out?"

"It took me only four weeks. You've known him more than twenty-five years, and you never tumbled to it."

"Jesus! That son of a bitch!" Portman jumped up. "Where is he? I'll kill him. And don't tell me you've hidden him someplace safe. We'll find him. No place is safe from us."

"I think you'll find that his current place is very safe from you. He's dead."

"Dead? You're lying!"

Tom held up his bloody shirt. "Do you think I got this playing Tiddlywinks?"

"*You* killed him?"

"He killed himself. We were struggling for his gun. It went off."

"Where's the body?"

"By now, in the morgue."

"The police have it? They're in on this now? Shit! What do they know?" Portman's face was livid with rage.

"Nothing you don't want them to know. And that's how it will stay, unless something happens to me or anyone close to me."

Portman sank down on his chair. "Tell me everything."

In the car on the way over, Tom had thought the story through. He had to modify it to protect Nora and also to keep himself from looking like a fool for leaving Foster alone after he had accused him of being the castrator. Of course, at that point he had believed Foster's alibi for last night. It wasn't until they were in Nora's office that all the pieces fell into place.

"I spent the entire day chasing down possibilities that all led to dead ends. Then it hit me that it had to be one of you guys. Foster was the one who fit the bill perfectly. I called him and said I had a lead and was coming over. He insisted on meeting at one of his fast-food hangouts."

"Typical," Portman grunted. "That guy should have OD'd on burgers and fries long ago."

"It was actually a smart move. Being in a public place can offer a kind of protection. Of course, when I told him what I'd worked out, he denied everything. He was obviously lying and more scared than a worker who has spent her final check from unemployment insurance. When I shot down his alibis, he got desperate. He threw all the other suspects at me, but I'd checked them out and they didn't hold up. Totally rattled, he came up with Denise Jackson."

"Who the hell is she?"

"Nora Malcolm's assistant."

Portman rolled his eyes.

"My reaction too, but Foster said she had the same last name as a man you guys put out of business and she must be looking for revenge. I pointed out that it was the same last name as Michael and Andrew and a million other Jacksons alive and dead, but he insisted she was the one and he'd prove it. Before I could stop him, he jumped up and ran out of the place, knocking down a chair to trip me as I took off after him. When I got into the street, he was gone. Must have jumped into a cab.

"I knew what he intended to do: kill her, then tell you she was the one and he had taken revenge for all his dear and stricken brothers. No one can question a corpse. I wanted to warn her, but her cell phone was off. I drove to her place, and she wasn't there. Then I called Nora Malcolm and asked her if she knew where Denise was. She told me you'd pulled the plug on the documentary and she and Denise were at her office, sorting through all the material for you. She also told me that Foster had just called and asked the same question. I told her to get Denise out of there and to tell her to go anyplace but home, and that she should leave too, but leave the door open for me. I hoped to get there before Foster and take him by surprise."

"And did you?"

"Unfortunately, no. He was waiting there with a gun when I arrived."

"And the two women?"

"Gone."

"So you jumped him and the gun went off."

Tom shook his head. "No way could I get to him without being killed. He was sitting behind a desk. I kept him talking, pushing all his buttons. Finally, he jumped up and ran around the desk. I was about to pounce when Nora Malcolm walked in and he aimed the gun at her. He wouldn't believe her when she said she didn't know where Denise had gone. It was while he was distracted, arguing with her, that I tackled him. He was stronger than I thought he'd be, and he put up a hell of a fight. Desperate men always do. Unfortunately, the gun went off before I could get it away from him."

"Sounds more fortunate than unfortunate to me. How much does the woman know about why he wanted her assistant? What did he tell her?"

"Nothing. The two of us were rolling around on the floor before he could get to that part."

"And you? What did you tell her?"

"There was no time for chit-chat. She'd called 911 the moment we started fighting, and the cops were already running down the hall when the gun went off."

"And the cops? What did you tell them?"

Tom repeated the version of events he had come up with. "You got real lucky, Tony. The detective on the case is an old friend of mine. He's not going to find any reason to doubt what I told him."

"And Nora? She accepted it too?"

"It seemed to make perfect sense to her. She's in a business where she often has to deal with screwballs. Besides, now that you've fired her from this project, she's eager to put it behind her and move on to her next one. It's over, Tony."

Portman swallowed the last of his drink, and looked down at his crotch. "Not for me it isn't."

"But for me it is." Tom picked up his laptop and shirt and got to his feet. "I mean it, Tony. Don't even think of trying anything. I've been keeping a complete record of this investigation, and it's all under seal with a legal agency that works closely with the district attorney's office. The events of this evening are on their way there right now. If anything happens to me or to anyone I love, one copy goes to the district attorney, another to *The New York Times*, a third to your favorite journalist, Fletcher Bowman. At that moment, you and all your Golden Guy brothers will be covered in shit that's been mixed with the new and improved Super Glue."

Portman jumped up, his face as red as Max's Hungarian borscht before the sour cream was added. "Fuck you!"

"No," Tom said quietly, politely. "Fuck you, Tony, and fuck all your rich, power-hungry friends. Don't disturb Boris, who may be reading a Russian rip-off of *Hustler*. I can see myself out."

He paused in the doorway. "Thanks for the shirt. I'll mail it back in the morning."

"To hell with the goddam shirt. Keep it. It's the only thing from Savile Row that a scumbag like you will ever get to wear." Portman had slumped back in his chair.

"You're right," Tom said. "But I don't want it. I'll donate it to the Salvation Army. It's a lousy fit. I'm a much bigger man."

It felt good to walk out on the expression that passed over Portman's face, the sour look of a man who had never before tasted defeat.

CHAPTER 39

NORA HAD changed into sweat pants and a Johns Hopkins sweatshirt. She looked as lovely and desirable in them as in her clinging silk robe.

"I made coffee," she said. "Or would you rather have something stronger?"

"Coffee's fine."

"Go sit down. I'll bring it in."

In the living room, a CD was on: Yo-Yo Ma playing Saint-Saens' "The Swan." Tom sank down on the sofa and closed his eyes. Beth had always called the cello the tears of the orchestra. She was right.

"Tired?" Nora was standing before him, a mug of coffee in each hand.

He took one from her. "It's been a long day."

"And night." She sat down, leaving the length of the coffee table between them. "So I was right when we met and I said you didn't look like a bookman to me. Who are you, and what are you really?"

"I'm Tom Berenson. And I really am a bookman, the owner of Beth's Book Nook in Brooklyn Heights."

She raised her eyebrows. "Go on."

"But before that, I was a cop, a detective, and a damn good one, I like to think."

"And now you moonlight as a private eye?"

"Not really. This was my first, and last, case. These guys made me an offer I couldn't refuse. Enough money to see Stephie through college, and an unbreakable agreement from Portman to keep his shopping mall out of our neighborhood."

"And in return?"

"I'd find out who was castrating the Golden Guys, the crème de la crème of Beta Alpha Beta Phi and the 1980 graduating class of GMU."

"And when you found him, you were going to kill him."

His gaze held hers. "I know what you're thinking, but you're wrong. I made it clear from the start that when I found the perpetrator, I'd turn him over to the police, where he'd be safe from their style of vigilante vengeance. I didn't kill Al Foster. That gun went off by accident, and it was his finger on the trigger. I didn't want him dead. I wish to God I had been able to get that damn gun away from him before it went off."

"What did you tell Tony Portman when you saw him?"

"I told him what happened and how I reported it to the police. I said also that all you overheard was the story I told the police."

"These guys are dangerous, Tom. Now that it's over, they're going to try to silence you. Permanently."

"That's not a realistic option for them. I've got a full report of my investigation under seal with an attorney. Anything happens to me or my family—even the most innocent-looking accident—and it's sent to the district attorney, the *Times,* and the rest of the media. Especially Fletcher Bowman's tabloids."

"Good." She looked relieved, but still uncomfortable. "Suddenly you've turned into a stranger."

"When you get down to it, we're all strangers, aren't we?"

She turned away and picked up her coffee mug. "Some are more strange than others. Who would have thought that Al Foster was castrating his fraternity brothers?"

"He wasn't."

She looked up, startled. "Do you mean he was right? It was Denise? Did you tell that to Tony?"

"No. I told you what I told Tony."

"Thank God. Thank you for covering for her. Have you talked to Denise?"

Tom shook his head.

"Then don't. I'll talk to her in the morning. I can't believe she'd harm anyone." Her hand was shaking as she put down her mug. "After I tell her what happened tonight, she's bound to come to her senses. We were planning to fly to New Orleans and start a documentary on Katrina, but I can cancel that. There are probably plenty of documentarians down there already. I've been intending to do something on the rain forest. I can have us on a plane and off to the Amazon by the end of the week. I guarantee you that she won't commit any more of these castrations."

Tom's eyes held hers. "I'm sure she won't too. Because she never committed any in the first place, did she?"

First, Nora looked bewildered. Then she paled. "You know." Two words, but her lips trembled as she said them.

Tom nodded.

"How? When?"

"Tonight. It all fell into place as I watched you trying to save Foster. That was no amateur first aid you were administering. Once a doctor, always a doctor. I'd thought that it was your husband who studied medicine, but it was you, wasn't it?"

"Yes, but I never lied to you about it."

"Right. You just let me jump to the wrong conclusions, and didn't bother to correct me." He rose and walked over to one of the bookcases. "You told me that Sid's parents were disappointed that he decided not to be a doctor."

"That's true."

"I'm sure it is, but you let me think that all these medical books were his when, actually, they're yours."

She gave a weak shrug of admittance.

"You also let me believe that you met while you were an undergraduate at Hopkins, but that's not true, either. You met Sid while you were in medical school at Hopkins. You didn't go to undergraduate college there, did you?"

She shook her head.

"I've checked the lists. There's a Norma Kransfield in the GMU class of 1982. Is that you? Or are you Naomi Horowitz, the salutatorian?"

"I'm not that smart. I'm Norma. Always hated that name. I finally dropped the *m* when Sid and I started our business."

"And the Renee Roberts in your class—is she the 'Aunt Ronnie' Leslie told me about? Your best friend from college days, the one who suffered from devastating depressions that finally drove her over the precipice into suicide? The friend whose suicide, Leslie said, put you into a deep depression of your own?"

Tears welled up in Nora's eyes, but she didn't answer. Her silence was answer enough.

"Arnold Simon told me that he turned to religion because he was plagued by the vile deeds in his past. Among them was one he didn't participate in but witnessed, his fraternity brothers' gang rape of two co-eds. He doesn't remember their names or faces, but he says he's still haunted by their screams."

Nora turned away and began fiddling with her coffee mug.

"Al Foster didn't take part in that rape, either. But he remembered the name of one of the girls—Renee Roberts. Said he saw her obituary in the *Times* awhile back."

"Funny that he should remember her name." Nora looked up, a flash of anger replacing the tears that had been in her eyes. "Back when we were at GMU, he didn't give a shit that she existed."

"Or Norma Kransfield, either, evidently. You're the other forgotten girl who was raped that night, aren't you?"

"'Forgotten girls,'" Nora repeated, shaking her head. "How easy it's been for those bastards to forget Ronnie and me, and all the other girls and women whose lives they've wrecked over the years. Well, I've given them something to remember us by."

"Are you going to tell me about it?" Tom asked into the silence that followed. "You owe me that," he added when she showed no sign of continuing.

She gave him a long, sad look, then sighed. "Yes, I suppose I do." She pushed away her coffee mug and stood up. "But I need something stronger than this."

She went into the kitchen and returned a moment later with a bottle of Johnnie Walker Black and two glasses filled with ice. She put down the glasses and held the bottle up to Tom. When he shook his head, she poured a sizeable splash into one of the glasses and sat down.

"Where do I begin?"

"The beginning is always the best place."

She took a long sip of her drink, her eyes filling with memories. "We were roommates. Two hardworking scholarship kids, the type teenagers call nerds these days. We hardly dated. We certainly weren't interested in the rich fraternity boys, especially not the jocks in Beta Alpha Beta Phi. Nor, of course, were any of them interested in the likes of mousy us. And then Ronnie, who was painfully shy, fell for one of them—Albert Foster. He was in her art class, and she was convinced that he wasn't like the others. Of course, he didn't know she was alive. I tried to get her to take the initiative, to go over and talk to him, to do something to make him notice her. But she couldn't bring herself to do it. She was miserable with longing. So I decided to be the mature one. I'd take matters in my own hands and help her out."

She shook her head. "When we're kids, we can be so goddam stupid and sure of ourselves. Why didn't I just mind my own damn business?" She took a swallow of the scotch, nearly draining the glass. "I worked in the library, and one afternoon I found myself checking out some books for Lyle Wayne. I screwed up my courage and told him that a friend and I would love to be invited to one of the Beta Alpha frat parties we'd heard so much about. The son of a bitch told me that there was going to be a party that very night at ten o'clock, and my friend and I must be sure to come.

"It took a bit of coaxing, but I finally convinced Ronnie we should go. I promised to stick to her side and help her strike up a conversation with Albert. I said I wouldn't leave until everything was going really well between them."

"And…?" Tom prompted her. He was tempted to reach out for the scotch to help him through what was coming. But the cop in him made him hold back. He needed a clear head.

"'And—*and!*'" The words broke on anger and pain. Nora jumped to her feet and began to pace. "And so, naïve little shit-heads that we were, we got ourselves all dressed up and went to the frat house." She sighed. "There was no party, of course, but they pretended there was going to be one. Said we were just the first to arrive. Albert wasn't there, either, but they assured us he was coming. They put on loud music, gave us each a drink. God knows what was in those drinks. Within minutes, our ears were ringing, our heads were spinning, and our legs had turned to rubber."

She drew a long, shuddering breath. "Tony Portman picked

Ronnie up and dumped her on the pool table. Neal Bernard and Lyle Wayne tried to pick me up, but they were drunk and couldn't get a handle on how to lift a girl who was six feet tall and fighting them the best she could when she was drugged out of her skull. They all found that hilarious. They decided one girl on the pool table was enough and settled for pinning me down on the floor. Then they all had at us. Over and over. And over again."

Nausea welled up in the back of Tom's throat. "You don't have to go on."

"Yes, I do," she insisted, tears welling up in her eyes. "You have to hear it. You have to know what those bastards did to us. But how can a man, even a good man like you, ever really understand? *Rape. Sodomy.* They're such mild words to cover such unspeakable acts. We screamed, we cried, we struggled, we begged. And they kept laughing and thinking up worse things to do to us. When we threw up, they took our vomit and—" She winced at the memory, then forced herself to go on. "And then there were the cue sticks. You can't have a gang rape on or near a pool table without using the cue sticks, can you? That's when Ronnie passed out. I wish to God I had too." She buried her face in her hands, and her shoulders shook with sobs.

Tom got up and went to her, but she shrank away from him. "No! Don't touch me." She pointed to the sofa. "Go back. Leave me alone. I just need a moment to pull myself together. Pour me another drink."

When Tom brought the glass to her, she held up her hand. It was as though she couldn't bear to take something from a man at that moment. "Put it on the table and sit down."

In another minute she had resumed her seat on the sofa and was taking a long, slow sip of the scotch, her eyes closed. She seemed to be willing herself to be calm. When she put the glass down, her hand was no longer trembling, and the sorrow and horror that had rocketed through her a short time before were replaced by an almost eerie stillness.

"They threw cold water on Ronnie to bring her to. And then they dragged us out and drove us to our dorm, and dumped us at the side entrance. They said that if we ever revealed what happened, they'd deny it, and we'd be in for a hell of a lot worse.

Somehow we managed to creep up to our room without being seen. Ronnie was a basket case, like a rag doll. No, more like a baby, just helpless and weeping. I cleaned her up and got her into bed. Then I took the longest shower of my life, but I knew I could never wash away the filth, the slime, the degradation. Never.

"We woke up in the morning so sick and sore we could barely move. I knew we should go to a doctor, but Ronnie was so traumatized and ashamed that she begged me to forget it. She was sure a doctor would call our parents, and, back then, she was probably right. Still, I was determined not to let the bastards get away with what they'd done. Without telling Ronnie, I went to see Professor Hanlon, the dean of students. I didn't mention Ronnie by name. Just told him that a friend and I had been raped and sodomized by the Beta Alpha Beta Phi's last night. Do you know what this renowned professor of abnormal psychology did?"

"I'm sure I can guess," Tom said. He'd seen and heard it so many times before. Too many times. "He blamed you and your friend."

Anger flared in Nora's eyes. "You bet your ass he did. First, this eminent psychologist tried to convince me that nothing had happened. That I was suffering from some kind of delusional hysteria and had made up the story. That those paragons of chivalry would never have done such a thing. When I insisted that they had and named every last one of the bastards who had taken part in the gang rape, Hanlon got furious. If anything had happened, he said, then my friend and I had asked for and encouraged it. After all, boys will be boys, and it's up to the girl to be realistic and set limits. Before he threw me out of his office, he warned me that if I dared to go to the police, he'd find out who my friend was and we'd both lose our generous scholarships to this prestigious school and be expelled with such bad records that we'd be lucky to be accepted by a community college full of, and I quote, 'mental retards and parolees.'" She took a long swallow of her drink.

Tom prodded her when she didn't continue. "I take it that you didn't go to the police."

"Of course I didn't go to the police! Young as I was, I realized that Hanlon's reaction would be like nothing compared to how the cops would handle us. I couldn't put Ronnie through that.

I couldn't do it to myself, either." She slammed down her glass. "God, Tom! We were just kids. Ronnie had skipped a grade in junior high and was only seventeen. I was just two months past my eighteenth birthday. There was no way we could take on the whole goddam establishment."

She turned her face to Tom, and suddenly she looked as young and vulnerable as she must have all those years ago. He thought of his Stephanie and her Leslie, two bright and eager teenagers who thought they could take on the world. Nora and Renee must have been just like them. Until those bastards struck. Nausea rose up in his throat, but rage pushed it down. He longed to reach out and wipe away the tears that were tracing their way down Nora's cheeks. But he knew that he dare not touch her.

"So what did you do?" he asked.

"What girls and women have been doing since the dawn of so-called civilization. We kept our mouths shut and tried to get on with our lives. But you never forget. The memory is always lurking in the shadows of your mind, ready to pounce and send you reeling." She got up and walked over to the window. "It was much worse for Ronnie. She was so timid and defenseless. I tried so hard to help her, but it was as though those bastards had ripped something out of her soul and left a gaping, bleeding hole inside it that would never heal. I blamed myself for it."

"It wasn't your fault. You were—" Tom tried to comfort her, but she whirled from the window and cut him off, furious.

"Yes, it was my fault! I was the one who got us the goddam invitation. I was the one who convinced her to go. I'll carry that with me till the day I die." She ran her hand through her hair. "When I was a kid, I read somewhere that if you save someone's life, you are responsible for that person. I don't know if that's reasonable. What I do know is that if you ruin someone's life, you are forever responsible for her. That's how I felt about Ronnie, and from that time on, I worked to keep her from going under. After graduation, I went to Hopkins for medical school, and she followed me there to get her Ph.D. in education.

"I wanted us to have normal lives, but I could never get her to date. I was wary of men, too. But then I met Sid. He was different, special, brilliant and funny, warm and loving. Most of all, he was patient and understanding. He gave me so much—the normalcy of a good marriage, the joy of our wonderful daughter, and an exciting life of adventure with our work in China. He deserved so much more than I could give him in return." She sighed and turned back to gaze out the window. "I miss him terribly. We had a good life."

"And Renee? What kind of life did she have? Al Foster told me that the *Times* gave her a short obituary. No one, except maybe a criminal or fabricated celebrity, gets a *Times* obituary of any size at all without having earned some recognition in a worthwhile sphere."

"She earned it, that obit. Her work was her life. She was a recognized expert in the field of early-childhood education. She taught at Hopkins, wrote several books that are used as texts and are often cited by educators and social workers. But that was it. That was her life. Nothing beyond it. At times it seemed almost enough to content her. But then those awful, black depressions would sneak up on her. She tried all kinds of therapies through the years, but nothing really worked. If I was around, I could usually pull her through. But I wasn't always around. I wasn't there for her when the last one hit. When she died, it was even more terrible for me than when Sid died. There was nothing I could have done to stop the blood clot that went speeding through his veins and hit his heart. But if I had been there, I could have pulled Ronnie through. I'd done it before."

Tom stood and walked over to her. He started to reach out to touch her shoulder, but pulled his hand back. "You're not to blame for her death."

"I'm to blame for not preventing it," she said, her back still turned to him.

"No. No one can stop a determined suicide. Your friend wasn't a kid anymore. She was an educated, adult woman. She and she alone was responsible for her death."

Nora whirled around in a fury. "The hell she was! Six fucking bastards who think they own the world and everyone on the planet are responsible for it. They started her long, slow death march more than twenty years ago when they raped her guts out. She didn't kill herself. *They* killed her." The hatred on her face sent a chill up Tom's spine.

"And you set out to make them pay."

"Not then. Back then, I was too angry and depressed to think straight. I longed to get revenge for Ronnie, but I was in the same kind of paralyzing black fog that had finally suffocated her. I couldn't eat, I couldn't work, I couldn't think. It was Leslie who finally pulled me out of it. She told me how frightened she was. She'd lost her father. She'd lost a woman who was as dear to her as a favorite aunt. And now she feared she was losing me too. I realized I had to get a grip on myself for her sake. It wasn't easy. I started looking around for a project that would interest me. I forced myself to reconnect with groups I had joined. And that's when everything began to come together. At a meeting of a sinology society that Sid and I belonged to, I got reacquainted with a brilliant woman who had for years been its president and driving force. After the meeting, the two of us went back to her place to talk. She sensed how troubled I was, and it was good to open up and tell her everything."

Nora turned and walked over to one of the bookcases that lined the walls. "I told you Sid was an expert on China and fluent in Chinese." She ran her hand along a shelf of books, pulled out a volume and stroked it. "That's true. But what is also true is that most of these books are mine. Between us, I was the authority on the dialects, the history, the one Sid depended on for precise, accurate translations."

Tom's head was spinning. He hadn't had a drink, yet he felt as if he had had one too many. "I don't understand," he said. "What has this got to do with what you did to Portman and the others?"

"It has everything to do with it. A year ago, in Hunan Province, a peasant woman died. No one knows Yang Huanyi's age, but she was certainly in her late nineties. She was thought to be the last woman fluent in Nushu, the secret script which poor illiterate Chinese women learned and used for centuries to communicate with each other about their emotions, their fears, their lives—things they never dared say aloud. Those who used Nushu were called 'sworn sisters.' When Huanyi died, it was believed that Nushu died with her. It was known that there were two aging Chinese women who had probably learned it from their grandmothers, but it wasn't really used as a means of communication and secret solace for women anymore. But there are more of us fluent in Nushu than the experts think. I'm one of them, and so is my friend from the society.

"I met Huanyi years ago when Sid and I were working in Hunan Province. She was an extraordinary woman, and a special bond grew between us, strong enough for her to recognize me as a sworn sister. She taught me the script, and we even corresponded occasionally, though not for many years. My friend and Huanyi were much closer. Huanyi didn't want the many secrets shared through the centuries by the sworn sisters to die with her, so she revealed them to my friend with a proviso: It was that the secrets would never be used for academic purposes but could be disclosed only to women in need. My friend recognized me as such a woman."

Tom shook his head. "I still don't understand."

"That's because you're not really listening. The problem with men is that they want everything immediately. They want the end at the beginning. Women start at the beginning and work through to the end. That's the only way to make sense of anything." She slipped the volume back on the shelf. "Listen, and you'll understand. I hope."

"I hope so too. Go on."

She told Tom how Nushu had been created by poor women to help them endure their bleak, oppressed lives—miserable arranged marriages, brutal husbands, tyrannical in-laws, drudgery from dawn till midnight, never-ending pregnancies, death of children from hunger and disease, the humiliation of rape. It offered not only a means of unburdening their hearts but it also passed along remedies that were centuries old. Among them were ways to cure sick children, and herbs and methods that would deal with rapists and abusive husbands.

"The last is what my friend is most interested in. She was the victim of date rape when she was in her twenties. She and her attacker still move in the same elite social circles. He's a governor now, one with presidential aspirations. She arranged for him to be seated beside her at one of the philanthropic dinners she sponsors. It was easy to slip the herbal mixture into his food. It's extremely potent. A smidgen is all it takes to put a bastard out of commission."

"How could she know it worked?"

Nora raised an eyebrow to indicate the foolishness of the question. "Its efficacy has been known for centuries. Still, she invited the man to her home a week later, indicating that after all those decades she was willing to let bygones be bygones, even start over. He was eager and delighted, but there was no way he could rise to the occasion. He never knew what had hit him."

"But that's not what you did to Portman and the others."

"Absolutely not. I used the alternative, more radical method. All the herbs were not always available to some of the sisters, so they had to resort to the alternative. They did it when the man involved was asleep. I did it my way because I needed the satisfaction of its being hands-on, and I wanted those bastards to know something had happened to them. Still, the procedure leaves them only a little sore, and they never really know something has happened till the next time they try to have sex. Even then, they can't be sure of the cause, which is why I always left them the note. I wanted them to *know*."

Tom drew a deep breath. "You're a trained doctor. You obviously have a scalpel. I can't believe that poor, illiterate women in the backwoods of China were performing the same procedure centuries ago."

Nora's eyes flashed. "Don't confuse poverty and illiteracy with stupidity. These women were smart and competent enough to work like oxen in the fields and in their hovels, to manage to keep their huge families fed and to nurse their children through illnesses that half the world has now forgotten ever existed. When desperation drove them, they could do it—and they did."

"How? There were no modern instruments available to them."

"You'd be surprised what can be accomplished with a sharpened chopstick."

Tom shivered at the thought. "It's hard to believe that men in China have been castrated for centuries."

"You make it sound like it happened to millions. If it had, if every man who deserved it had been altered, perhaps China would never have had such a huge population. Nushu was used only by women in the Hunan province, and probably only the tiniest fraction of those who were raped, sodomized and brutalized ever resorted to this remedy. Like their sisters around the world even today, the great majority kept quiet and endured their lives of subjugation and abuse. Justice doesn't exist for them. But here, now, thanks to Huanyi and my friend, some of us can at last get justice."

"You mean there are more 'sworn sisters'? More women doing what you've done?"

"Maybe not exactly what I've done. We don't keep statistics like baseball fans with their strikeouts and home runs. Most, I would think, prefer the herbal method. My friend has dedicated herself to finding us and bringing us together, a small cadre of rape victims whose attackers have gone free and who are angry enough and strong enough to avenge the crime, and to retaliate for victims who are incapable of exacting their own revenge. And we don't call ourselves 'sworn sisters.' My friend considers that term sacred, belonging only to the original communicators in Nushu, and I agree with her. We call ourselves Hecate's Sisters."

"Hecate, the three-faced goddess of the crossroads, the night, witchcraft and all things evil."

"Not all things evil. You forget that she helped Demeter find Persephone in the depths of hell and then rescue her from the ravages of Hades for three-quarters of the year. Like Hecate, we know we can't succeed completely in our mission, but we're working on it."

It was all too much. Tom was beginning to wonder if Nora was unhinged, if she was making this up about a small cadre of female vigilantes. And then he remembered what Foster had told him earlier that evening about the surge of unexplained cases of impotence he had been reading about in his urology journals.

"This cadre," he said. "How big is it?"

She took a breath and thought a moment. "A hundred, maybe. I don't know the exact number, nor is it wise for me to know it. But my friend is able to keep in close contact with them all."

"She gives them their assignments?"

"Yes. No one can act on her own. Everything must be report-ed and investigated. We don't want anyone hit who doesn't richly deserve being sent into his own personal hell."

"How many have *you* done?"

"Just the ones you know about. Actually, I thought at first that I might have to start and stop with Neal Bernard. He and some of the others were in Nantucket when I went back to put the final touches on the whale documentary. Unfortunately, he was the only one who went for solitary walks along the beach. I wasn't sure that I'd ever get to the others, but then the Golden Guys documentary came my way. It was as if fate, or maybe Hecate, had handed it to me. You know the rest."

"And who's next on your list?"

"No one. I'm done. I made it clear to my friend from the outset that this was strictly personal. That I would handle only the men who had brutalized Ronnie and me. There are plenty of sisters to take care of the other bastards out there." She shook her head. "You look so appalled. But what would you do if you discovered Stephanie had been gang raped by a bunch of rich fraternity boys, and you knew who they were?"

"I'd want to cut off their balls and kill them."

"You'd want to, but you wouldn't, would you? You're a po-liceman, and you'd go by the book and want the law to do its thing. And what would happen? It would be your daughter who would be put on trial, by the world-class lawyers that their families would hire. The guys would probably go free, or at best be put on probation."

"You're thinking of how it was years ago. It's different today." Even as he said it, the words sounded hollow to him.

She raised an eyebrow. "I think you've been away from the police force too long. Studies show that campus rape is on the rise. One out of five coeds are attacked, and the guys who do it are almost never expelled. Their apologists shrug off the crime. They say the boys are young, and their judgment was impaired by liquor. It's chalked up to youthful indiscretion. The boys will know better when they're older, and the hell with their victims. Well, I can tell you that once a rapist, always a rapist. There is no way that a boy who has raped a girl is ever going to take no for an answer from a woman when he's a man. We can't find them all, but the sisters are seeing to it that at least some of these sons of bitches won't keep on raping. And, damn it, we're relishing every minute of it."

He flinched at the hatred in her eyes.

Suddenly, her faced softened, and she reached out and touched his arm. "I'm sorry," she said, and she looked like the Nora he had known from the beginning of their relationship. "Not for what I've done," she added. "I'll never regret that. What I regret is what it's done to you, to us. I told you at the start that you shouldn't get involved with a woman like me. You should have listened. I tried to stop it, remember? But you kept coming back, and what we had was so good, so sweet...."

Tom felt as though his heart was in a vise, and he was acutely aware of every slow, painful beat. "But not good enough or sweet enough to end your mission."

"That had to come first. Oh, Tom! Why didn't you listen to me?"

"For the same reason that you kept letting me come back."

"What we had was beautiful, but it was only make-believe. You fell in love with a woman who no longer existed."

"But she existed once."

"That was long before you came into my life. I can't go back. We can't go back. No one can ever go back." She sighed. "And now it's time for the next step. I have done my thing, the thing I had sworn to do. Are you now going to do your thing and turn me over to the police?"

"Why? Portman and his friends have never reported any crime. They'd never admit to what happened."

"But they hired you to find out who did it. Will you do me a favor? Will you wait till Denise and I are off in the rain forest before you tell them?"

"Portman already knows who the castrator was. You were there when the police took his body away."

She gazed at him in silence. Then, so quietly he almost didn't hear it, she said, "Thank you." She looked away, then turned her eyes back on him. "I guess that's it, then. I guess this is good-bye."

"I guess it is." It hurt to get the words past the ache in his throat.

Slowly they walked down the hall, then paused at the door.

"When I was working on the documentary, I discovered something no one was supposed to know. These men were planning to rig the next election and take over the country. Did you know that?"

"I found it out along the way too."

"Well, what I've done has put a stop to that."

"Or only slowed it down. These guys own the banks and Wall Street. With their hedge funds, buyouts, mortgage and credit manipulations, they're on their way to owning the whole country anyway, if they don't own one hundred percent of it already. They can make or break the world's economy. Even if they destroy it, they've got it set so they'll come out on top. Being impotent isn't going to stop them."

"But it's bound to keep them from enjoying it fully."

"Absolutely," Tom agreed. "Henry Kissinger assures us that power is a great aphrodisiac. But what good is that great aphrodisiac if...."

She was unable to resist a smile. "You have a point there."

"Tell me, those guys are big. Former football players, still in pretty good shape. How did you manage it? They always said their attacker was huge."

"That was just their pride talking. But you forget that I'm as tall as most of them, taller than a few. Besides, I'm in better shape—a black belt in both karate and judo. And no one should ever underestimate the element of surprise, or the determination of a woman on a mission."

"And there really are many more like you out there?"

"Many more." She frowned. "Are you planning to report us?"

"Do you really think anyone would believe me?"

"Certain tabloids and cable channels...."

"I doubt even them. Though maybe that could be a good thing. It might spread the word among the creeps of the world that they should mind their manners and keep their pants zipped."

As Tom smiled at this unlikely prospect, she reached out and touched his cheek. "I'm going to miss that smile," she said, her voice husky.

He put his hand over hers, but she quickly pulled it away and reached to open the door.

"Good-bye, Tom. You deserve so much better. Someday, you'll find it."

"I'm not sure I want to." Each word was like a knife in his heart. "It hurts too much."

He saw the sparkle of tears in her eyes as she closed the door behind him.

CHAPTER 40

TOM DROVE BACK to Brooklyn on automatic pilot, his thoughts choked off by a dense cloud of depression. The sense of loss and disappointment was so sharp he could almost taste it. The pain was not as exquisite as when Beth died, but it came close. Very close.

Somehow he navigated the tunnel, the streets, the traffic lights, found a parking space, and walked the few blocks home.

The first thing that hit him when he entered his apartment was the savory aroma of chicken soup mixed with the fragrance of fresh-baked challah. Max had been busy all day, preparing for the holiday. Tom closed his eyes and inhaled, letting the pungent scent seep through him, bringing with it sweet memories of Rosh Hashanahs past—his mother's kitchen, Beth's kitchen.... The smell was like a cathartic, slipping past his nostrils and into his veins, cleansing him of the degradation he had felt, working for vicious manipulators like Tony Portman and his friends, being exposed to their depraved world of arrogance, greed and excess. But there was no relief from the pain of losing Nora, the Nora his imagination had created out of a sweet, desperate longing.

Max had left the light on in the kitchen for him in case he came home hungry. On the counter, two round challahs rested on cooling racks, gleaming in their golden glory. Round, to symbolize the cycle of the new year and the circle of life. As Tom reached out and touched one, his eyes misted, brightening its glaze.

He switched off the light and started toward his room, pausing in front of Stephanie's closed door. He knew she would be asleep, but still he made the polite gesture of knocking gently. Then he turned the knob and tiptoed in. Gertrude was curled at the foot of the bed. She opened one eye, stood up and stretched, circled a few times, then settled down again.

Stephanie slept on her side, her dark hair tumbling across her pillow, one arm stretched out above her head, as though reaching for a beautiful dream. Tom smiled and smoothed her hair. She looked so grown up—and yet still so much like a little girl. His little girl. He wanted so much to be by her side always, to protect her from the ugliness, the harshness that lurked along life's twists and turns. But the choice wasn't his. Like every child before and after her, she had to make her own way along life's circuitous path.

As he bent down and kissed her cheek, Stephanie opened her eyes. "Hi, Dad." Her voice was husky from sleep. "What time is it?"

"Late. Go back to sleep."

But she propped herself up on her elbow. "Have a good day?"

He turned out his hand. "So-so."

"Sorry. It was kind of crazy here. Grandpa's gone all out for *Erev* Rosh Hashanah. I think he really wants to impress Mrs. Alexander."

"Well, you know what that kosher deli ad used to say about the way to a woman's heart...."

"'Take her out for pastrami sandwich.'" Stephanie laughed. "Maybe it will work for Nora too. Grandpa said you were going to invite her. Is she coming?"

Tom shook his head.

"Bummer. We were hoping we'd meet her." She was looking at him expectantly, as though he would come up with another day, another occasion.

"Well, not tomorrow," he said. He didn't add, *Not ever.* He smoothed her hair. "Go back to sleep. Before you know it, it will be morning and time for school."

She sent him an air kiss and stretched out. "'Night. See you in the morning."

"See you in the morning." The words wrapped him in a familiar, comforting warmth as he closed the door behind him.

That warmth had dissipated a few minutes later when he lay down in his own bed. A bed that felt big and lonely once more. He sighed and pulled up the blankets. The cold, painful lump had returned to the back of his throat and was working its way up to press behind his eyes.

Suddenly, the bed shook. There was a pause, and then he felt a pressure slowly moving up his legs, up past his knees, past his thighs, up to his belly and chest, where it stopped. He opened his eyes and found two green eyes gazing down at him. For the first time since Beth's death, Gertrude had returned to their bed.

"Cats know how we feel before we do," Beth used to say. "They know when we need them."

Tom reached out and scratched Gertrude behind her ear. "Welcome back, old girl," he whispered. He knew it was probably just for the night. But somehow he sensed that it was just for the night that he needed her nearby, with all the memories she brought with her. Tomorrow he would be stronger. Tomorrow he could cope.

Gertrude turned her head and ran her pink, rough tongue along his hand in a rare and gentle cat kiss. Then she curled herself into a ball on his chest and settled down to sleep. He ran his hand over the warm circle of her body, and it reminded him of the plump spheres of Max's challahs. The cycle of the year. The circle of life.

Tomorrow at sundown, the ancient cycle of a new year would begin. Together, he and Stephanie and Max—his family (and with Mrs. Alexander, who might eventually be joining it)—would usher in 5765, lighting and blessing the candles, the bread, the wine. They would eat Max's delicious meal, then go to the synagogue, where, surrounded by friends, they would thank God for bringing them to this season and pray that the new year would be a good year, a peaceful year for all of them and for all humanity.

And so the Days of Awe would begin, the ten days between Rosh Hashanah and that holiest of days, Yom Kippur. Ten days of reflection and repentance, for on Yom Kippur God can be asked to forgive only his people's sins against Him. For all worldly sins, forgiveness must be sought from those who have been wronged—and given freely to those who have wronged us.

Tom sighed. He had much to reflect on. Did he have much to repent? He wasn't sure, but as a vision of Nora flitted across his closed eyes he knew he had much to regret. Could he forgive her? Not for what she had done to others. That wasn't his business, nor was it in his power to do. It was between her and them. But could he forgive her for what she had done to him? Yet, what had she done to him? She had reawakened him to love and life. Could he forgive her for destroying it all?

Could she forgive *him*? For he had reawakened her too. Then he had walked out of her life, perhaps when she needed him most. As they stood there at her door, though, he had seen in her eyes that she would never hold it against him. Surely he could forgive her also. He loved her too much not to.

And so he would begin the new year with forgiveness in his heart. It was the forgetting that would be impossible.

On his chest, Gertrude began kneading the blanket and purring. He ran his hand over her soft, silky fur. She looked up at him as though she wanted to remind him of something, add something. And then he heard it—an echo of Beth's voice from deep in his heart. "Time makes all things possible," he heard her whisper, and a sudden, sweet peace slipped over him. He smiled. It took time to complete the cycle of a year. Time that brought with it healing and renewal and hope. Time that made all things possible, even the rekindling of a love that had once been so right that surely, someday, it would be right again....

If you enjoyed this book—and I hope that you did—please consider posting a review at Amazon.com and www.goodreads.com. Thank you.

Barbara Brett

BOOK CLUB DISCUSSION QUESTIONS

1. *Secret Agenda* centers around multimillionaire Wall Streeters who brought our economy to its knees and have emerged from the debacle richer and more powerful than ever. Someone is making them pay for it in a way that is more devastating to men than murder. Do you think the punishment fits the crime?

2. All of the victims attended the prestigious Gouverneur Morris University and are members of the elite Beta Alpha Beta Phi, one of the oldest fraternities in the United States. Known as the Golden Guys back then, they brought the university and the fraternity to the height of fame with their prowess on the football field. How do you feel about fraternities and their influence on college students and society?

3. Back when they were still undergraduates, the Golden Guys vowed that within twenty-five years of their graduation they would take over the nation just as they always took over the football field. That time has now arrived. Given the positions they have achieved, do you think they should be able to realize their goal?

4. Among the Golden Guys we meet are Tony Portman, the real estate mogul; Bob Michaelson, known as the Hedge Fund Honcho; Albert Foster, the Park Avenue urologist; Neal Bernard, the high-powered Wall Street litigator; Nicholas Hammond III, known as the Take-Over King; Doug

McGrath, the popular movie star; scientist Jason Gilbert, winner of the Nobel Prize; and United States Senator Lyle Wayne. Do any of them remind you of people you know or people you have read about in the news?

5. Another Golden Guy, who could also be in the castrator's sights, is the Reverend Arnold Simon. Years ago, he gave up his wealth and life of privilege to work with society's outcasts—and he has vowed to force his fraternity brothers to repent their misdeeds and change their ways. What did you think of him and of his work with those in need?

6. Tom Berenson, the retired police lieutenant who now owns a bookstore in Brooklyn, is the man the Golden Guys seek out to find their attacker. At first he is reluctant to get involved with these men, but when they make him an offer that will save his business and put his daughter, Stephanie, through college, he relents. Do you think he was right to take on the case?

7. Tom's wife, Beth, died two years ago, but we learn a great deal about her and their relationship through Tom's memories. How would you describe Beth? What do you think of her and of the marriage she and Tom had?

8. So that he can meet the victims and potential victims at one time and in one place, Tom is invited to the Golden Guys' twenty-fifth anniversary celebration at Gouverneur Morris University. What did you think of the lavish event? Were you surprised by some of the interactions that took place between some of the fraternity brothers?

9. At the anniversary celebration, Tom meets Nora Malcolm, the TV producer who is filming a documentary about the Golden Guys. He is told that she should be able to help him with background material on the men. What do you think of Nora and of her assistant, Denise Jackson, and of their attitude toward the men they are filming?

10. As Tom and Nora work together, they realize that they have a great deal in common. Both, however, are struggling to get over lost love. Were you pleased to see the warmth they felt for each other blossom into an affair? Did you hope that what they felt for each other could help them get past their loss and build a future together?

11. Among the many suspects Tom is investigating is Vittorio Capperrelli, the macho wrestler and sports entrepreneur, whose sexy actress wife appears to have slept with all the victims. What do you think of Vittorio and of the private meeting he demands with Tom?

12. Tom's father-in-law, Max, who stayed on after Beth's death, plays a big role in Tom's life. Did you like Max? Why? What did you think of the advice he gave Tom about his relationship with Nora?

13. At the home of Golden Guy Albert Foster, Tom meets Madison, Foster's daughter. Madison is the same age as Tom's daughter, Stephanie. Compare the two girls. What do you think of them?

14. Were you surprised when Tom discovers who the castrator is? What did you think of the motive?

15. Throughout his investigation, Tom has known that he and his family are in danger, that the Golden Guys will not want them around after the culprit is caught. Do you think that the steps he has taken to protect himself and his family will work?

SIZZLE

Barbara Brett

Prologue

Spring 1988

WHEN MARIETTA WYLFORD was making love with a man she didn't care for, which was more often than not these days, she found it helpful to close her eyes and focus her mind on the first and last ride she had taken on the Coney Island Cyclone at the age of fifteen. A rather pimply boy named Tommy Something had talked her into it, and when their lead car reached the crest of the first incline, he grabbed her in his scrawny arms and clamped his wet lips on hers. The forces of gravity and wind velocity kept them glued together for the rest of the ride. Unable to disentangle herself, Marietta (she was just plain Marianne back then) clung to him, moaning and shrieking into his mouth as their car hurtled from peaks into valleys and catapulted from valleys onto peaks. Afterward, Tommy swaggered along by her side, convinced that he had given her the sex thrill of her life. She saw no reason to disillusion him by revealing that he disgusted her and that her reaction had been sheer animal panic evoked by speeding through space at such a terrifying rate, especially not after he bought her a huge stuffed panda. In the twenty-three years that had slipped through her fingers since that hot, sticky July night, she had made excellent and lucrative use of that memory.

Now, just when her mind had taken her halfway up the sharpest incline of her imaginary roller coaster, a dense weight plummeted down on her chest, making the air whoosh out of her lungs and into her companion's mouth. She managed to free her lips from his and to whisper as passionately as she could with the little breath she had left, "Don't stop now, darling."

His head dropped onto her pillow.

She lay there for a moment, staring up at the rainbow prisms the crystal chandelier cast on her ceiling in the soft pink glow of the nightlight. Never had she felt such an oppressive weight. It crushed her breasts until they threatened to become concave. But the pain and the pressure were as nothing compared to the icy fear that had begun to pulsate from the dark recesses of her mind and radiate all through her body.

Her tongue darted out and moistened her dry lips. "Darling . . ." she whispered. "Darling...are you all right?"

There was no answer from the slack lips pressed against her cheek.

She closed her eyes and slowly turned her head. It took every ounce of courage she had to open them. When she did, she found herself staring into a pair of glasslike blue eyes that she knew could not see her, would never see again.

"Oh, my God!" she cried. With a strength born of necessity, she thrust off the body and groped for a pulse in his wrist and throat. When chest massage and mouth-to-mouth resuscitation both failed, she succumbed to the horror of the situation, and ran into the bathroom, vomited, and sank down on the floor.

She lay there, curled in womb position on the powder-pink carpet, her head pressed against the hard, cold porcelain of the bowl, telling herself that it wasn't true, that it couldn't be true. But finally she had to admit that it was. That was when the trembling began.

"Do something," she told herself through chattering teeth. "You can't just lie here—you have to do something."

She pulled herself to her feet and walked over to the white-and-gold French provincial telephone on the Lucite table beside the pink marble bathtub. She dialed a number and, while it rang, took a cigarette from a pink Wedgwood box and lit it with a matching lighter.

Be home, she repeated silently with each ring. *Please, please be home.*

On the fifth ring a rather breathless female voice came over the wire.

"Melanie," Marietta said, "Philip Bailey just died while we were in bed. What do I do?"

"Oh, my God! Are you sure he's dead?"

"Of course I'm sure."

"Have you called for an ambulance?"

"Are you out of your mind? I can't have him found naked in my bed."

"Well, you can't just have your maid put him out with the garbage in the morning. You have to call for an ambulance immediately. Any delay would sound fishy to the police."

"But he's in my bed, and he's naked."

"Since when have you been such a puritan?"

"I'm not a puritan. I'm a businesswoman, and I refuse to jeopardize the deal we were working on. God knows, I'm sorry for Philip, but that doesn't change the fact that the stock he was about to sell me will go to his wife now, and she'll never let me have it if she knows how he died."

"Get him dressed. Tell the police and the medics that he was taking a nap."

Her hands began to tremble. "Melanie, I can't touch him."

"You have to. What are you wearing?"

She glanced into a mirror. "One false eyelash and some hair spray."

"First call nine-one-one. Then get yourself dressed as though you were going out to dinner. I'll be over in five minutes. Pray that the cops are slow getting there."

An officer answered the 911 phone on the fifth ring, and sounded so efficient as he took down her information that Marietta was tempted to tell him not to rush the ambulance over, that she had things to do before it arrived.

She hung up the phone and ran into her bedroom to dress. Though she knew it was there, it somehow came as a shock to find Philip Bailey's body still sprawled across her bed. It lay as it had fallen when she had struggled out from beneath it, legs on the side at an angle that would have been awkward even for a contortionist, upper torso flat on its back, arms flung wide in a grotesque welcoming gesture. The eyes were the worst—those staring, unseeing eyes. She knew she should close them, but she couldn't bring herself to do it. Instead, she reached for the silk sheet that had tumbled to the floor and pulled it over his face.

The blue of the sheet reminded her of cloudless spring skies and of heaven. She wondered fleetingly if there was a heaven. Philip Bailey would know by now. But only from hearsay. She doubted very much that he would be an inhabitant.

Not since her days of whirlwind changes during fashion shows had she dressed so quickly. In less than three minutes, her navy Yves Saint Laurent suit looked as though it had never been taken off. Unable to locate her missing false eyelash, she pulled off the remaining one, reglossed her lips, and combed her shoulder-length red hair.

She was picking up Philip's clothing when the doorman rang her on the intercom.

"Yes, William?" she said, praying he wouldn't announce the arrival of the ambulance.

"Miss Danielle is here to see you, Mrs. Wylford."

"Thank you, William. I'm also expecting an ambulance. A friend visiting me has taken deathly ill. It should be here at any moment."

"I'll send the medics right up, ma'am." William's tone held the proper mixture of servility and humanitarian concern.

Marietta had the door open before Melanie could ring the bell. Closing it, she said, "The ambulance hasn't arrived. So far, so good."

"I'll bet you haven't dressed him yet," Melanie said, her brown eyes scanning Marietta's face. She was ten years younger and four inches shorter than Marietta, but her lack of makeup, angular body, and severe attire occasionally made people take her for the older of the two.

Marietta shook her head. "Melanie, I—"

But Melanie didn't wait for her to finish the thought. "Come on," she said, brushing past her and heading for the bedroom. "The *Post* printed another one of its bitchy editorials about the delay in response to emergency calls. The cops will be trying to break the sound barrier for the next few days."

By the time Marietta caught up with her in the bedroom, Melanie had pulled down the sheet.

"Couldn't you at least have closed his eyes?" she asked. Gently, she reached over and performed this final service. "Rest in peace," she whispered, her face suddenly filled with tenderness. Then she turned back to Marietta, all business again. "You'll have to help me. I can't do this by myself."

Marietta nodded. "I'll be all right now. I just couldn't touch him while I was alone."

Melanie picked up Philip's black silk socks from the floor and handed one to Marietta. "I've never known you to be squeamish. In your office, you make life-and-death decisions about corporations and careers every day."

"This is different. I don't like being out of control. It scares me."

The socks were the easiest to put on. The rest of the clothes posed a real problem: Philip Bailey was well over six feet tall and weighed two hundred and forty pounds, more than both women put together. For a moment the two stared at his hulking frame, feeling at a loss. Then Melanie picked up his undershorts from the floor. "Come on. If the Druids could build Stonehenge without modern technology, we can dress a corpse."

"They had more than just seconds to do it in," Marietta reminded her, but she reached for Philip's trousers.

Working together, they slipped the shorts and trousers up past Philip's knees. Then Melanie knelt on the bed, slipped her shoulders under his thighs, and hoisted him up like a wheelbarrow while Marietta pulled the two garments over his buttocks and belly.

"Thank God he considered himself too macho for an undershirt," Marietta said as Melanie eased herself out from under his legs.

By rolling him first on one side and then on the other, they managed to slip his shirt on without ripping it. They decided to dispense with his tie and jacket, on the theory that he would have shed them if he had gone into the bedroom to lie down because he wasn't feeling well. Just as they finished buttoning his shirt and shoving it into his pants, the intercom buzzed.

"The ambulance guys are on their way up, ma'am," William announced.

"Did he have anything to eat here?" Melanie asked.

"A few martinis, some Stilton cheese, some caviar."

"Good. Tell them that. Say he came here to take you to dinner. You had some cocktails first, and then he said he wasn't feeling well. You suggested that he lie down for a while. A little later, when you went in to see how he was feeling, you found him dead and called for an ambulance."

Marietta nodded and ran a hand through her hair. "Do I look all right?"

"You always look all right." Suddenly, Melanie's face paled. "Damn! We forgot to zip his fly." She ran to the bedroom and returned just as Marietta was opening the door.

The policemen were solicitous, the ambulance attendants swift and efficient. Within ten minutes the necessary information had been taken down and they left with the mortal remains of Philip J. Bailey, American publishing genius. The policemen followed the covered stretcher, one of them with Philip's jacket and shoes tucked under his arm.

Marietta closed the door after them and leaned against it. "How was I?" she asked.

"As always, you were magnificent. You had the perfect blend of reserve and concern one would expect from a person who had a strictly business relationship with the deceased."

"Well, it was strictly business. All I was doing in that bed was negotiating a special stock option and offering him a sweetener he'd never get from Harrison Kendricks."

Melanie gave her a level look. "He wasn't interested in any kind of deal with Kendricks. We both know you're the one he wanted to sell *Sizzle* to."

"All right. So I'd had a couple of drinks and I was high on them and on the news he'd just told me. He said he'd gotten some information on Kendricks that was guaranteed to force him to back off. It all combined to make me feel horny." She sighed. "He may have been a genius in the magazine world, but the guy was nothing special in bed."

"Considering what happened, maybe he wasn't feeling up to par."

Marietta dismissed the subject with a wave of her hand and walked into the living room. There, surrounded by the antique furniture she had collected over the years—the ivory-brocade-covered

Louis XVI gilt-wood sofa, the Louis XV beechwood bergères, the tulipwood writing tables and ormolu-mounted worktables, the eighteenth-century paintings and decorations, and the Waterford crystal chandelier—she began to relax. "God, I could use a drink," she said, collapsing on the sofa. "Is there anything left in the pitcher?"

Melanie walked across the room to the bar that had been handcrafted to resemble an elongated Louis XV commode. She inspected the monogrammed Steuben martini pitcher. "It's empty."

"Make us a few, will you?"

"What did you do with the gin and vermouth," Melanie asked, looking around, "polish them off?"

"They should be there." Marietta straightened up and peered over at the bar. "No, wait—Philip made the drinks in the kitchen. He must have left them there."

As Melanie passed the cocktail table, Marietta gestured toward the martini glasses that stood next to a sterling silver tray set out with dishes of crackers and caviar and cheese. "Get rid of this on your way, please. It depresses me."

Melanie cleared the table and disappeared into the kitchen. A few seconds later she was back with the Gilbey's and vermouth.

Marietta had slipped off her shoes and stretched her long legs out on the sofa. She didn't speak until after she had taken two big swallows of her drink. "What's going to happen now?"

Melanie placed the well-filled martini pitcher on the cocktail table within easy reach and curled up on the other end of the sofa. "His family will be notified. There'll be an autopsy to determine cause of death. The fact that he was dressed won't fool the medical examiner, Mari. He'll know that Philip wasn't merely counting sheep when he died."

"Damn. Maybe we should have washed him."

"There wasn't time, and it wouldn't have helped. Don't worry. I'll make a few well-placed phone calls. The news shouldn't leak out. Do you know his wife?"

"We've never met."

"You'll have to pay your respects to her before the funeral and attend the service. Otherwise, she'll jump to conclusions, and so will the public."

"They'll jump to them anyway."

"Not if you make it hard for them. No one can carry it off better than you. When you do visit his wife, though, no matter how itchy you are to get your hands on her shares, you're not to talk business."

"I'll leave that to an emissary," Marietta said, giving her a meaningful look. "We're not going to be able to drag our feet on this, you know. Kendricks's bankers announced his intention to make a hostile raid Monday. This is Wednesday. That leaves us only seventeen business days before the SEC will allow him to start buying up shares."

"I thought you said Bailey had something on Kendricks that was bound to make him back off."

"Yes, but he hadn't told Kendricks—or me, either, damn it. When I asked him what he'd found out, he said that the fewer people who were in on the secret, the stronger his position would be. The only hint he would give me was saying something like, 'Dallas would prove to be Kendricks's Achilles heel.' And then he died before I could get any more out of him."

"So that's why you let him get you in bed."

Instead of responding, Marietta finished her drink and poured herself another. "Philip probably found out some dirt about the newspaper Kendricks bought down there, or about some of his real estate."

"I can't imagine anyone finding anything Kendricks would want suppressed. He's never made a secret of the fact that he's a bastard. He revels in his reputation. The whole world knows he was a mercenary in Africa twenty-five years ago and has used the same killer tactics he learned there to build his publishing empire. He started it off by inheriting his family's newspaper from his brother under pretty suspicious circumstances, but he never tried to hide that fact either."

Marietta brightened. "Maybe that's it. Maybe Philip discovered proof that Kendricks killed his brother."

"As far as I know, his brother never set foot in this country. He died in England. I think Philip was snowing you because he knew it was the only way you'd let him into your bed."

Marietta shook her head. "He knew something, I'm sure of

it. He was too confident, too exultant to have been putting on an act."

"Then if it was something he could find out, I'm sure you can learn what it was too. He must have proof of it somewhere. He wouldn't be relying on hearsay."

"Yes, but where's the proof?"

Melanie shrugged. "In a safe or a safe-deposit box, maybe. Maybe in his desk at the office."

"I doubt that he'd let it out of his sight." Marietta jumped up, almost knocking over the pitcher. "His attaché case! I forgot to give it to the policemen. It's still in the hall closet." She ran from the room and returned a moment later with a brown leather case bearing the gold monogram *P.J.B.*

"As your lawyer, Mari, I have to tell you that you can't open that. It should be delivered to his heirs intact. I'll take it with me when I leave."

"For God's sake, Melanie—"

"Of course," Melanie cut her off, standing up and stretching, "I have no idea what you might or might not do while I'm in the john."

The moment Melanie was out of the room, Marietta opened the case. Its contents were disappointing: an advance issue of *Sizzle* with Diane von Furstenberg on the cover, the late-city edition of that morning's *Times*, a Xerox copy of an edited manuscript, an advertising contract with Tiffany's, a bottle of Maalox No. 2 tablets, a pair of soiled socks. She returned the items, snapped the case shut, and shook her head as Melanie reentered the room.

"Would you like to spend the night at my place?" Melanie asked.

"No, thanks."

"Would you like me to stay here, then?"

"No. I'll be all right. I'll sleep in one of the guest rooms."

Melanie picked up the attaché case and headed for the door. She paused there for a moment, studying Marietta, her eyes full of concern. "Are you sure you're all right?"

"Of course I am." A note of impatience crept into Marietta's voice. "I was shaken for a moment when it happened. That was to be expected. But it was only for a moment." She opened the door, and Melanie walked out into the hall. "Make those phone calls you mentioned and see to it that everything is done exactly as it should be. I don't want any loose ends. I'll see you at the office tomorrow. Nine sharp."

She closed the door briskly. She was in control again.

Read more at Amazon/Kindle

Made in the USA
Lexington, KY
21 April 2018